JASON LUTES
JAR *of* FOOLS

DRAWN AND QUARTERLY PUBLICATIONS

ACKNOWLEDGEMENTS | This book is respectfully dedicated to Rachel Bers, Edwin Brubaker, Abigail Gross, Thomas Hart, Robert Jazz, Megan Kelso, Benjamin Leff, Jon Lewis, Carolyn Lutes and Philip Lutes, Howard Rigberg, Allison Schwartz, James Sturm, Michel Vrána, Chris Ware, and Deborah Zeidenberg, who collectively provided the inspiration and support necessary to its completion.

Special thanks to Scott McCloud and the Xeric Foundation.

First published (in a different form) in 1994 by Penny Dreadful Press.
First complete edition published in 1997 by Black Eye Books.
This edition published in 2001 by Drawn & Quarterly.
ISBN 1-896597-39-4
Printed in Canada.
10 9 8 7 6 5 4 3 2

Publication design
by Michel Vrana and Jason Lutes.
Publisher: Chris Oliveros

Drawn & Quarterly
Post Office Box 48056
Montreal, Quebec
Canada H2V 4S8

Free Catalogue available upon request.

Website: www.drawnandquarterly.com
E-mail: info@drawnandquarterly.com

for Rachel

part one

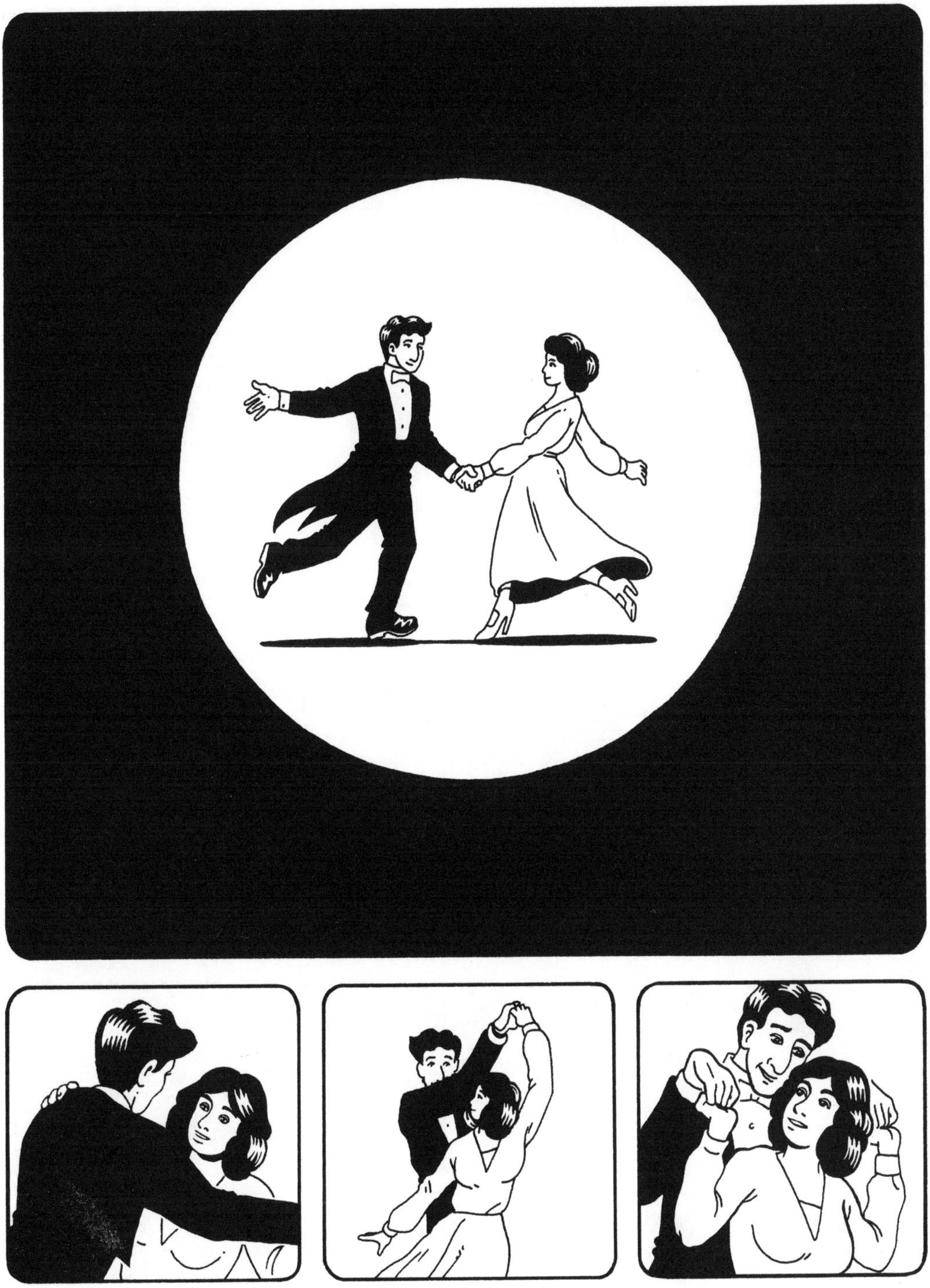

God...
I forgot what a desolate place this is.

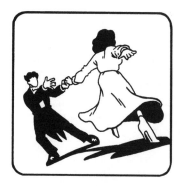

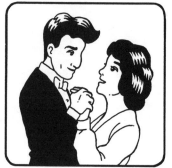

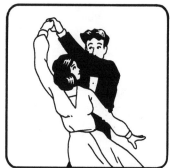

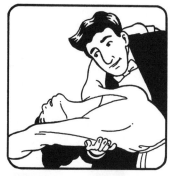

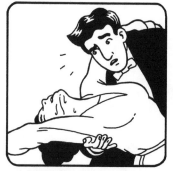

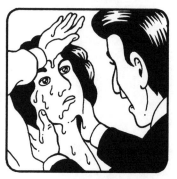

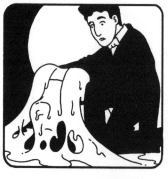

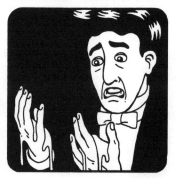

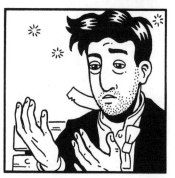

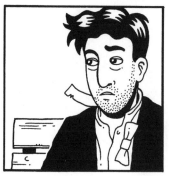

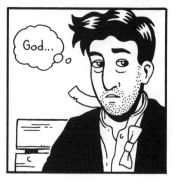

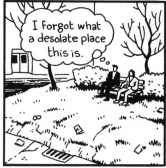

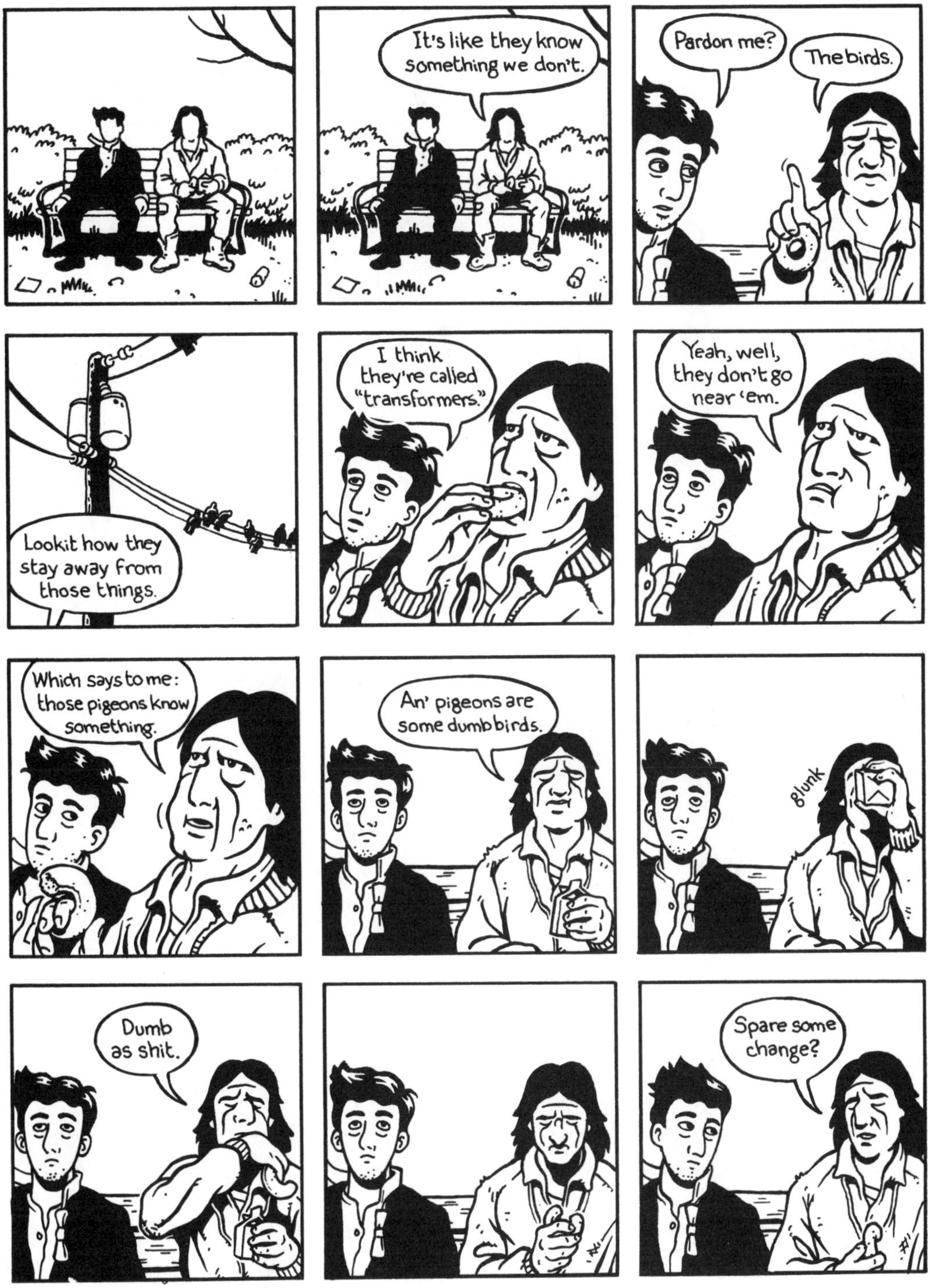
It's like they know something we don't.
Pardon me?
The birds.
Lookit how they stay away from those things.
I think they're called "transformers."
Yeah, well, they don't go near 'em.
Which says to me: those pigeons know something.
An' pigeons are some dumb birds.
glunk
Dumb as shit.
Spare some change?

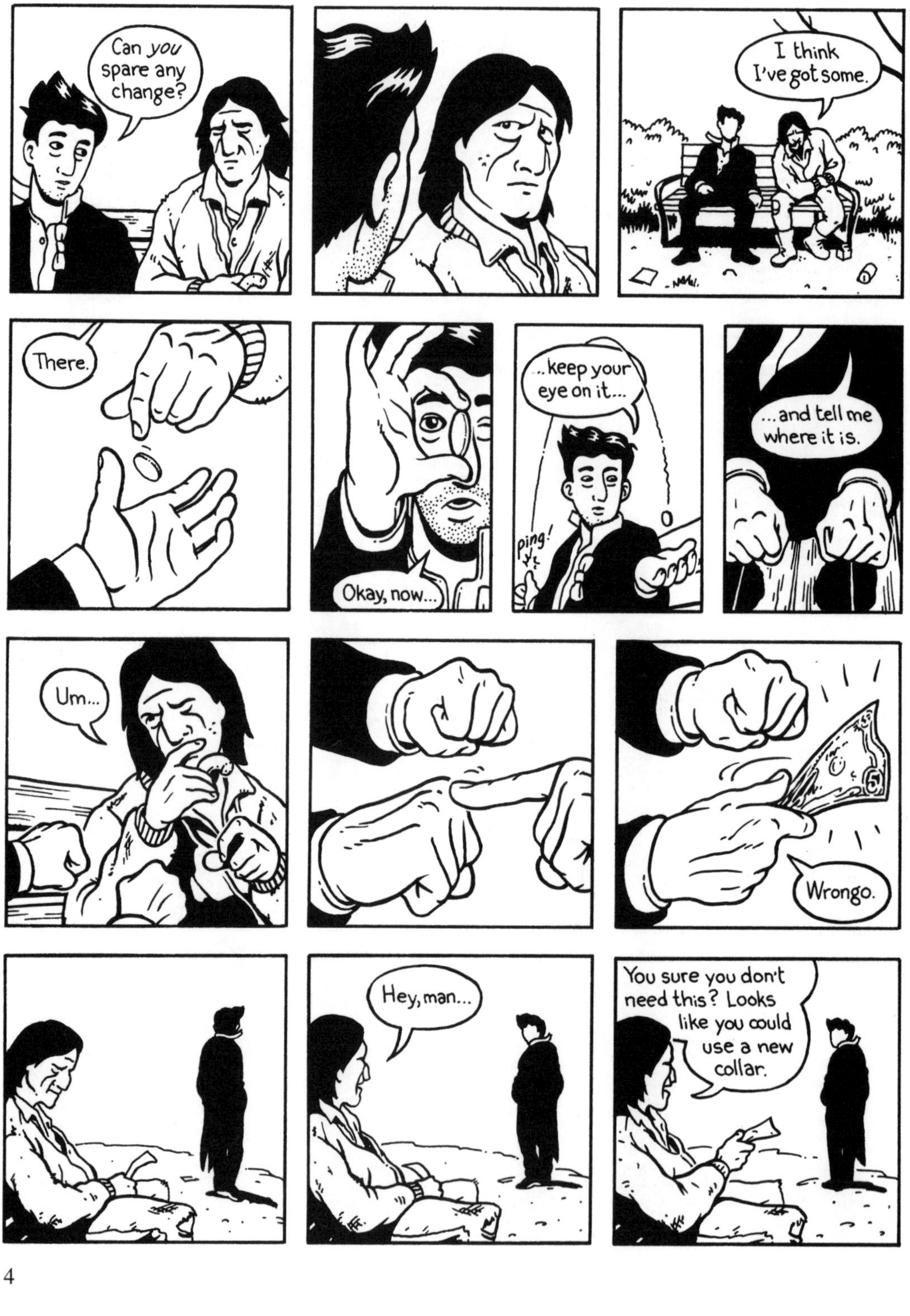
Can you spare any change?
I think I've got some.
There.
Okay, now...
...keep your eye on it...
ping!
...and tell me where it is.
Um...
Wrongo.
Hey, man...
You sure you don't need this? Looks like you could use a new collar.

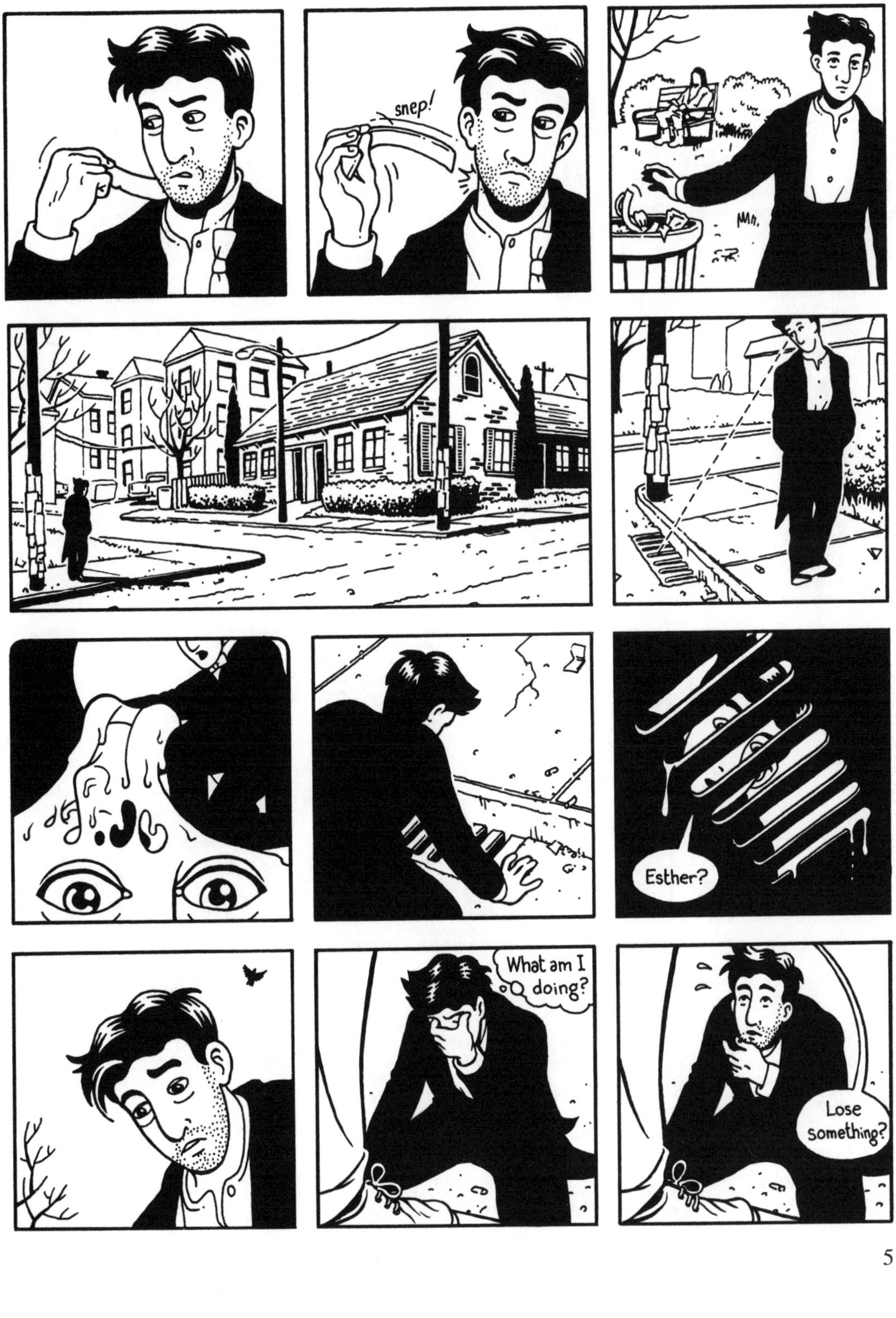
snep!
Esther?
What am I doing?
Lose something?

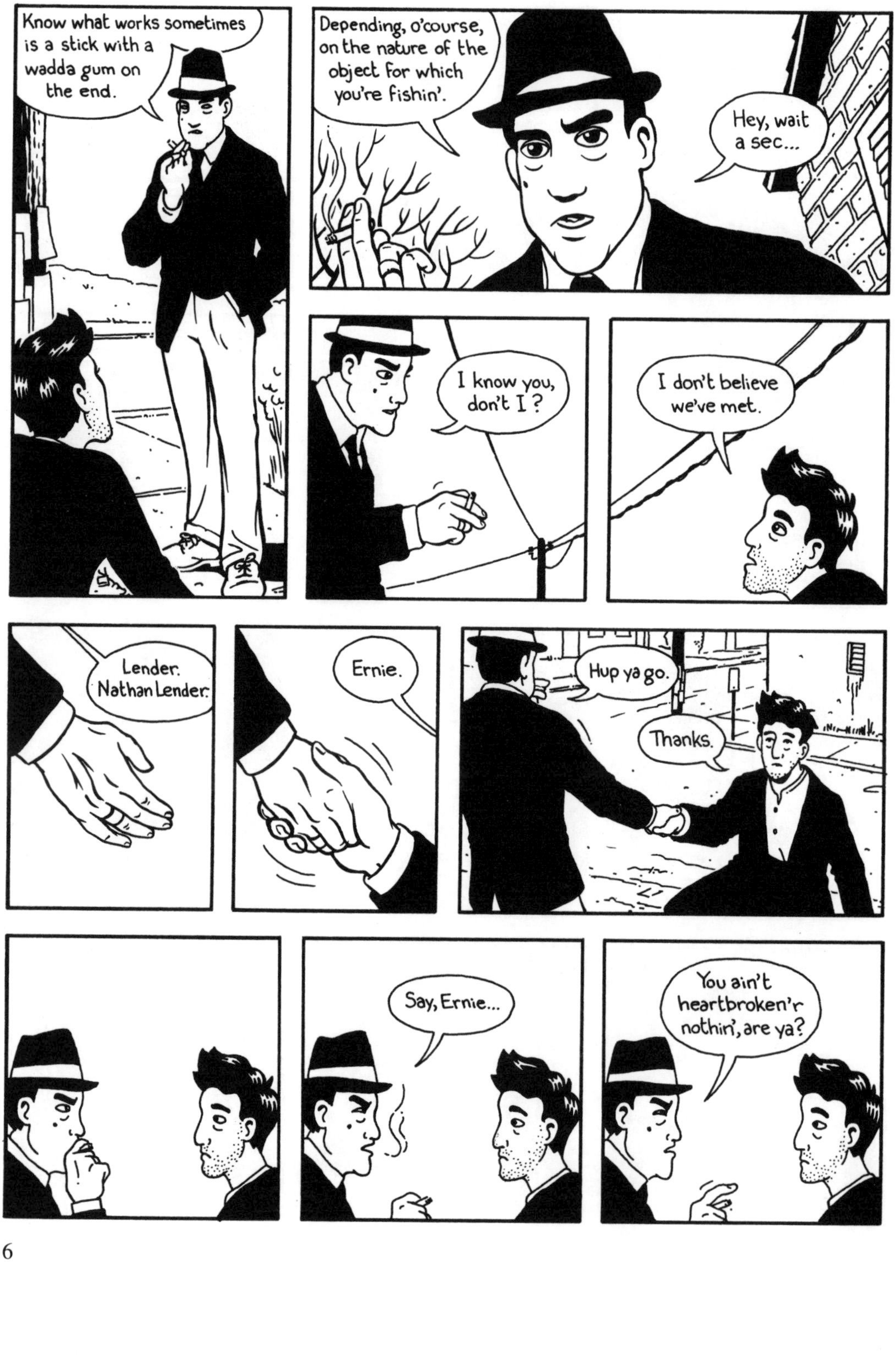
Know what works sometimes is a stick with a wadda gum on the end.
Depending, o'course, on the nature of the object for which you're fishin'.
Hey, wait a sec...
I know you, don't I?
I don't believe we've met.
Lender. Nathan Lender.
Ernie.
Hup ya go.
Thanks.
Say, Ernie...
You ain't heartbroken'r nothin', are ya?

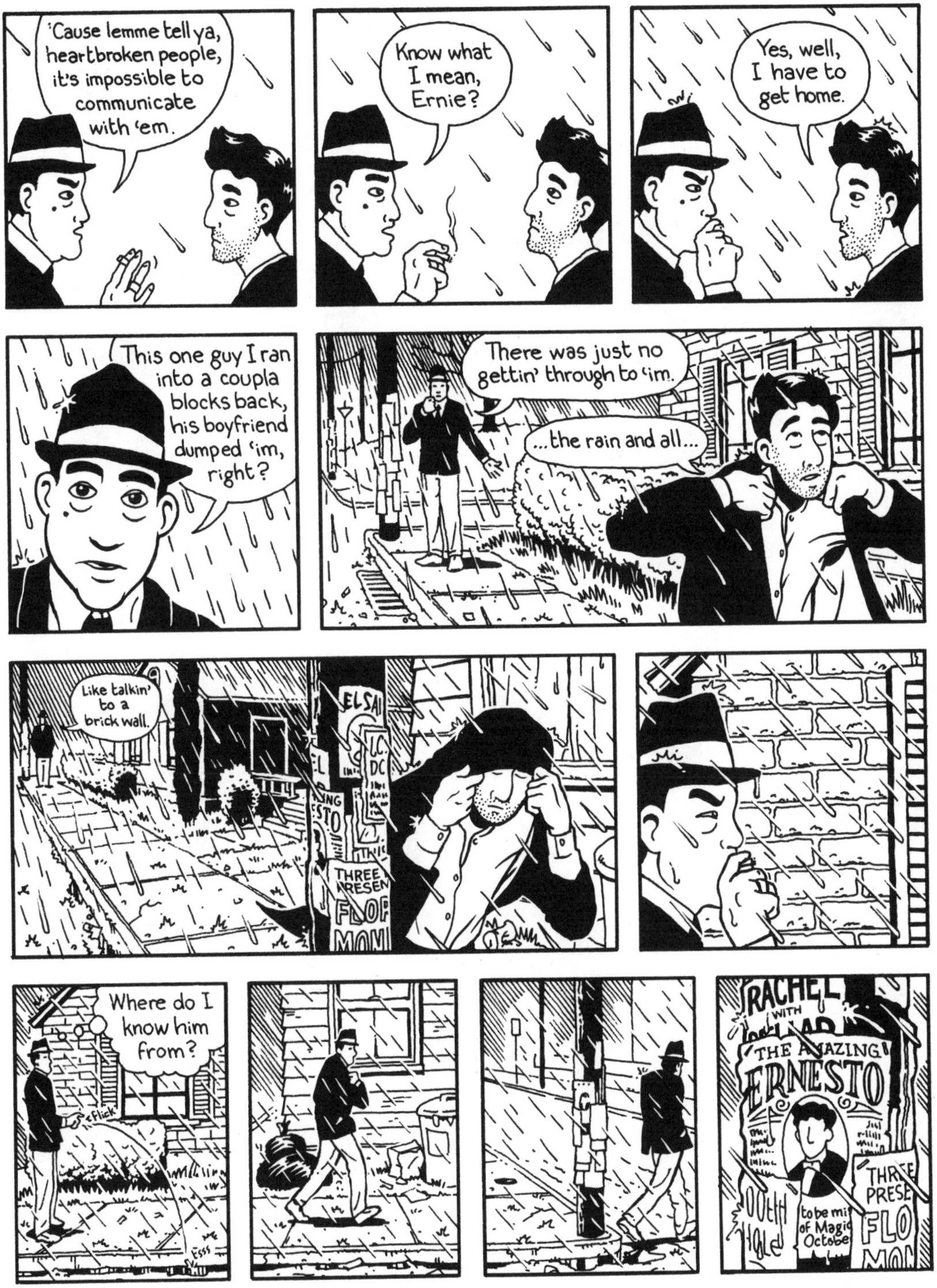
'Cause lemme tell ya, heartbroken people, it's impossible to communicate with 'em.
Know what I mean, Ernie?
Yes, well, I have to get home.
This one guy I ran into a coupla blocks back, his boyfriend dumped 'im, right?
There was just no gettin' through to 'im.
...the rain and all...
Like talkin' to a brick wall.
Where do I know him from?
Flick
Esss
RACHEL
WITH
THE AMAZING
ERNESTO

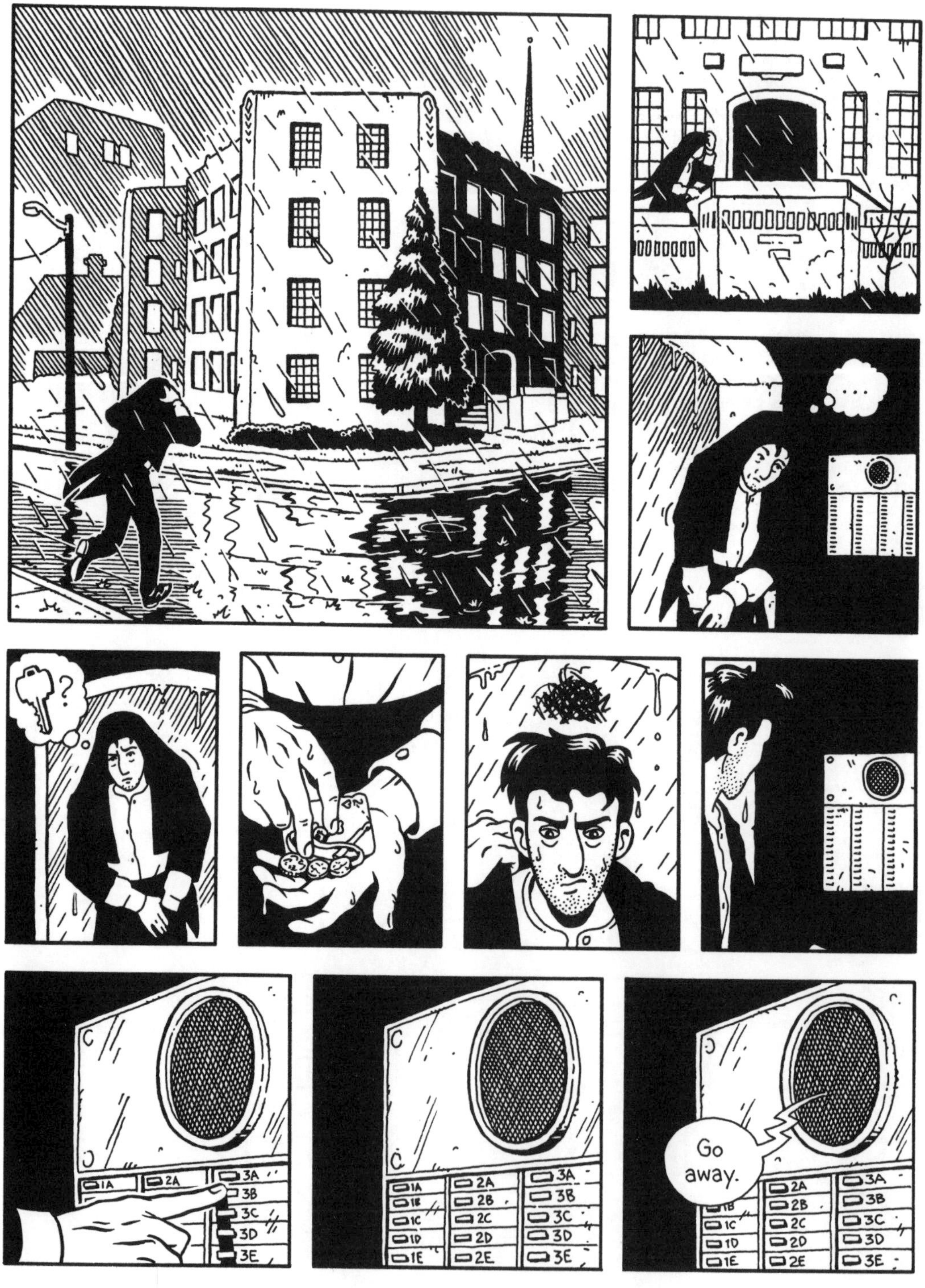

...
?
1A
2A
3A
3B
3C
3D
3E
1A
1B
1C
1D
1E
2A
2B
2C
2D
2E
3A
3B
3C
3D
3E
Go away.
1B
1C
1D
1E
2A
2B
2C
2D
2E
3A
3B
3C
3D
3E

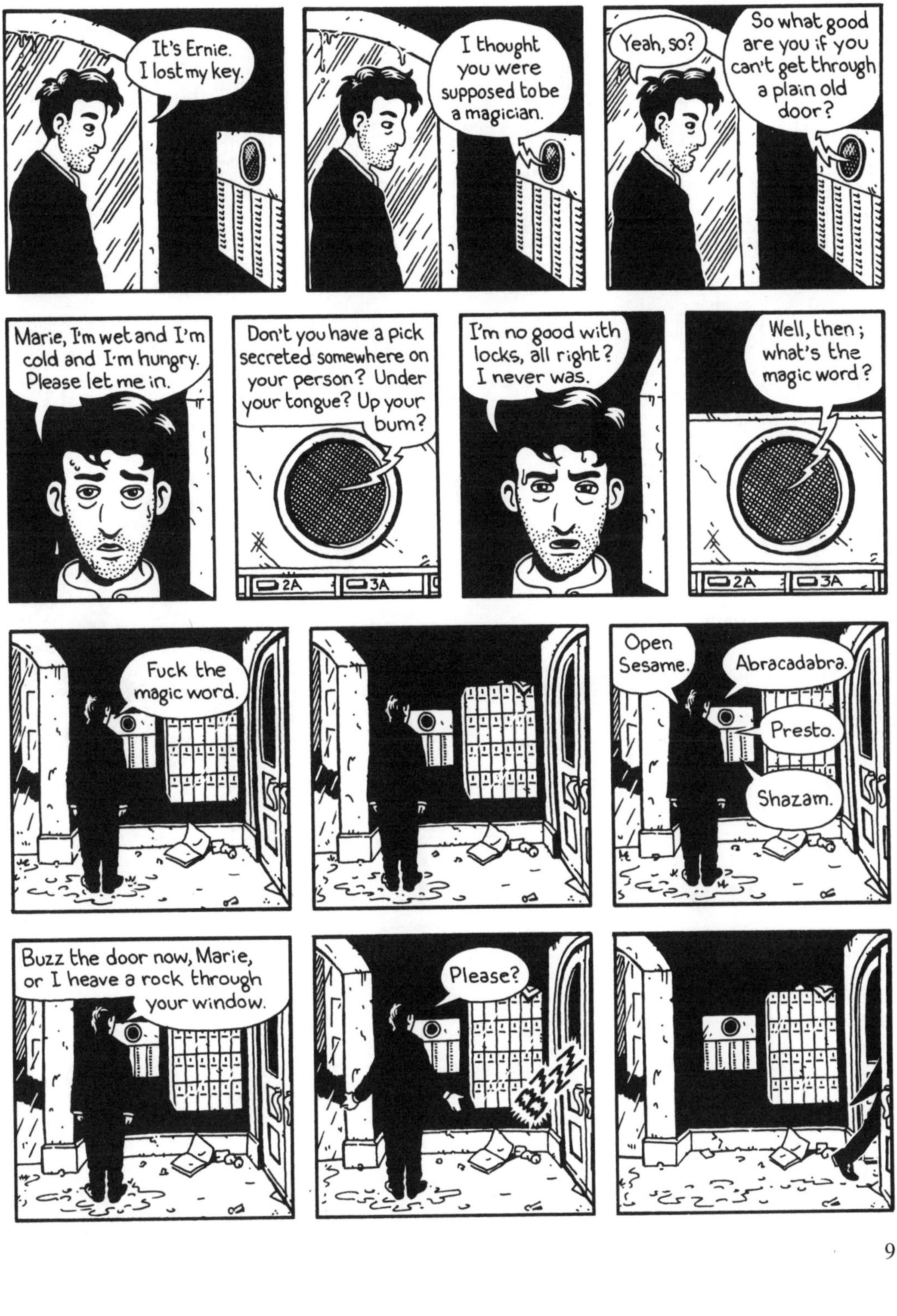
It's Ernie. I lost my key.
I thought you were supposed to be a magician.
Yeah, so?
So what good are you if you can't get through a plain old door?
Marie, I'm wet and I'm cold and I'm hungry. Please let me in.
Don't you have a pick secreted somewhere on your person? Under your tongue? Up your bum?
2A
3A
I'm no good with locks, all right? I never was.
Well, then; what's the magic word?
2A
3A
Fuck the magic word.
Open Sesame.
Abracadabra.
Presto.
Shazam.
Buzz the door now, Marie, or I heave a rock through your window.
Please?
BZZZ

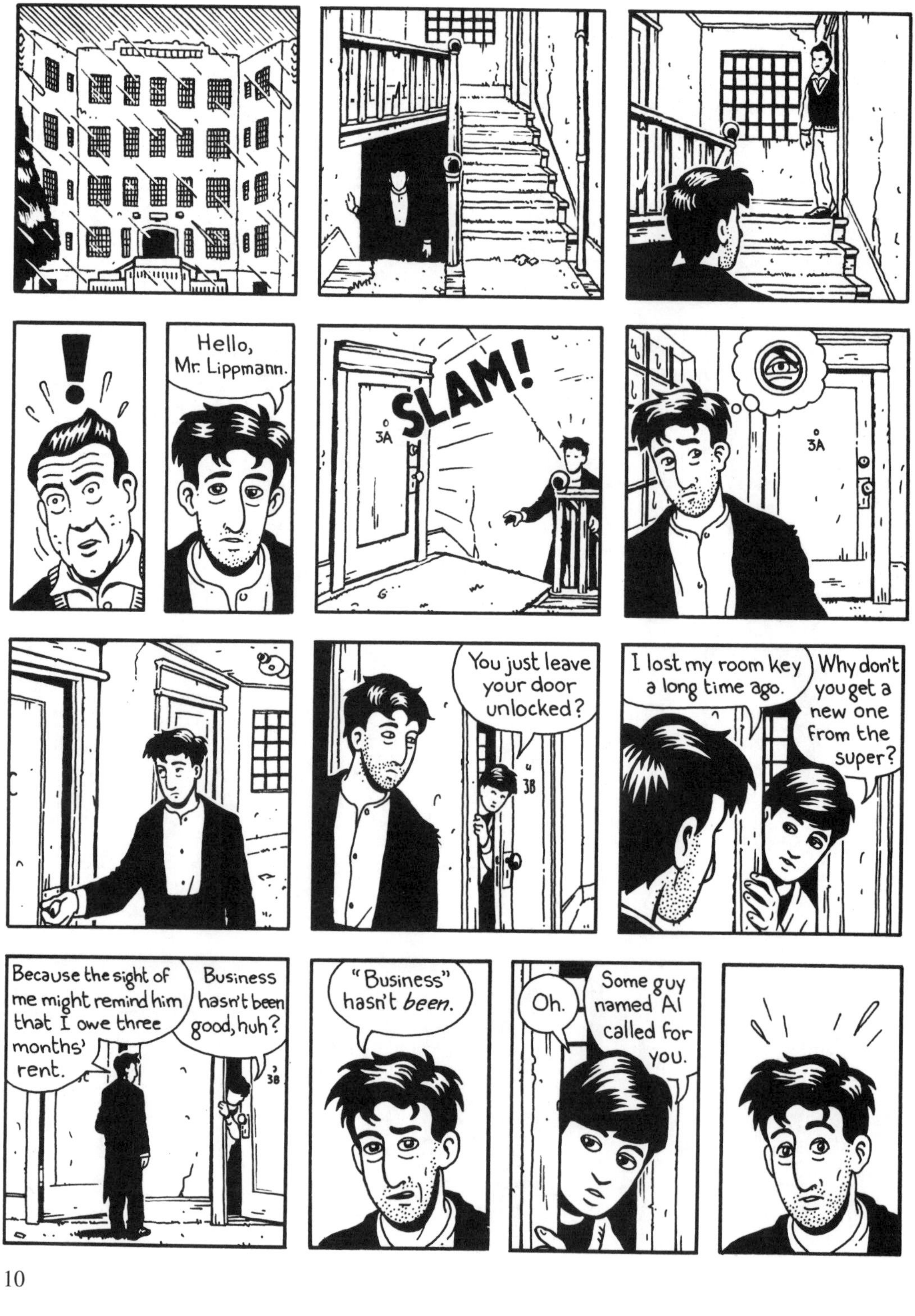
!
Hello, Mr. Lippmann.
SLAM!
3A
3A
You just leave your door unlocked?
3B
I lost my room key a long time ago.
Why don't you get a new one from the super?
Because the sight of me might remind him that I owe three months' rent.
Business hasn't been good, huh?
3B
"Business" hasn't *been*.
Oh.
Some guy named Al called for you.

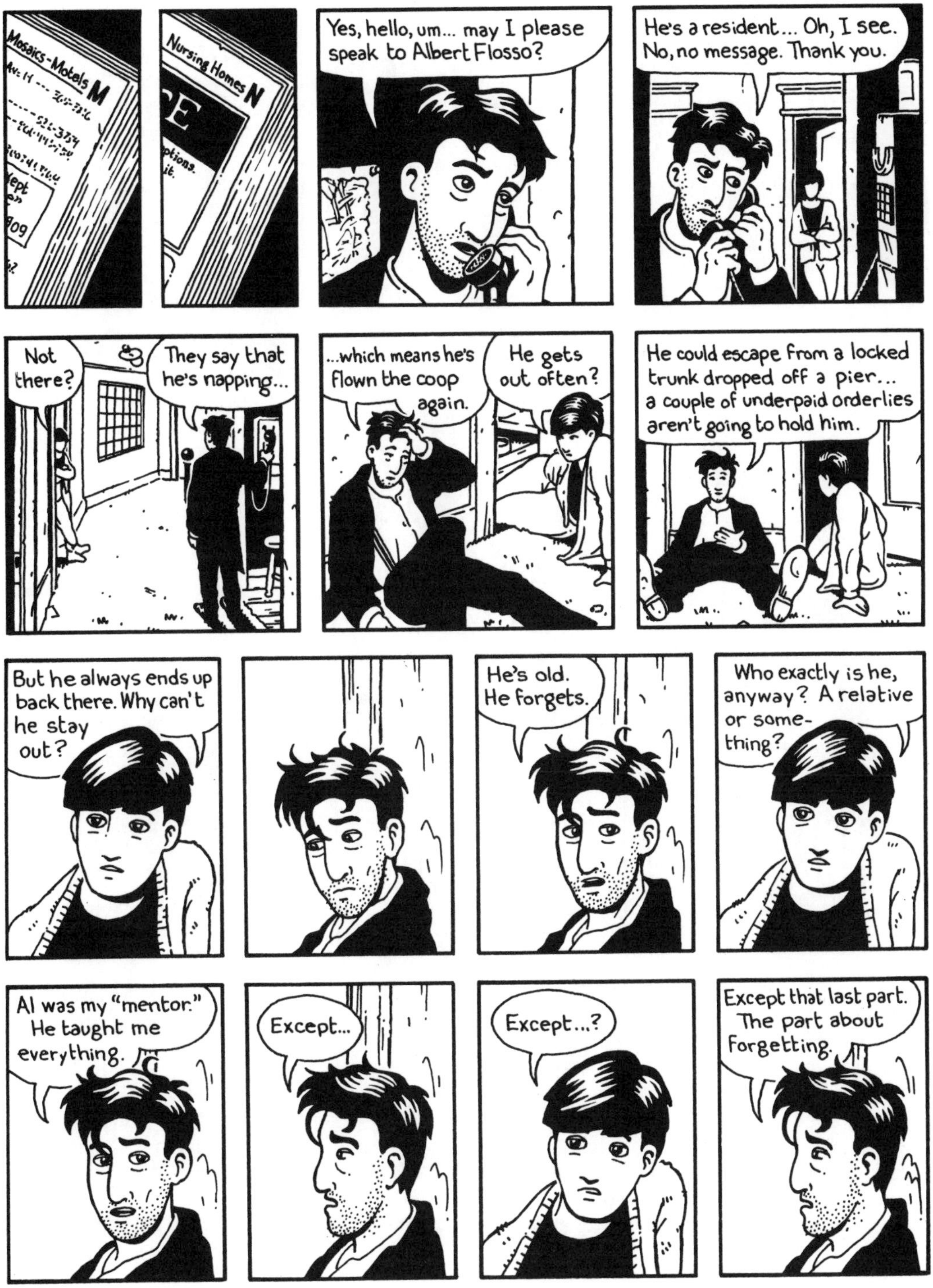
Mosaics-Motels M
Nursing Homes N
Yes, hello, um... may I please speak to Albert Flosso?
He's a resident... Oh, I see. No, no message. Thank you.
Not there?
They say that he's napping...
...which means he's flown the coop again.
He gets out often?
He could escape from a locked trunk dropped off a pier... a couple of underpaid orderlies aren't going to hold him.
But he always ends up back there. Why can't he stay out?
He's old. He forgets.
Who exactly is he, anyway? A relative or something?
Al was my "mentor." He taught me everything.
Except...
Except...?
Except that last part. The part about forgetting.

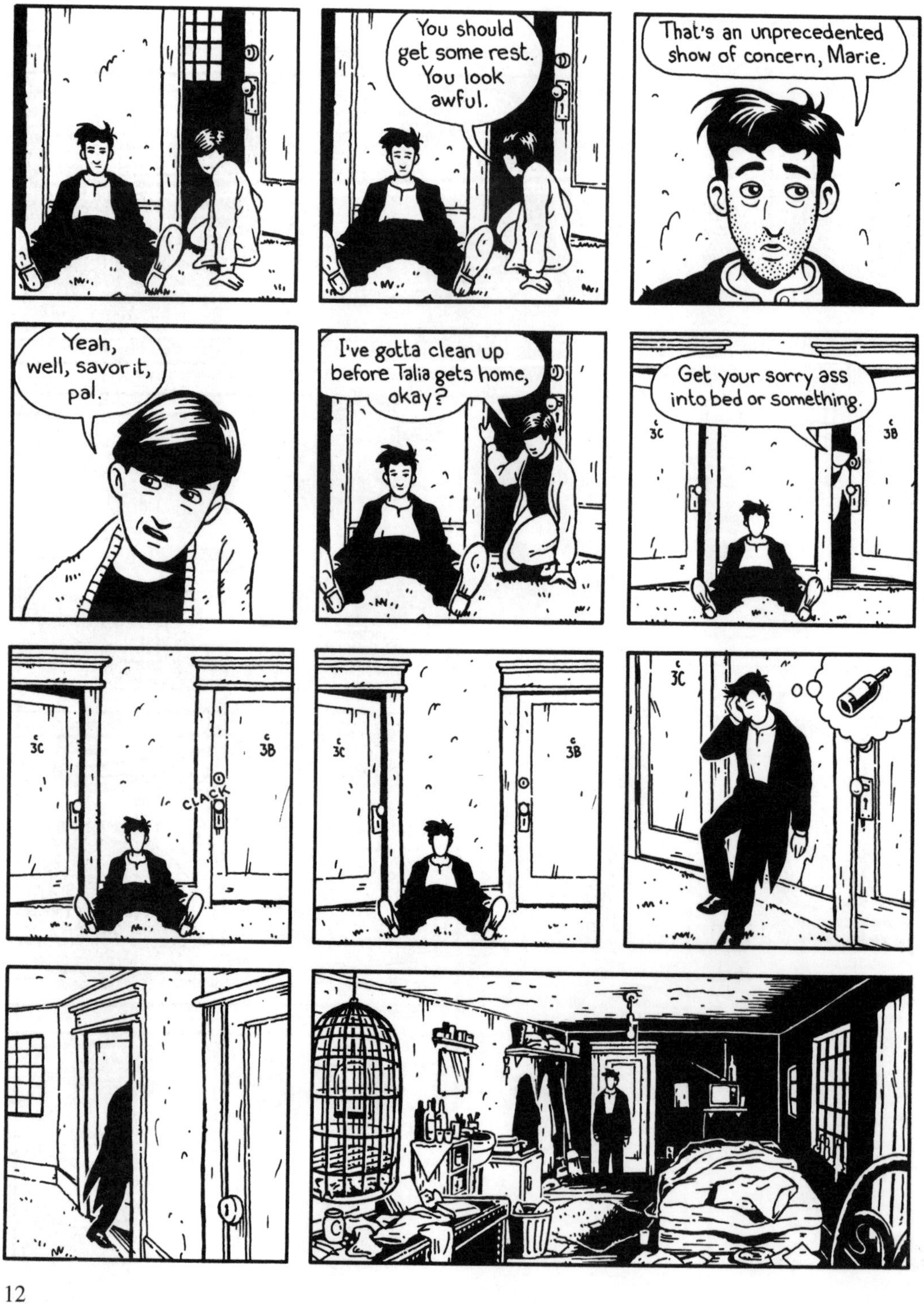
You should get some rest. You look awful.
That's an unprecedented show of concern, Marie.
Yeah, well, savor it, pal.
I've gotta clean up before Talia gets home, okay?
Get your sorry ass into bed or something.
3C
3B
3C
3B
CLACK
3C
3B
3C

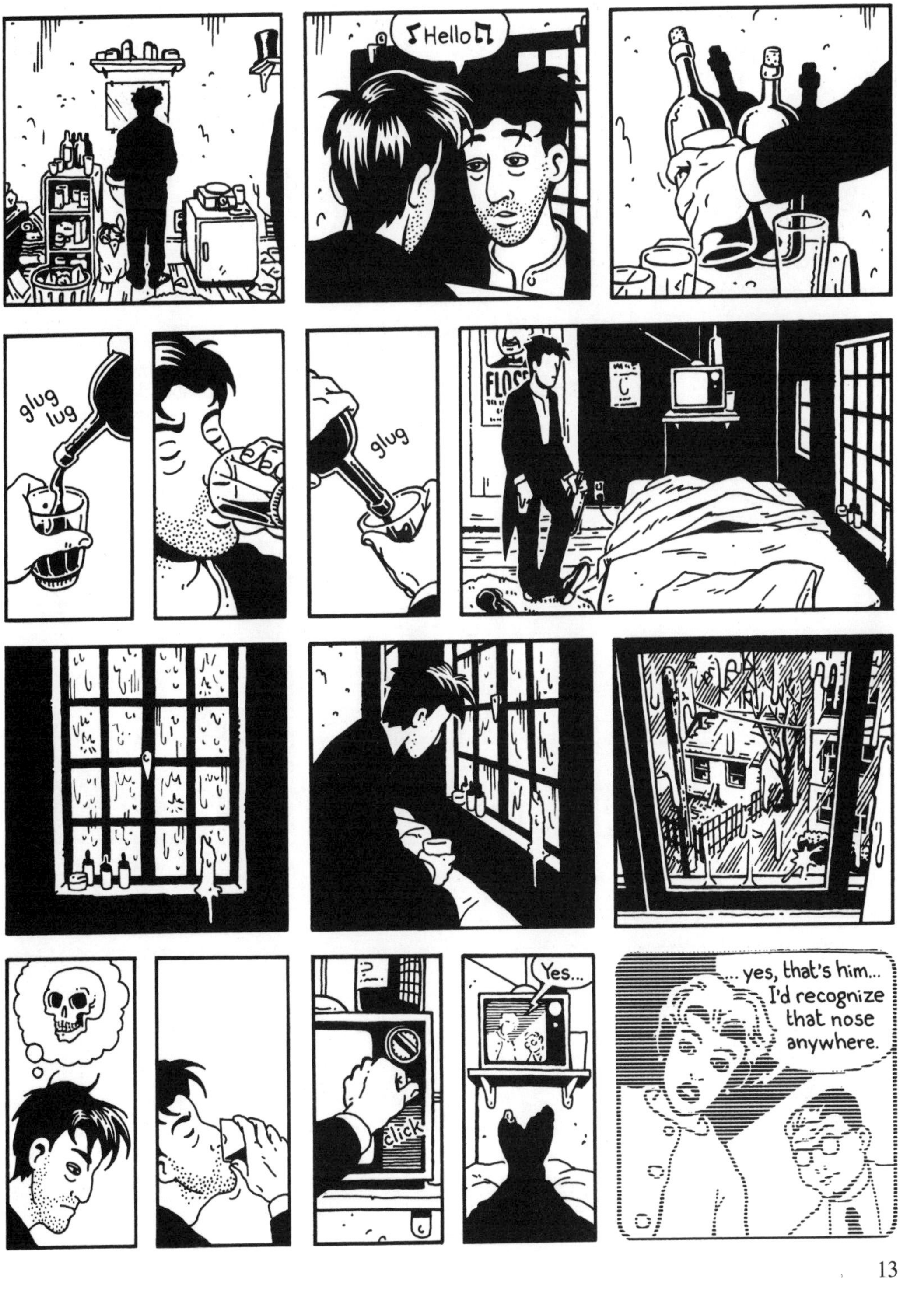
Hello
glug
lug
glug
FLOS
click
Yes...
... yes, that's him...
I'd recognize
that nose
anywhere.

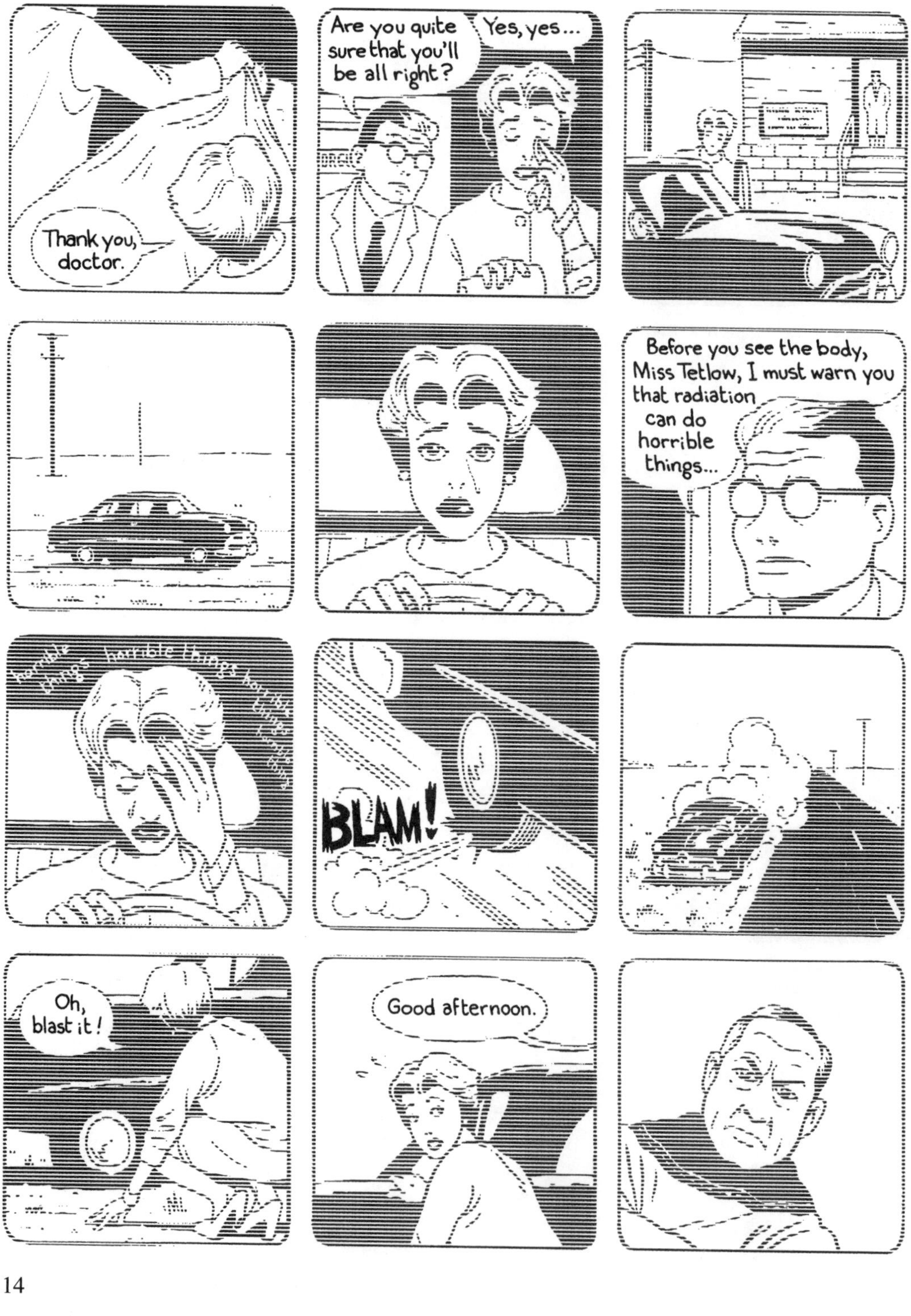
Thank you, doctor.
Are you quite sure that you'll be all right?
Yes, yes...
Before you see the body, Miss Tetlow, I must warn you that radiation can do horrible things...
horrible things horrible things
BLAM!
Oh, blast it!
Good afternoon.

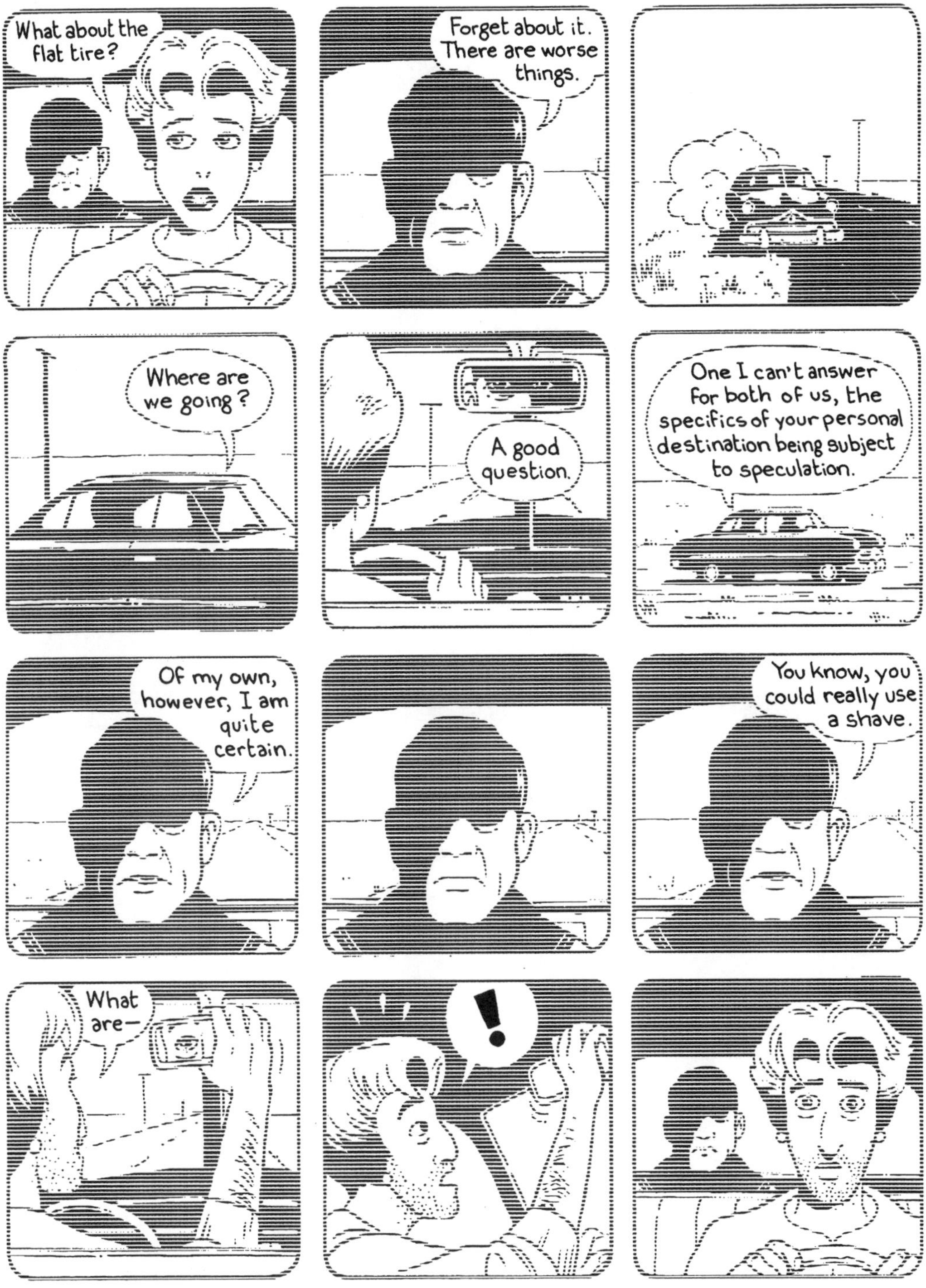
What about the flat tire?
Forget about it. There are worse things.
Where are we going?
A good question.
One I can't answer for both of us, the specifics of your personal destination being subject to speculation.
Of my own, however, I am quite certain.
You know, you could really use a shave.
What are—
!

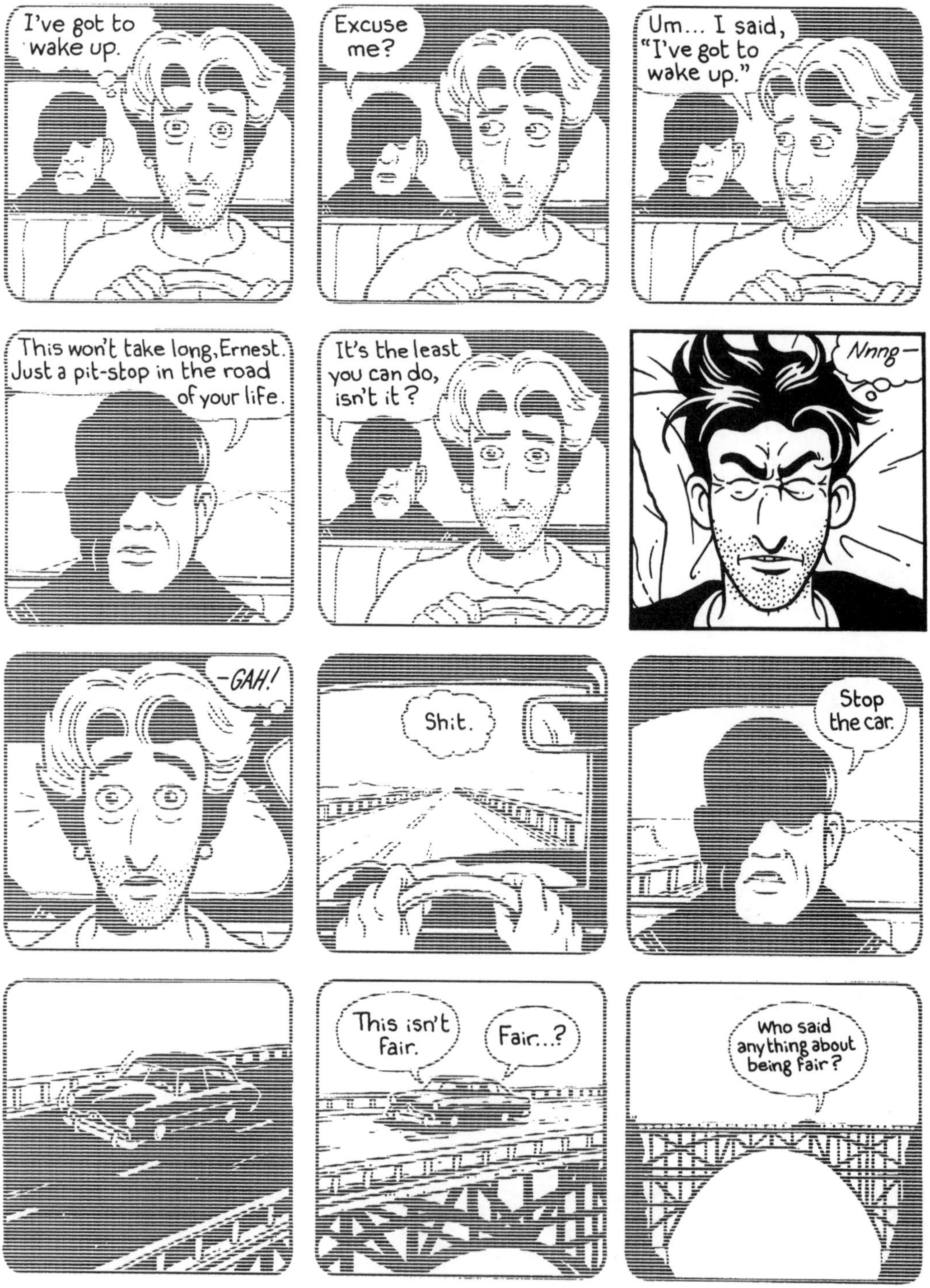
I've got to wake up.
Excuse me?
Um... I said, "I've got to wake up."
This won't take long, Ernest. Just a pit-stop in the road of your life.
It's the least you can do, isn't it?
Nnng—
—GAH!
Shit.
Stop the car.
This isn't fair.
Fair...?
Who said anything about being fair?

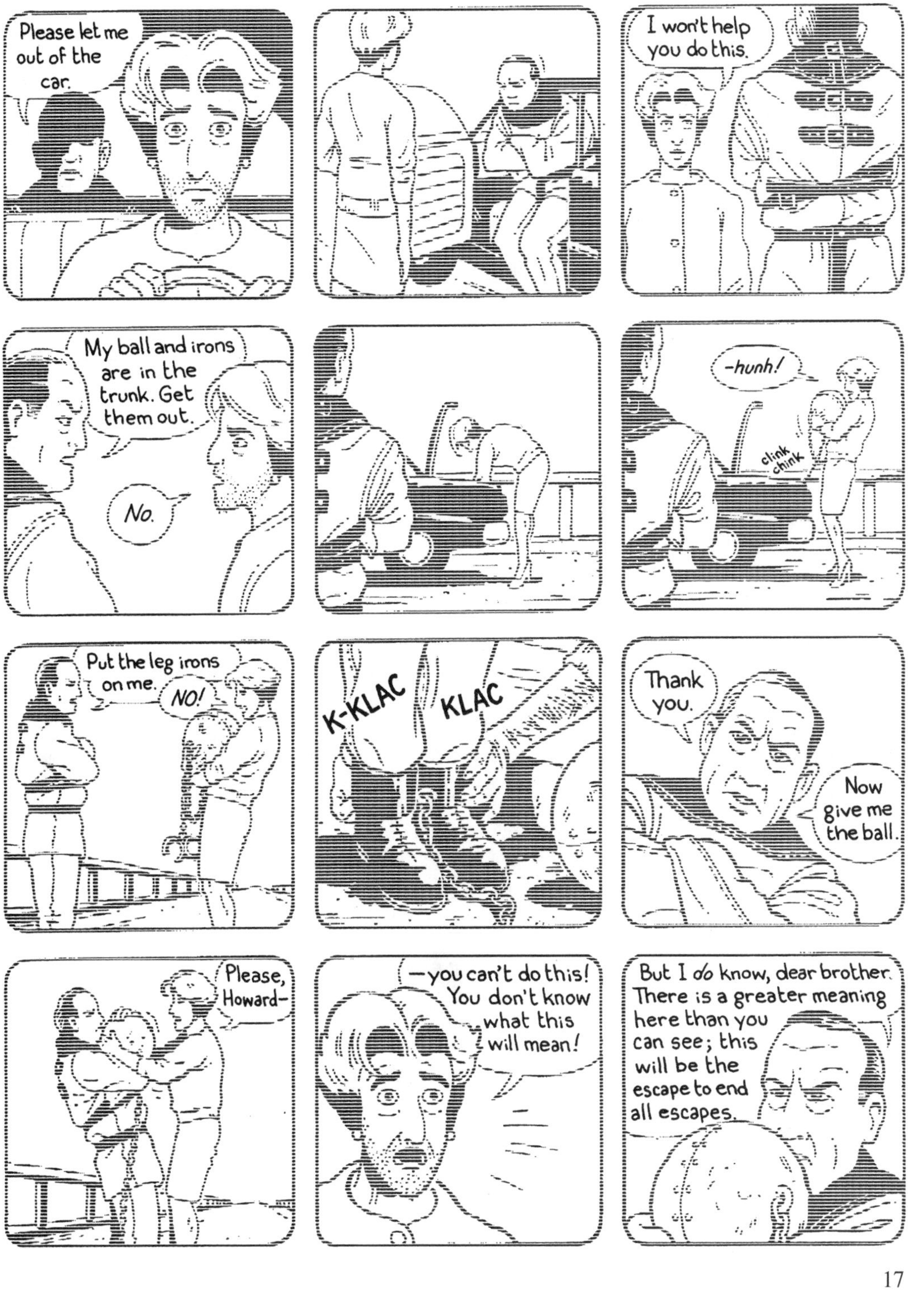

Please let me out of the car.
I won't help you do this.
My ball and irons are in the trunk. Get them out.
No.
-hunh!
clink chink
Put the leg irons on me.
NO!
K-KLAC
KLAC
Thank you.
Now give me the ball.
Please, Howard-
—you can't do this! You don't know what this will mean!
But I do know, dear brother. There is a greater meaning here than you can see; this will be the escape to end all escapes.

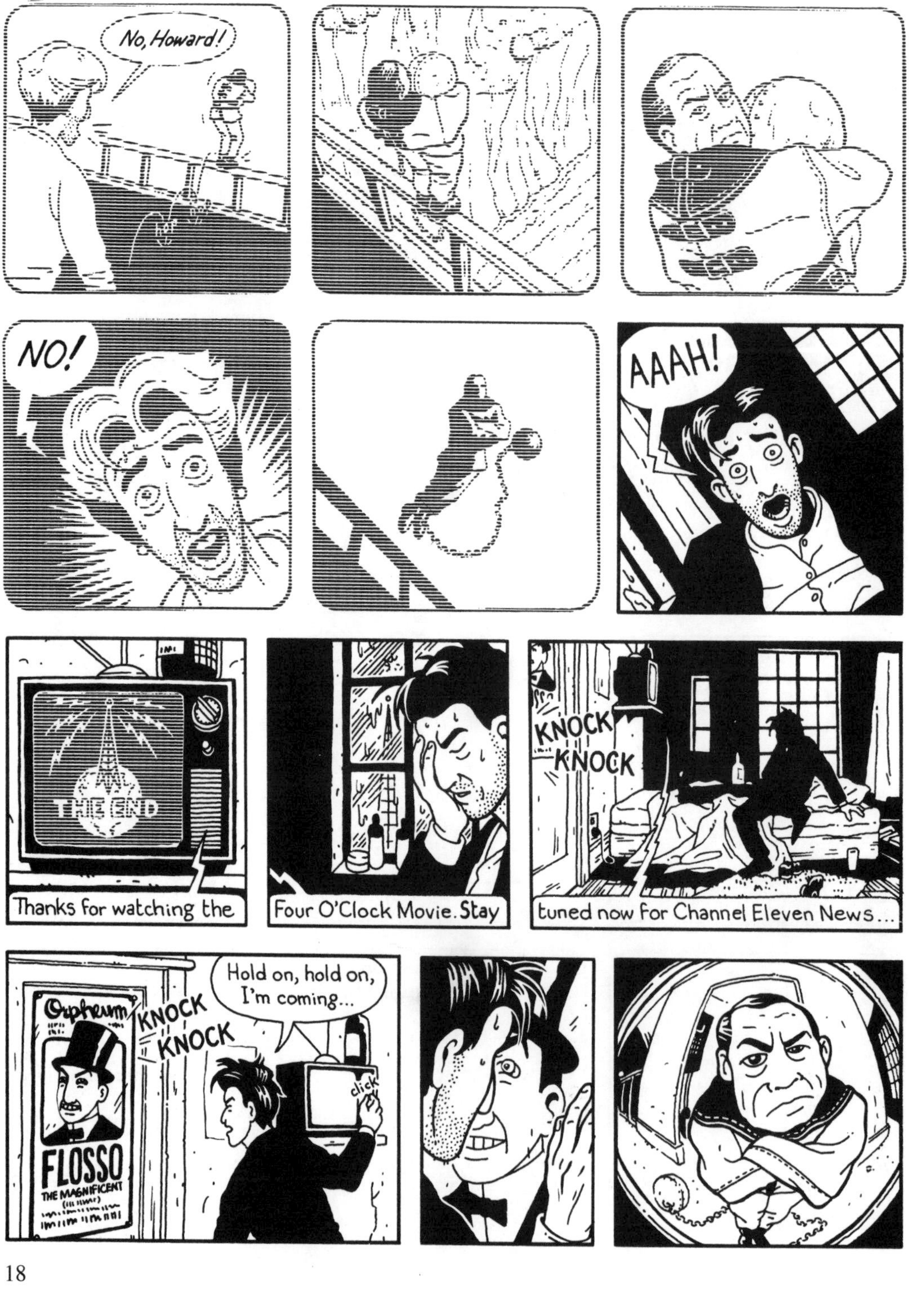
No, Howard!
NO!
AAAH!
THE END
Thanks for watching the
Four O'Clock Movie. Stay
KNOCK
KNOCK
tuned now for Channel Eleven News...
Orpheum
FLOSSO
THE MAGNIFICENT
KNOCK
KNOCK
Hold on, hold on, I'm coming...
click

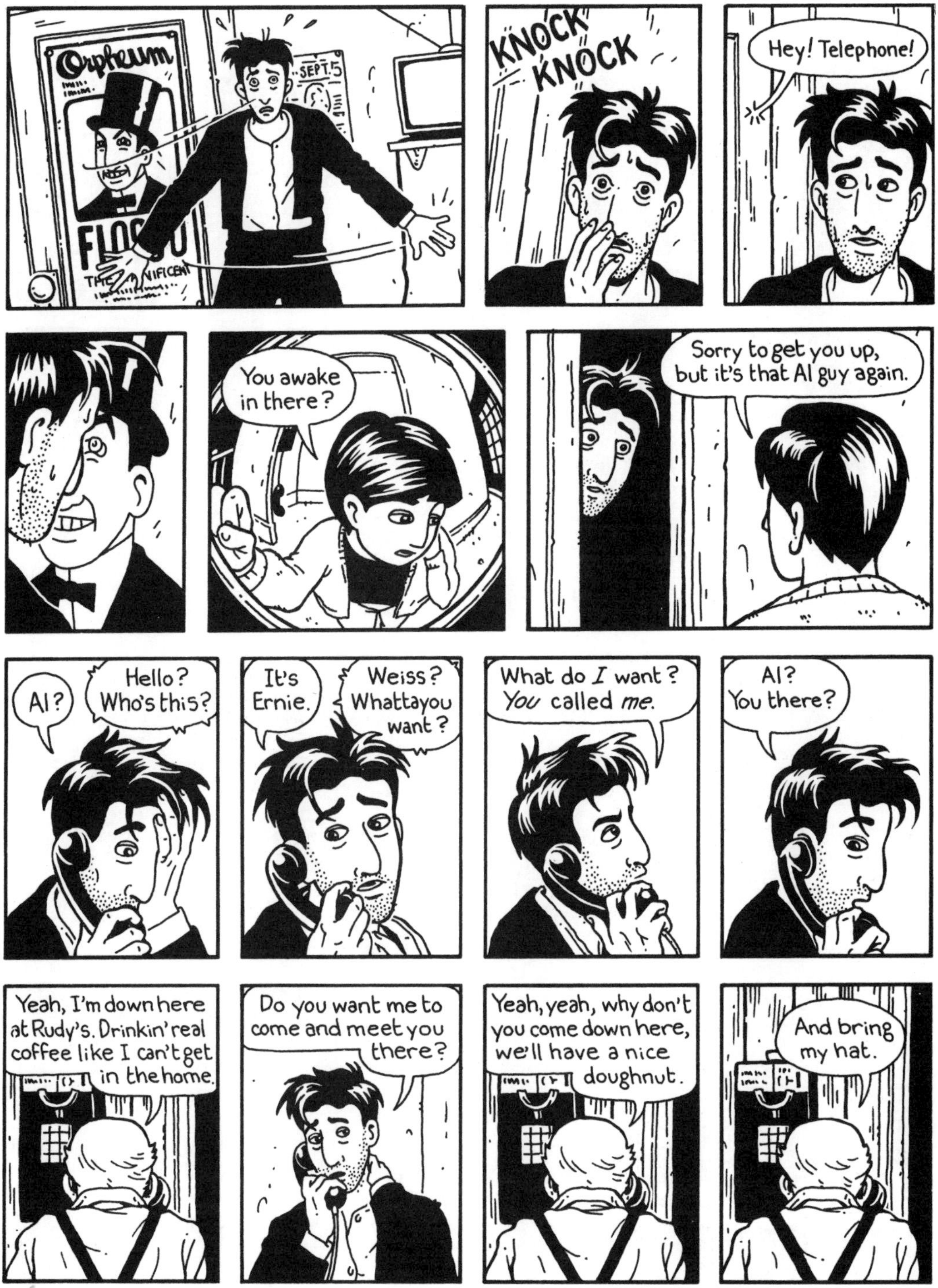
Orpheum
SEPT. 5
FLO
THE
NIFICEN
KNOCK
KNOCK
Hey! Telephone!
You awake in there?
Sorry to get you up, but it's that Al guy again.
Al?
Hello? Who's this?
It's Ernie.
Weiss? Whattayou want?
What do *I* want? *You* called *me*.
Al? You there?
Yeah, I'm down here at Rudy's. Drinkin' real coffee like I can't get in the home.
Do you want me to come and meet you there?
Yeah, yeah, why don't you come down here, we'll have a nice doughnut.
And bring my hat.

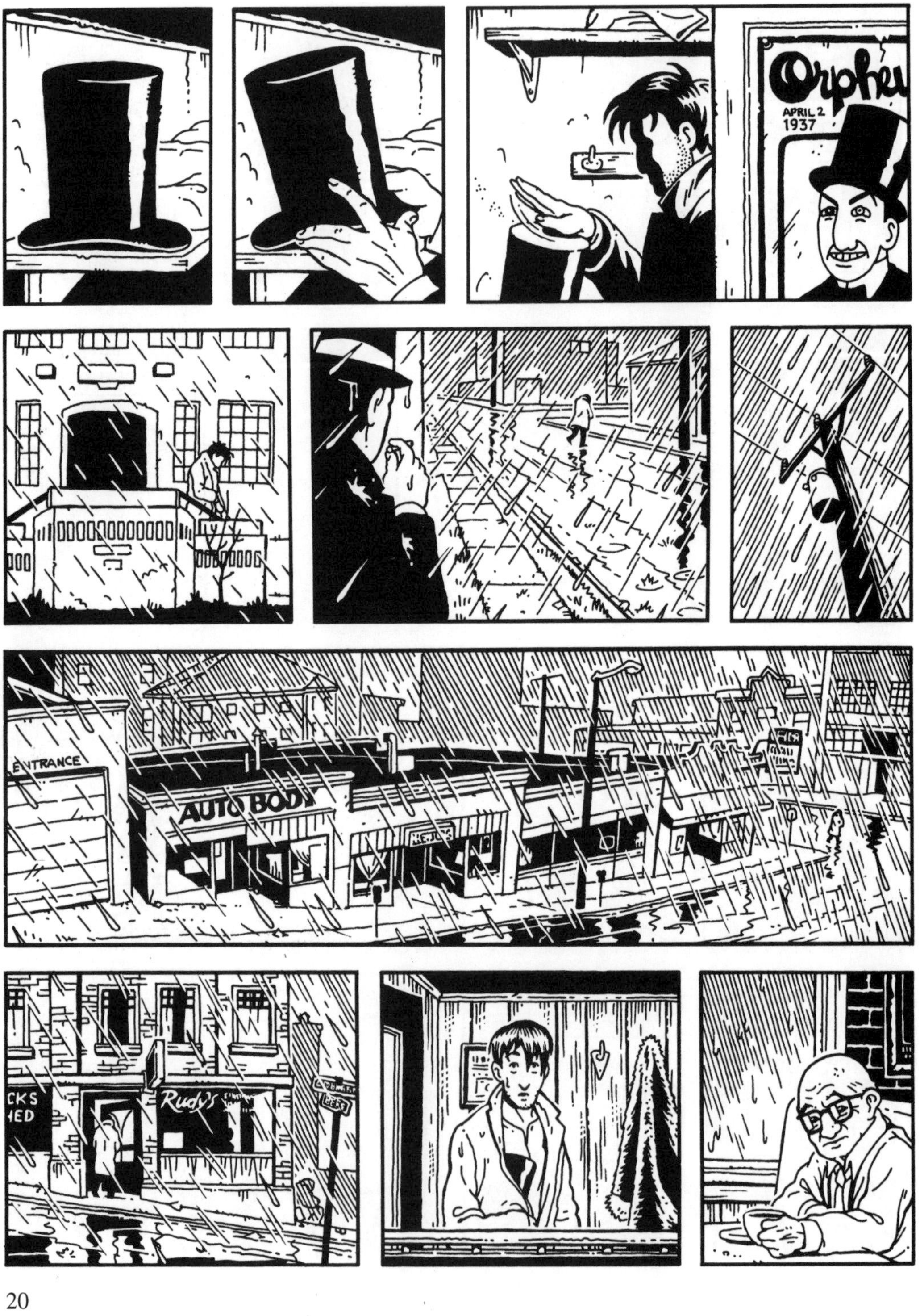
Orpheu
APRIL 2
1937
ENTRANCE
AUTO BODY
CKS
HED
Rudy's

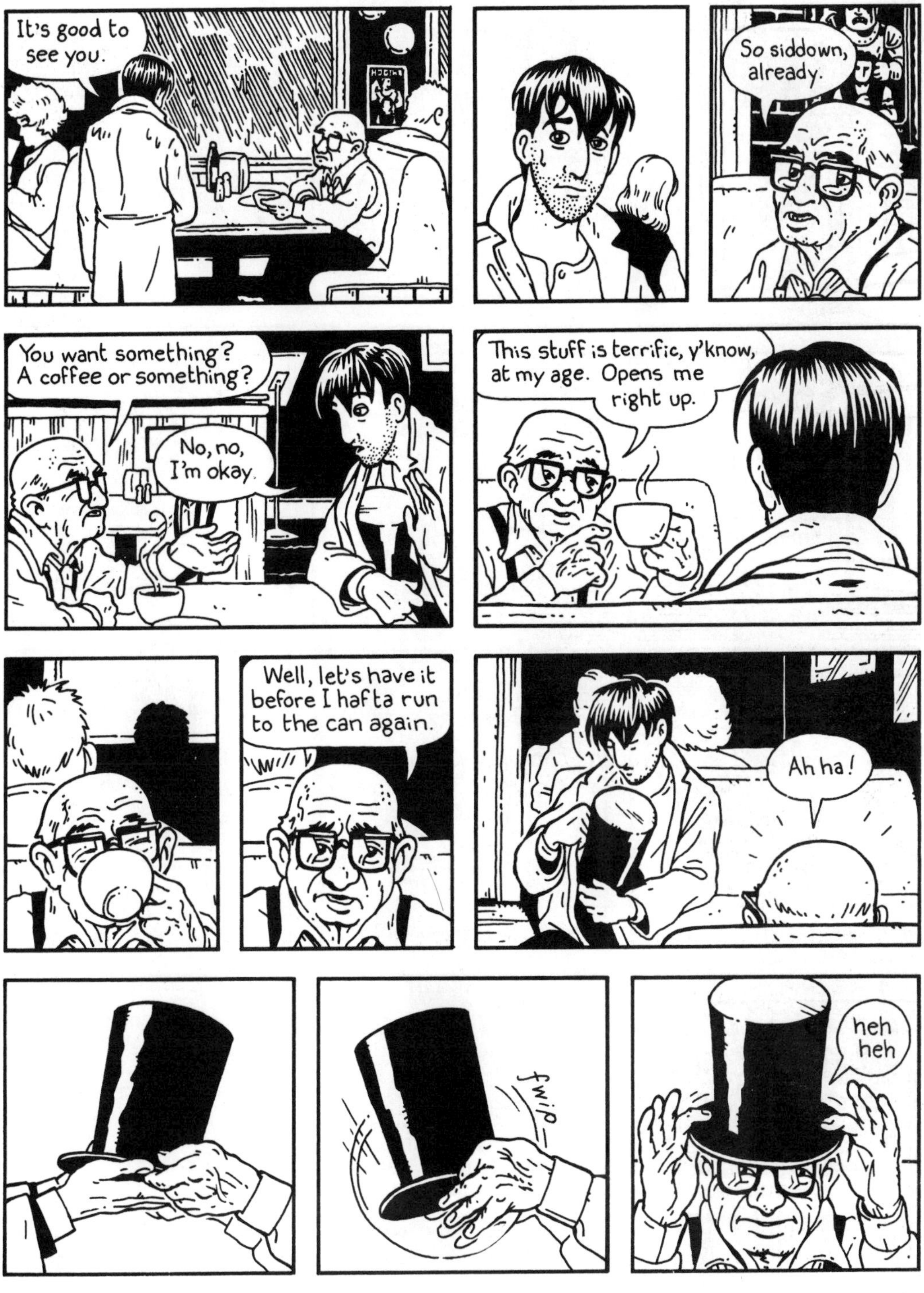
It's good to see you.
So siddown, already.
You want something? A coffee or something?
No, no, I'm okay.
This stuff is terrific, y'know, at my age. Opens me right up.
Well, let's have it before I hafta run to the can again.
Ah ha!
fwip
heh heh

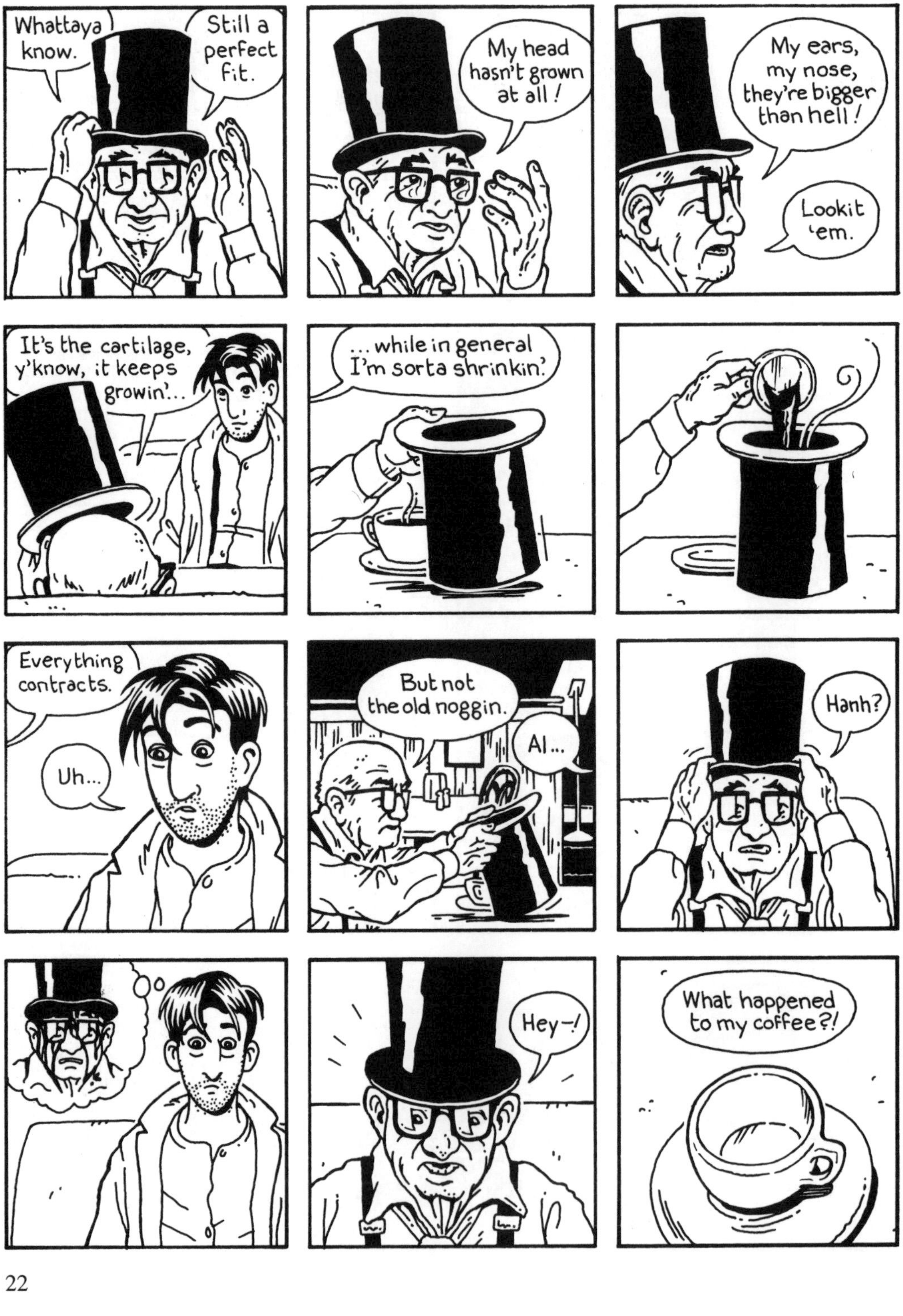
Whattaya know.
Still a perfect fit.
My head hasn't grown at all!
My ears, my nose, they're bigger than hell!
Lookit 'em.
It's the cartilage, y'know, it keeps growin'...
... while in general I'm sorta shrinkin'.
Everything contracts.
Uh...
But not the old noggin.
Al...
Hanh?
Hey-!
What happened to my coffee?!

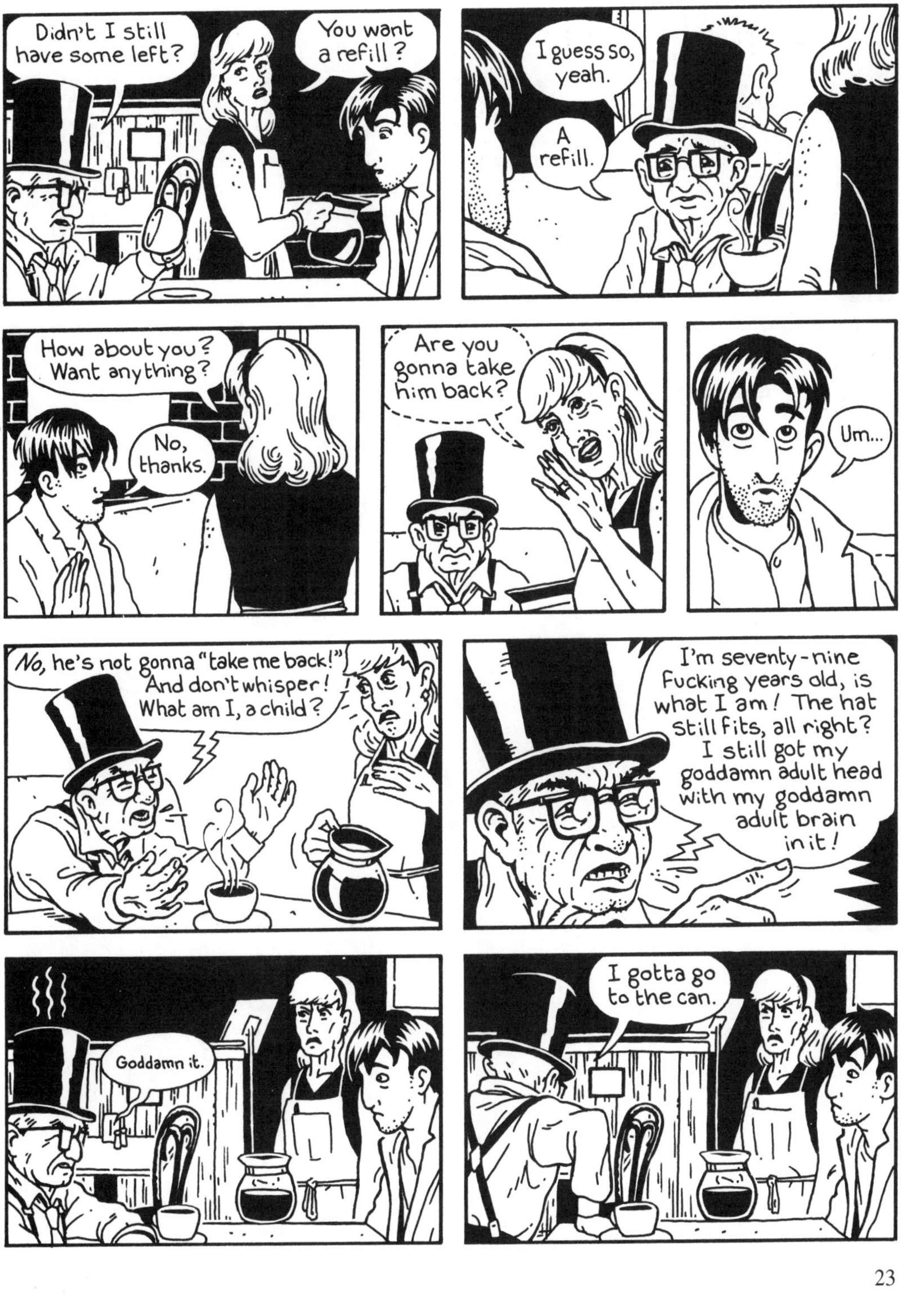
Didn't I still have some left?
You want a refill?
I guess so, yeah.
A refill.
How about you? Want anything?
No, thanks.
Are you gonna take him back?
Um...
No, he's not gonna "take me back!" And don't whisper! What am I, a child?
I'm seventy-nine fucking years old, is what I am! The hat still fits, all right? I still got my goddamn adult head with my goddamn adult brain in it!
Goddamn it.
I gotta go to the can.

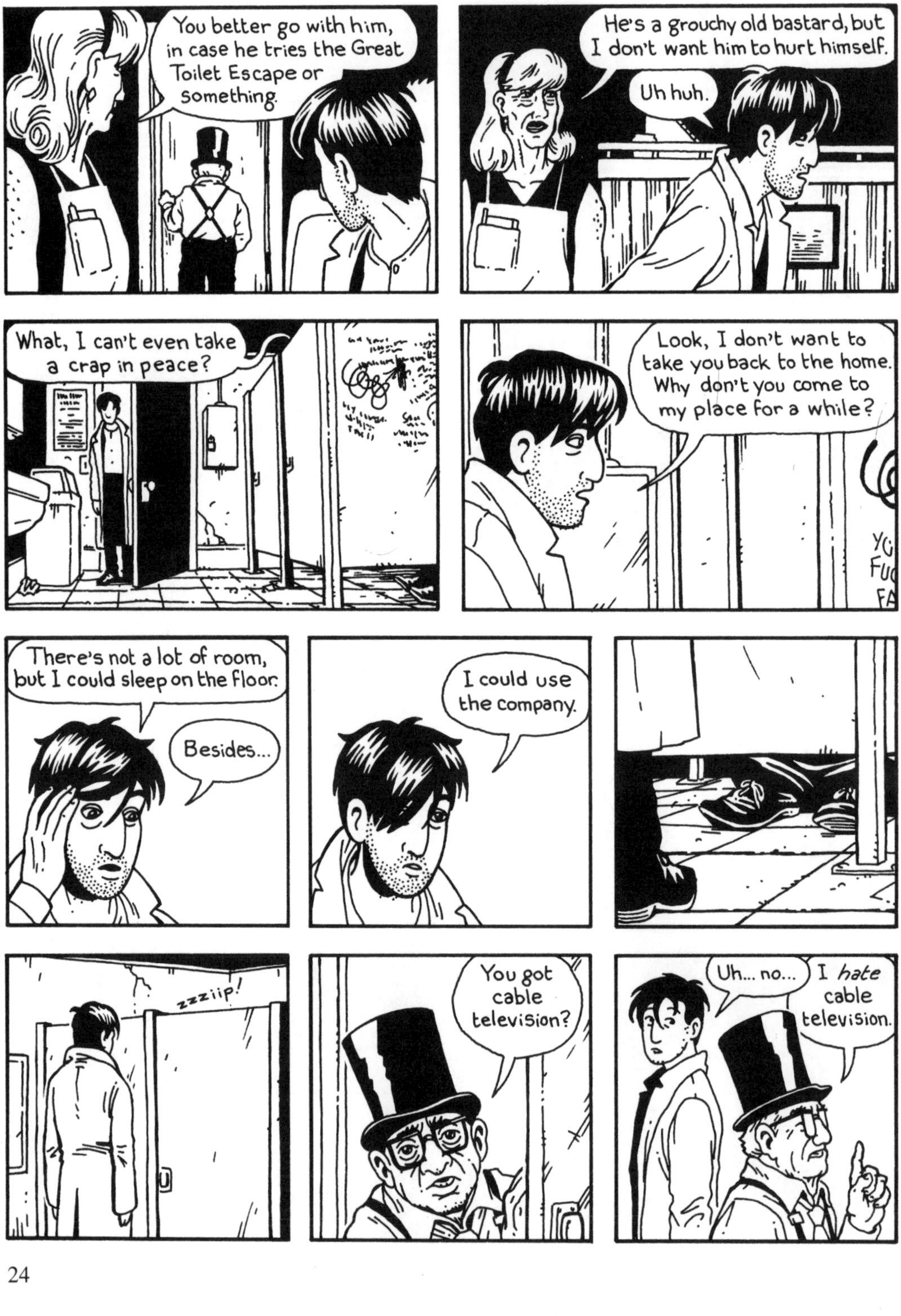
You better go with him, in case he tries the Great Toilet Escape or something.
He's a grouchy old bastard, but I don't want him to hurt himself.
Uh huh.
What, I can't even take a crap in peace?
Look, I don't want to take you back to the home. Why don't you come to my place for a while?
There's not a lot of room, but I could sleep on the floor.
Besides...
I could use the company.
zzziip!
You got cable television?
Uh... no...
I *hate* cable television.

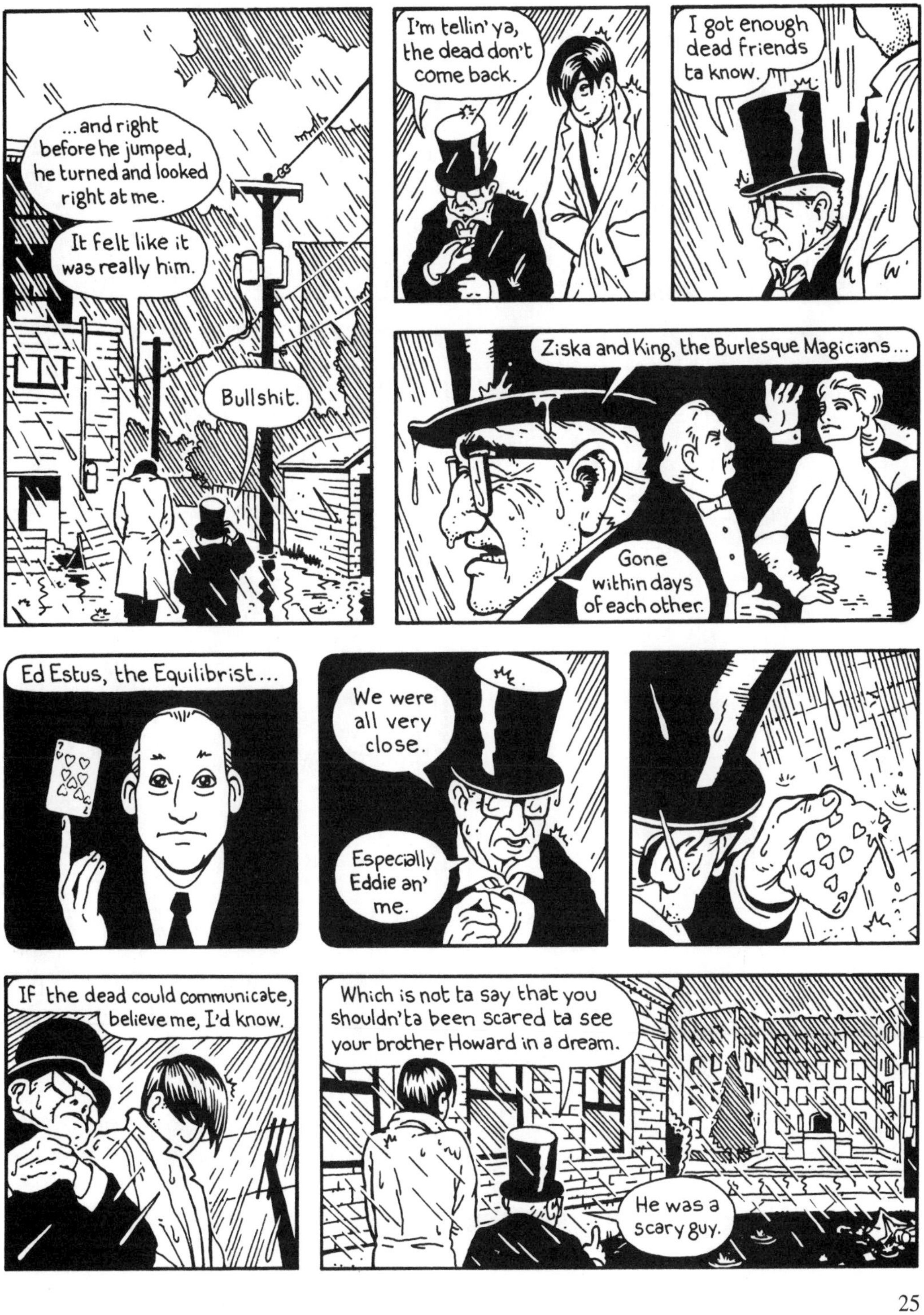
...and right before he jumped, he turned and looked right at me.
It felt like it was really him.
Bullshit.
I'm tellin' ya, the dead don't come back.
I got enough dead friends ta know.
Ziska and King, the Burlesque Magicians...
Gone within days of each other.
Ed Estus, the Equilibrist...
We were all very close.
Especially Eddie an' me.
If the dead could communicate, believe me, I'd know.
Which is not ta say that you shouldn'ta been scared ta see your brother Howard in a dream.
He was a scary guy.

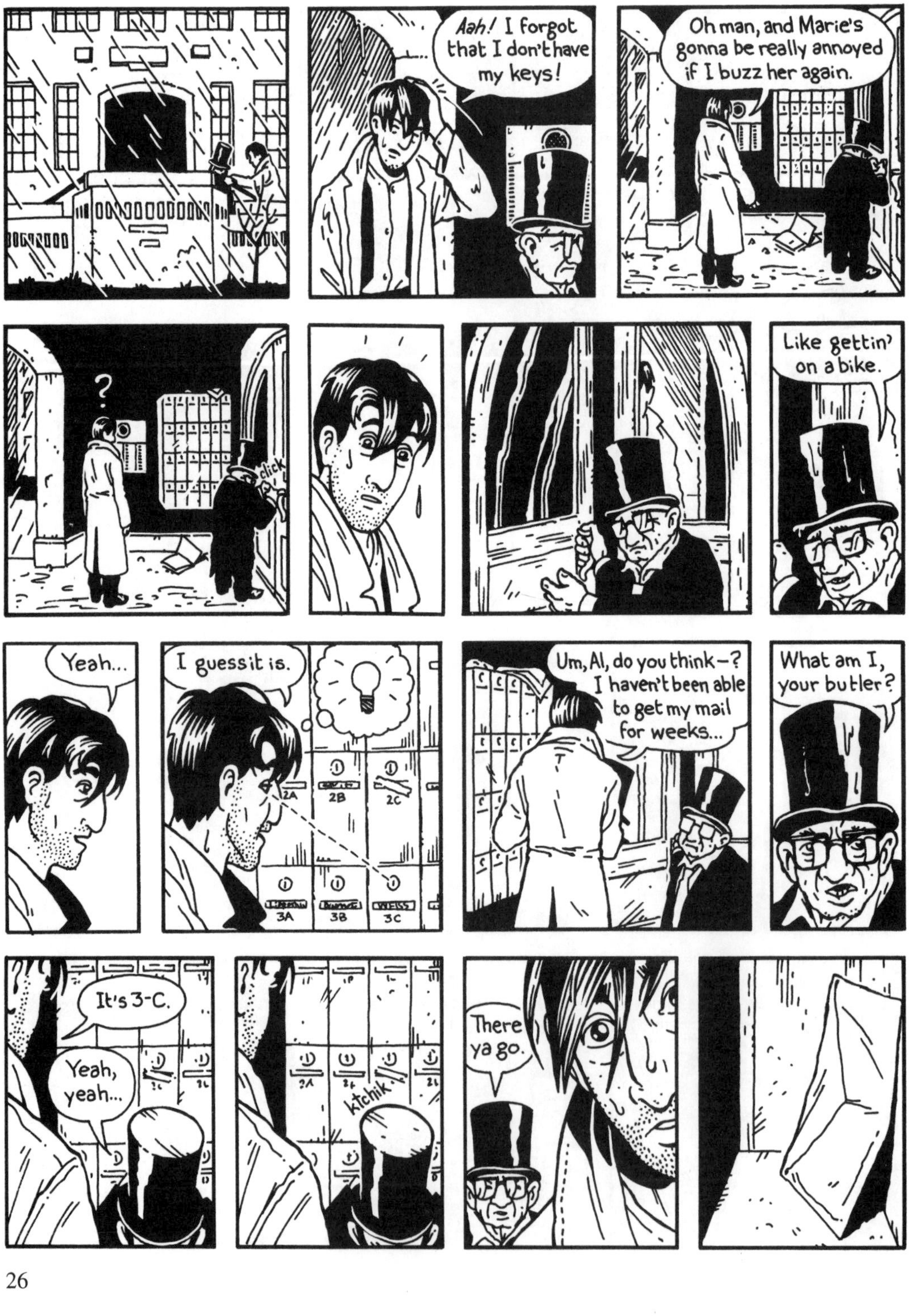
Aah! I forgot that I don't have my keys!
Oh man, and Marie's gonna be really annoyed if I buzz her again.
?
click
Like gettin' on a bike.
Yeah...
I guess it is.
2A
2B
2C
WEISS
3A
3B
3C
Um, Al, do you think—? I haven't been able to get my mail for weeks...
What am I, your butler?
It's 3-C.
Yeah, yeah...
ktchik
There ya go.

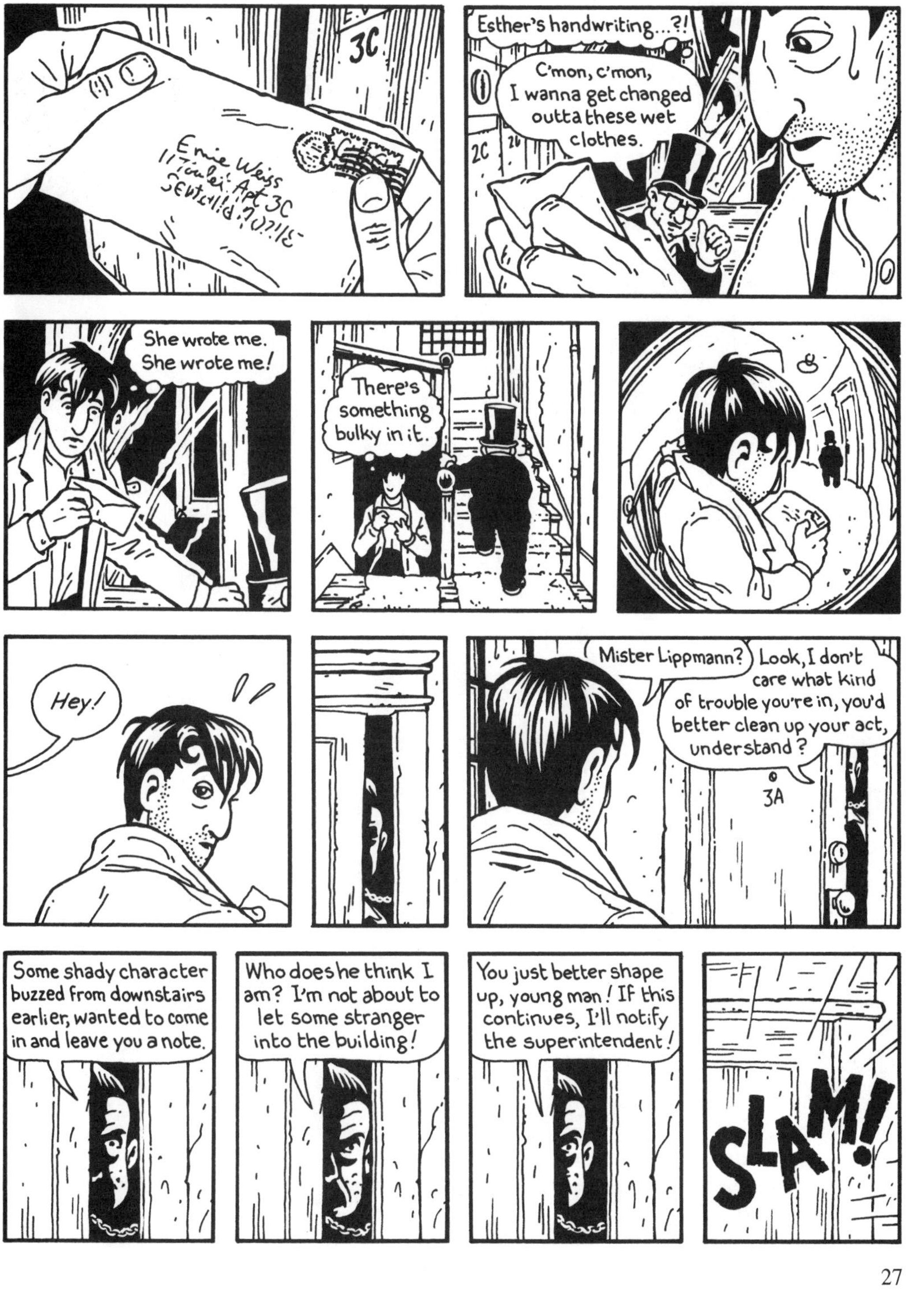
3C
Esther's handwriting...?!
C'mon, c'mon, I wanna get changed outta these wet clothes.
2C
She wrote me. She wrote me!
There's something bulky in it.
Hey!
Mister Lippmann?
Look, I don't care what kind of trouble you're in, you'd better clean up your act, understand?
3A
Some shady character buzzed from downstairs earlier, wanted to come in and leave you a note.
Who does he think I am? I'm not about to let some stranger into the building!
You just better shape up, young man! If this continues, I'll notify the superintendent!
SLAM!

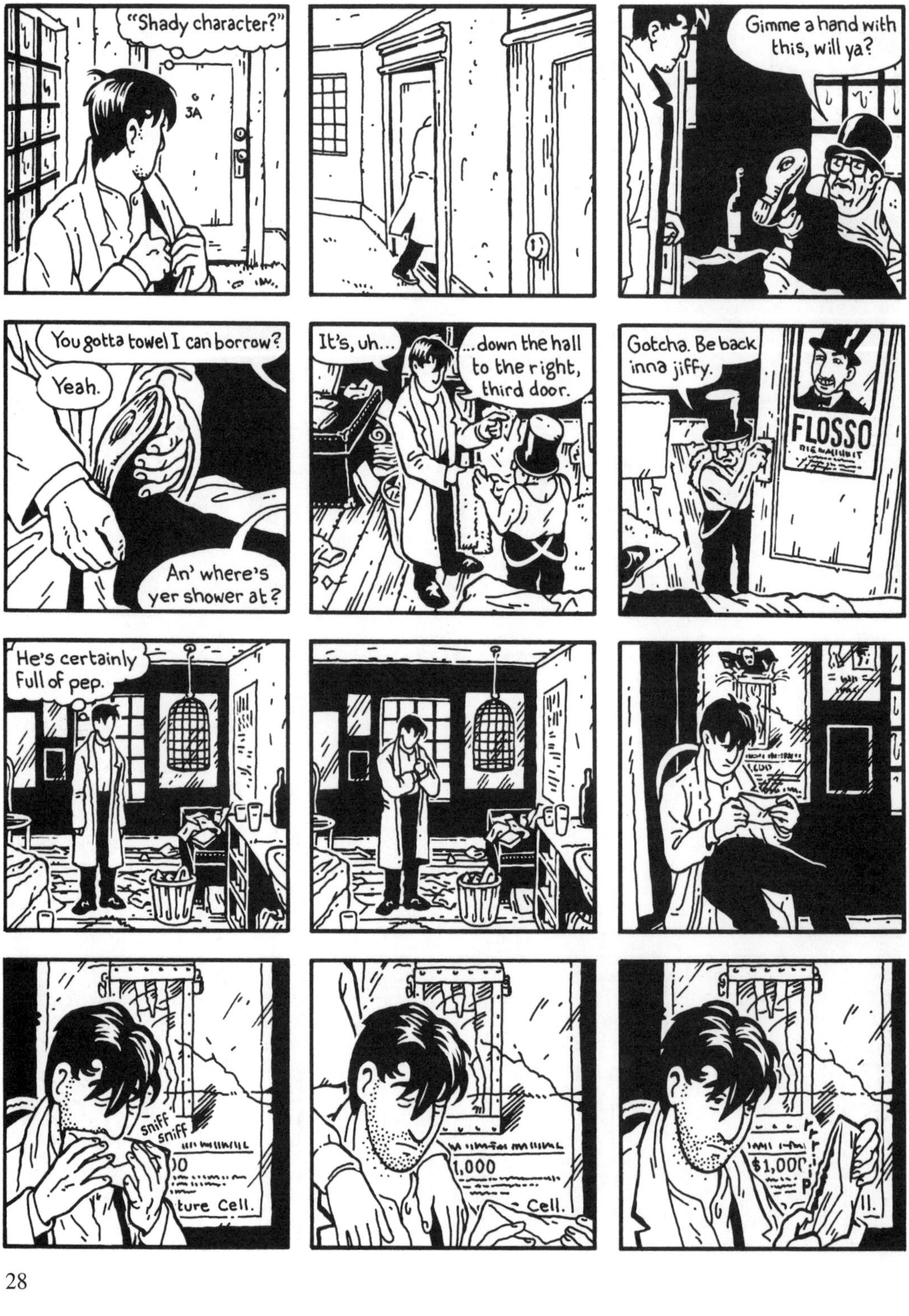
"Shady character?"
3A
Gimme a hand with this, will ya?
You gotta towel I can borrow?
Yeah.
An' where's yer shower at?
It's, uh...
...down the hall to the right, third door.
Gotcha. Be back inna jiffy.
FLOSSO
He's certainly full of pep.
sniff sniff
ture Cell.
1,000
Cell.
$1,000

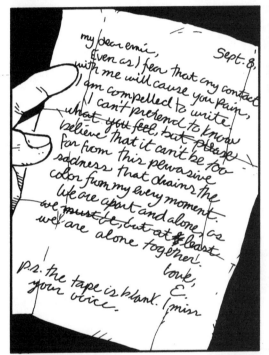

my dear emie,
(even as) I fear that my contact
with me will cause you pain,
I am compelled to write.
I can't pretend to know
what you feel, but please
believe that it can't be too
far from this pervasive
sadness that drains the
color from my every moment.
We are apart and alone, as
we must be, but at least
we are alone together!
love,
E.
p.s. the tape is blank. I miss
your voice.

Sept. 8,

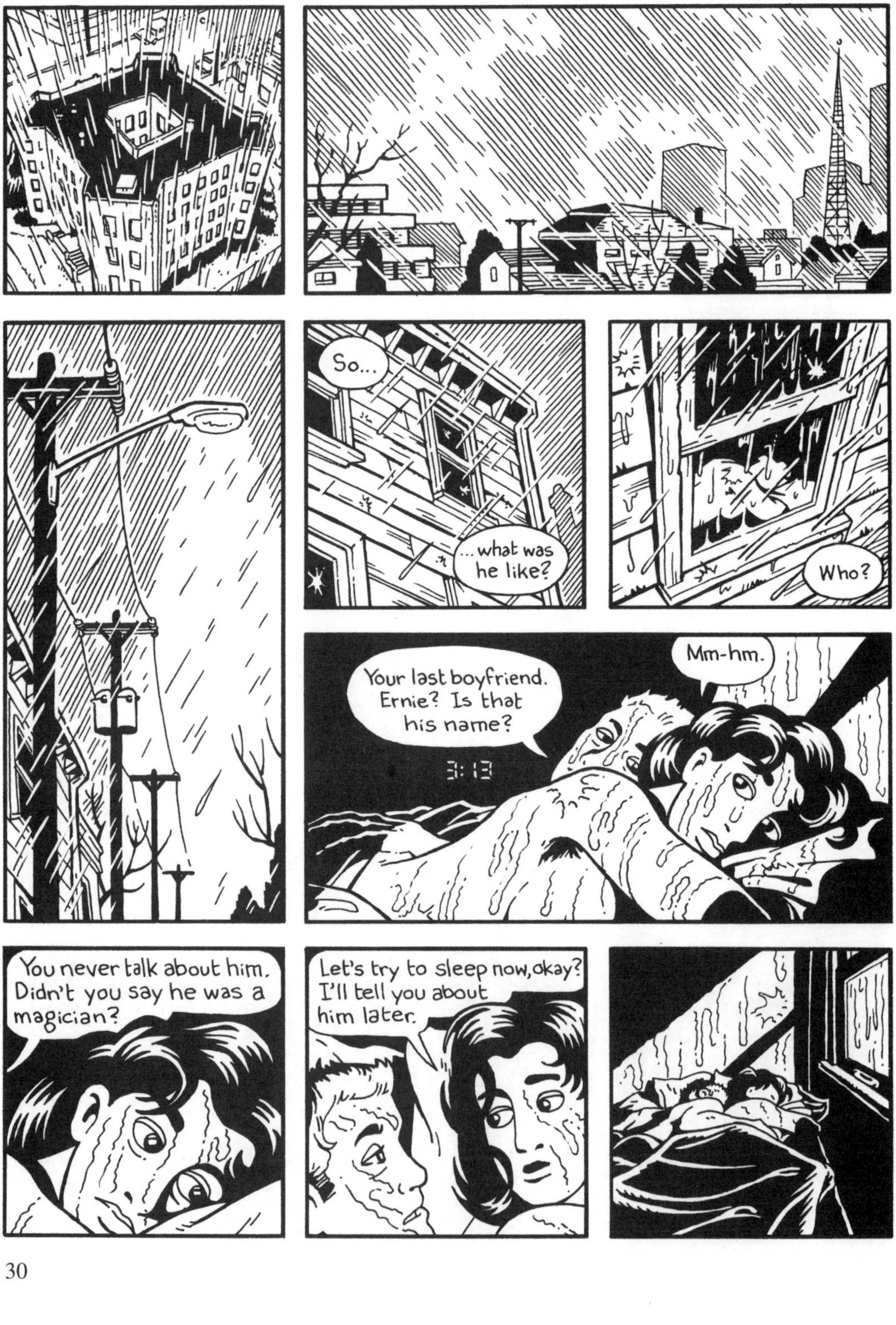
So...
...what was he like?
Who?
Your last boyfriend. Ernie? Is that his name?
Mm-hm.
3:13
You never talk about him. Didn't you say he was a magician?
Let's try to sleep now, okay? I'll tell you about him later.

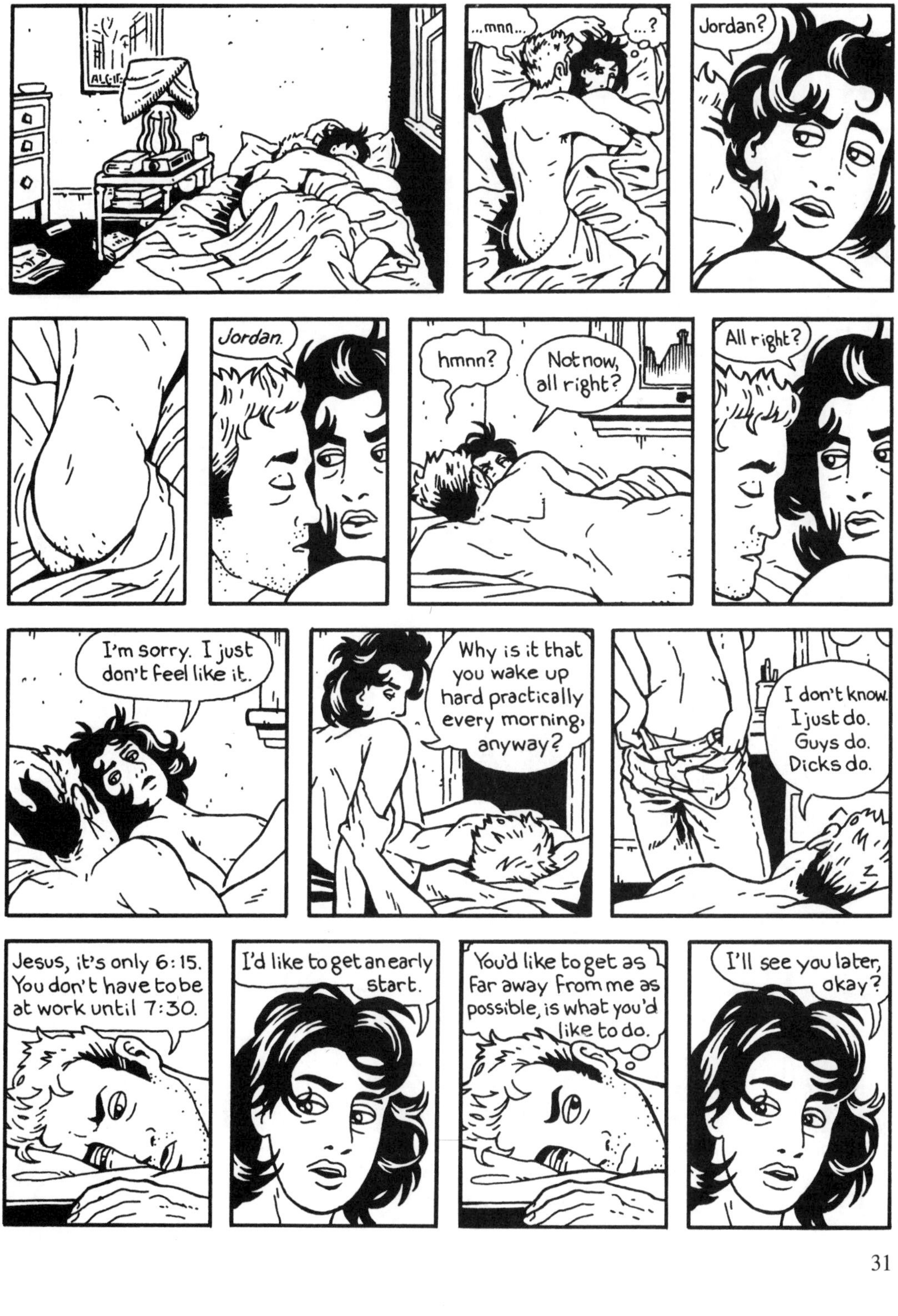
...mnn...
...?
Jordan?
Jordan.
hmnn?
Not now, all right?
All right?
I'm sorry. I just don't feel like it.
Why is it that you wake up hard practically every morning, anyway?
I don't know. I just do. Guys do. Dicks do.
Jesus, it's only 6:15. You don't have to be at work until 7:30.
I'd like to get an early start.
You'd like to get as far away from me as possible, is what you'd like to do.
I'll see you later, okay?

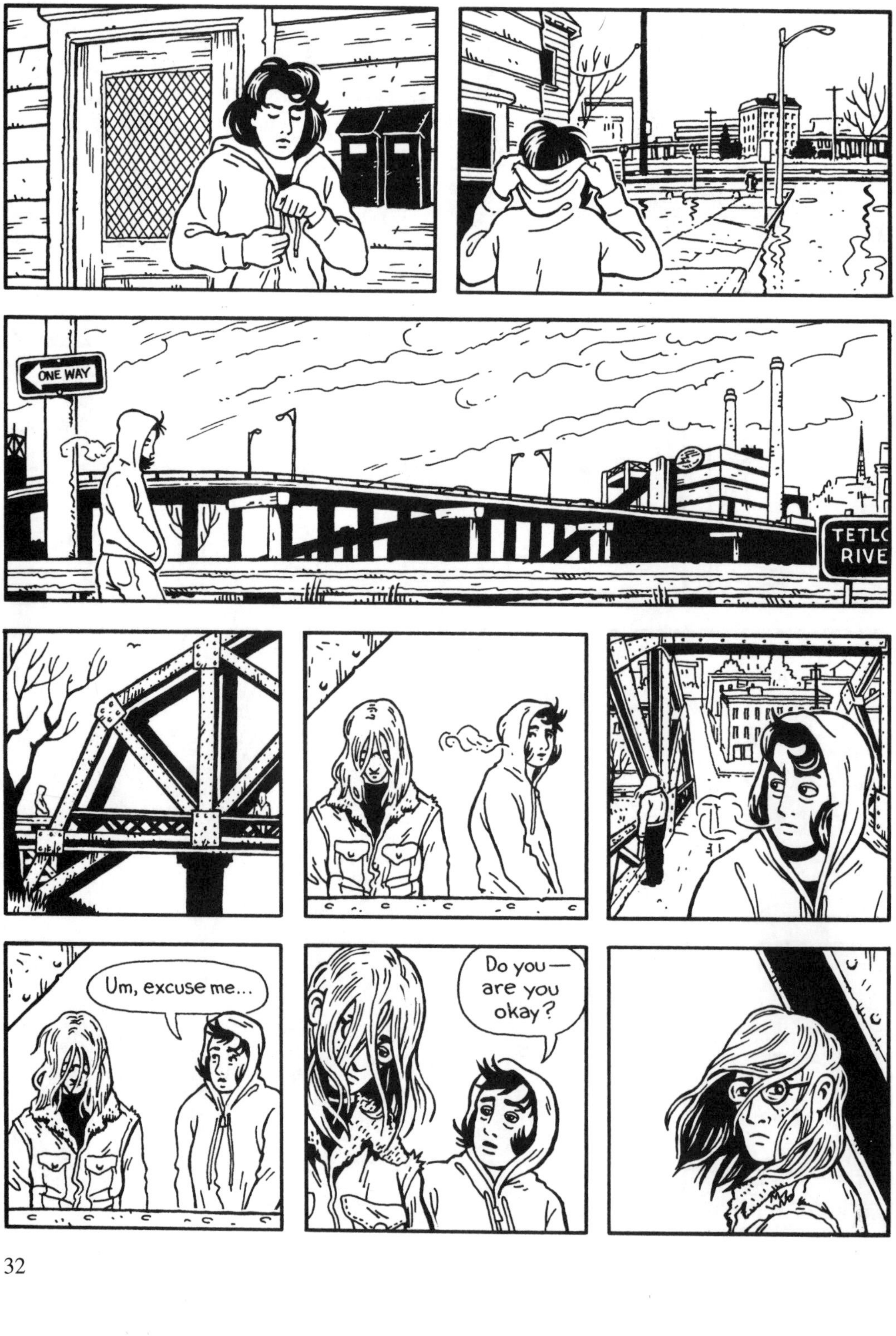
ONE WAY
TETLO
RIVE
Um, excuse me...
Do you— are you okay?

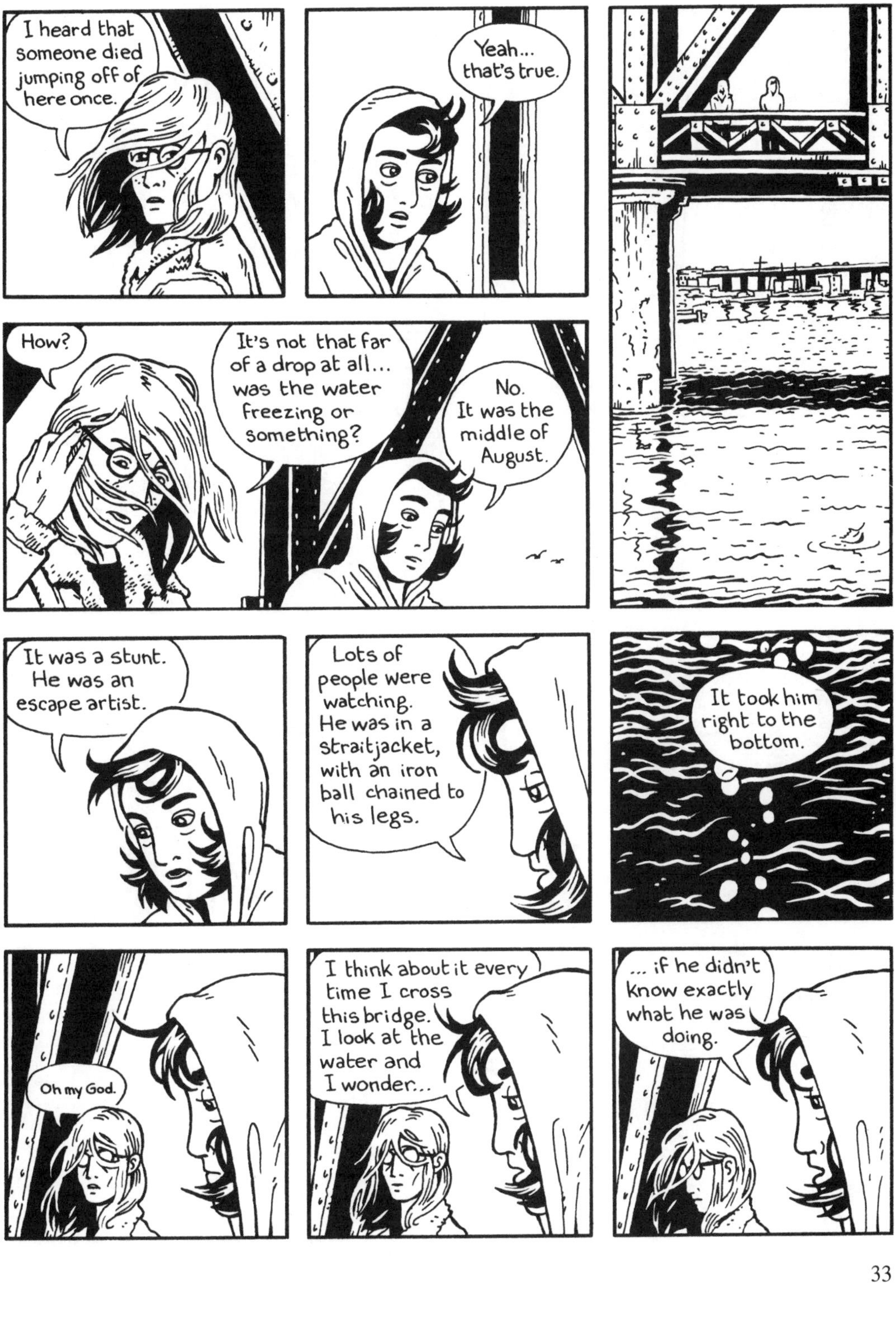
I heard that someone died jumping off of here once.
Yeah... that's true.
How?
It's not that far of a drop at all... was the water freezing or something?
No. It was the middle of August.
It was a stunt. He was an escape artist.
Lots of people were watching. He was in a straitjacket, with an iron ball chained to his legs.
It took him right to the bottom.
Oh my God.
I think about it every time I cross this bridge. I look at the water and I wonder...
... if he didn't know exactly what he was doing.

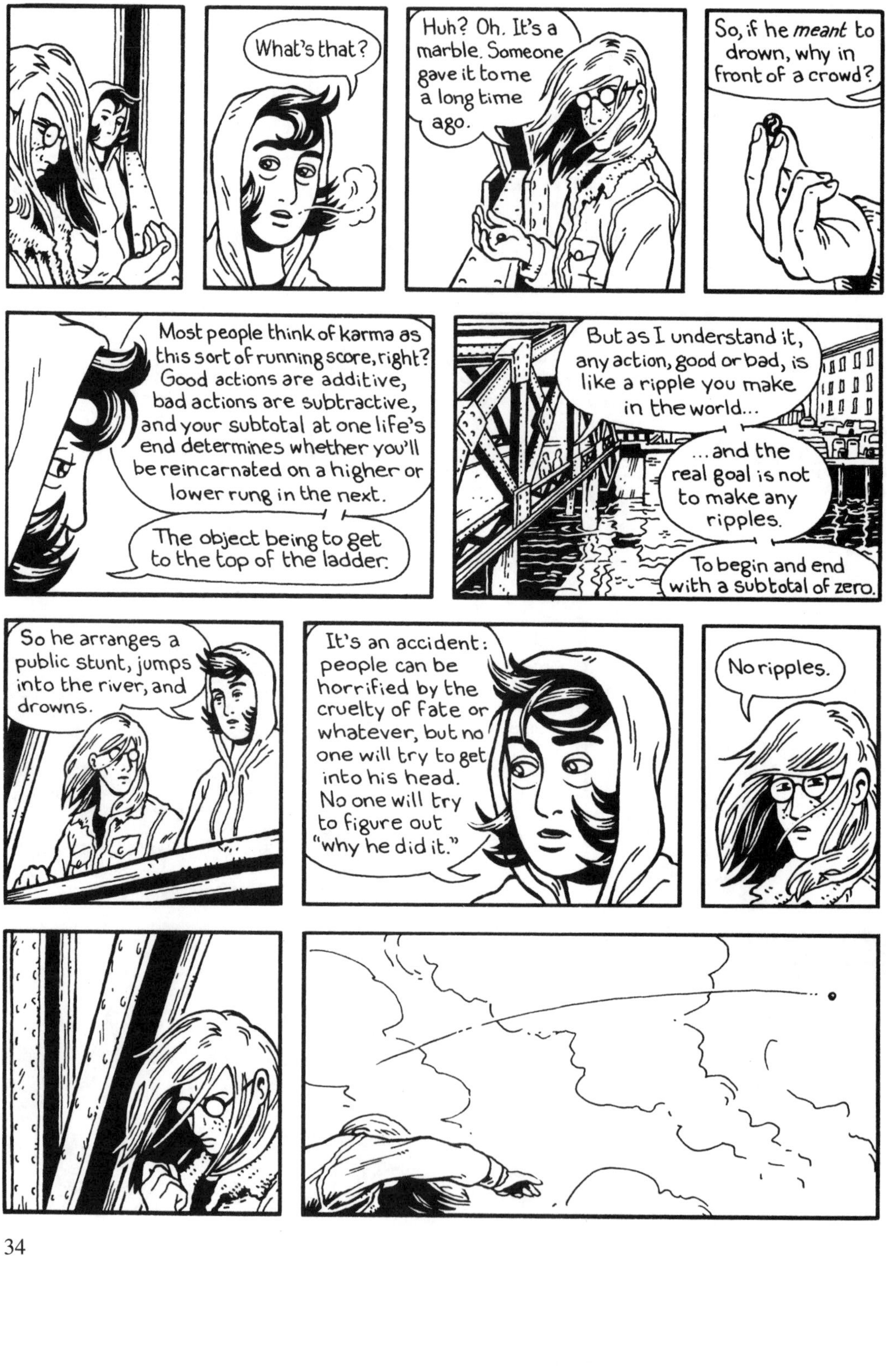
What's that?
Huh? Oh. It's a marble. Someone gave it to me a long time ago.
So, if he *meant* to drown, why in front of a crowd?
Most people think of karma as this sort of running score, right? Good actions are additive, bad actions are subtractive, and your subtotal at one life's end determines whether you'll be reincarnated on a higher or lower rung in the next.
The object being to get to the top of the ladder.
But as I understand it, any action, good or bad, is like a ripple you make in the world...
...and the real goal is not to make any ripples.
To begin and end with a subtotal of zero.
So he arranges a public stunt, jumps into the river, and drowns.
It's an accident: people can be horrified by the cruelty of fate or whatever, but no one will try to get into his head. No one will try to figure out "why he did it."
No ripples.

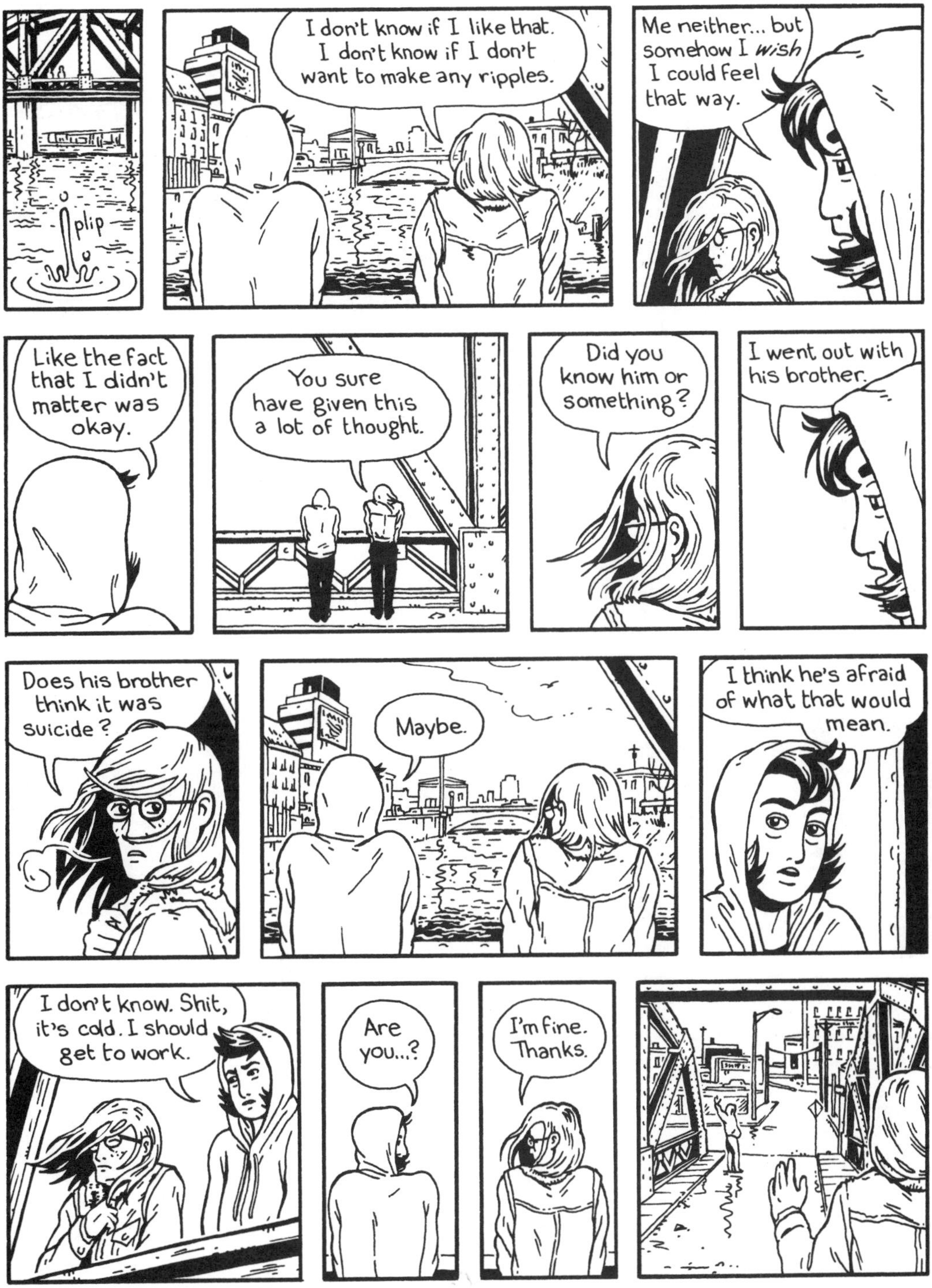
plip
I don't know if I like that. I don't know if I don't want to make any ripples.
Me neither... but somehow I *wish* I could feel that way.
Like the fact that I didn't matter was okay.
You sure have given this a lot of thought.
Did you know him or something?
I went out with his brother.
Does his brother think it was suicide?
Maybe.
I think he's afraid of what that would mean.
I don't know. Shit, it's cold. I should get to work.
Are you...?
I'm fine. Thanks.

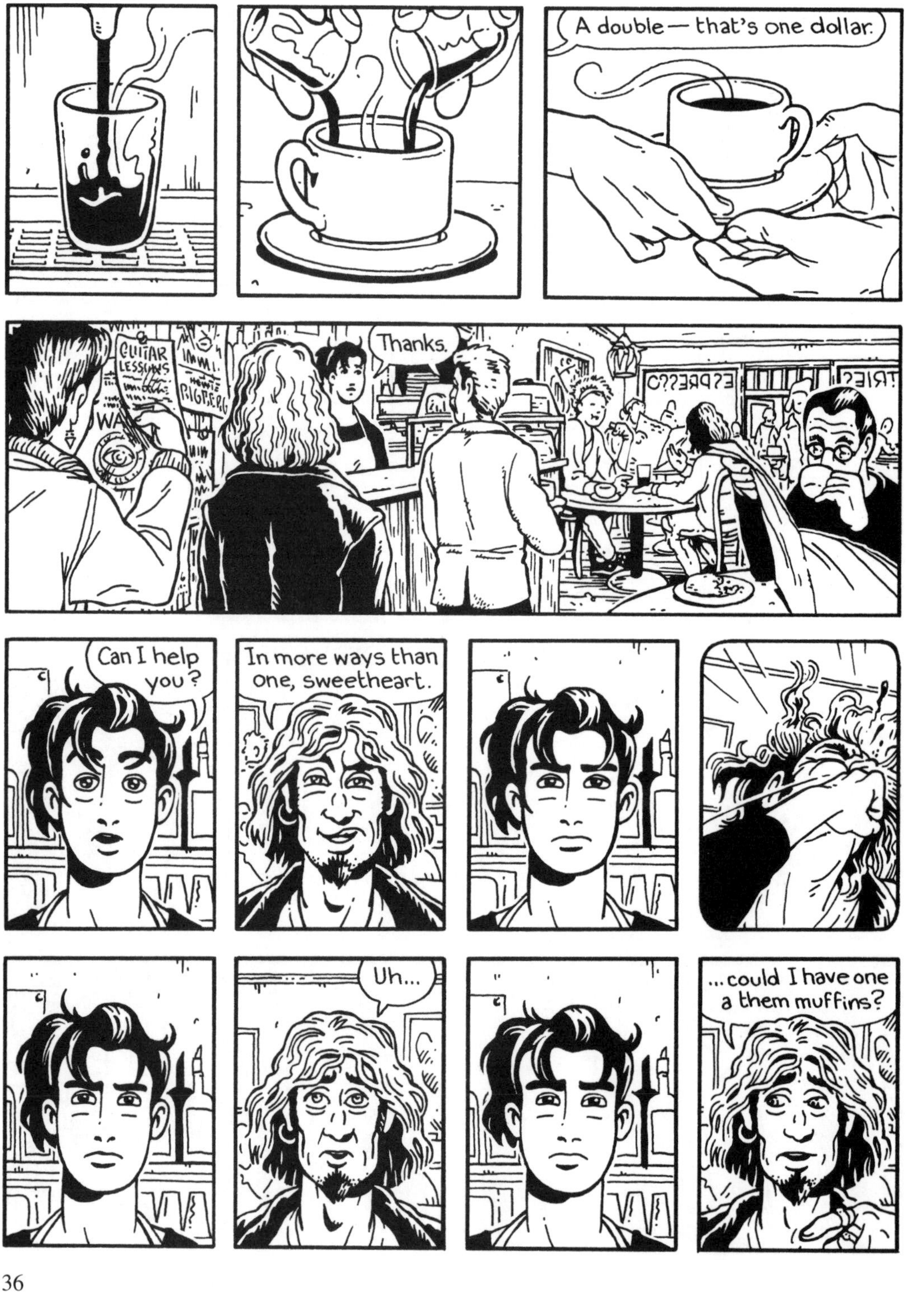
A double — that's one dollar.
Thanks.
GUITAR LESSONS
ESPRESSO
Can I help you?
In more ways than one, sweetheart.
Uh...
...could I have one a them muffins?

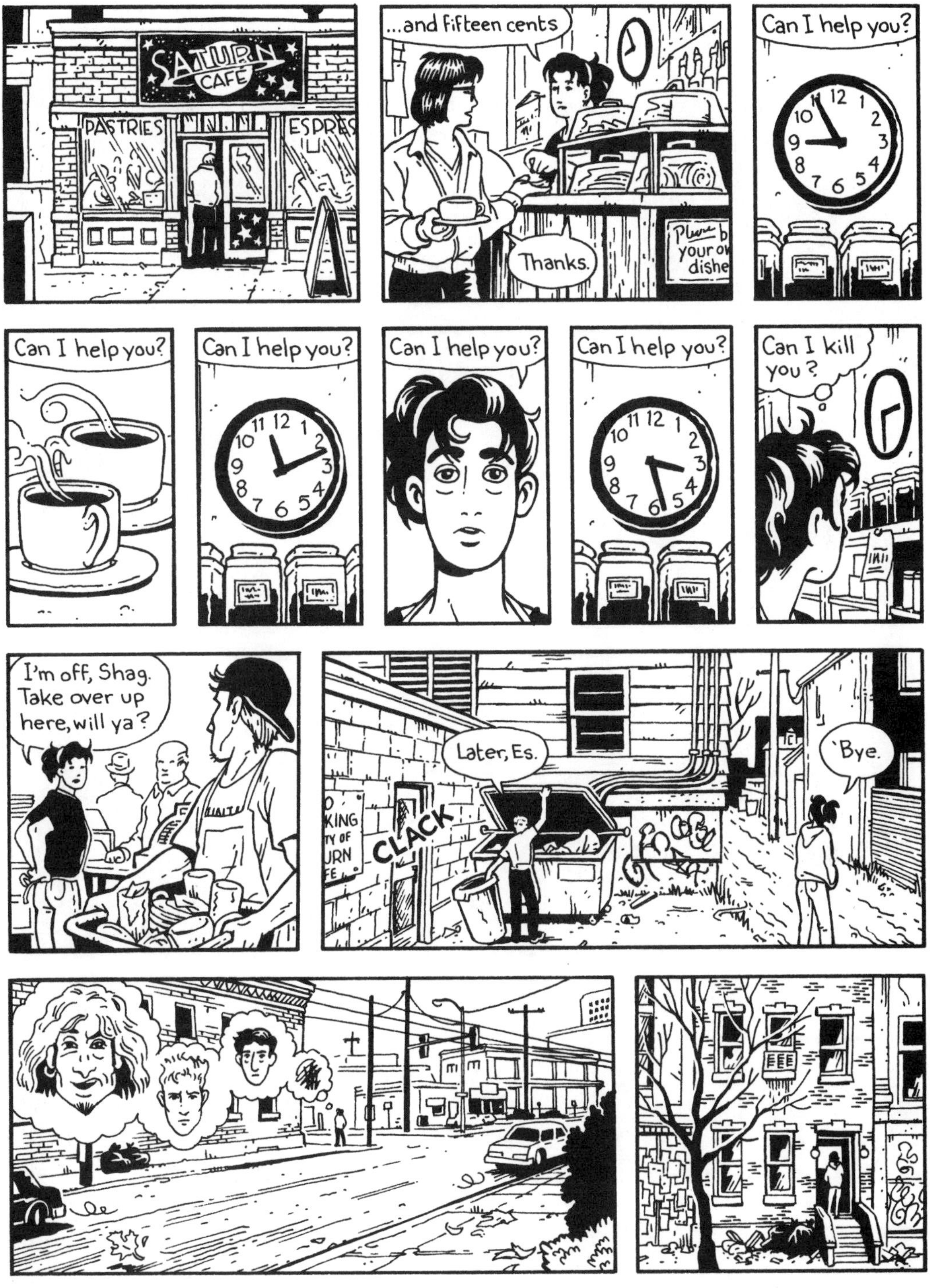

SATURN CAFÉ
PASTRIES
ESPRES
...and fifteen cents
Thanks.
Can I help you?
Can I help you?
Can I help you?
Can I help you?
Can I help you?
Can I kill you?
I'm off, Shag. Take over up here, will ya?
Later, Es.
CLACK
`Bye.

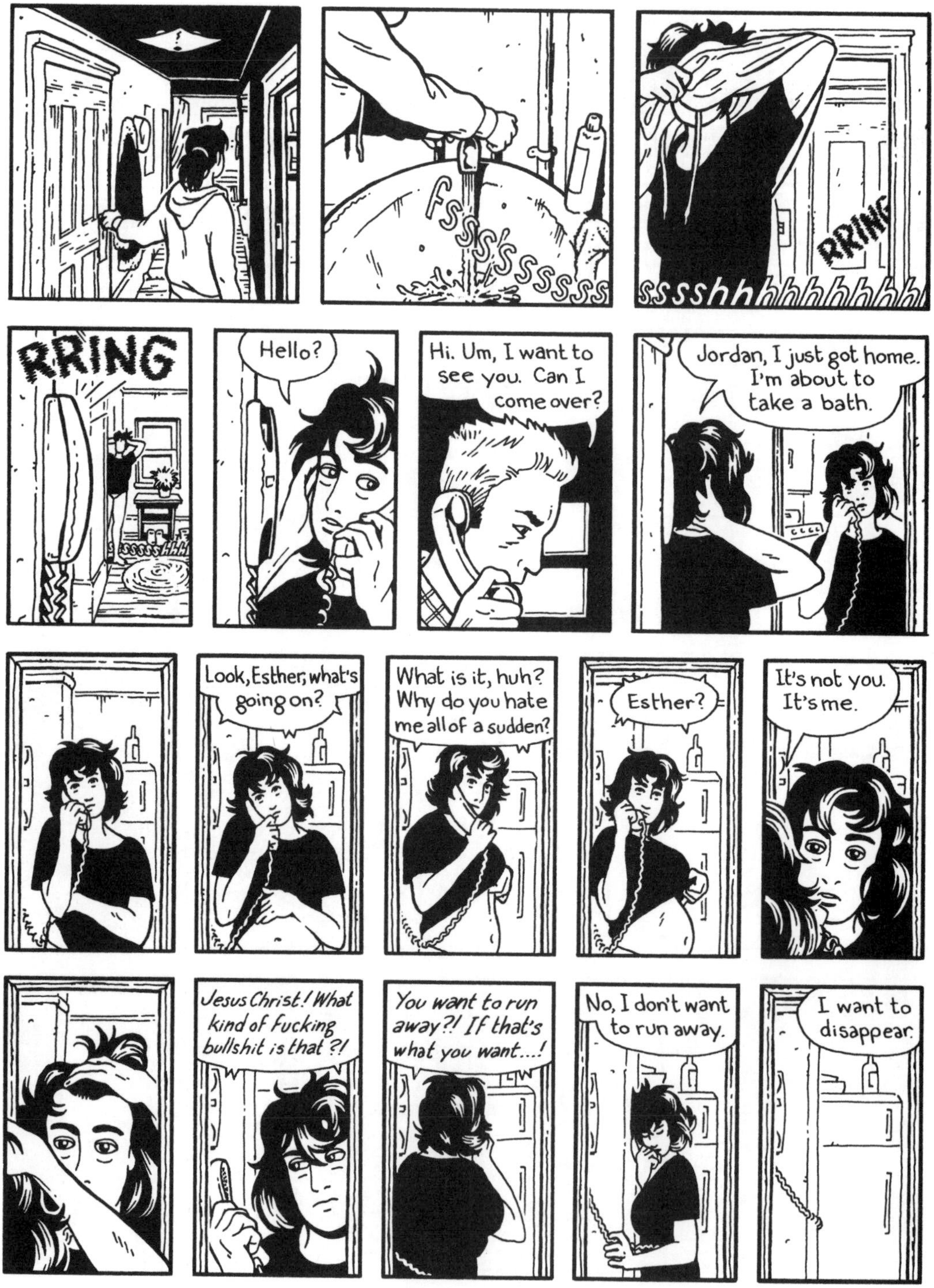

fsssssssssss
ssssshhhhhhhhhh
RRING
RRING
Hello?
Hi. Um, I want to see you. Can I come over?
Jordan, I just got home. I'm about to take a bath.
Look, Esther, what's going on?
What is it, huh? Why do you hate me all of a sudden?
Esther?
It's not you. It's me.
Jesus Christ! What kind of fucking bullshit is that?!
You want to run away?! If that's what you want...!
No, I don't want to run away.
I want to disappear.

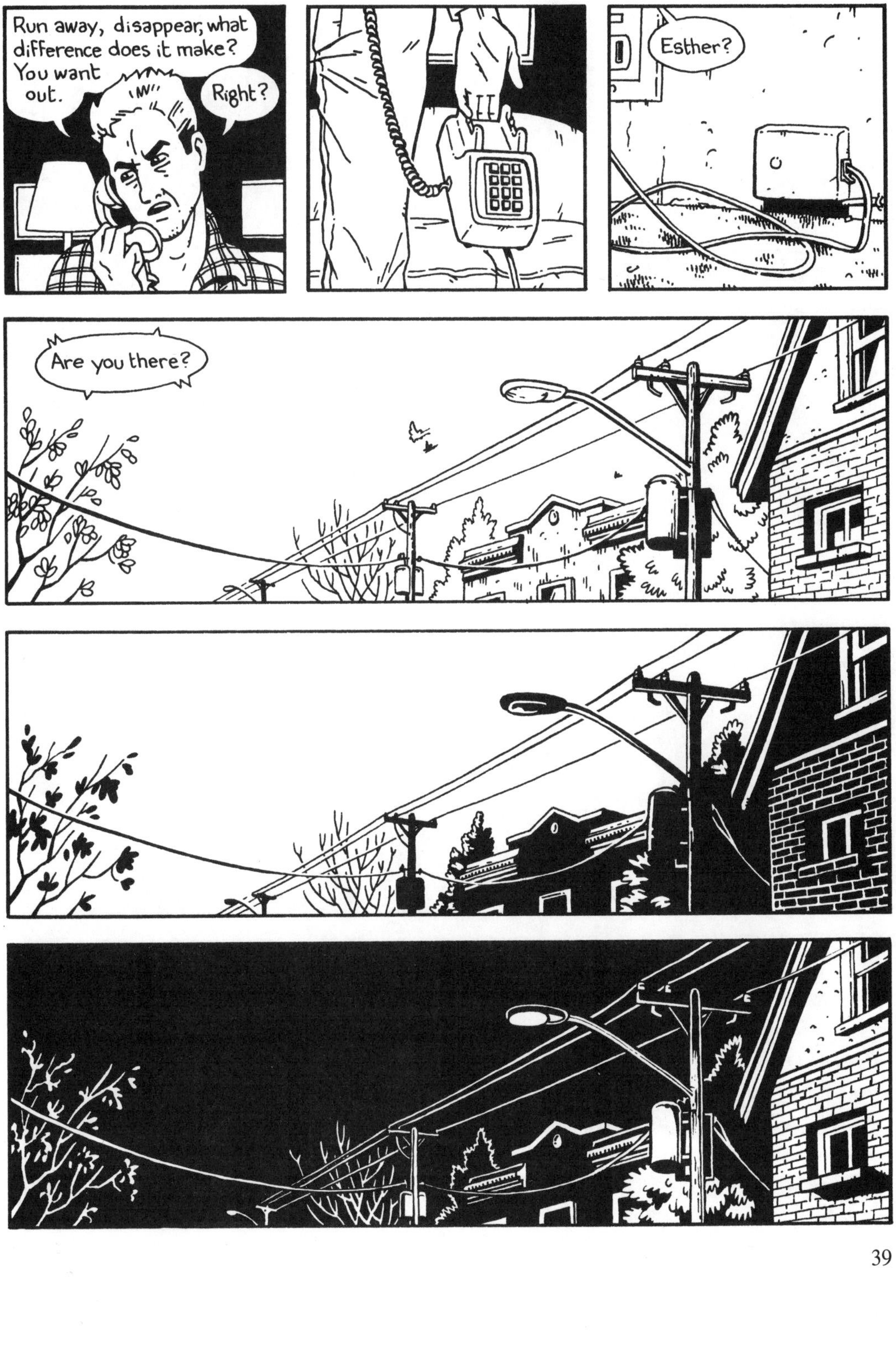

Run away, disappear, what difference does it make? You want out.
Right?
Esther?
Are you there?

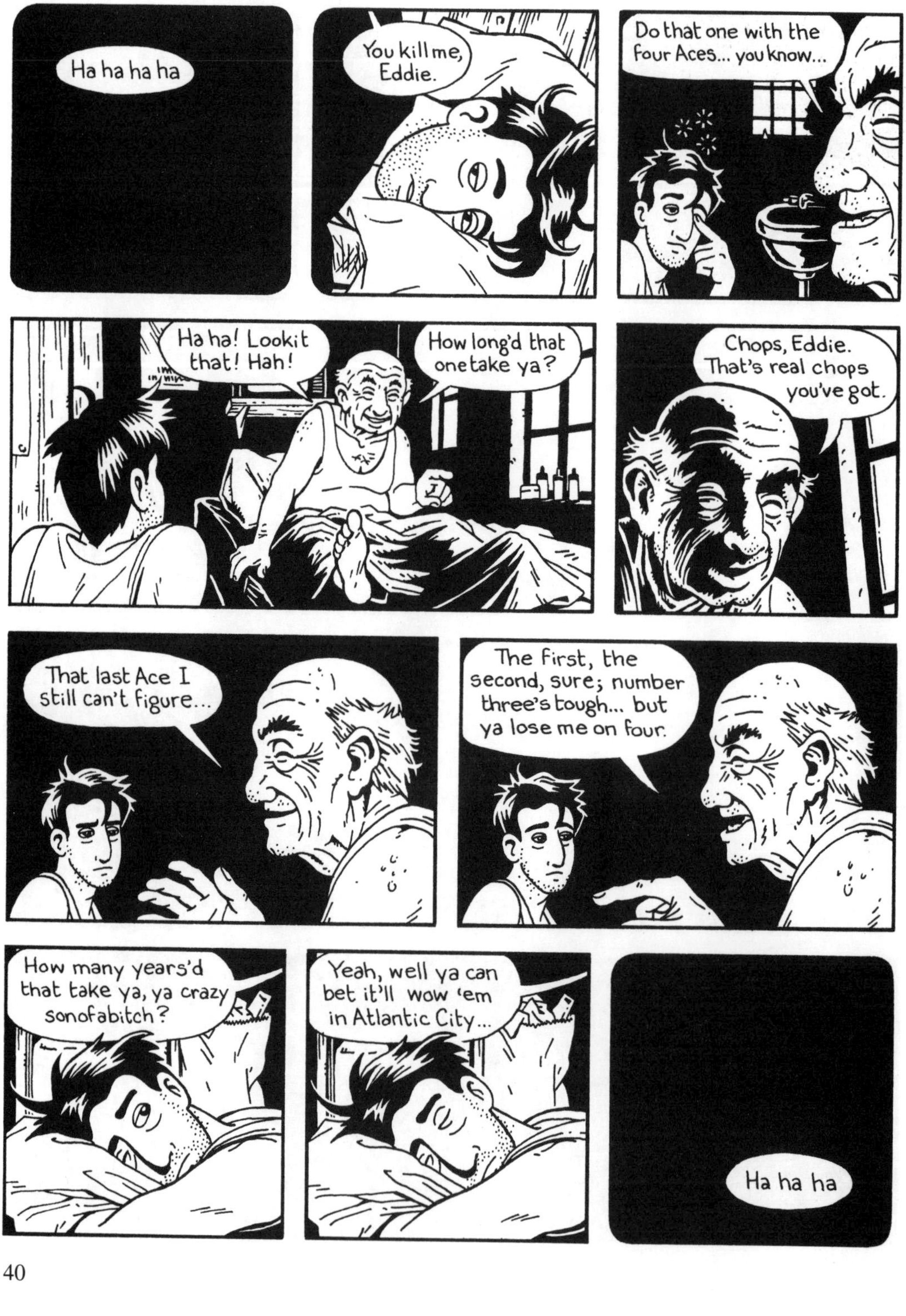
Ha ha ha ha
You kill me, Eddie.
Do that one with the four Aces... you know...
Ha ha! Lookit that! Hah!
How long'd that one take ya?
Chops, Eddie. That's real chops you've got.
That last Ace I still can't figure...
The first, the second, sure; number three's tough... but ya lose me on four.
How many years'd that take ya, ya crazy sonofabitch?
Yeah, well ya can bet it'll wow 'em in Atlantic City...
Ha ha ha

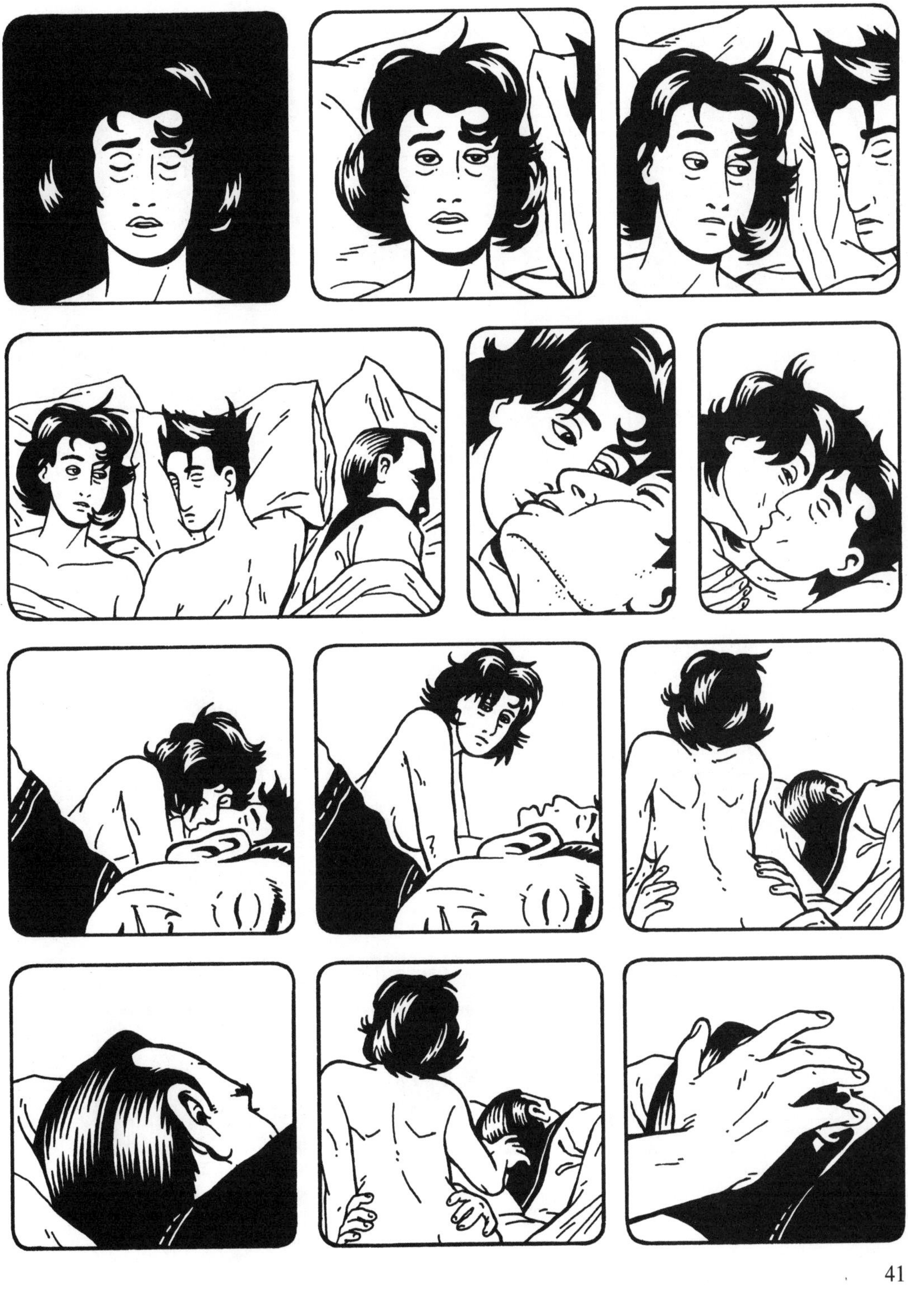

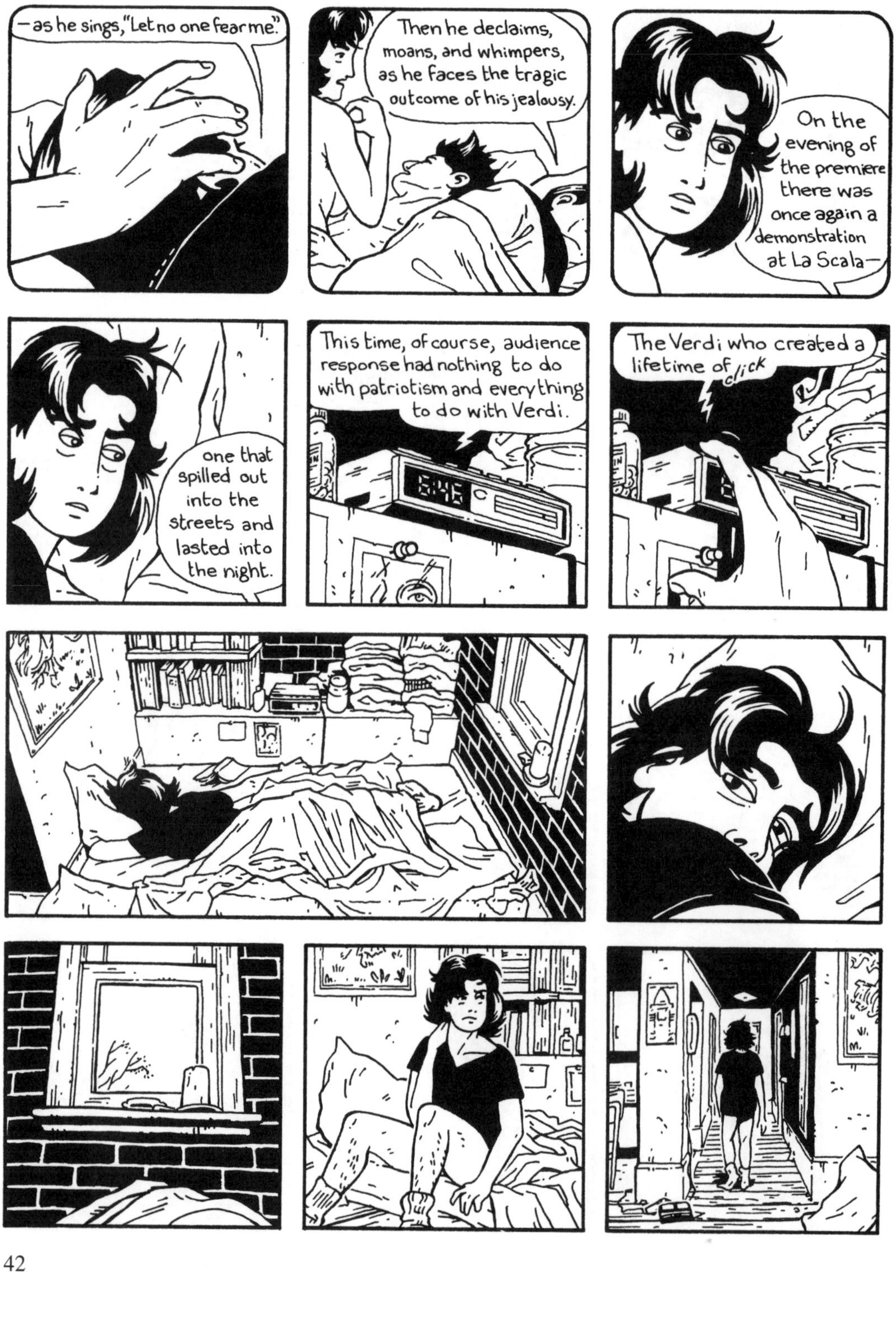
—as he sings, "Let no one fear me."
Then he declaims, moans, and whimpers, as he faces the tragic outcome of his jealousy.
On the evening of the premiere there was once again a demonstration at La Scala—
one that spilled out into the streets and lasted into the night.
This time, of course, audience response had nothing to do with patriotism and everything to do with Verdi.
The Verdi who created a lifetime of
click

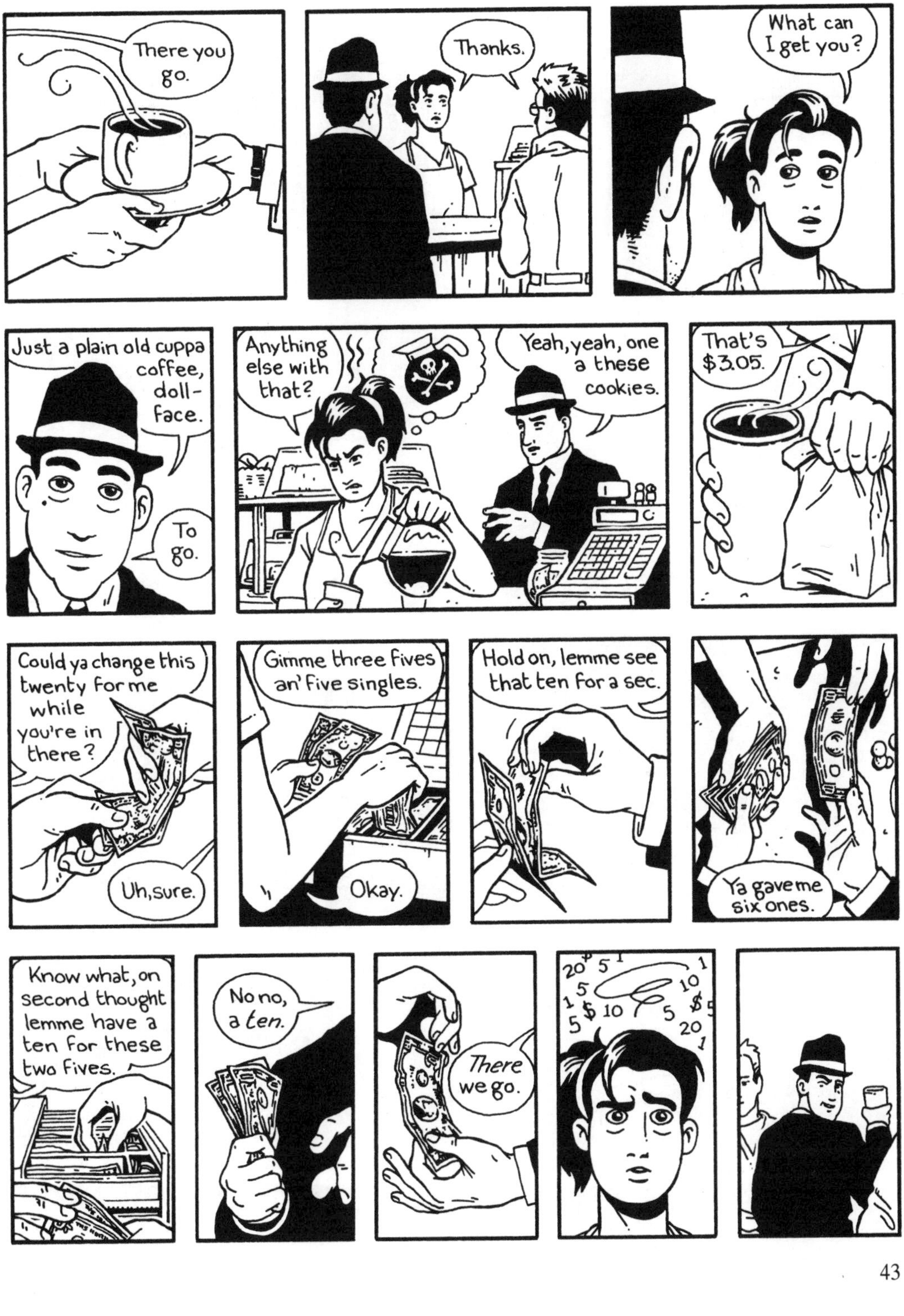

There you go.
Thanks.
What can I get you?
Just a plain old cuppa coffee, doll-face.
To go.
Anything else with that?
Yeah, yeah, one a these cookies.
That's $3.05.
Could ya change this twenty for me while you're in there?
Uh, sure.
Gimme three fives an' five singles.
Okay.
Hold on, lemme see that ten for a sec.
Ya gave me six ones.
Know what, on second thought lemme have a ten for these two fives.
No no, a *ten*.
There we go.
20 5 1 1 5 10 1 $ 10 5 $ 5 5 20 1

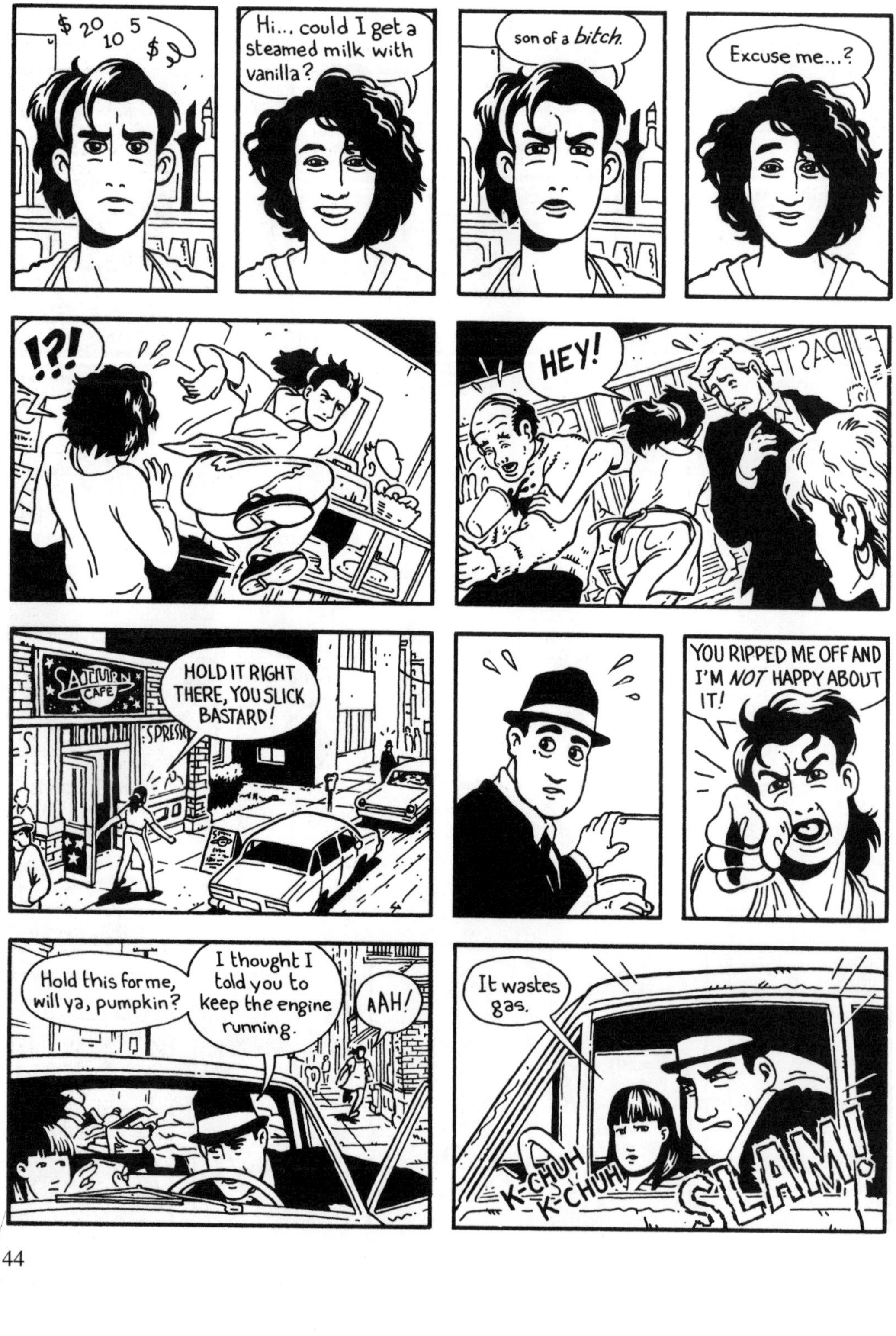
$ 20 10 5 $
Hi... could I get a steamed milk with vanilla?
son of a bitch.
Excuse me...?
!?!
HEY!
SATURN CAFÉ
ESPRESSO
HOLD IT RIGHT THERE, YOU SLICK BASTARD!
YOU RIPPED ME OFF AND I'M NOT HAPPY ABOUT IT!
Hold this for me, will ya, pumpkin?
I thought I told you to keep the engine running.
AAH!
It wastes gas.
K-CHUH K-CHUH
SLAM!

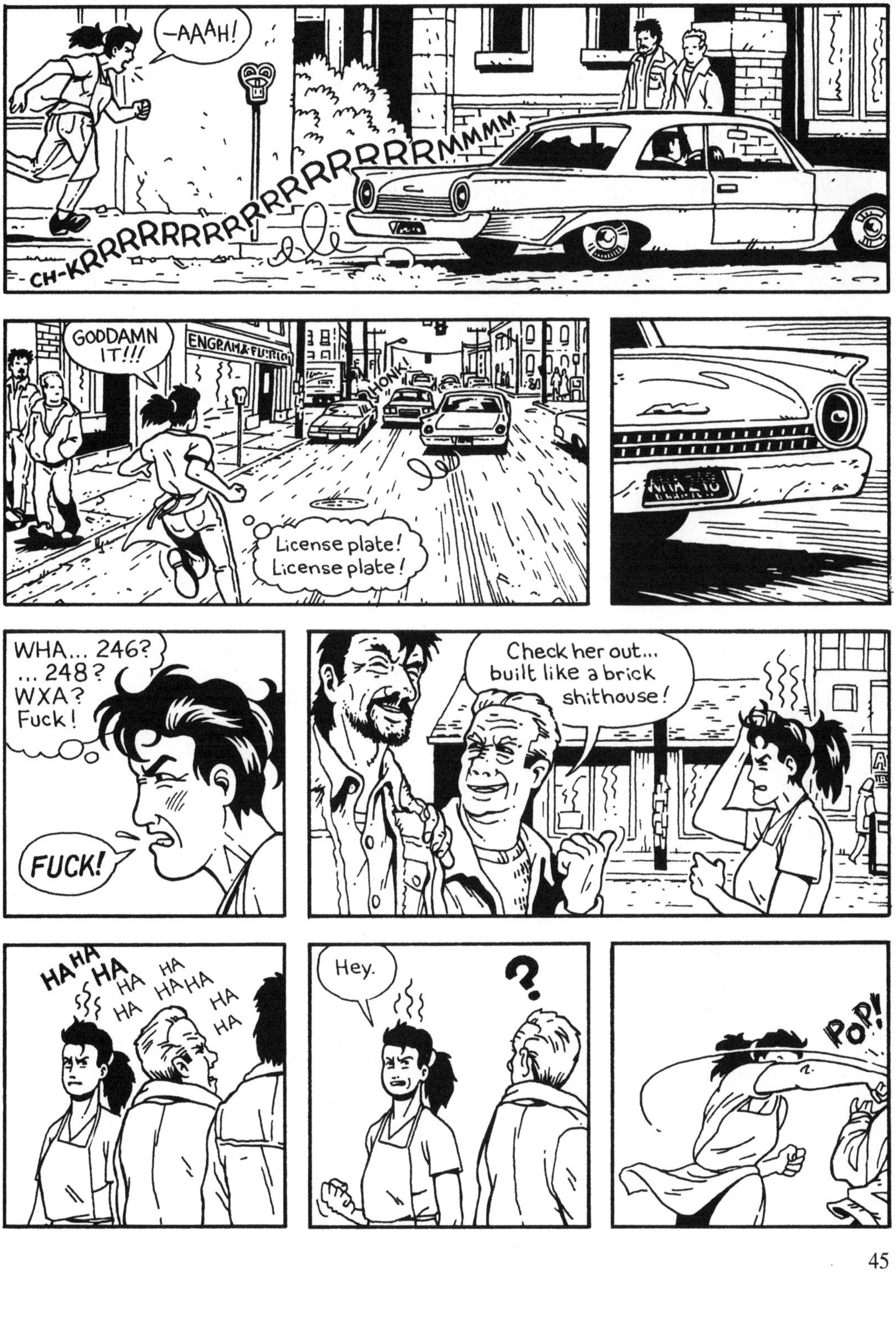
–AAAH!
CH-KRRRRRRRRRRRRRRRRRMMMM
GODDAMN IT!!!
HONK!
License plate! License plate!
WHA... 246? ... 248? WXA? Fuck!
FUCK!
Check her out... built like a brick shithouse!
HAHA HA HA HA HAHA HA HA HA
Hey.
?
POP!

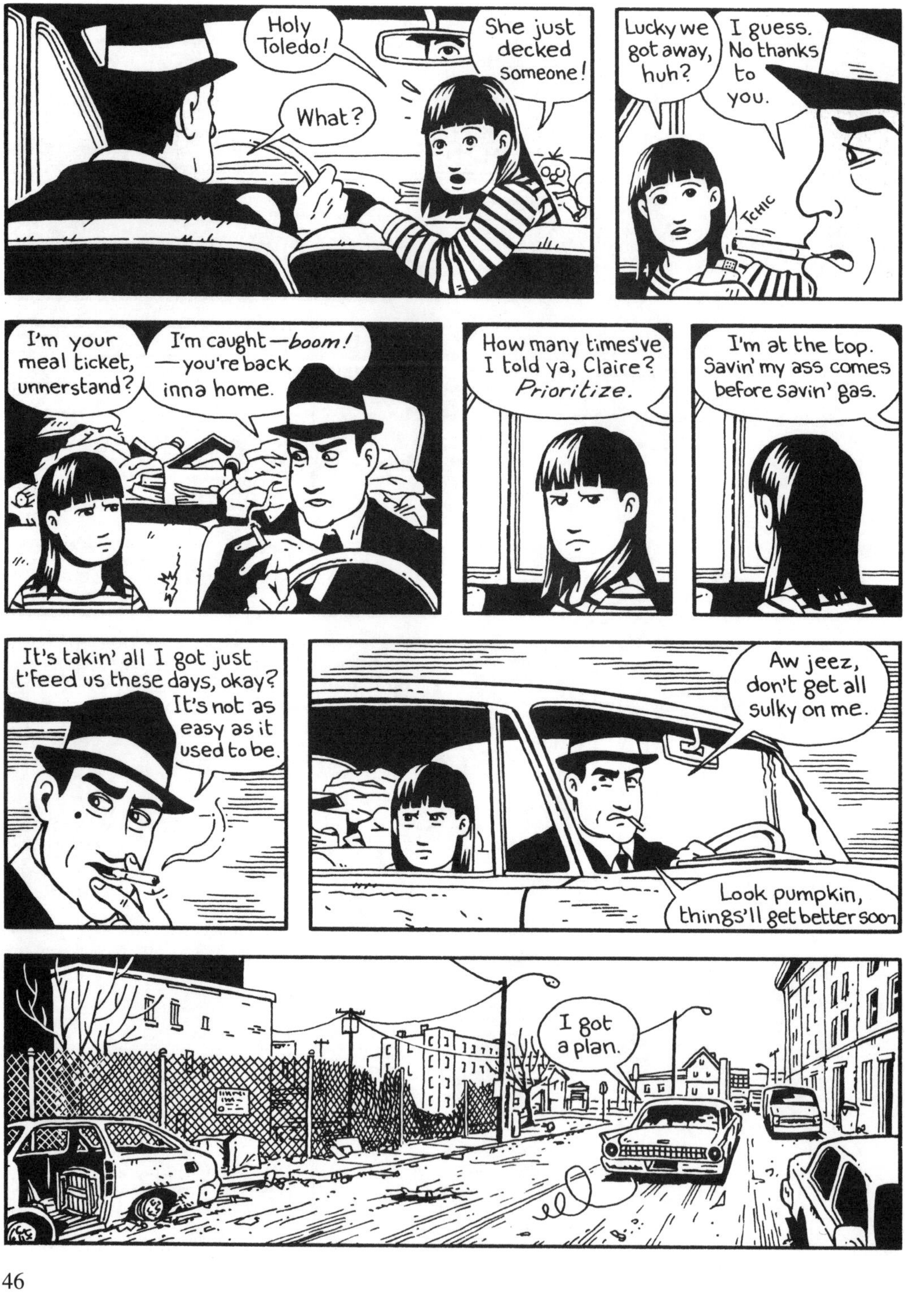
Holy Toledo!
What?
She just decked someone!
Lucky we got away, huh?
I guess. No thanks to you.
TCHIC
I'm your meal ticket, unnerstand?
I'm caught—*boom!* —you're back inna home.
How many times've I told ya, Claire? *Prioritize.*
I'm at the top. Savin' my ass comes before savin' gas.
It's takin' all I got just t'feed us these days, okay? It's not as easy as it used to be.
Aw jeez, don't get all sulky on me.
Look pumpkin, things'll get better soon.
I got a plan.

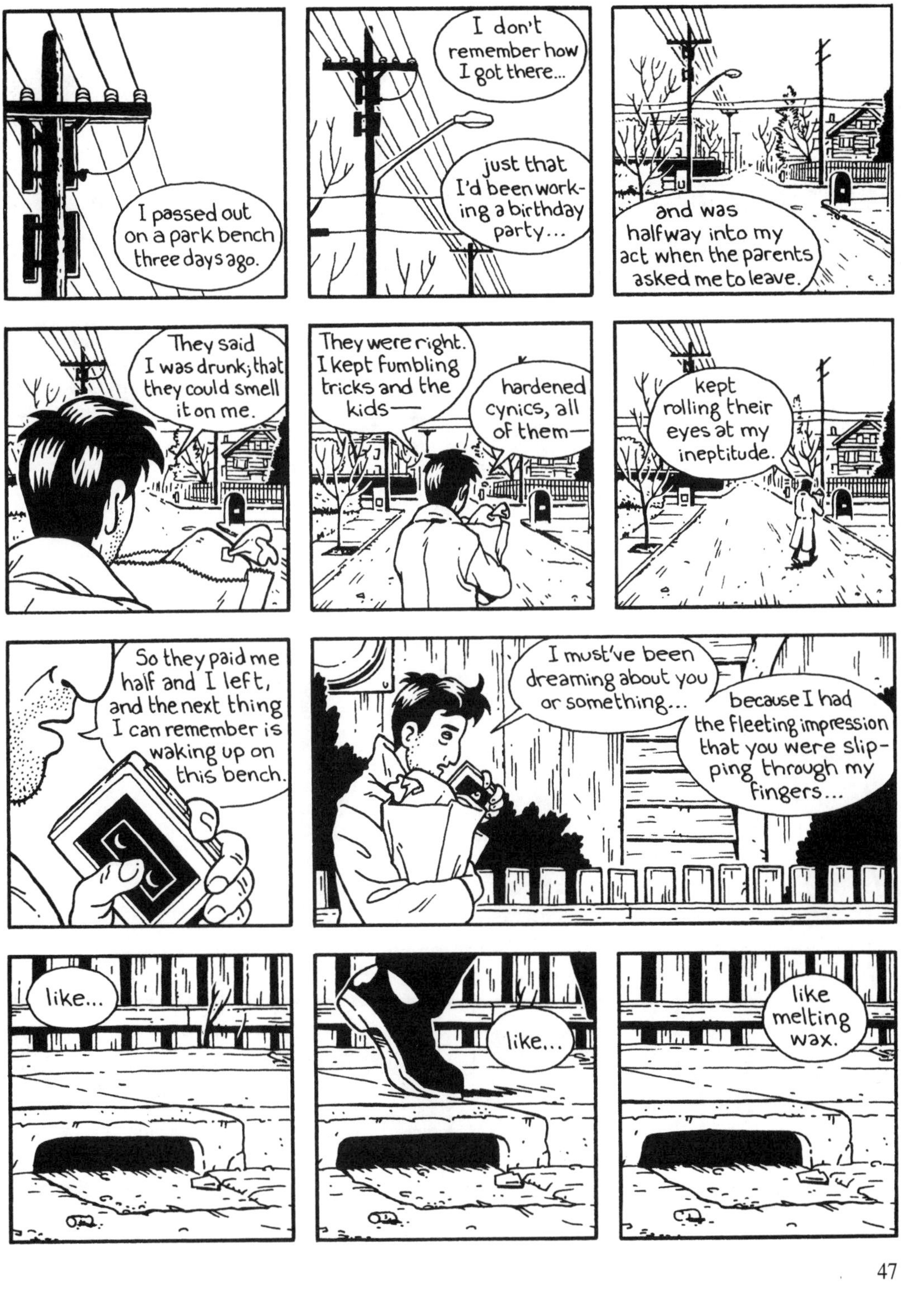
I passed out on a park bench three days ago.
I don't remember how I got there...
just that I'd been working a birthday party...
and was halfway into my act when the parents asked me to leave.
They said I was drunk; that they could smell it on me.
They were right. I kept fumbling tricks and the kids—
hardened cynics, all of them—
kept rolling their eyes at my ineptitude.
So they paid me half and I left, and the next thing I can remember is waking up on this bench.
I must've been dreaming about you or something...
because I had the fleeting impression that you were slipping through my fingers...
like...
like...
like melting wax.

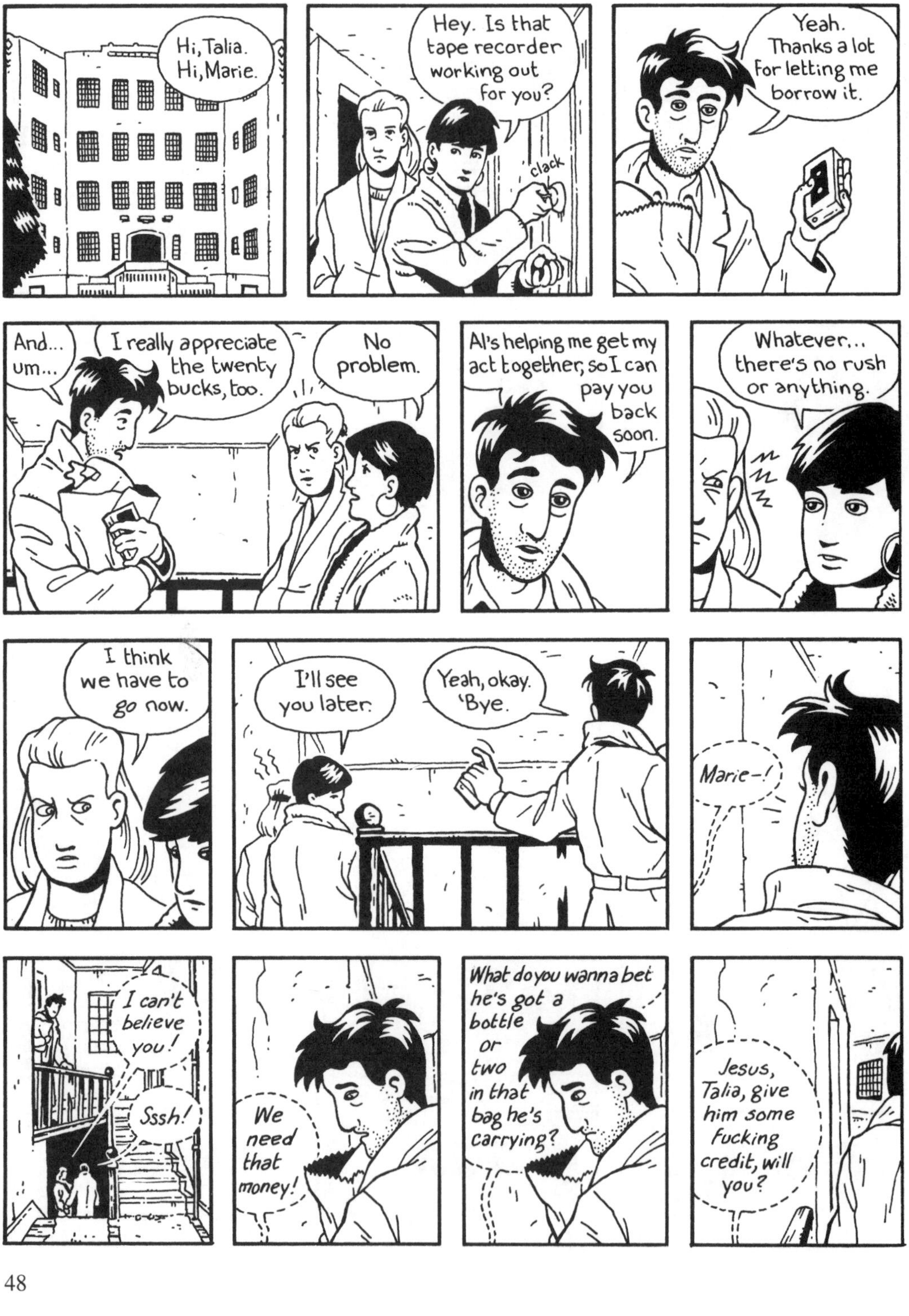
Hi, Talia. Hi, Marie.
Hey. Is that tape recorder working out for you?
clack
Yeah. Thanks a lot for letting me borrow it.
And... um...
I really appreciate the twenty bucks, too.
No problem.
Al's helping me get my act together, so I can pay you back soon.
Whatever... there's no rush or anything.
I think we have to go now.
I'll see you later.
Yeah, okay. 'Bye.
Marie–!
I can't believe you!
Sssh!
We need that money!
What do you wanna bet he's got a bottle or two in that bag he's carrying?
Jesus, Talia, give him some fucking credit, will you?

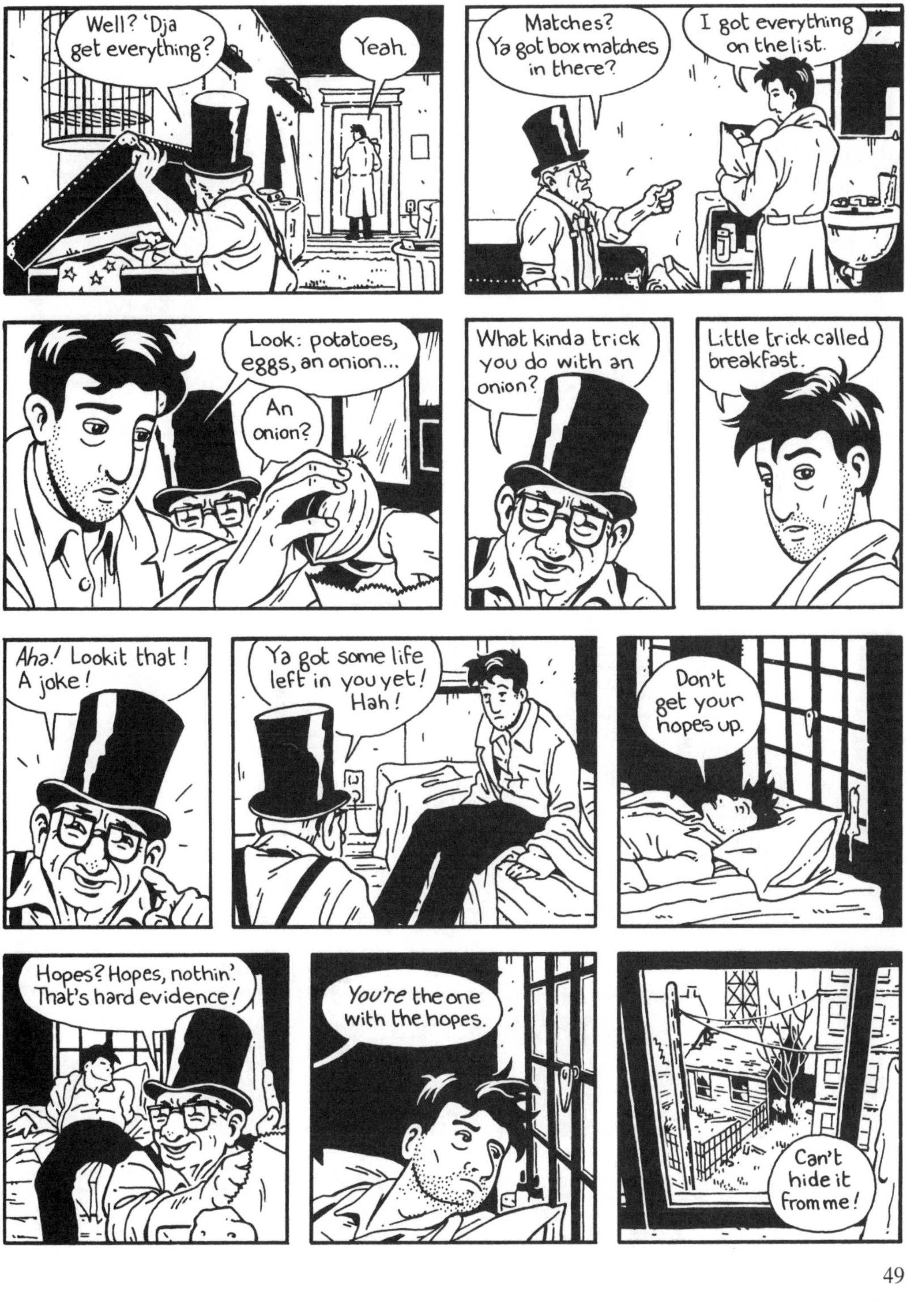
Well? 'Dja get everything?
Yeah.
Matches? Ya got box matches in there?
I got everything on the list.
Look: potatoes, eggs, an onion...
An onion?
What kinda trick you do with an onion?
Little trick called breakfast.
Aha! Lookit that! A joke!
Ya got some life left in you yet! Hah!
Don't get your hopes up.
Hopes? Hopes, nothin'. That's hard evidence!
You're the one with the hopes.
Can't hide it from me!

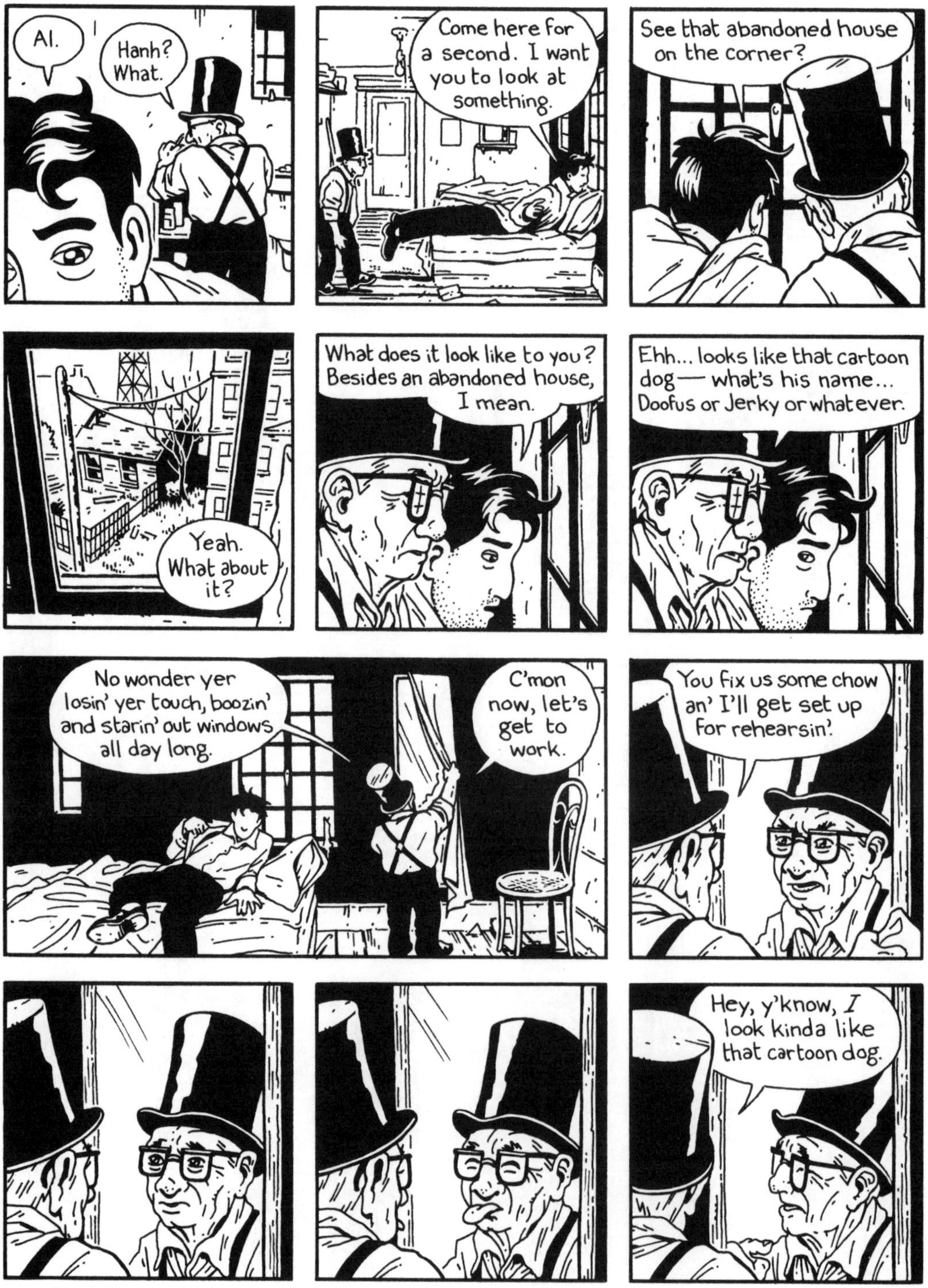
Al.
Hanh? What.
Come here for a second. I want you to look at something.
See that abandoned house on the corner?
Yeah. What about it?
What does it look like to you? Besides an abandoned house, I mean.
Ehh... looks like that cartoon dog — what's his name... Doofus or Jerky or whatever.
No wonder yer losin' yer touch, boozin' and starin' out windows all day long.
C'mon now, let's get to work.
You fix us some chow an' I'll get set up for rehearsin'.
Hey, y'know, *I* look kinda like that cartoon dog.

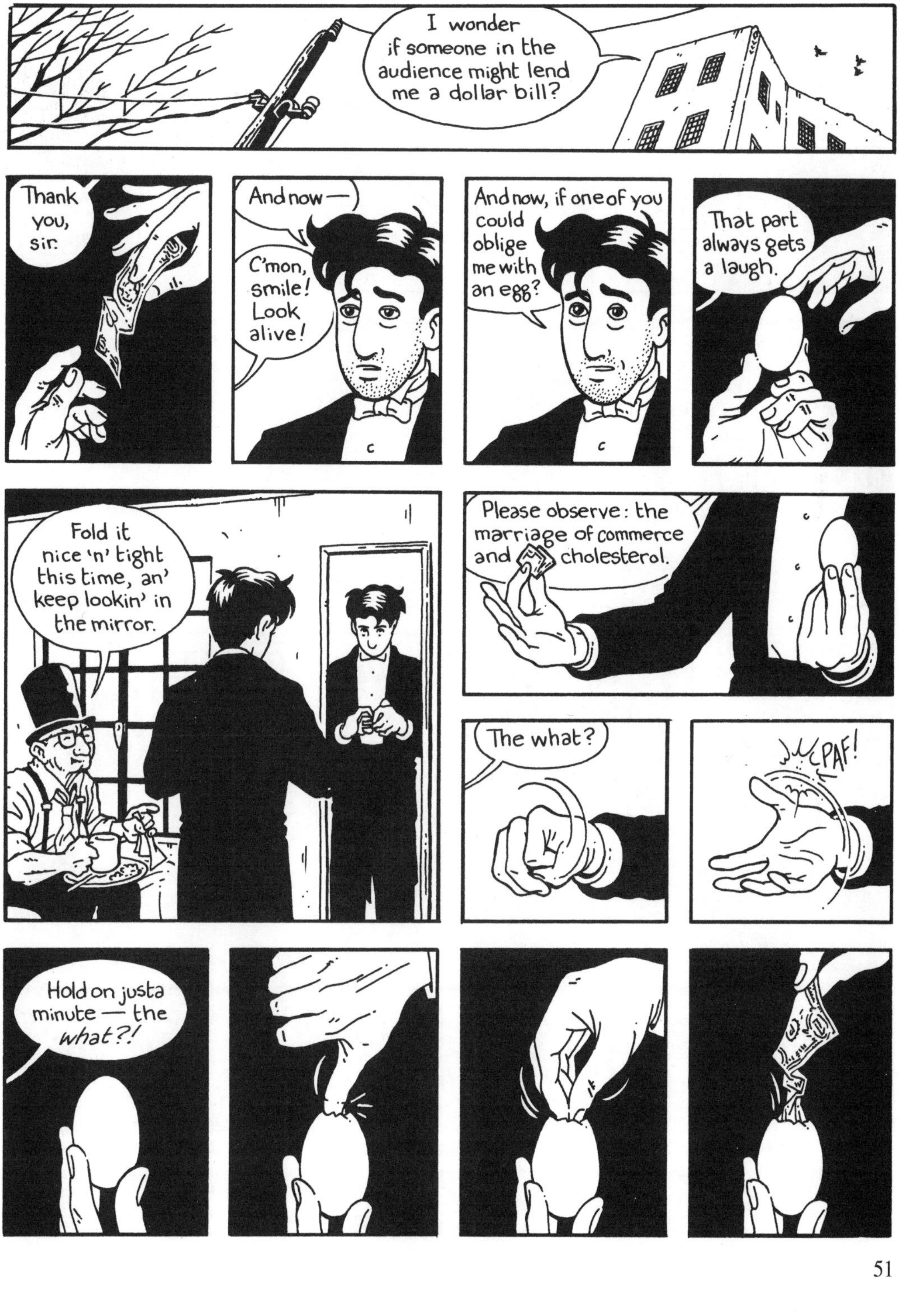
I wonder if someone in the audience might lend me a dollar bill?
Thank you, sir.
And now—
C'mon, smile! Look alive!
And now, if one of you could oblige me with an egg?
That part always gets a laugh.
Fold it nice 'n' tight this time, an' keep lookin' in the mirror.
Please observe: the marriage of commerce and cholesterol.
The what?
PAF!
Hold on justa minute — the *what?!*

I was trying to be funny. I don't like using money in tricks.

No no no — "Can someone in the audience lend me an egg," *that's* funny.

You're talkin' over people's heads, here! Ya wanna distract 'em, not make 'em feel like rubes!

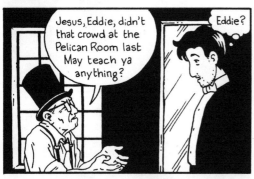Jesus, Eddie, didn't that crowd at the Pelican Room last May teach ya anything?

Eddie?

They were right there with ya, until that crack about Myrna Loy and the Dalai Lama!

Al—

Al, it's me, Ernie! Not Eddie, Ernie!

I gotta go for a walk.

CLACK

Orpheum

FLOSSO
THE MAGNIFICENT

I pulled off the sleight pretty well, didn't I?

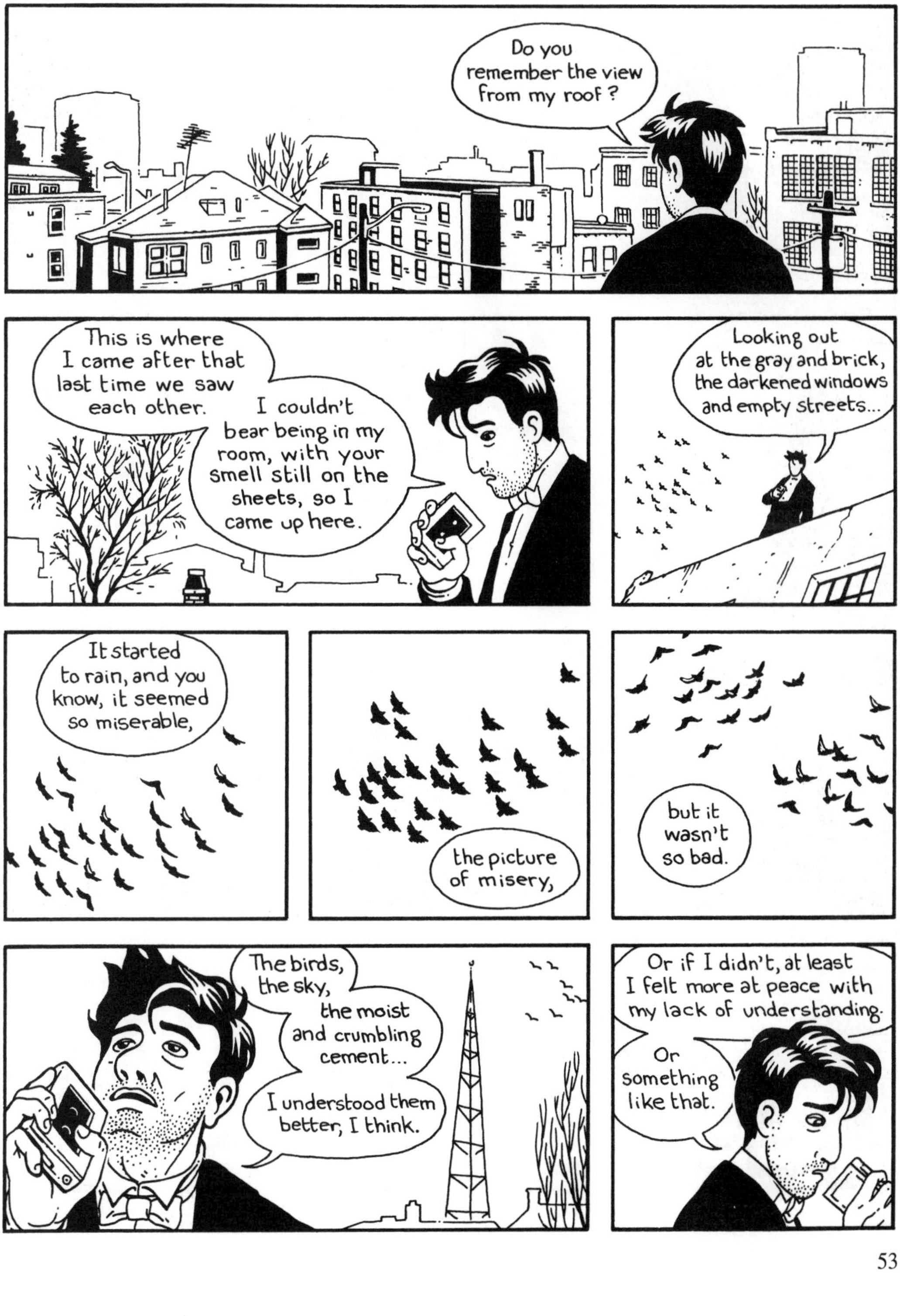
Do you remember the view from my roof?
This is where I came after that last time we saw each other.
I couldn't bear being in my room, with your smell still on the sheets, so I came up here.
Looking out at the gray and brick, the darkened windows and empty streets...
It started to rain, and you know, it seemed so miserable,
the picture of misery,
but it wasn't so bad.
The birds, the sky,
the moist and crumbling cement...
I understood them better, I think.
Or if I didn't, at least I felt more at peace with my lack of understanding.
Or something like that.

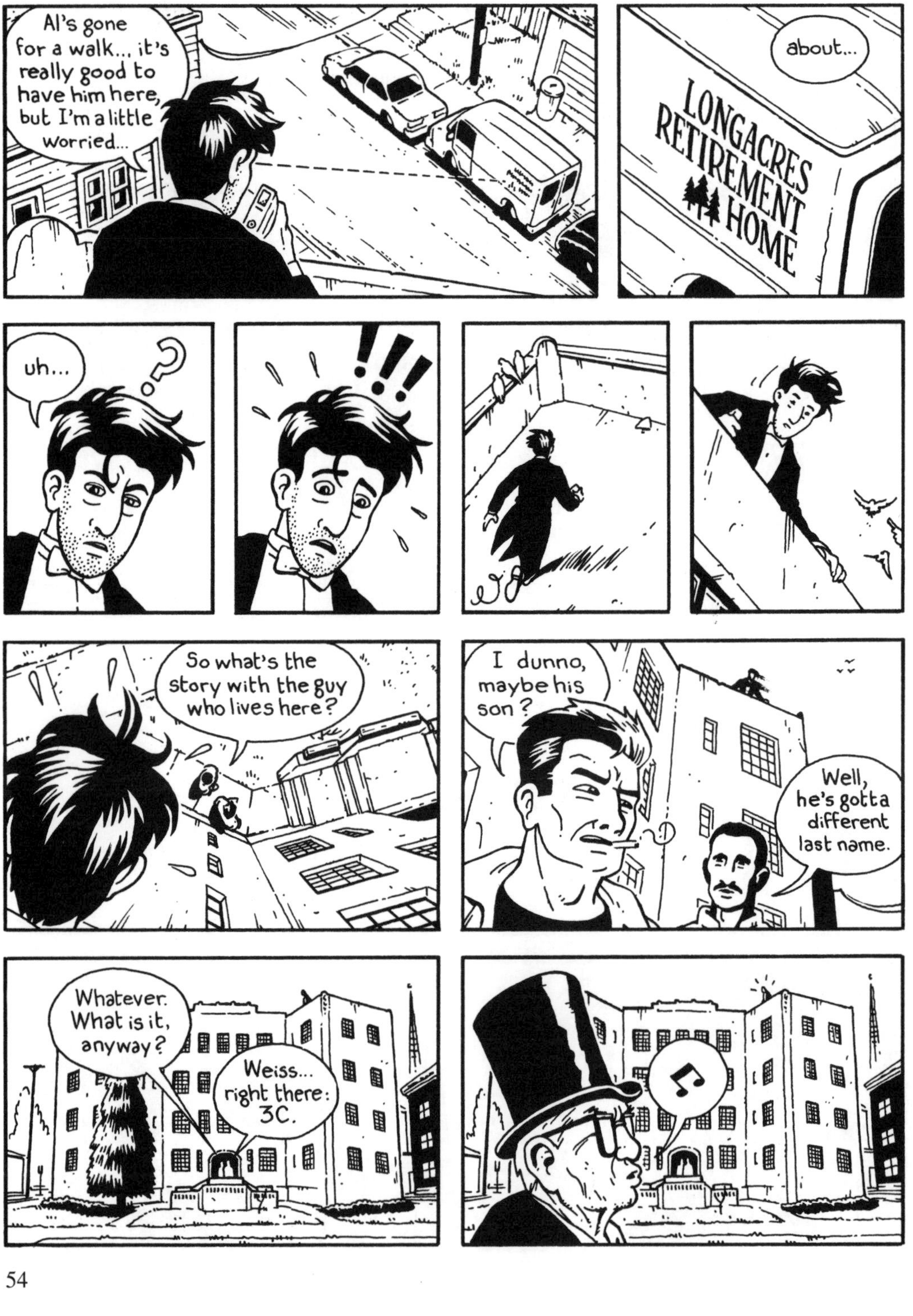
Al's gone for a walk..., it's really good to have him here, but I'm a little worried...
about...
LONGACRES RETIREMENT HOME
uh...
So what's the story with the guy who lives here?
I dunno, maybe his son?
Well, he's gotta different last name.
Whatever. What is it, anyway?
Weiss... right there: 3C.

They're going to take him back!

Warn him, warn him— I've got to warn him!

No answer.

I'll try one a the neighbors.

So listen, we gotta be sure t'search 'im before he goes in the van... he's always carryin' a pick or two.

Okay.

That's what I'm thinkin', that's what I'm thinkin'...

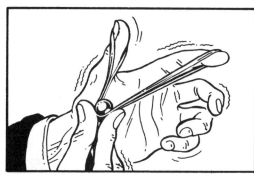

Come on... somebody... which one belongs to the super?

♪♫

thwip!

tup!

?!

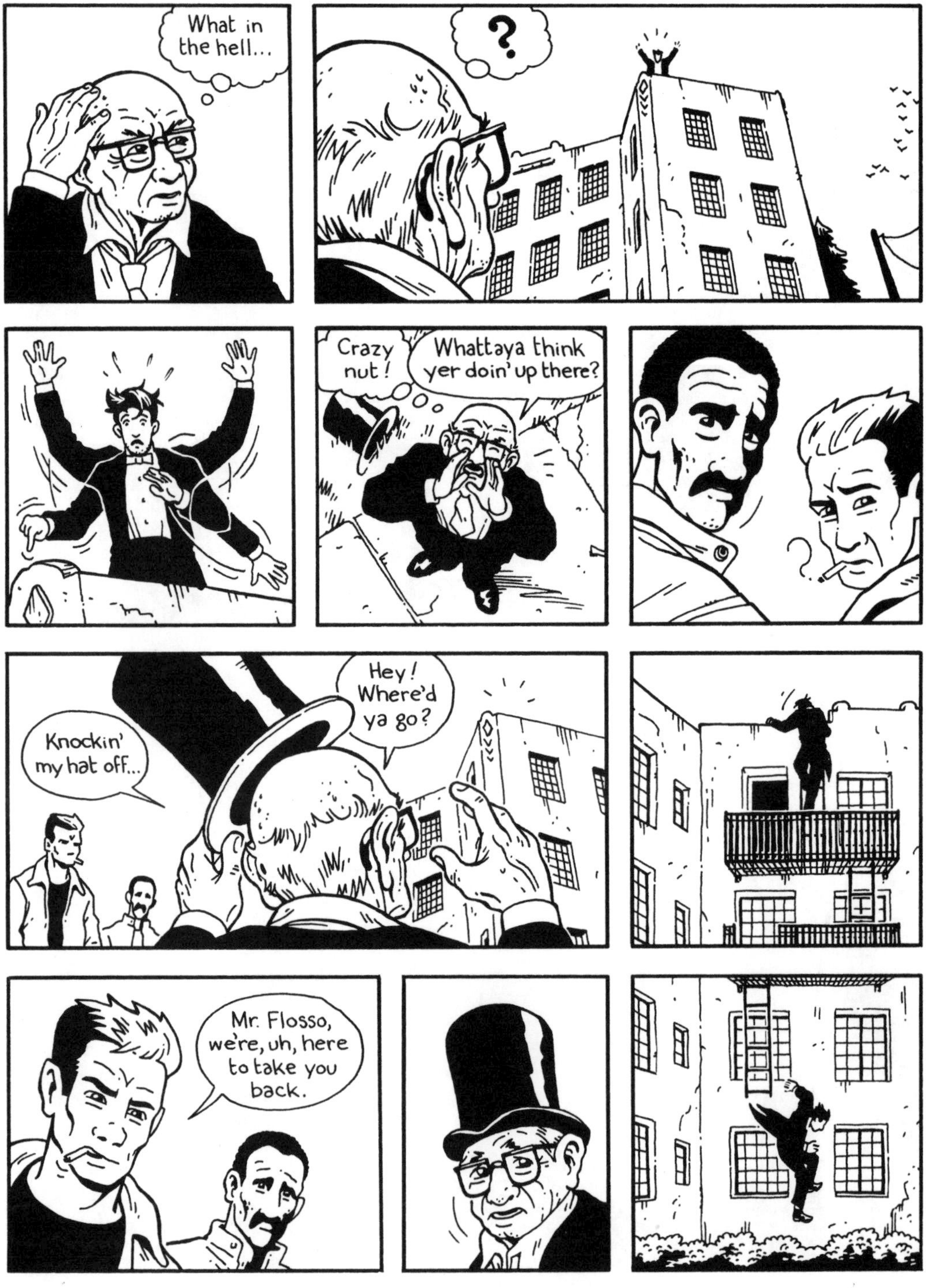
What in the hell...
?
Crazy nut!
Whattaya think yer doin' up there?
Hey! Where'd ya go?
Knockin' my hat off...
Mr. Flosso, we're, uh, here to take you back.

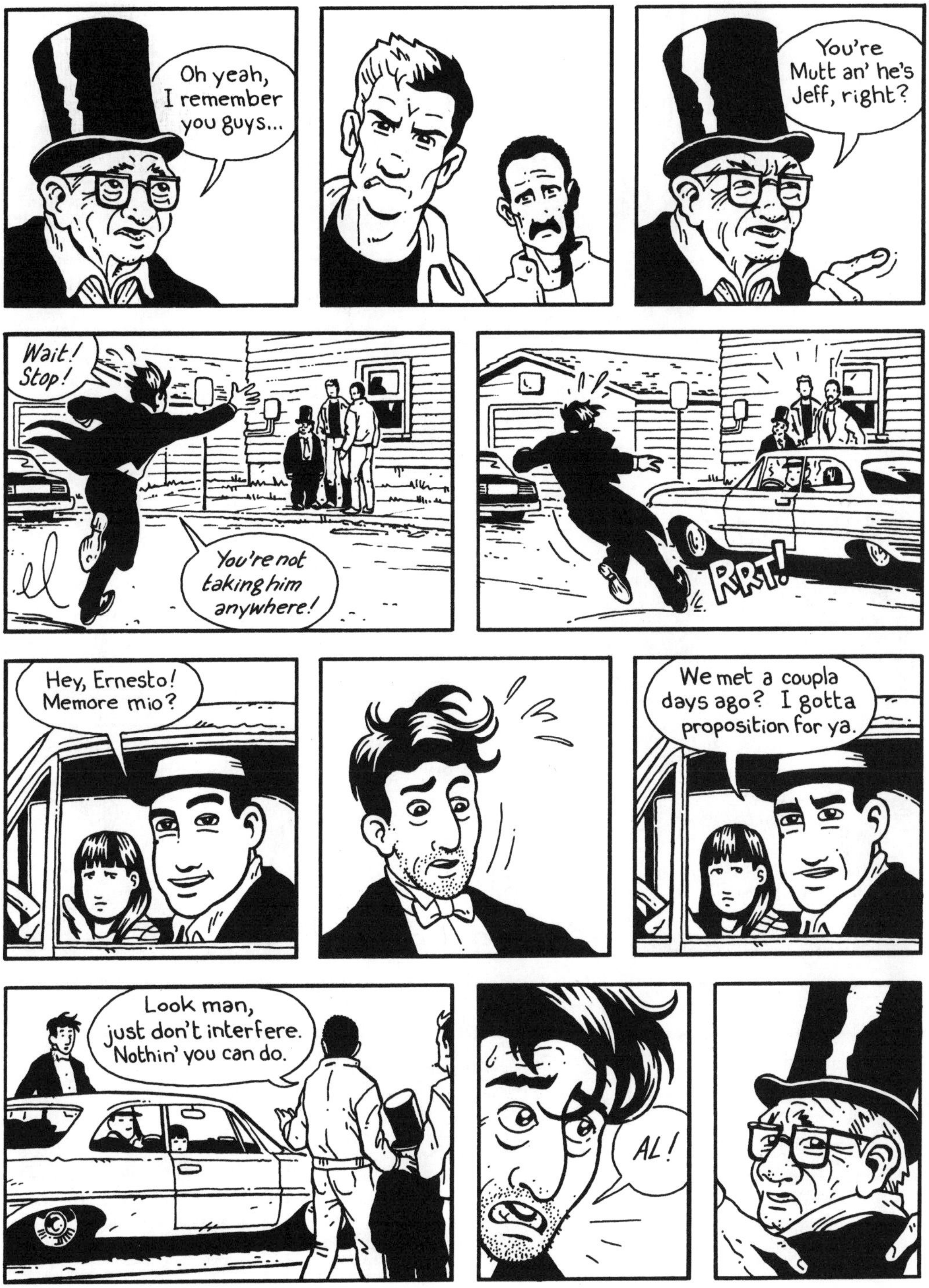
Oh yeah, I remember you guys...
You're Mutt an' he's Jeff, right?
Wait! Stop!
You're not taking him anywhere!
RRT!
Hey, Ernesto! Memore mio?
We met a coupla days ago? I gotta proposition for ya.
Look man, just don't interfere. Nothin' you can do.
AL!

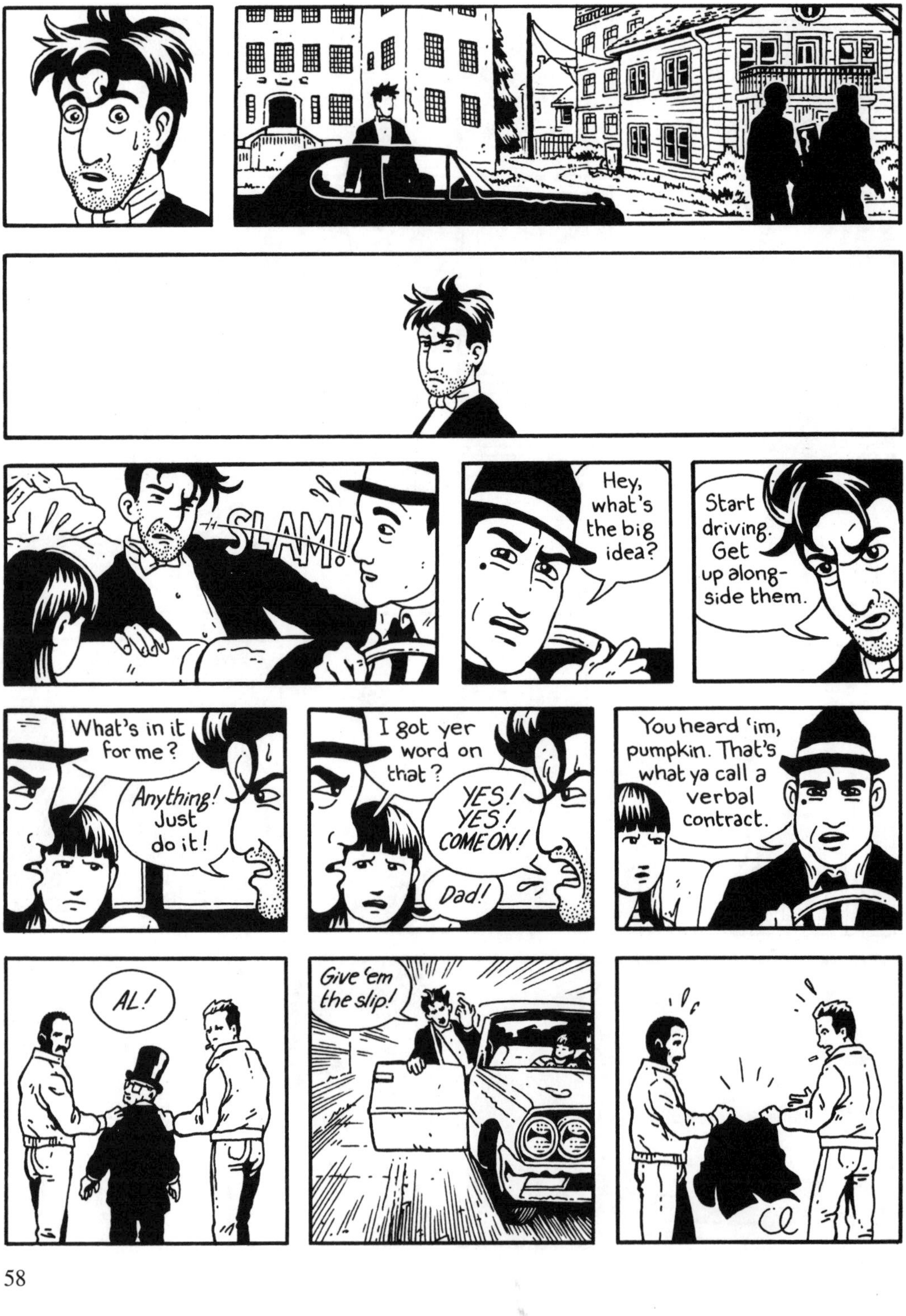
SLAM!
Hey, what's the big idea?
Start driving. Get up alongside them.
What's in it for me?
Anything! Just do it!
I got yer word on that?
YES! YES! COME ON!
Dad!
You heard 'im, pumpkin. That's what ya call a verbal contract.
AL!
Give 'em the slip!

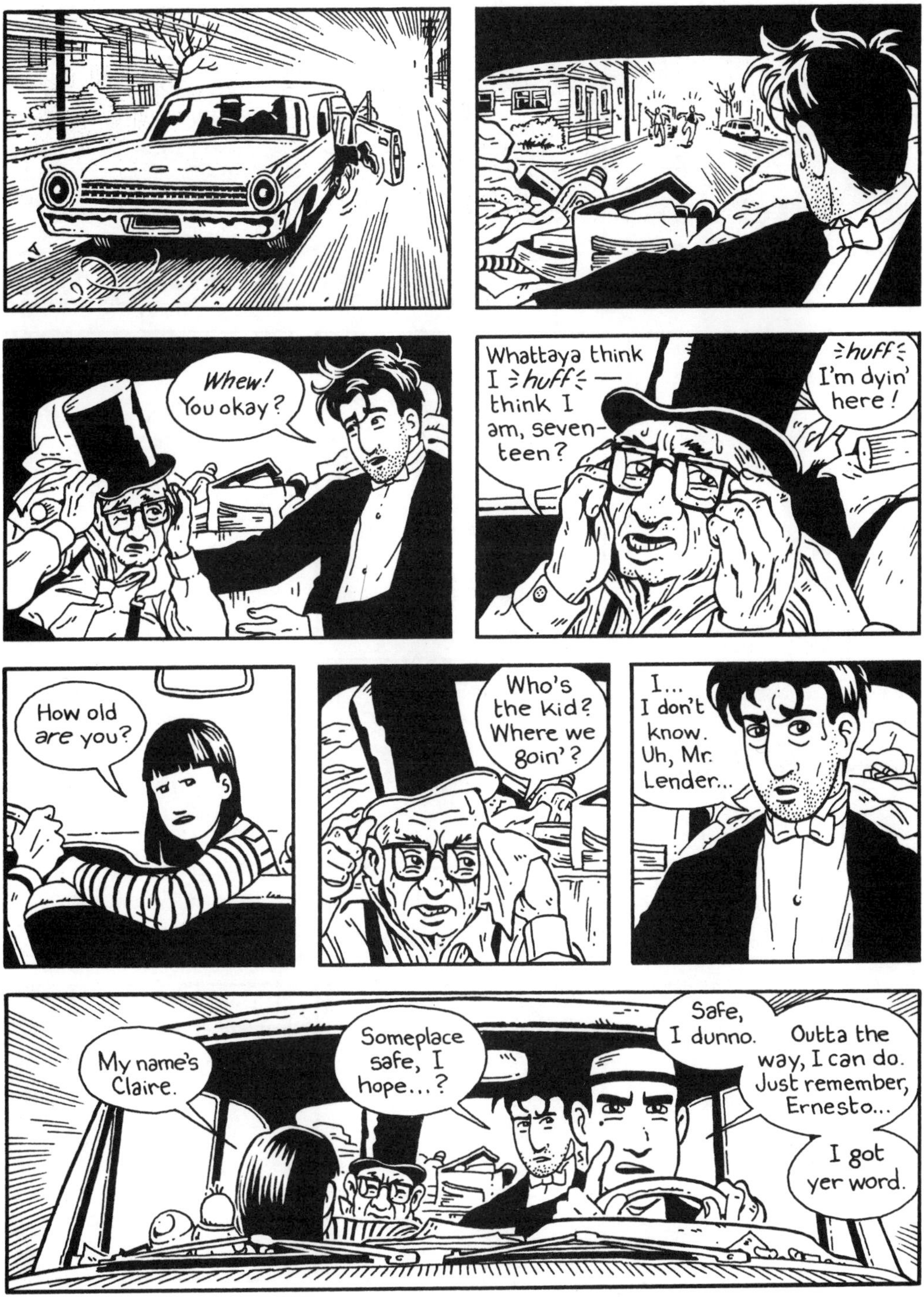
Whew!
You okay?
Whattaya think I huff — think I am, seventeen?
huff I'm dyin' here!
How old are you?
Who's the kid? Where we goin'?
I... I don't know. Uh, Mr. Lender...
My name's Claire.
Someplace safe, I hope...?
Safe, I dunno.
Outta the way, I can do. Just remember, Ernesto...
I got yer word.

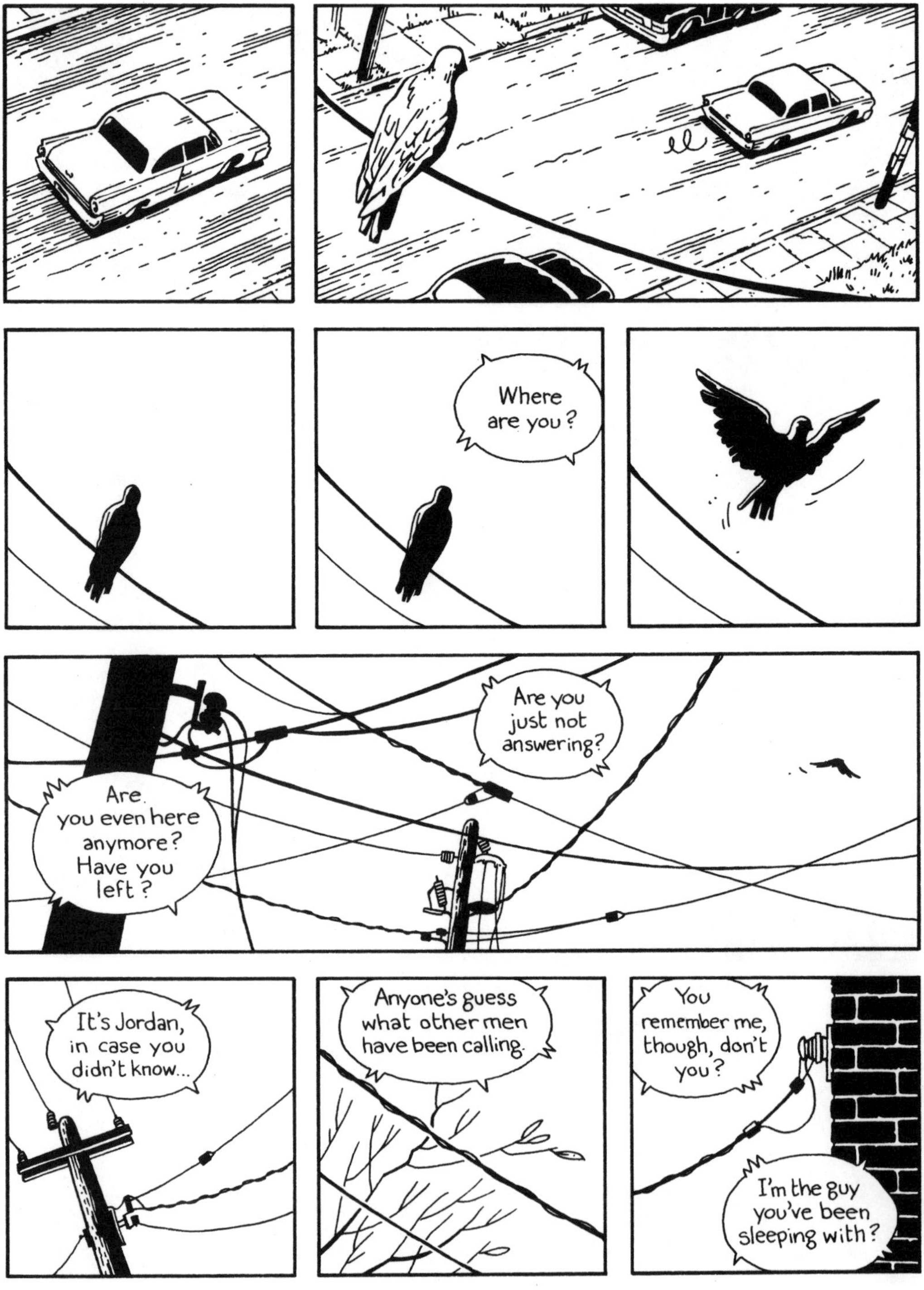
Where are you?
Are you just not answering?
Are you even here anymore? Have you left?
It's Jordan, in case you didn't know...
Anyone's guess what other men have been calling.
You remember me, though, don't you?
I'm the guy you've been sleeping with?

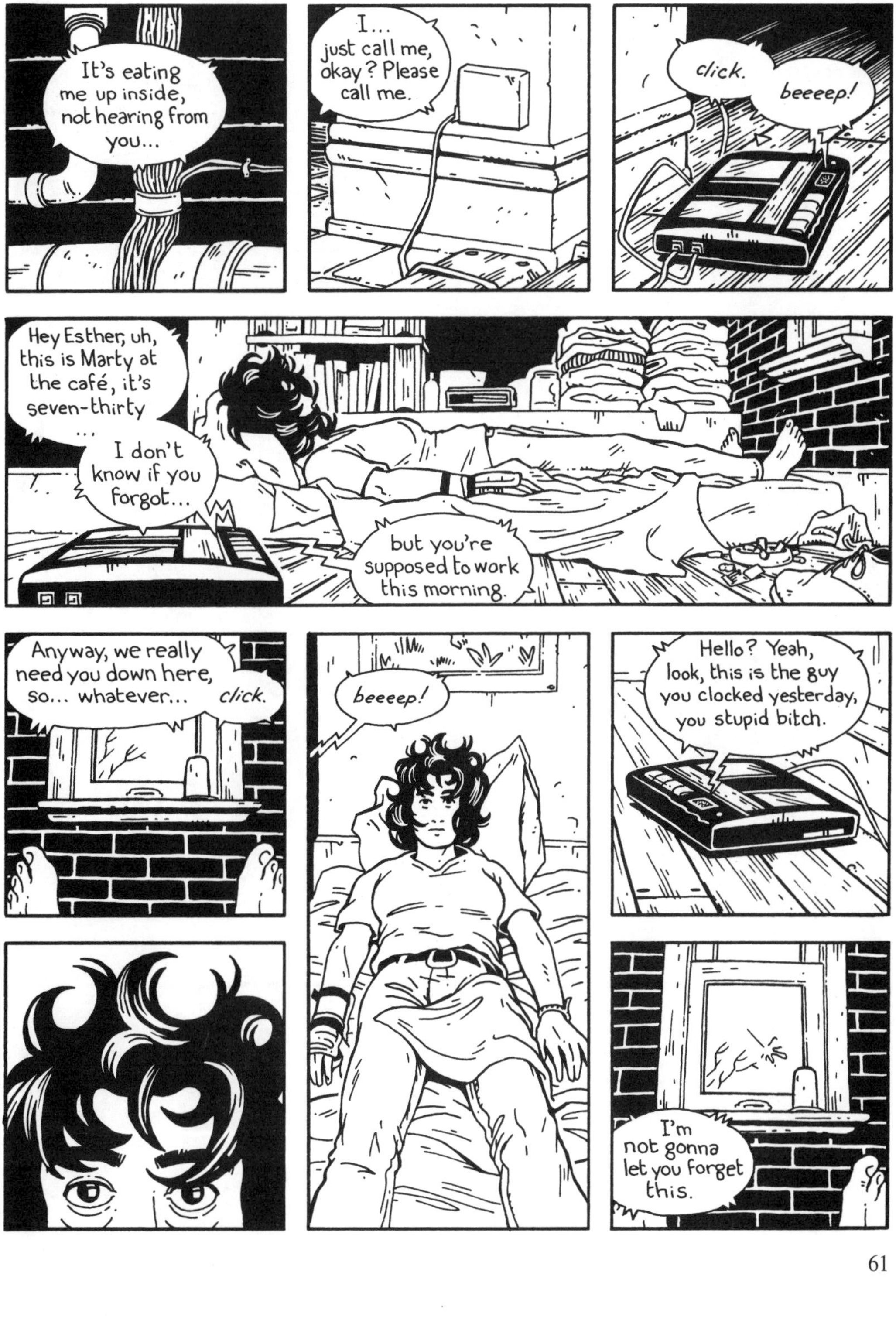
It's eating me up inside, not hearing from you...
I... just call me, okay? Please call me.
click.
beeeep!
Hey Esther, uh, this is Marty at the café, it's seven-thirty ...
I don't know if you forgot...
but you're supposed to work this morning.
Anyway, we really need you down here, so... whatever...
click.
beeeep!
Hello? Yeah, look, this is the guy you clocked yesterday, you stupid bitch.
I'm not gonna let you forget this.

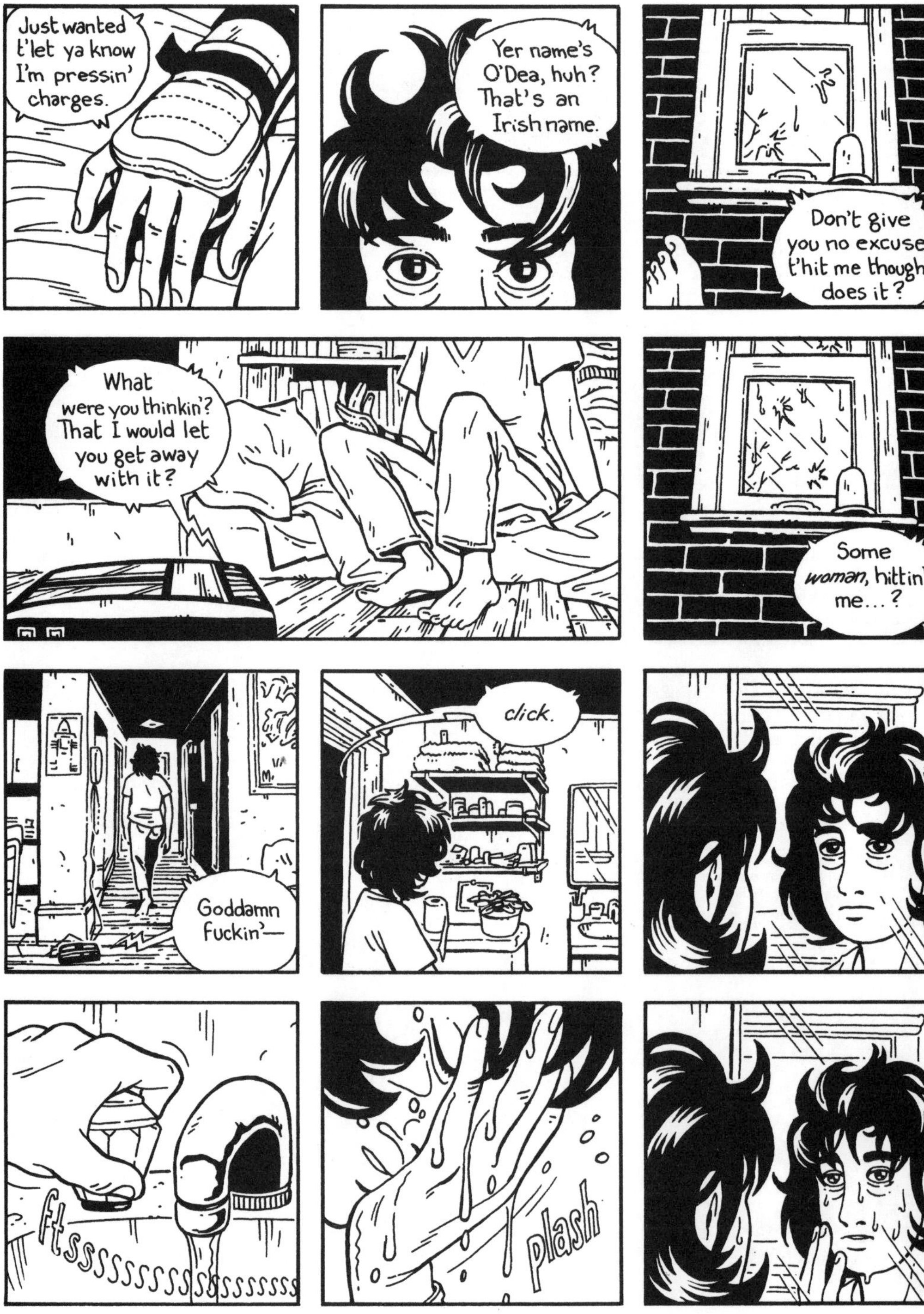

Just wanted t'let ya know I'm pressin' charges.
Yer name's O'Dea, huh? That's an Irish name.
Don't give you no excuse t'hit me though, does it?
What were you thinkin'? That I would let you get away with it?
Some *woman*, hittin' me...?
Goddamn fuckin'—
click.
ftsssssssssssssssssss
plash

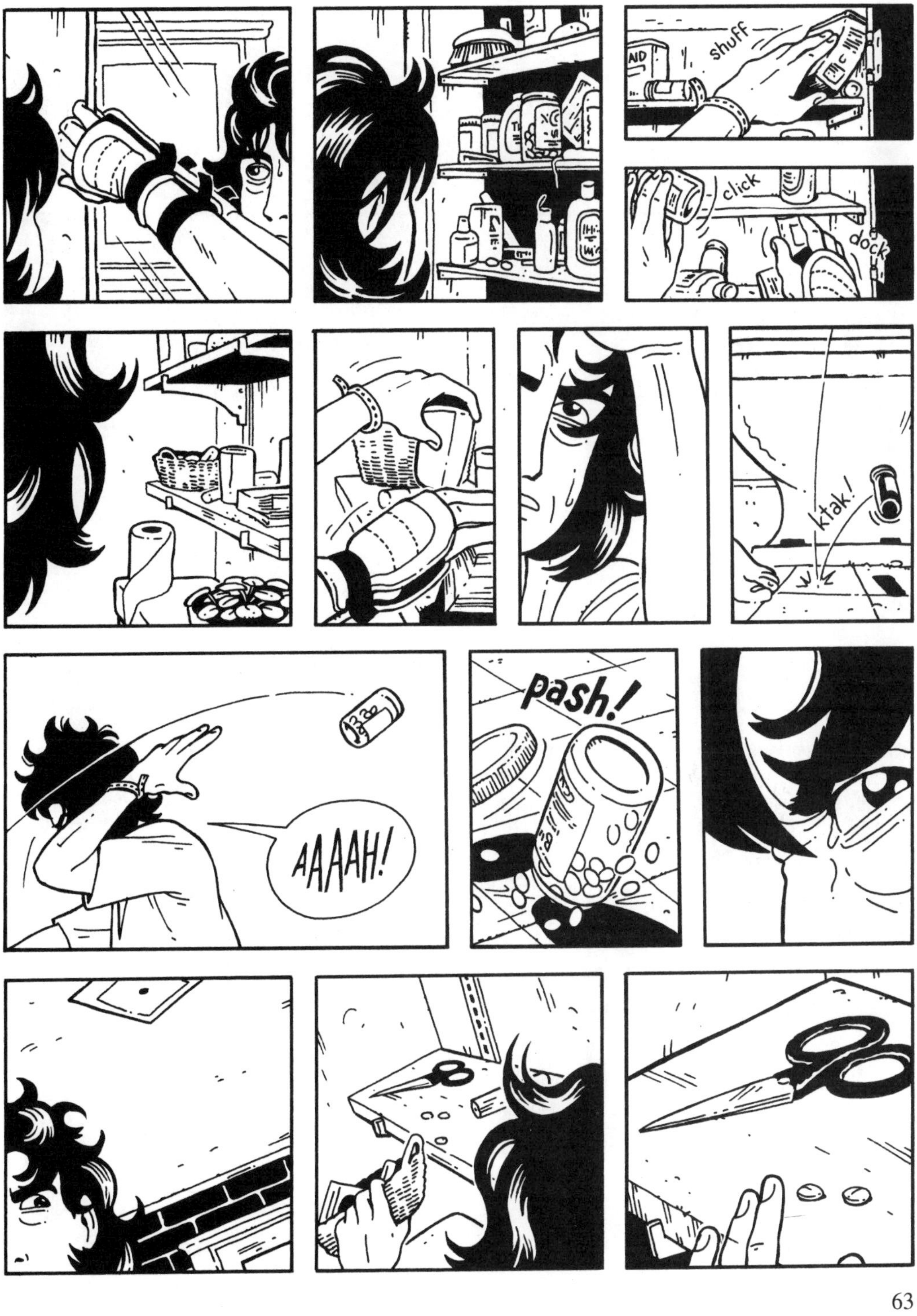
shuff
click
dock
ktak!
AAAAH!
pash!

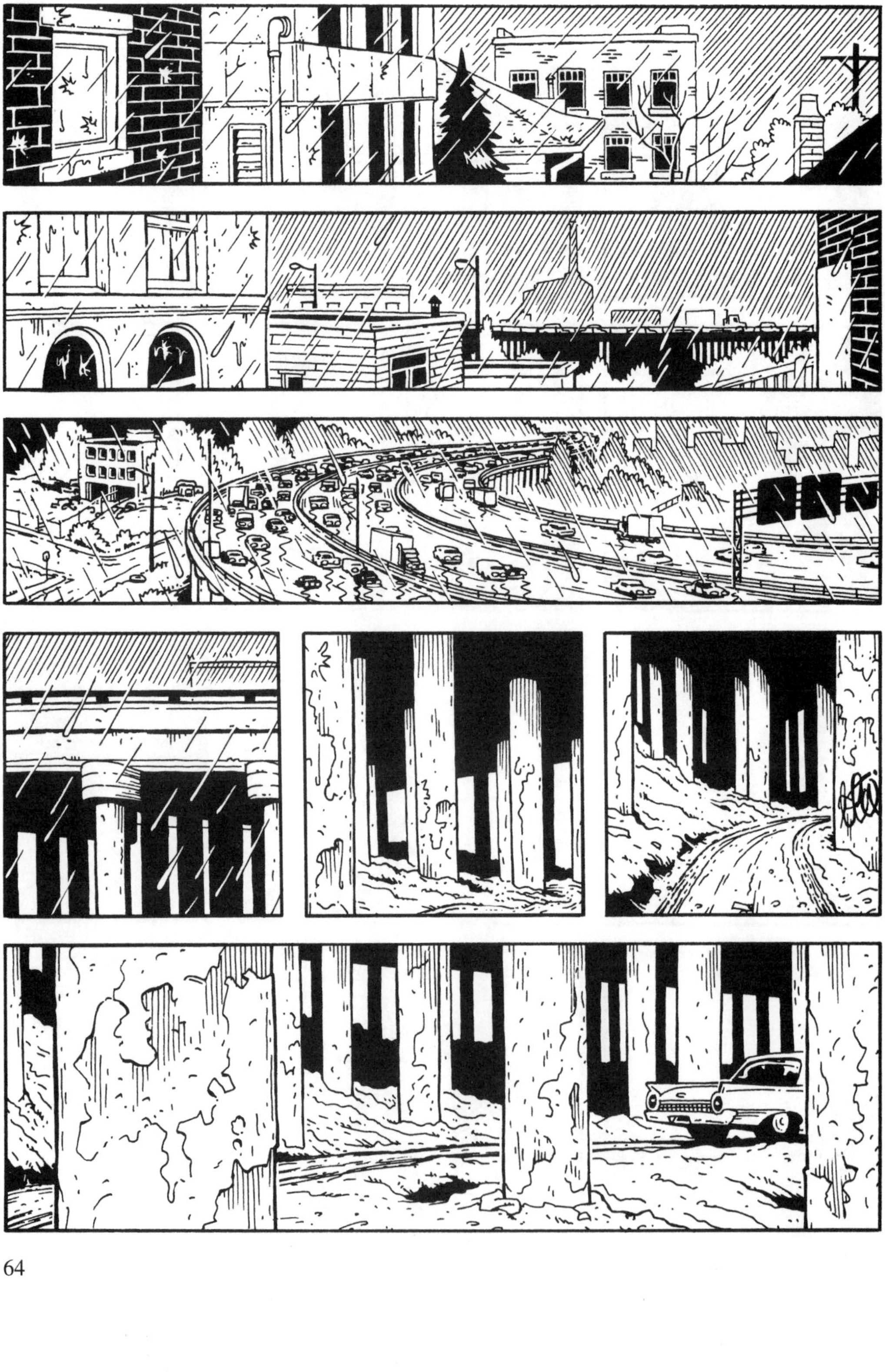

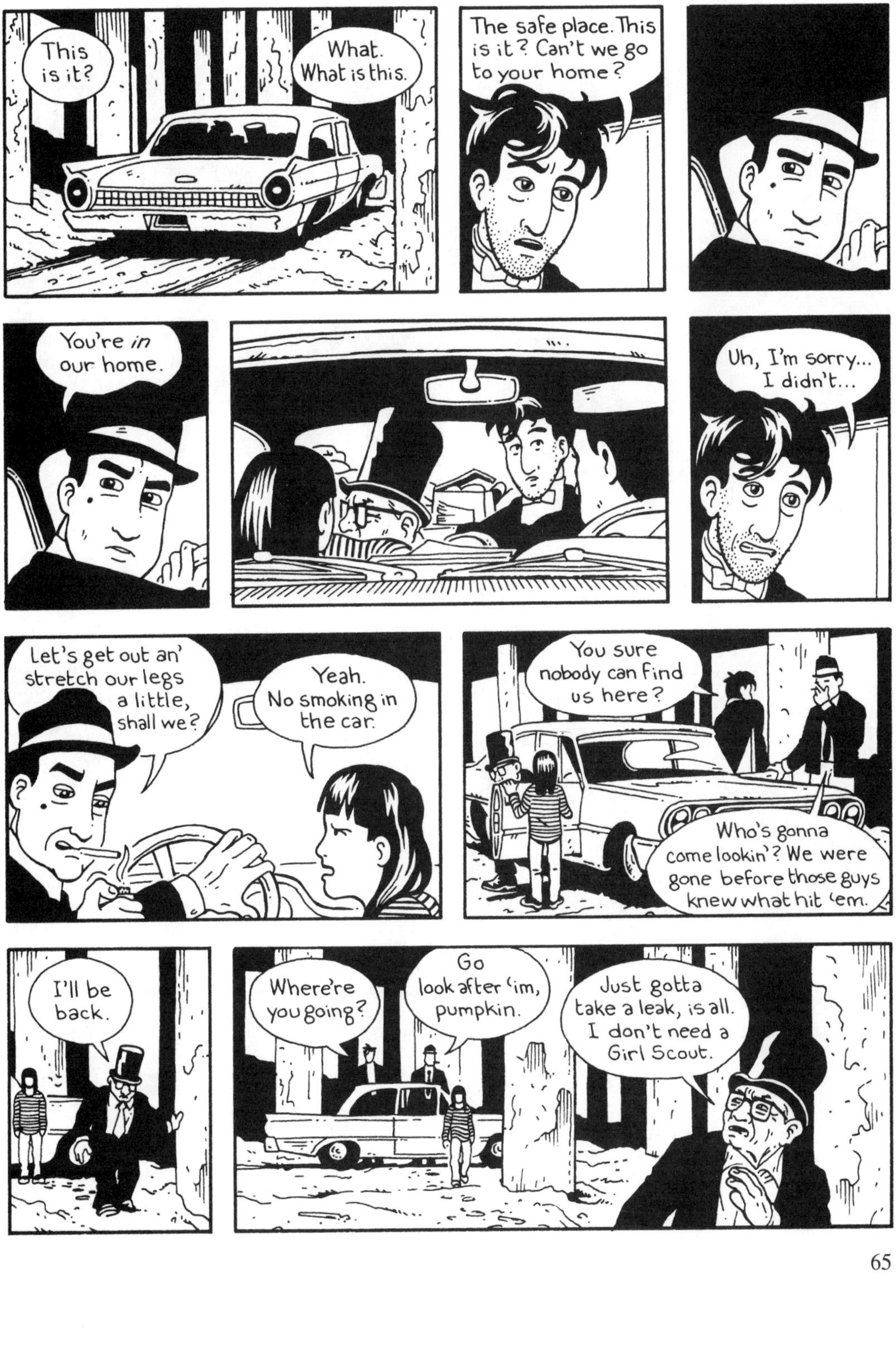
This is it?
What. What is this.
The safe place. This is it? Can't we go to your home?
You're *in* our home.
Uh, I'm sorry... I didn't...
Let's get out an' stretch our legs a little, shall we?
Yeah. No smoking in the car.
You sure nobody can find us here?
Who's gonna come lookin'? We were gone before those guys knew what hit 'em.
I'll be back.
Where're you going?
Go look after 'im, pumpkin.
Just gotta take a leak, is all. I don't need a Girl Scout.

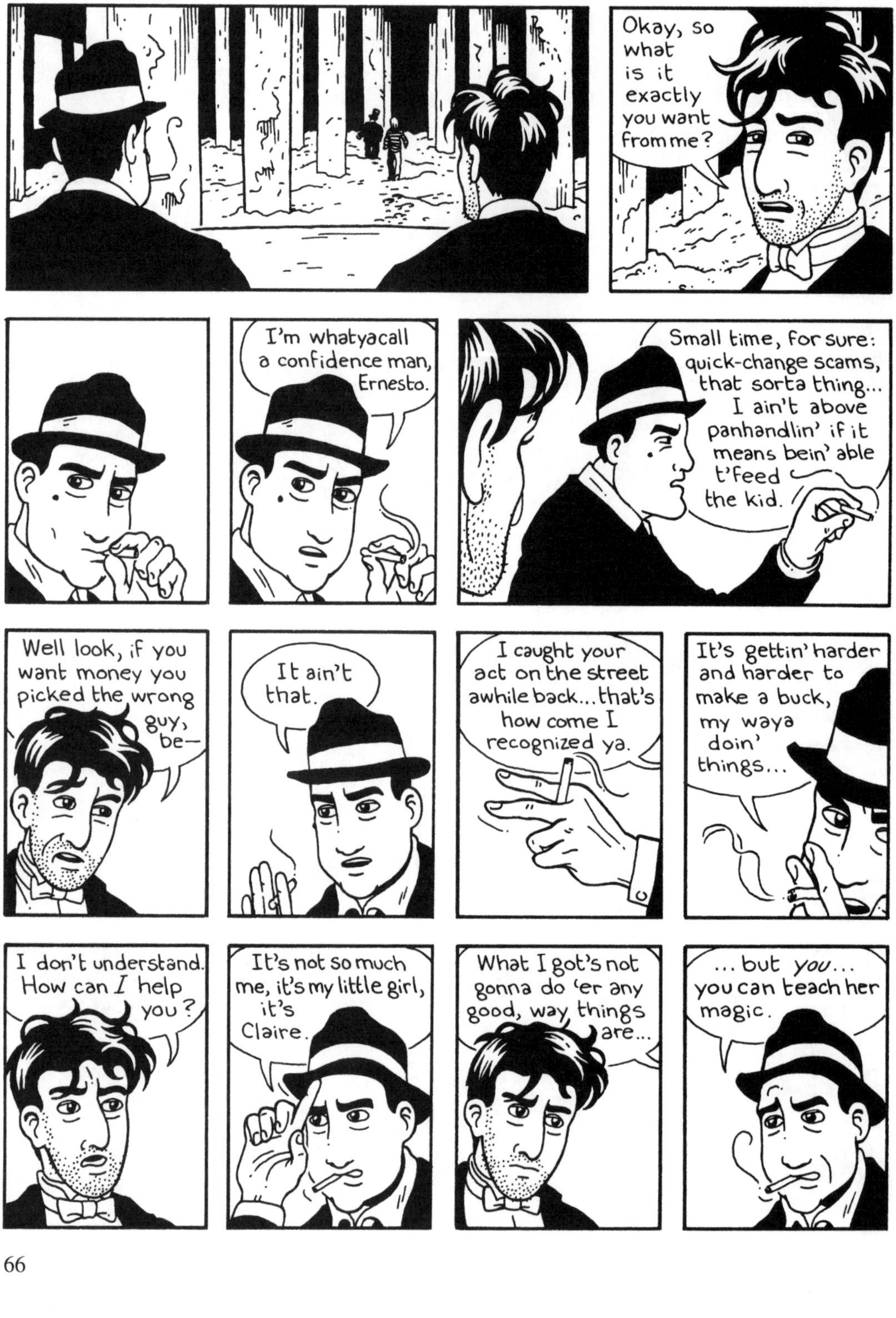
Okay, so what is it exactly you want from me?
I'm whatyacall a confidence man, Ernesto.
Small time, for sure: quick-change scams, that sorta thing... I ain't above panhandlin' if it means bein' able t'feed the kid.
Well look, if you want money you picked the wrong guy, be—
It ain't that.
I caught your act on the street awhile back... that's how come I recognized ya.
It's gettin' harder and harder to make a buck, my waya doin' things...
I don't understand. How can *I* help you?
It's not so much me, it's my little girl, it's Claire.
What I got's not gonna do 'er any good, way things are...
... but *you*... you can teach her magic.

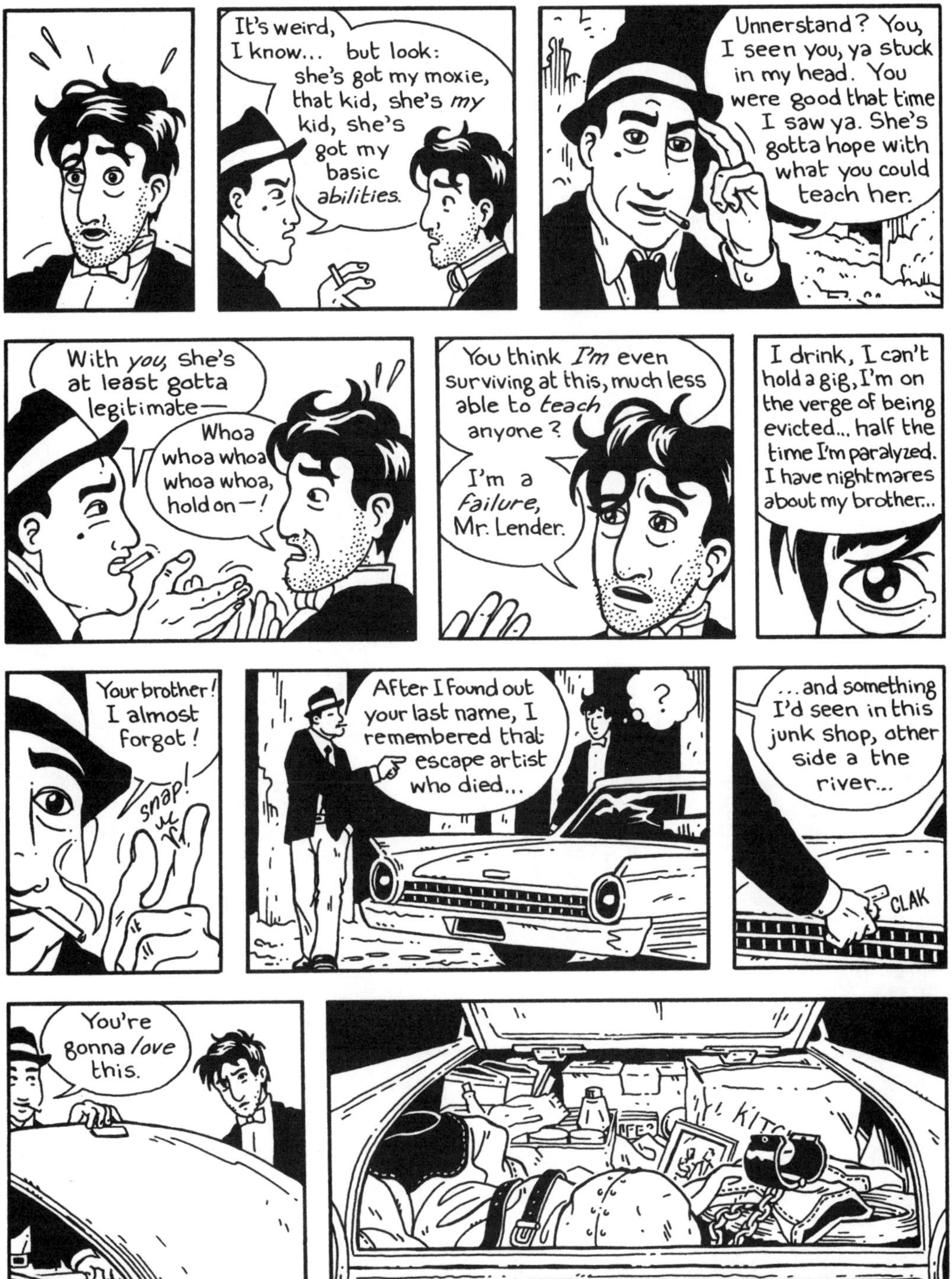
It's weird, I know... but look: she's got my moxie, that kid, she's *my* kid, she's got my basic *abilities*.
Unnerstand? You, I seen you, ya stuck in my head. You were good that time I saw ya. She's gotta hope with what you could teach her.
With *you*, she's at least gotta legitimate—
Whoa whoa whoa whoa whoa, hold on—!
You think *I'm* even surviving at this, much less able to *teach* anyone?
I'm a *failure*, Mr. Lender.
I drink, I can't hold a gig, I'm on the verge of being evicted... half the time I'm paralyzed. I have nightmares about my brother...
Your brother! I almost forgot!
snap!
After I found out your last name, I remembered that escape artist who died...
?
...and something I'd seen in this junk shop, other side a the river...
CLAK
You're gonna *love* this.

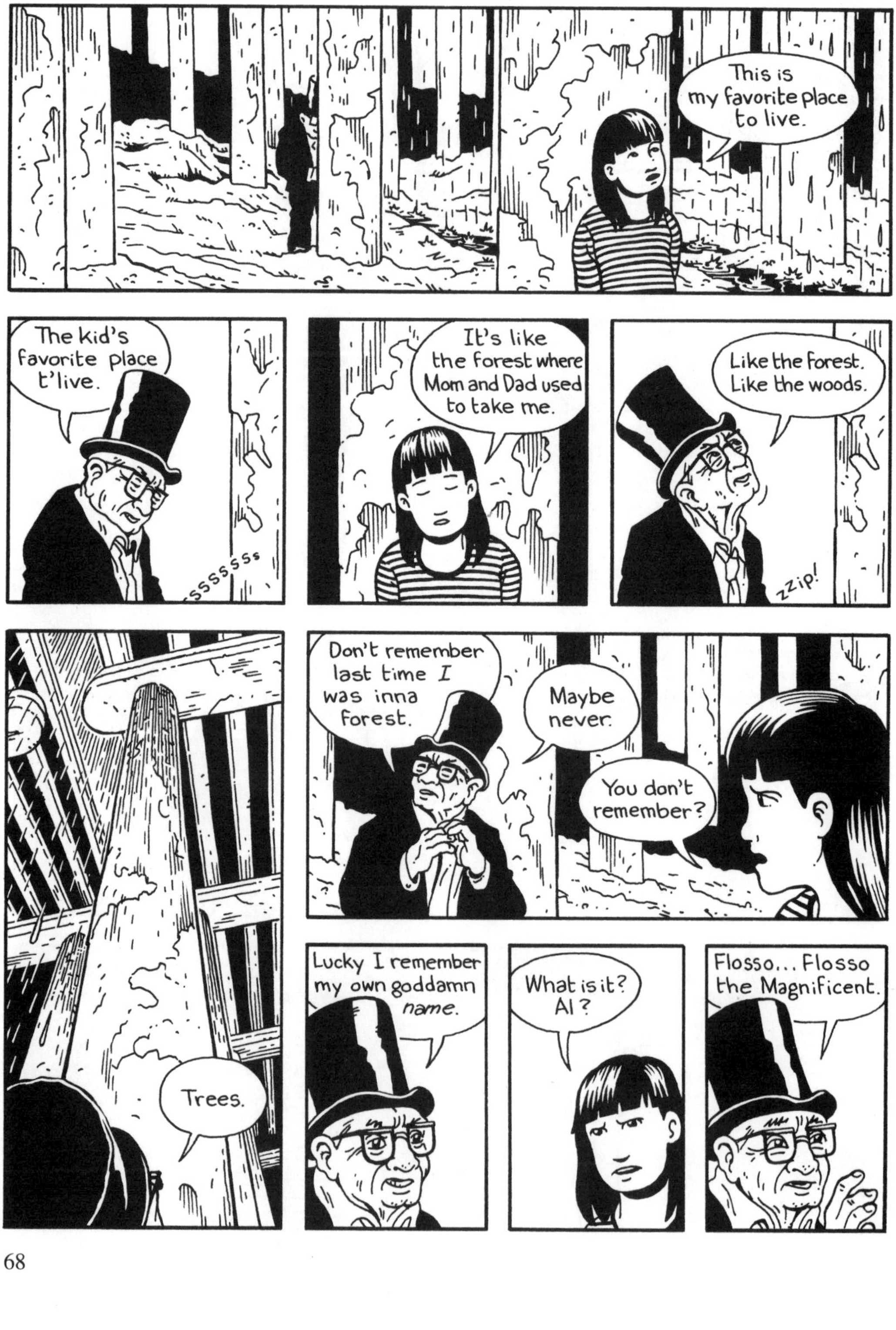
This is my favorite place to live.
The kid's favorite place t'live.
SSSSSSSS
It's like the forest where Mom and Dad used to take me.
Like the forest. Like the woods.
zzip!
Trees.
Don't remember last time *I* was inna forest.
Maybe never.
You don't remember?
Lucky I remember my own goddamn *name*.
What is it? Al?
Flosso... Flosso the Magnificent.

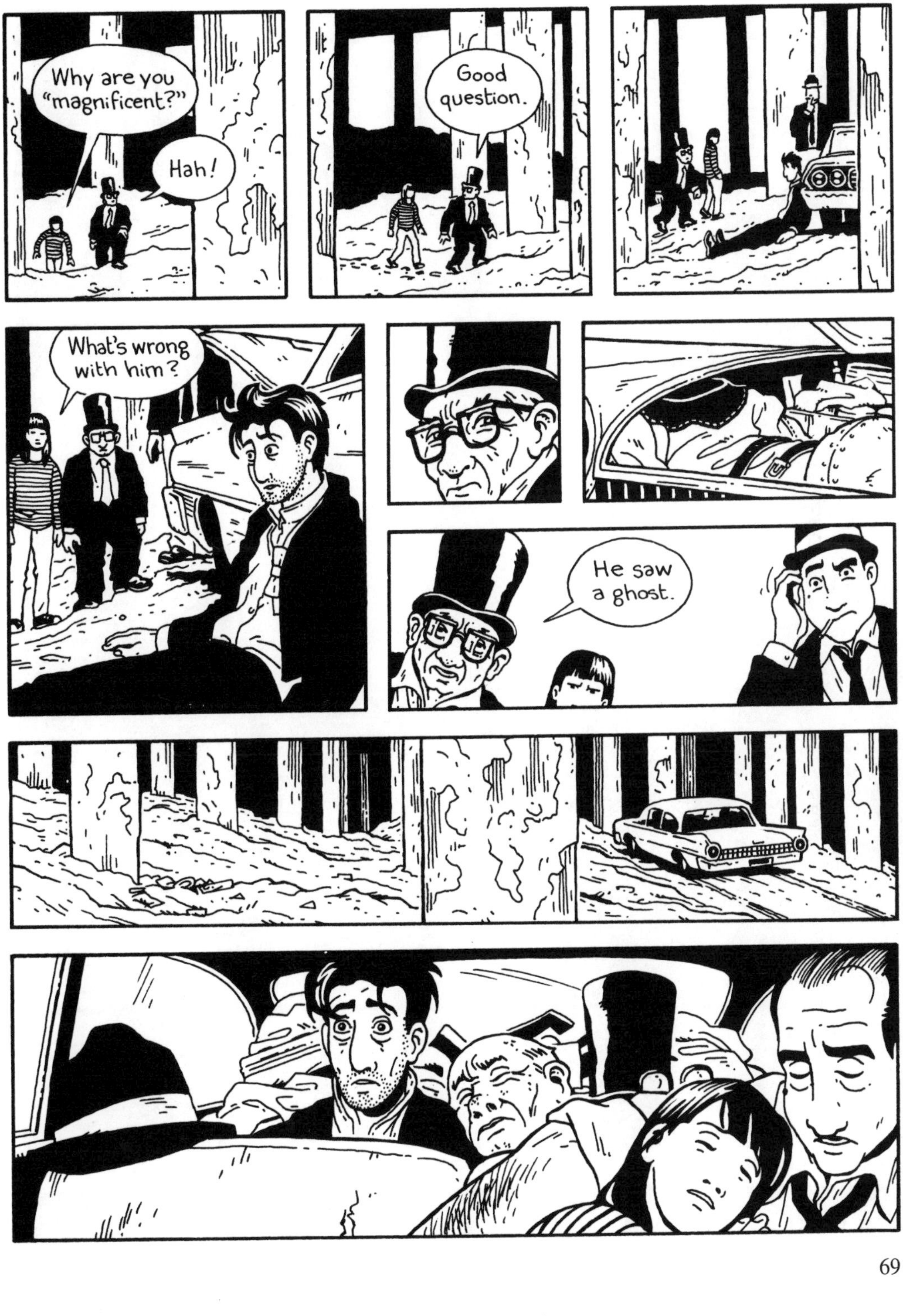
Why are you "magnificent?"
Hah!
Good question.
What's wrong with him?
He saw a ghost.

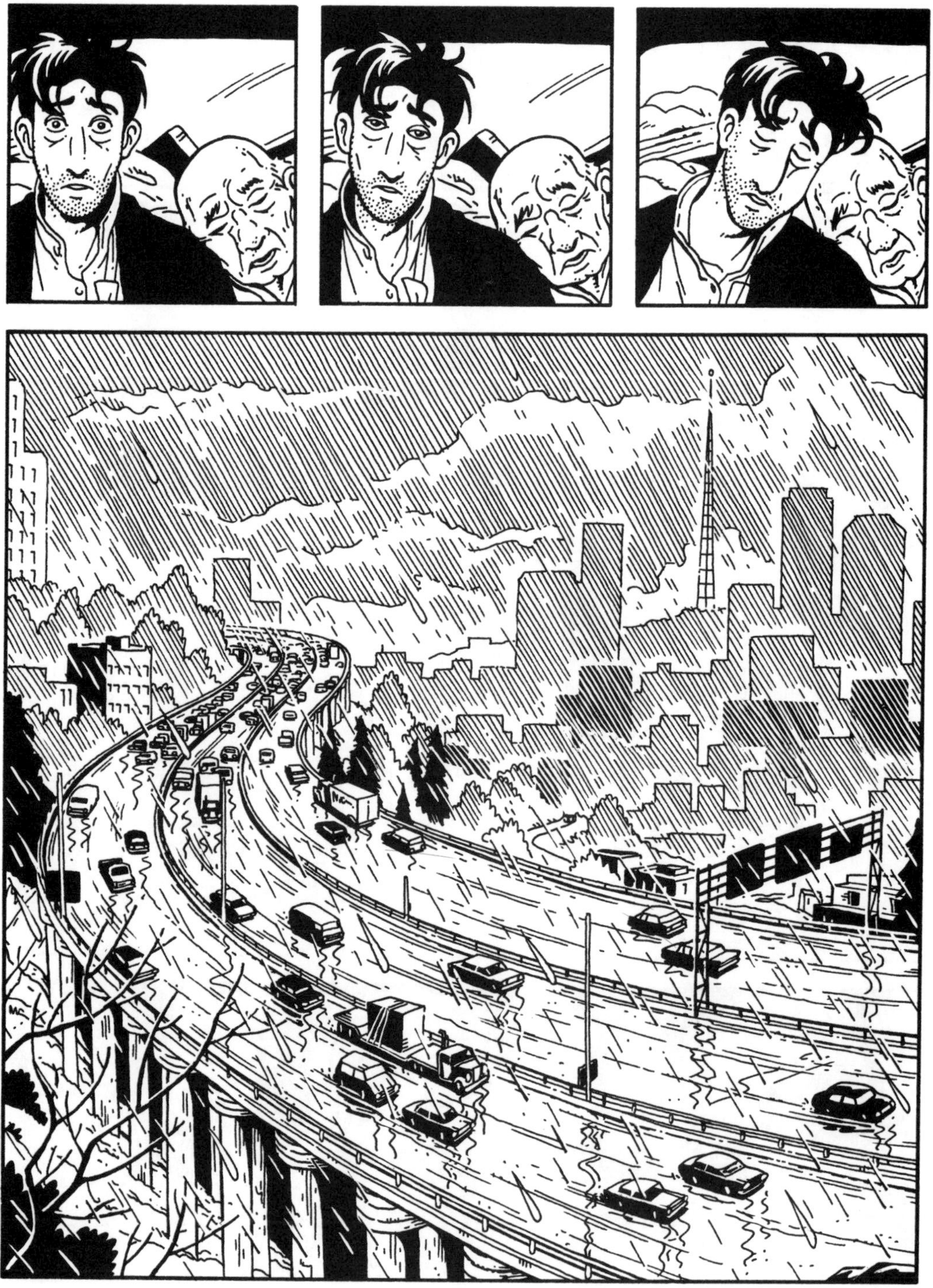

part two

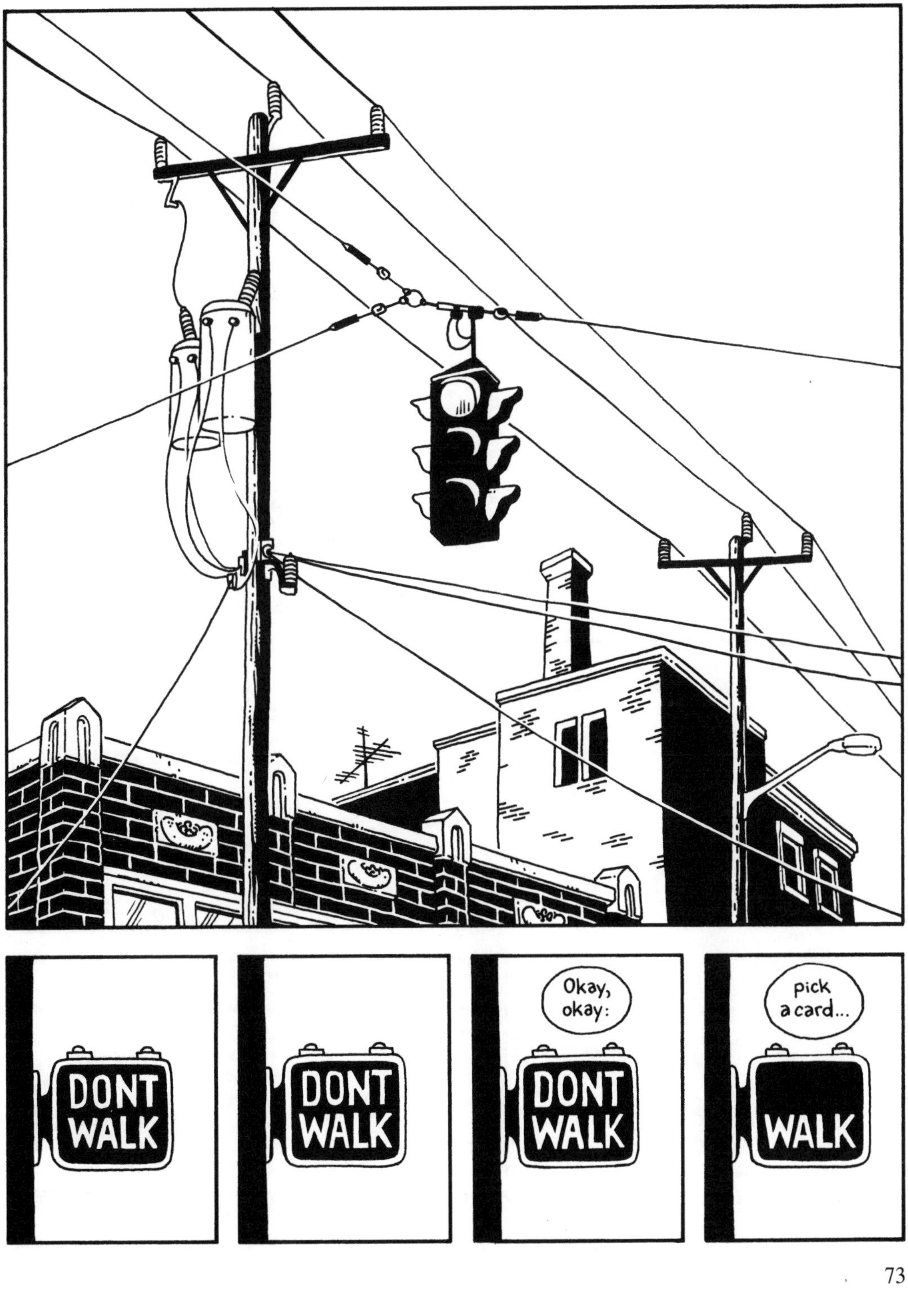
DONT
WALK
DONT
WALK
Okay, okay:
DONT
WALK
pick a card...
WALK

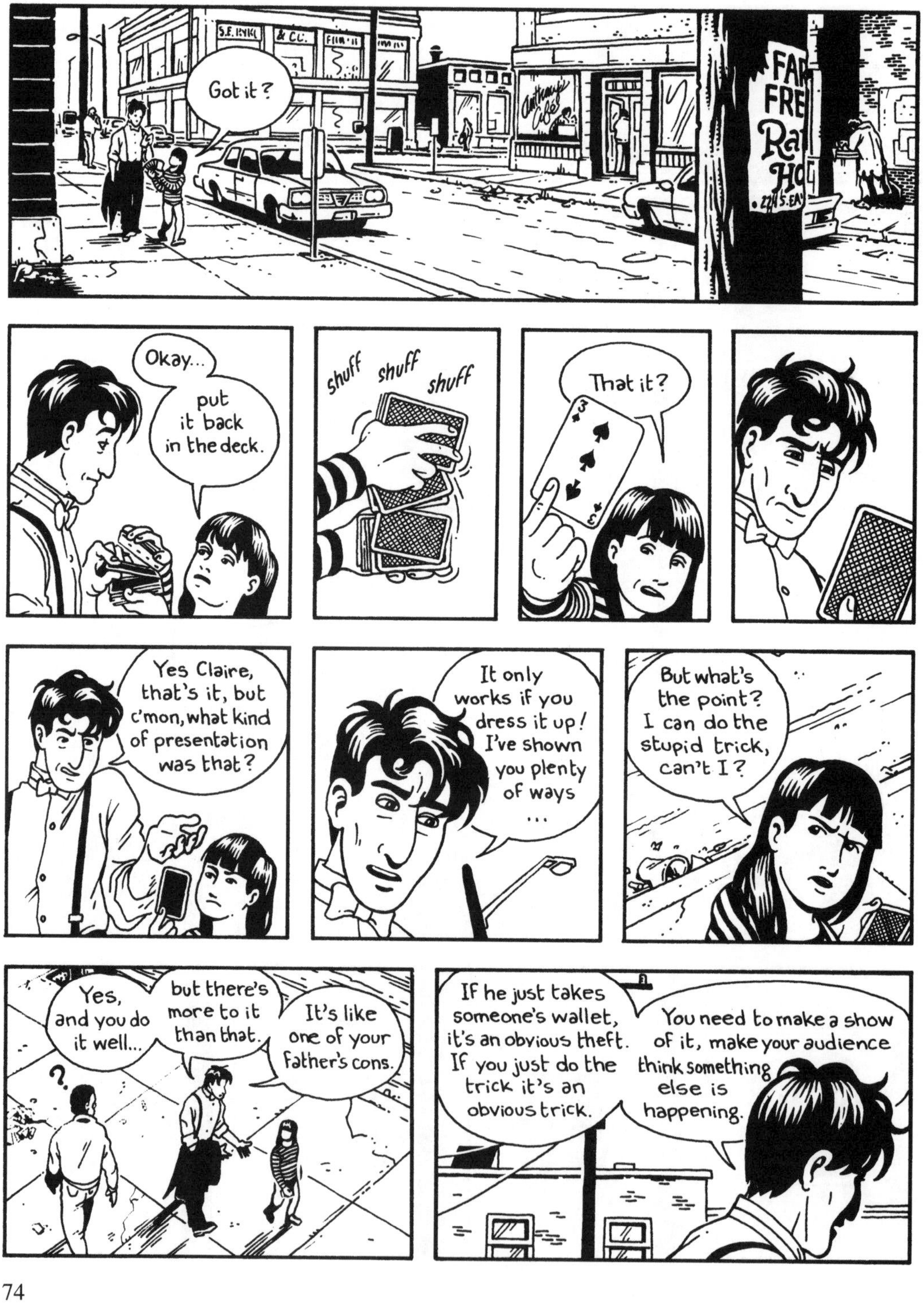

Got it?
Okay...
put it back in the deck.
shuff shuff shuff
That it?
Yes Claire, that's it, but c'mon, what kind of presentation was that?
It only works if you dress it up! I've shown you plenty of ways ...
But what's the point? I can do the stupid trick, can't I?
Yes, and you do it well...
but there's more to it than that.
It's like one of your father's cons.
If he just takes someone's wallet, it's an obvious theft. If you just do the trick it's an obvious trick.
You need to make a show of it, make your audience think something else is happening.

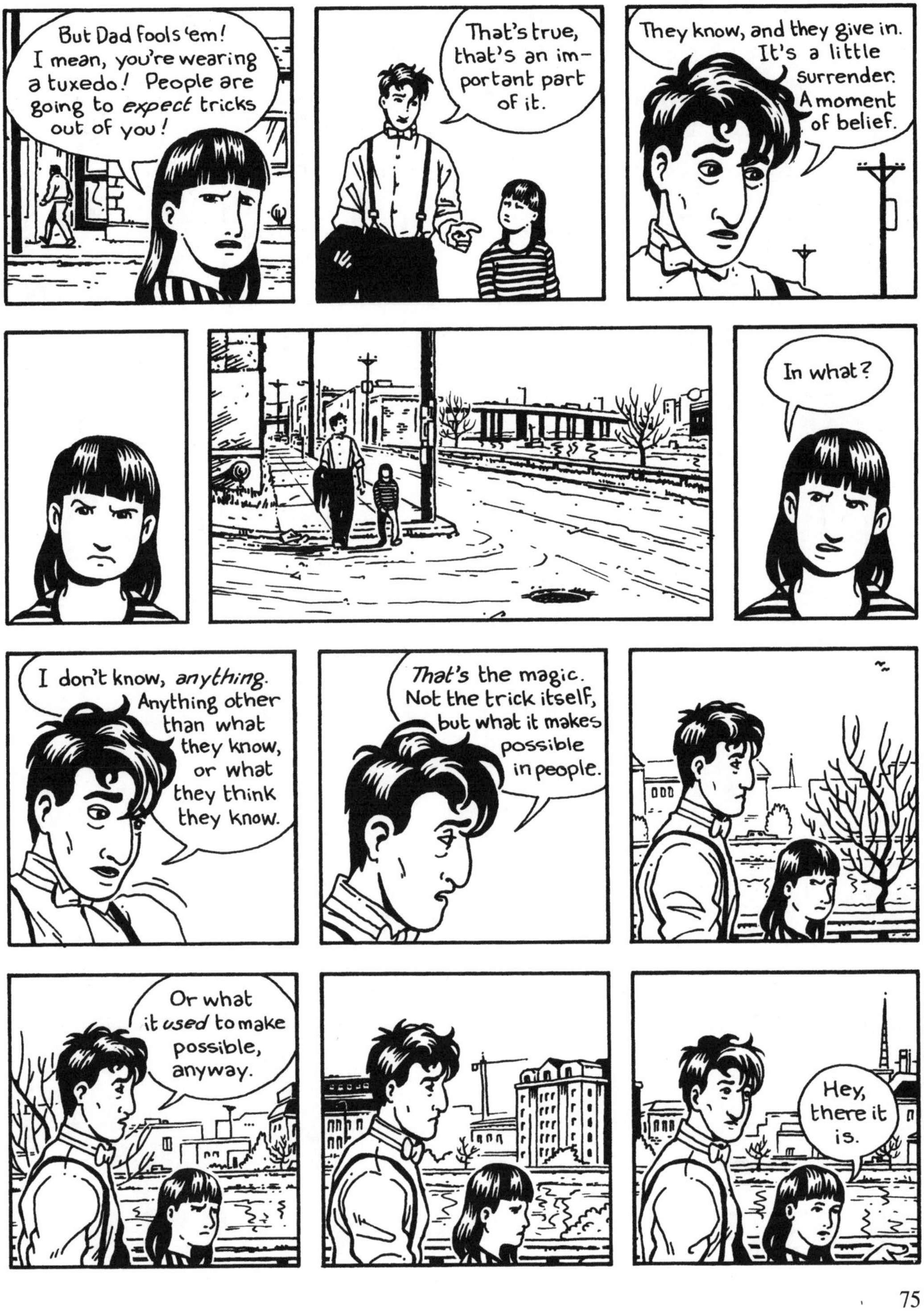
But Dad fools 'em! I mean, you're wearing a tuxedo! People are going to *expect* tricks out of you!
That's true, that's an important part of it.
They know, and they give in. It's a little surrender. A moment of belief.
In what?
I don't know, *anything*. Anything other than what they know, or what they think they know.
That's the magic. Not the trick itself, but what it makes possible in people.
Or what it *used* to make possible, anyway.
Hey, there it is.

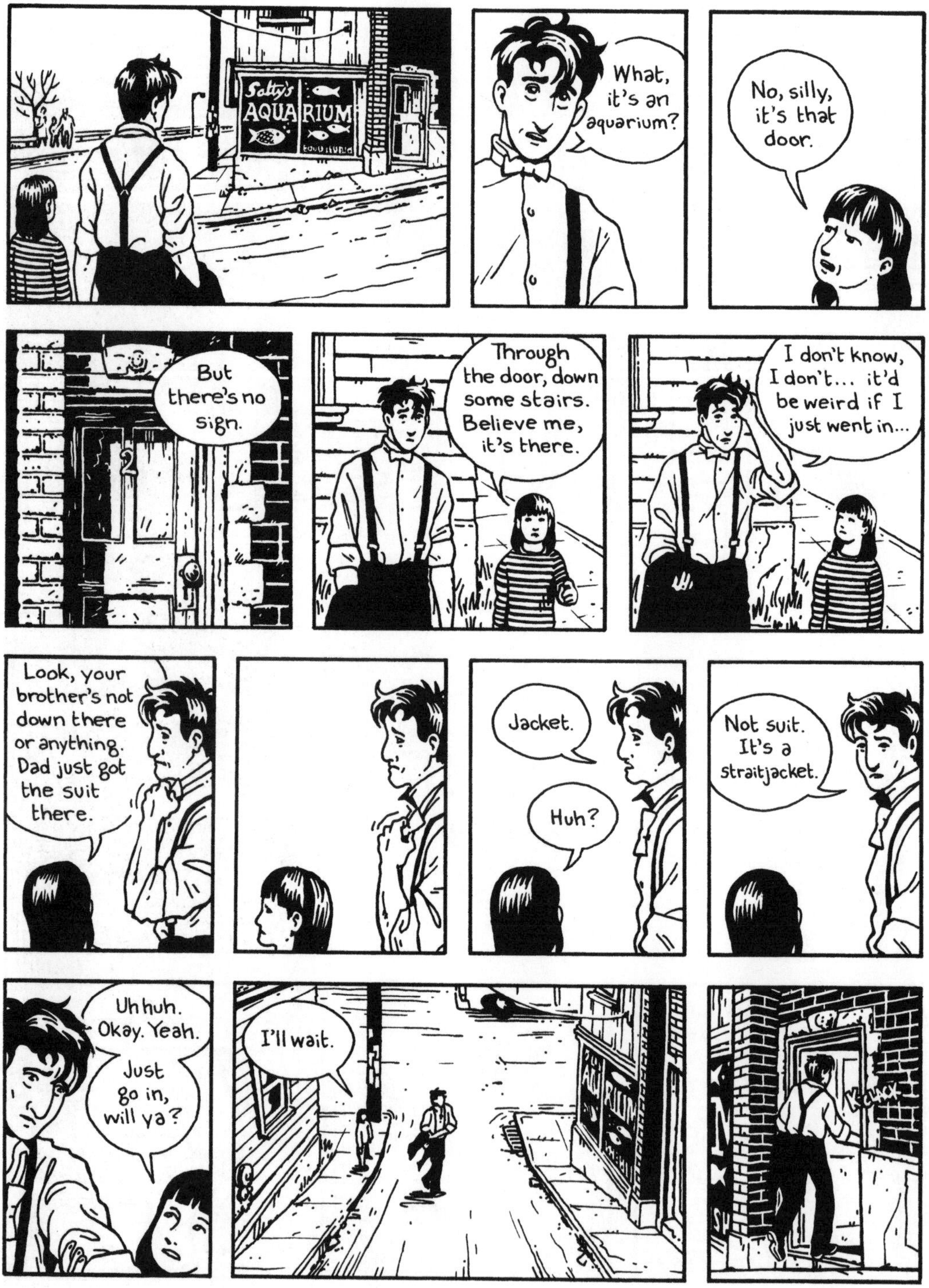
Salty's
AQUARIUM
What, it's an aquarium?
No, silly, it's that door.
But there's no sign.
Through the door, down some stairs. Believe me, it's there.
I don't know, I don't... it'd be weird if I just went in...
Look, your brother's not down there or anything. Dad just got the suit there.
Jacket.
Huh?
Not suit. It's a straitjacket.
Uh huh. Okay. Yeah.
Just go in, will ya?
I'll wait.

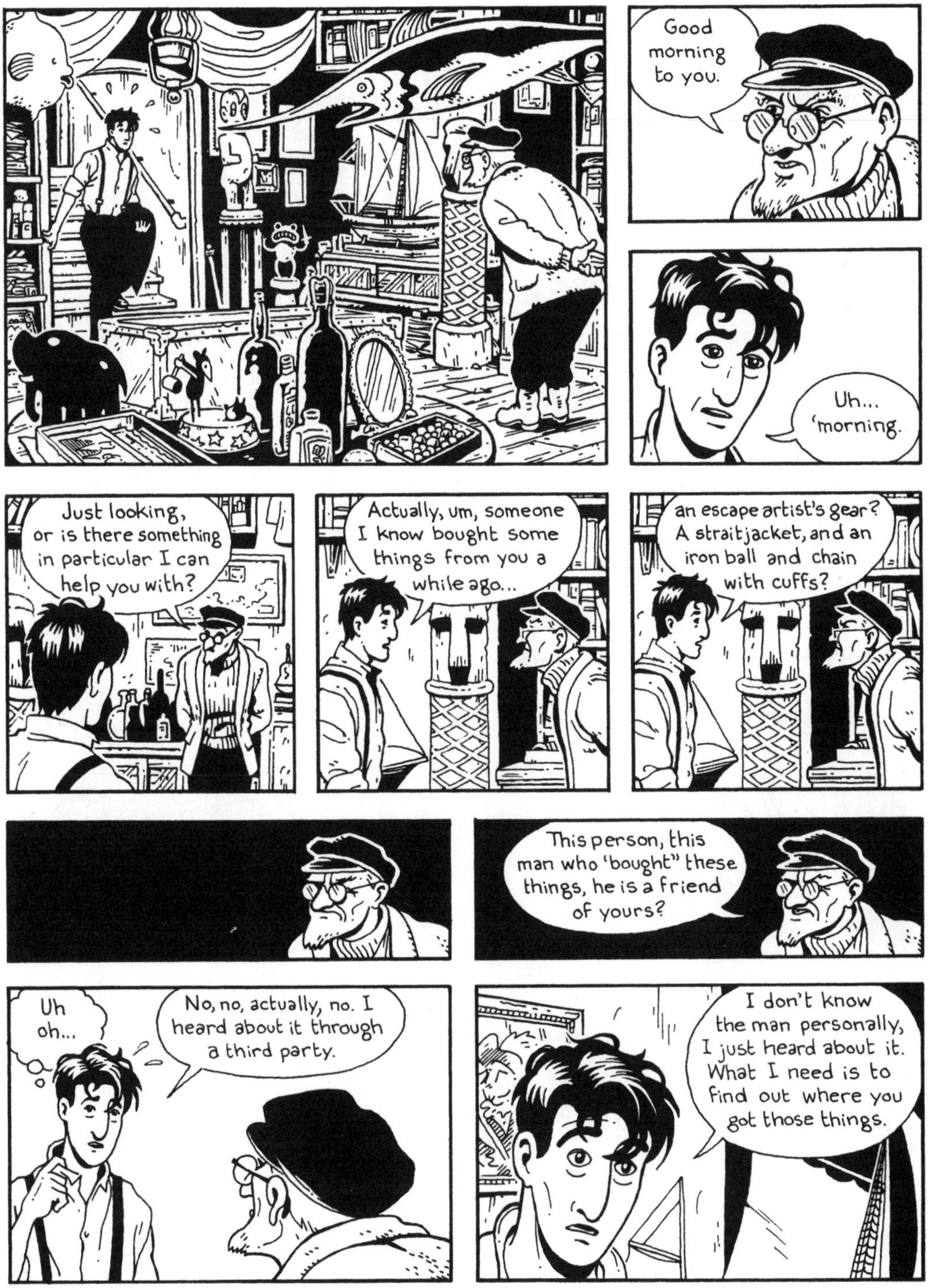
Good morning to you.
Uh... 'morning.
Just looking, or is there something in particular I can help you with?
Actually, um, someone I know bought some things from you a while ago...
an escape artist's gear? A straitjacket, and an iron ball and chain with cuffs?
This person, this man who 'bought" these things, he is a friend of yours?
Uh oh...
No, no, actually, no. I heard about it through a third party.
I don't know the man personally, I just heard about it. What I need is to find out where you got those things.

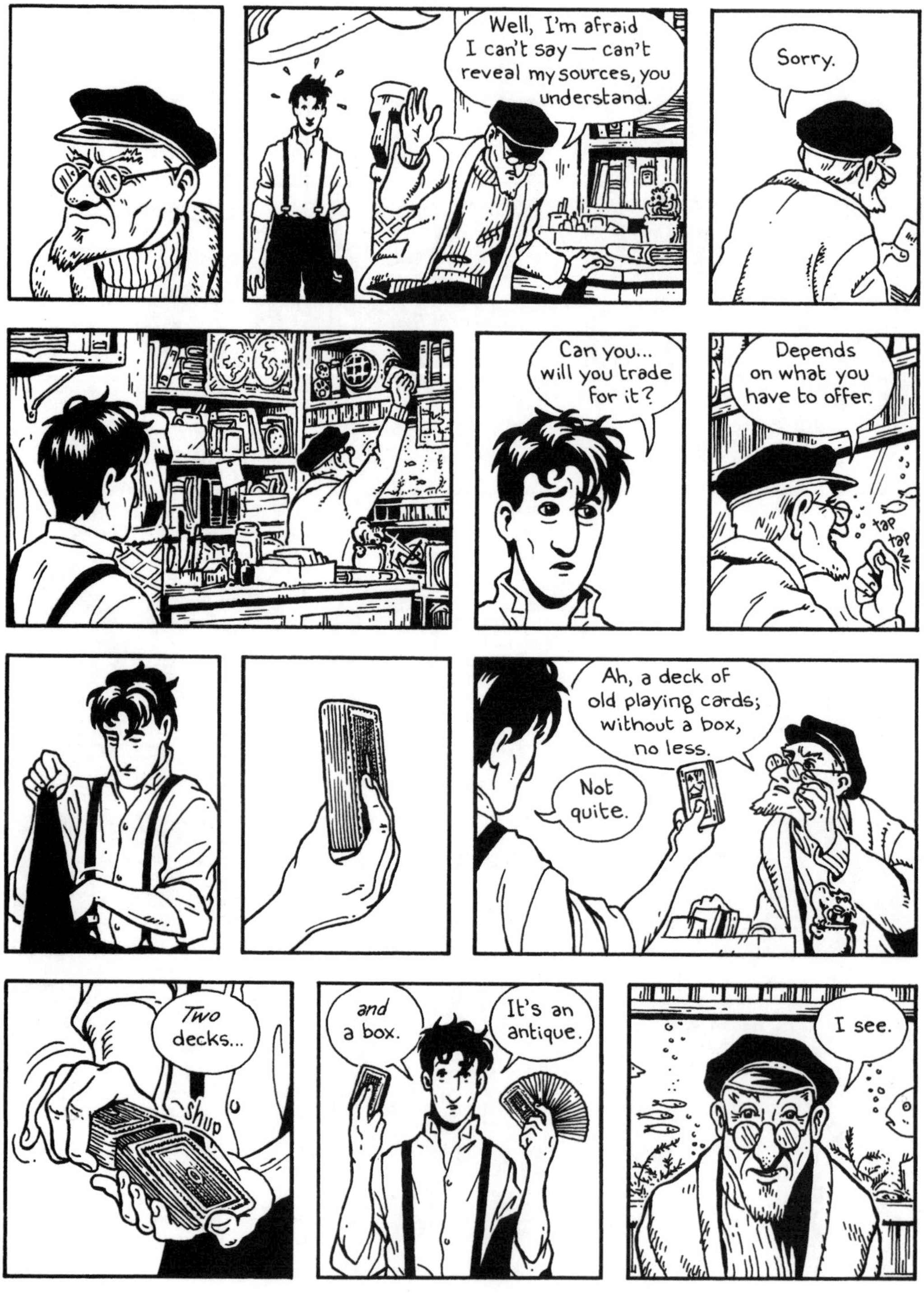
Well, I'm afraid I can't say — can't reveal my sources, you understand.
Sorry.
Can you... will you trade for it?
Depends on what you have to offer.
tap tap
Ah, a deck of old playing cards; without a box, no less.
Not quite.
Two decks...
shup
and a box.
It's an antique.
I see.

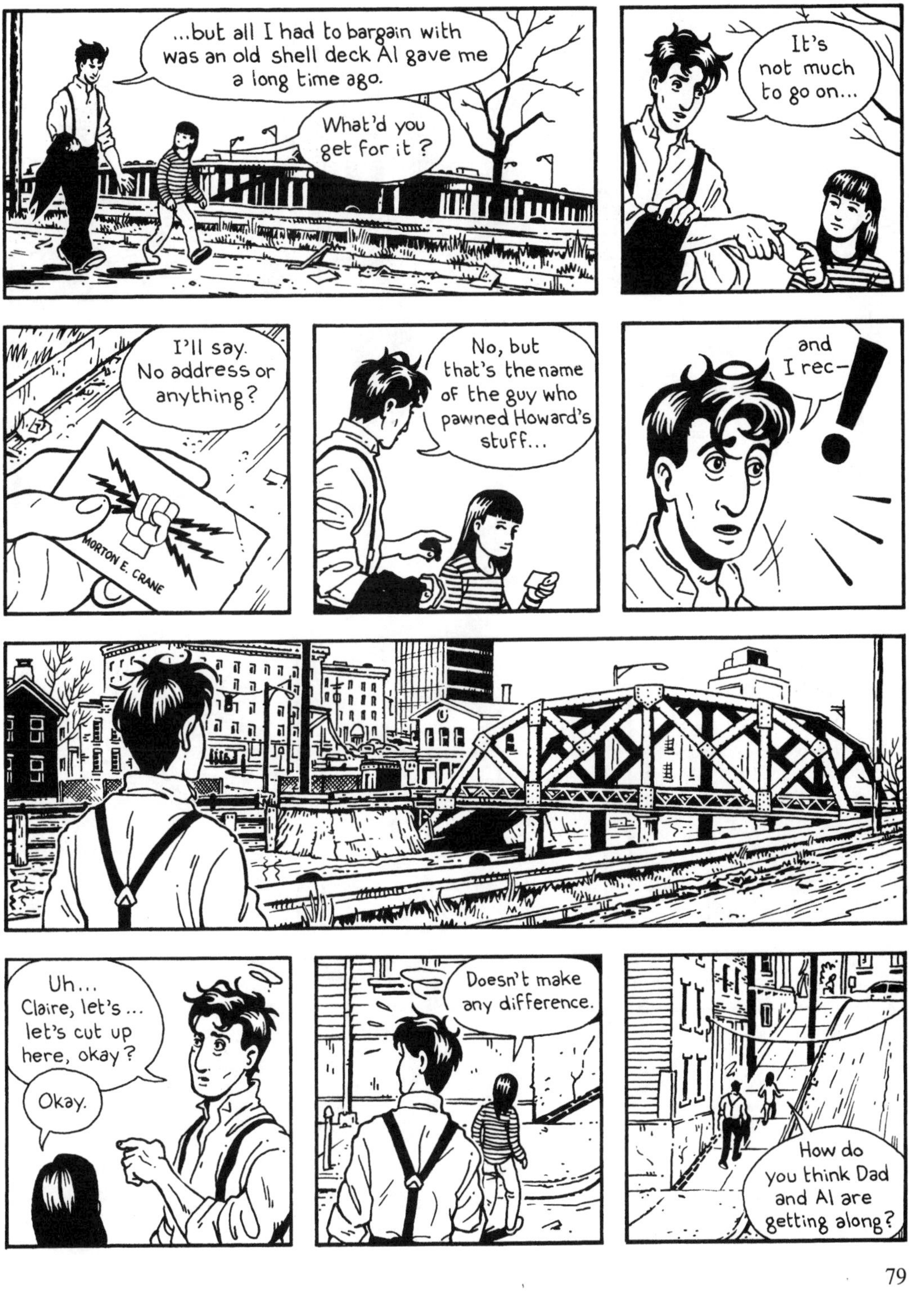
...but all I had to bargain with was an old shell deck Al gave me a long time ago.
What'd you get for it ?
It's not much to go on...
I'll say. No address or anything?
MORTON E. CRANE
No, but that's the name of the guy who pawned Howard's stuff...
and I rec—
!
Uh... Claire, let's... let's cut up here, okay?
Okay.
Doesn't make any difference.
How do you think Dad and Al are getting along?

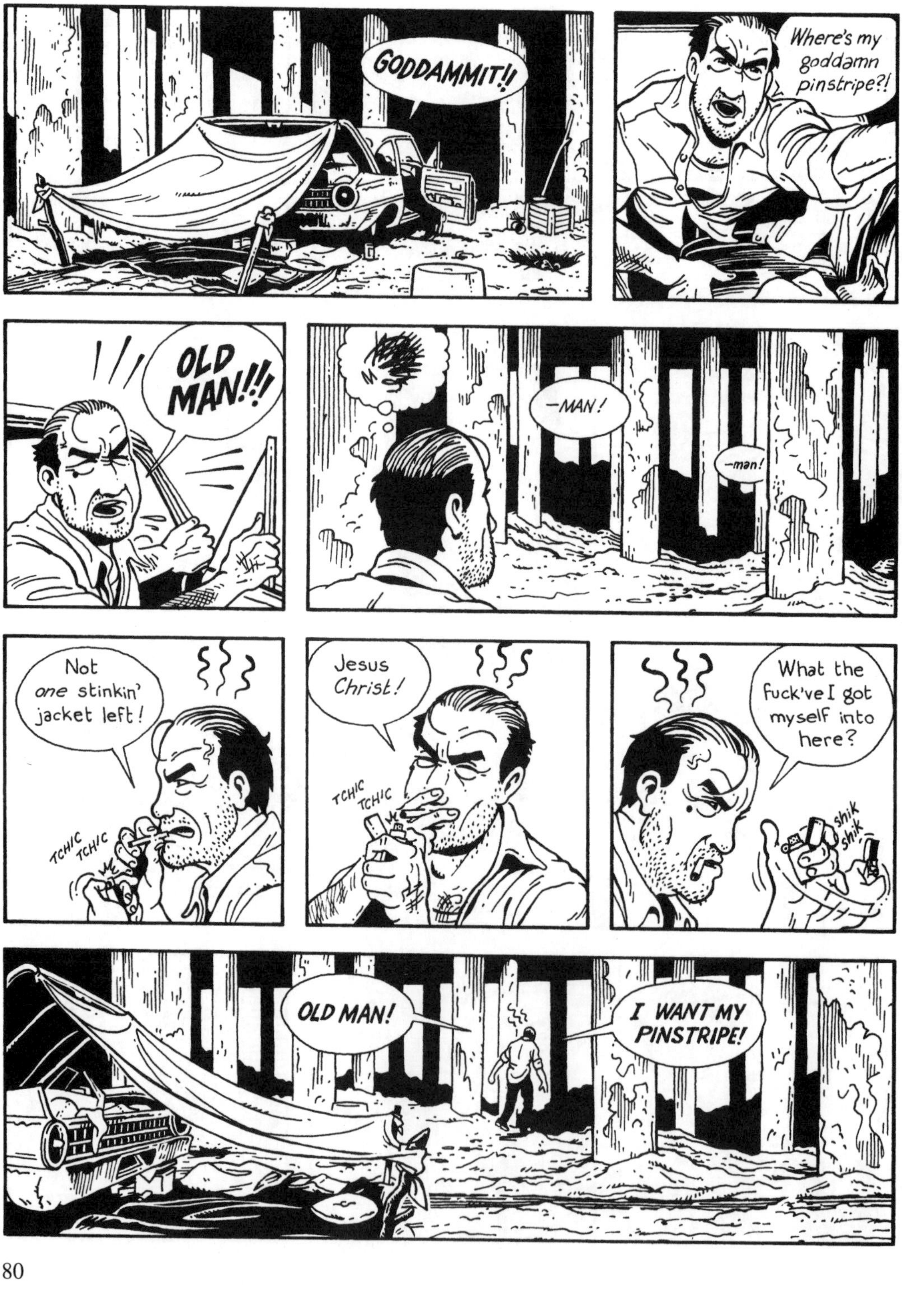
GODDAMMIT!!
Where's my goddamn pinstripe?!
OLD MAN!!!
—MAN!
—man!
Not one stinkin' jacket left!
TCHIC TCHIC
Jesus Christ!
TCHIC TCHIC
What the fuck've I got myself into here?
shik shik
OLD MAN!
I WANT MY PINSTRIPE!

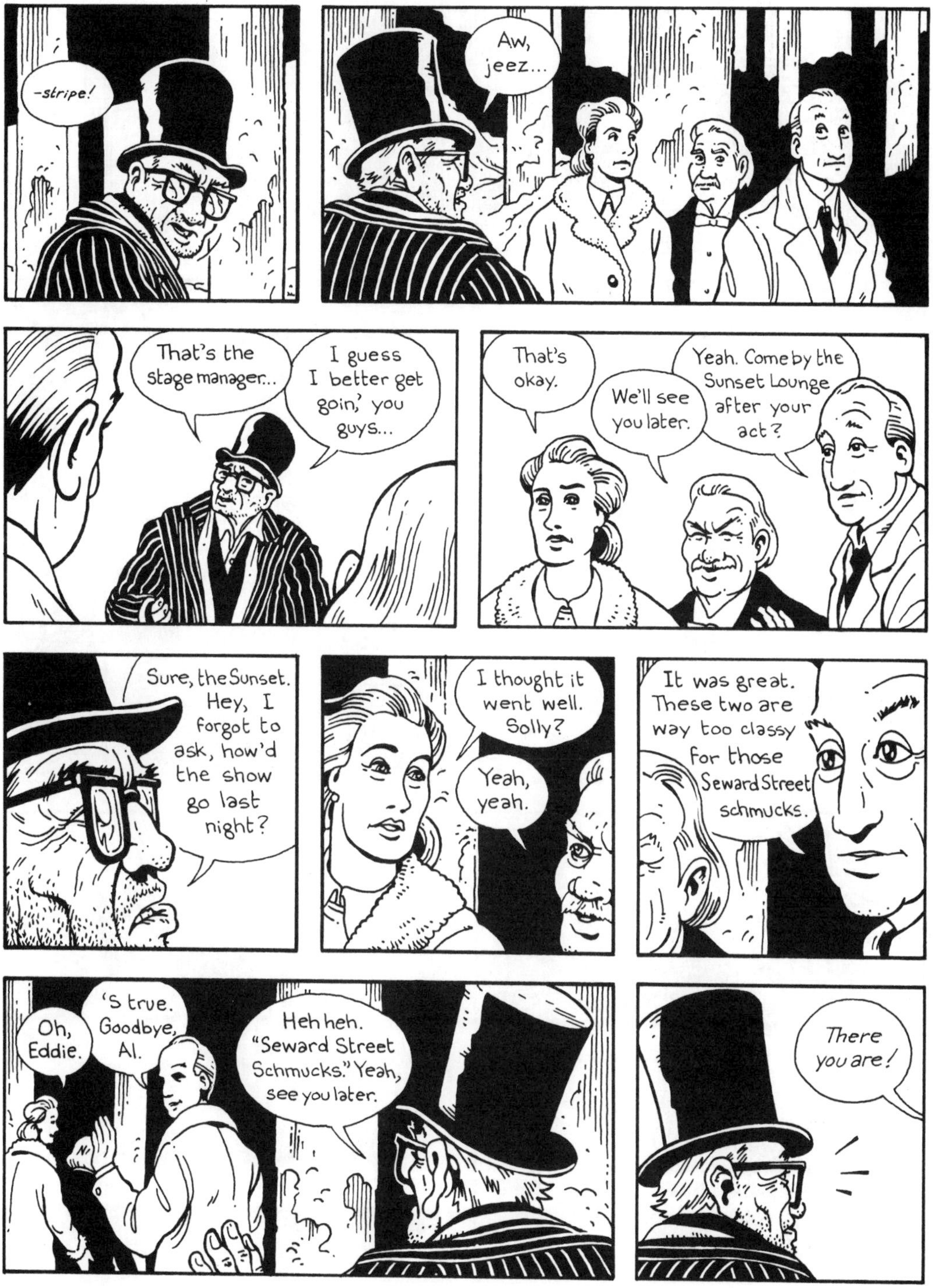

–stripe!
Aw, jeez...
That's the stage manager...
I guess I better get goin,' you guys...
That's okay.
We'll see you later.
Yeah. Come by the Sunset Lounge after your act?
Sure, the Sunset. Hey, I forgot to ask, how'd the show go last night?
I thought it went well. Solly?
Yeah, yeah.
It was great. These two are way too classy for those Seward Street schmucks.
Oh, Eddie.
'S true. Goodbye, Al.
Heh heh. "Seward Street Schmucks." Yeah, see you later.
There you are!

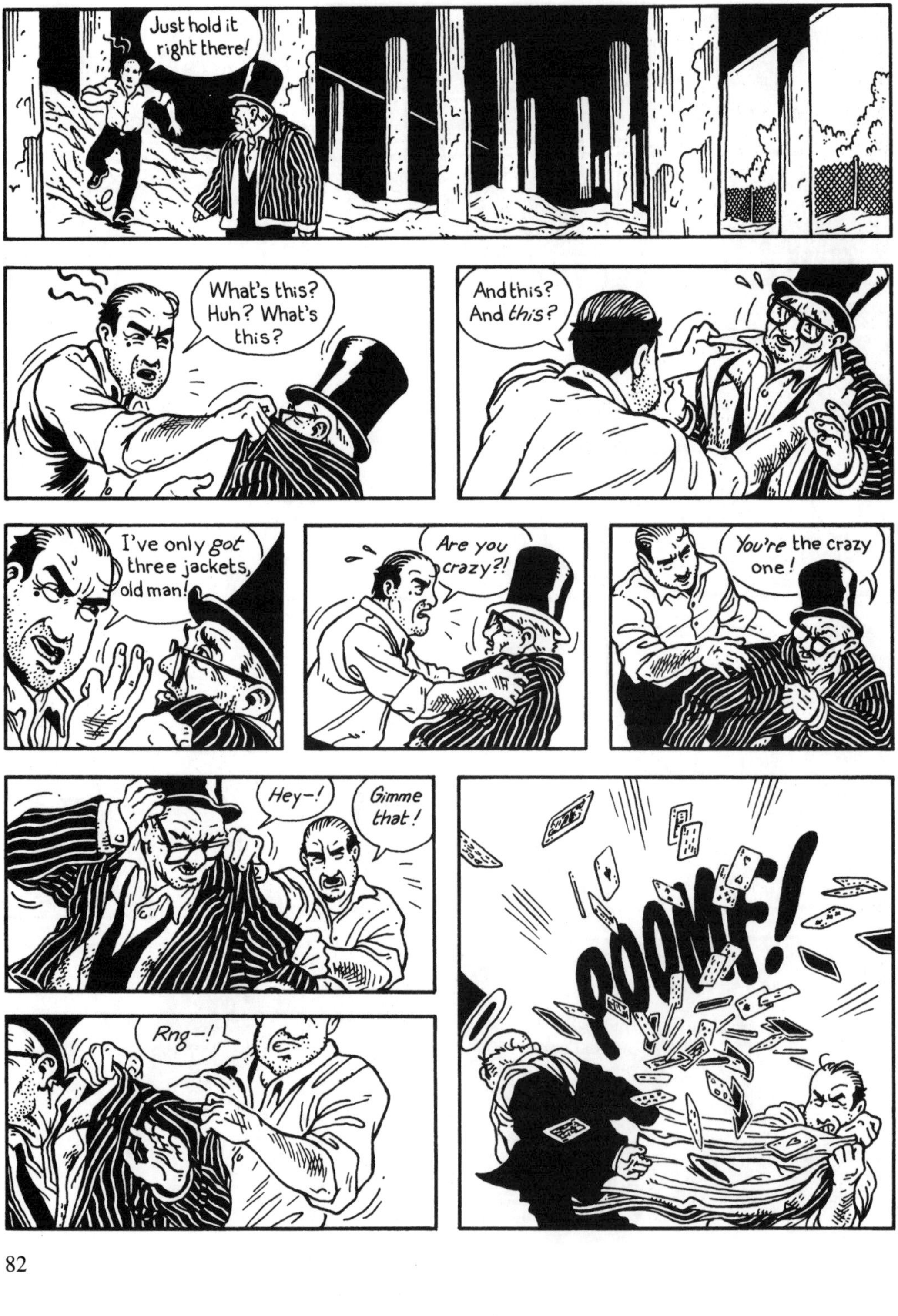
Just hold it right there!
What's this? Huh? What's this?
And this? And *this*?
I've only *got* three jackets, old man!
Are you crazy?!
You're the crazy one!
Hey–!
Gimme that!
Rng–!
POOMF!

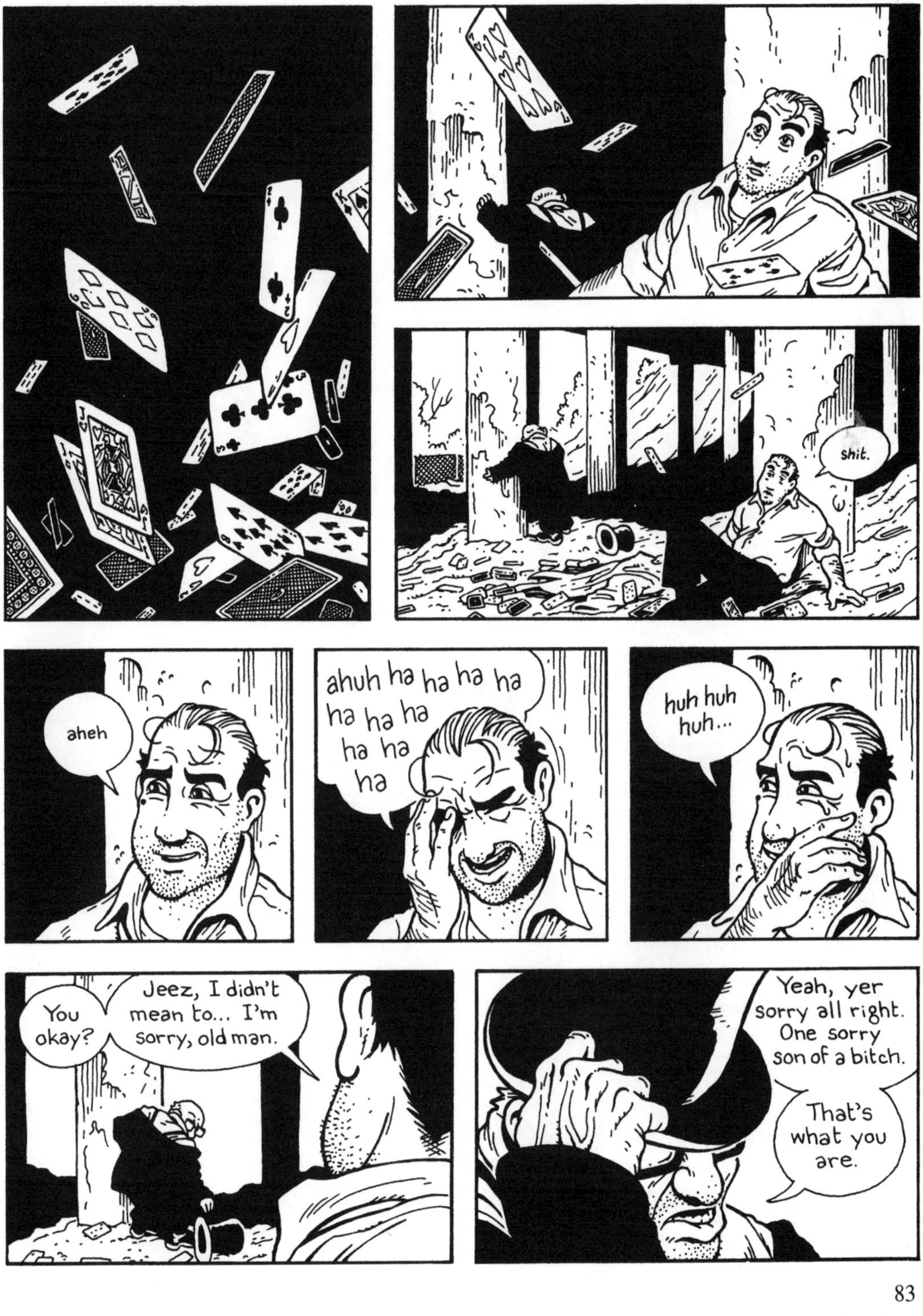
shit.
aheh
ahuh ha ha ha ha ha ha ha ha ha ha
huh huh huh...
You okay?
Jeez, I didn't mean to... I'm sorry, old man.
Yeah, yer sorry all right. One sorry son of a bitch.
That's what you are.

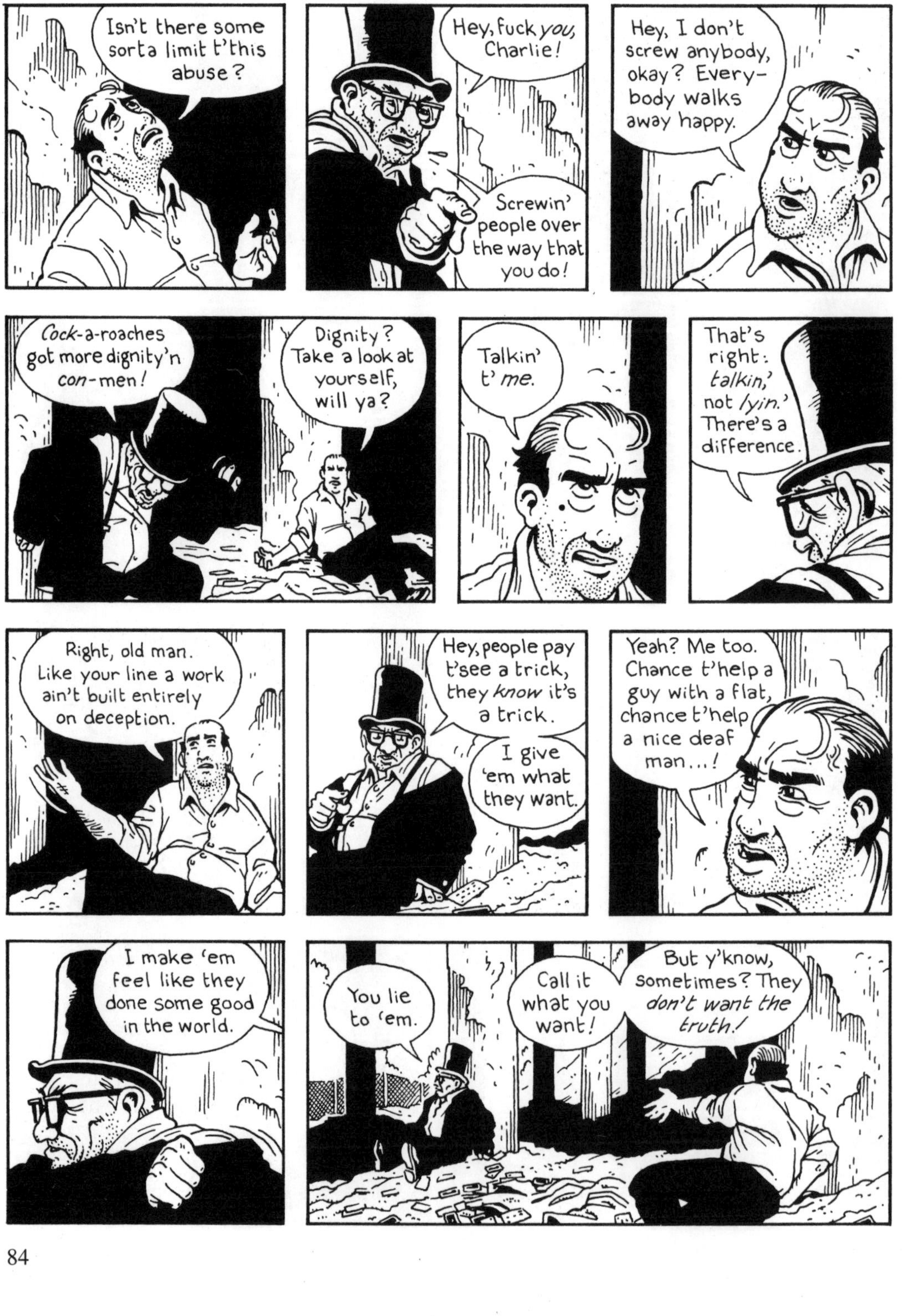
Isn't there some sorta limit t'this abuse?
Hey, fuck *you*, Charlie!
Screwin' people over the way that you do!
Hey, I don't screw anybody, okay? Every-body walks away happy.
Cock-a-roaches got more dignity'n *con*-men!
Dignity? Take a look at yourself, will ya?
Talkin' t' *me*.
That's right: *talkin,'* not *lyin.'* There's a difference.
Right, old man. Like your line a work ain't built entirely on deception.
Hey, people pay t'see a trick, they *know* it's a trick.
I give 'em what they want.
Yeah? Me too. Chance t'help a guy with a flat, chance t'help a nice deaf man...!
I make 'em feel like they done some good in the world.
You lie to 'em.
Call it what you want!
But y'know, sometimes? They *don't want the truth!*

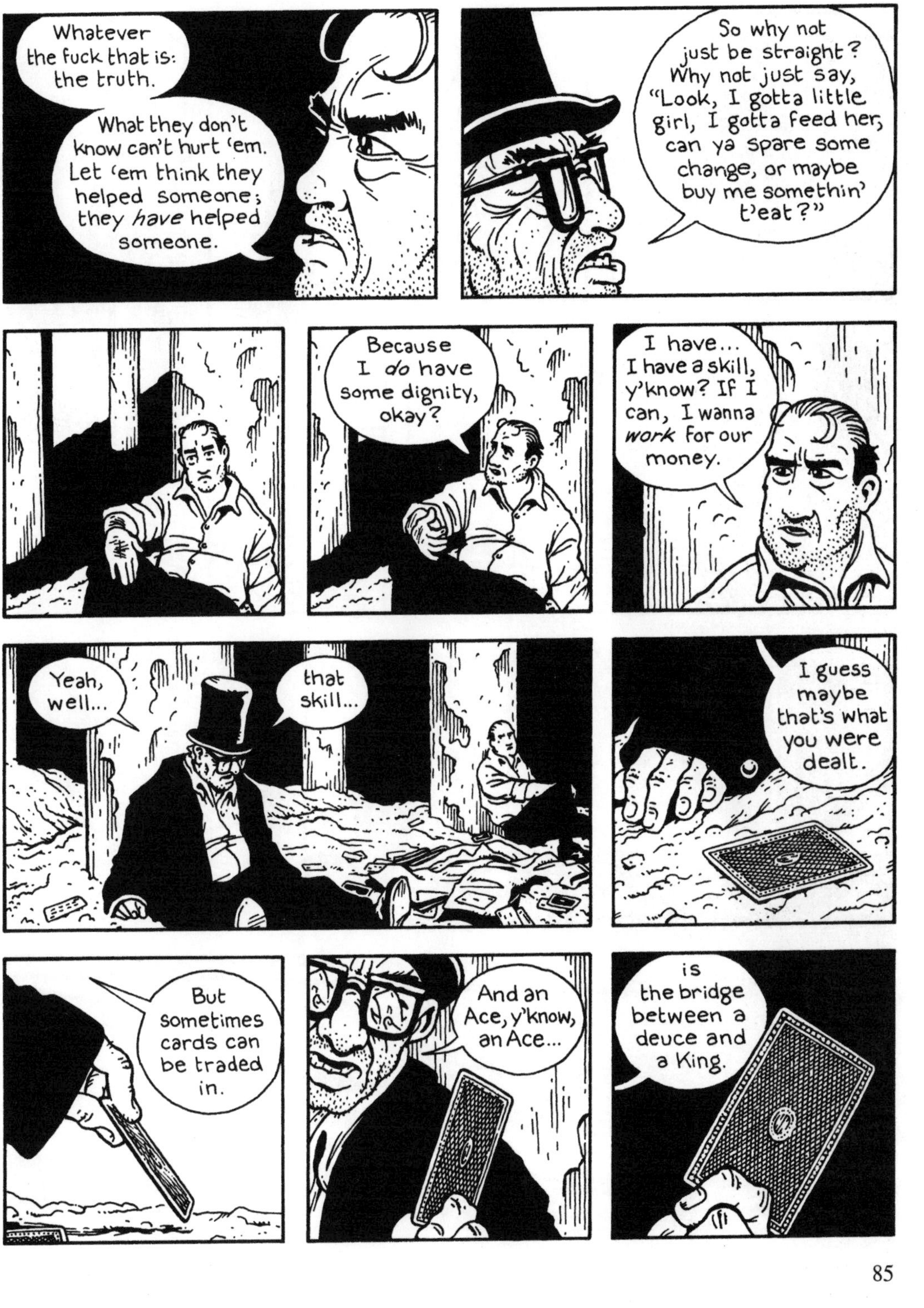
Whatever the fuck that is: the truth.
What they don't know can't hurt 'em. Let 'em think they helped someone; they *have* helped someone.
So why not just be straight? Why not just say, "Look, I gotta little girl, I gotta feed her, can ya spare some change, or maybe buy me somethin' t'eat?"
Because I *do* have some dignity, okay?
I have... I have a skill, y'know? If I can, I wanna *work* for our money.
Yeah, well...
that skill...
I guess maybe that's what you were dealt.
But sometimes cards can be traded in.
And an Ace, y'know, an Ace...
is the bridge between a deuce and a King.

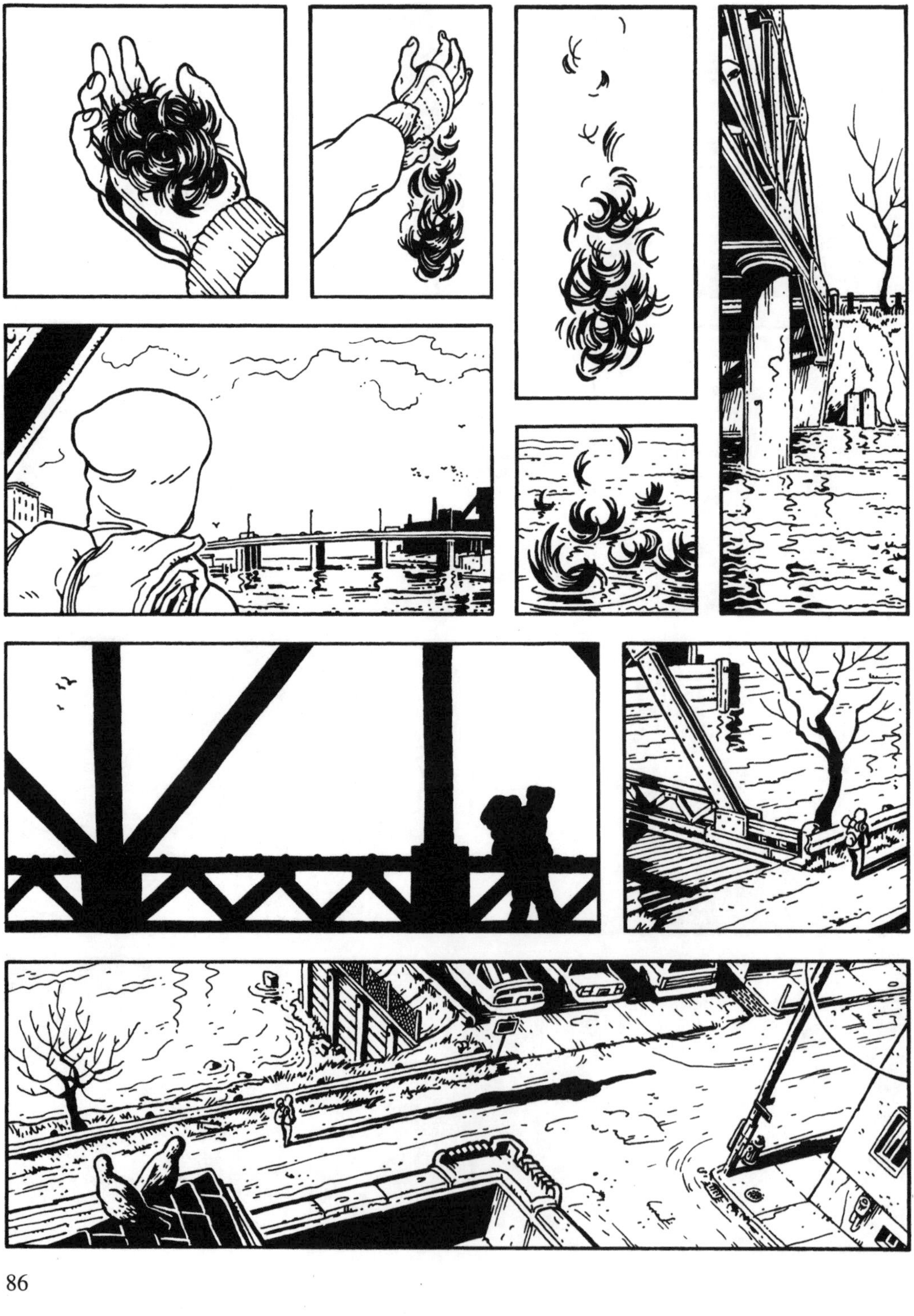

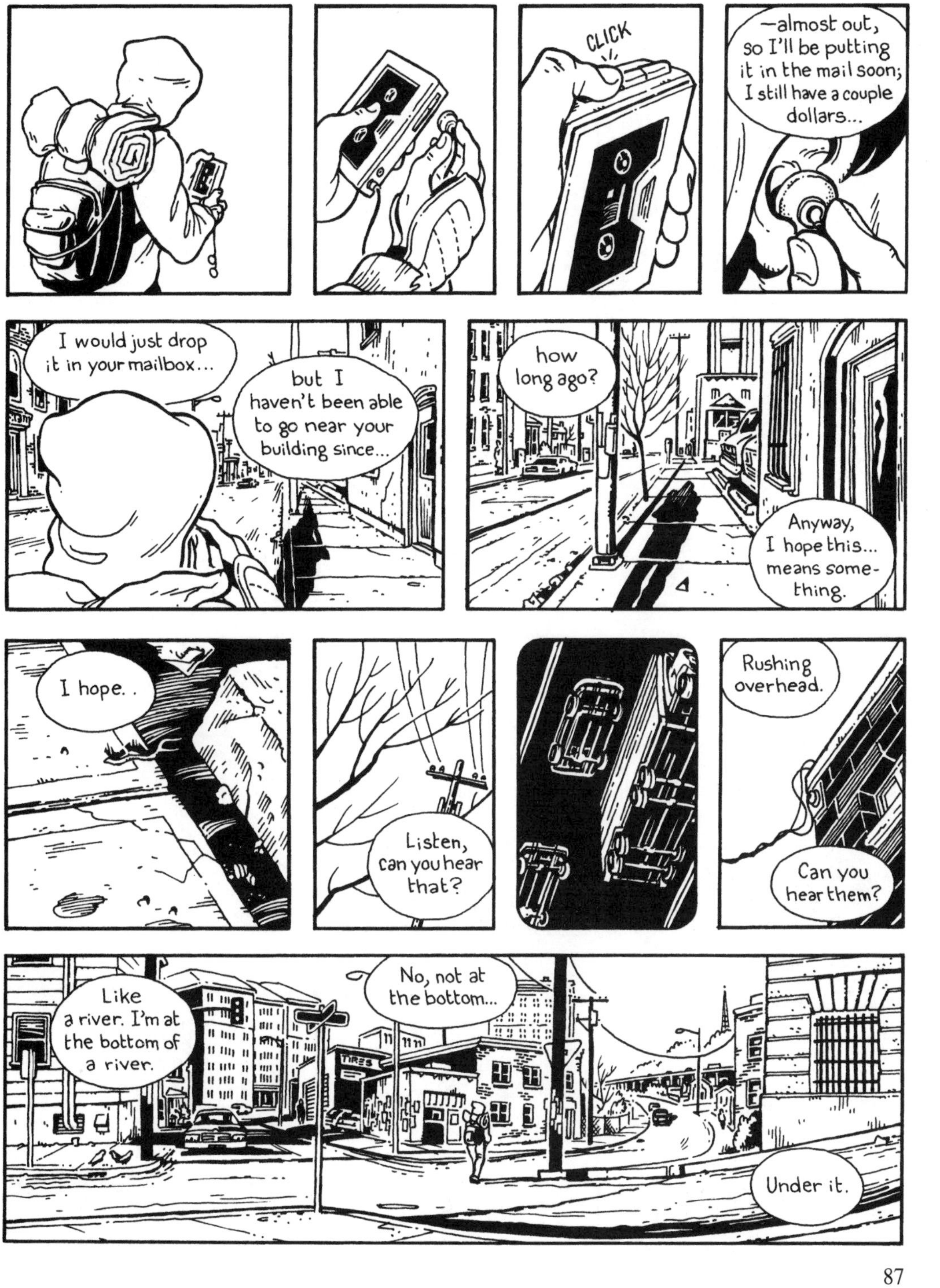
CLICK
—almost out, so I'll be putting it in the mail soon; I still have a couple dollars...
I would just drop it in your mailbox...
but I haven't been able to go near your building since...
how long ago?
Anyway, I hope this... means some-thing.
I hope. .
Listen, can you hear that?
Rushing overhead.
Can you hear them?
Like a river. I'm at the bottom of a river.
No, not at the bottom...
TIRES
Under it.

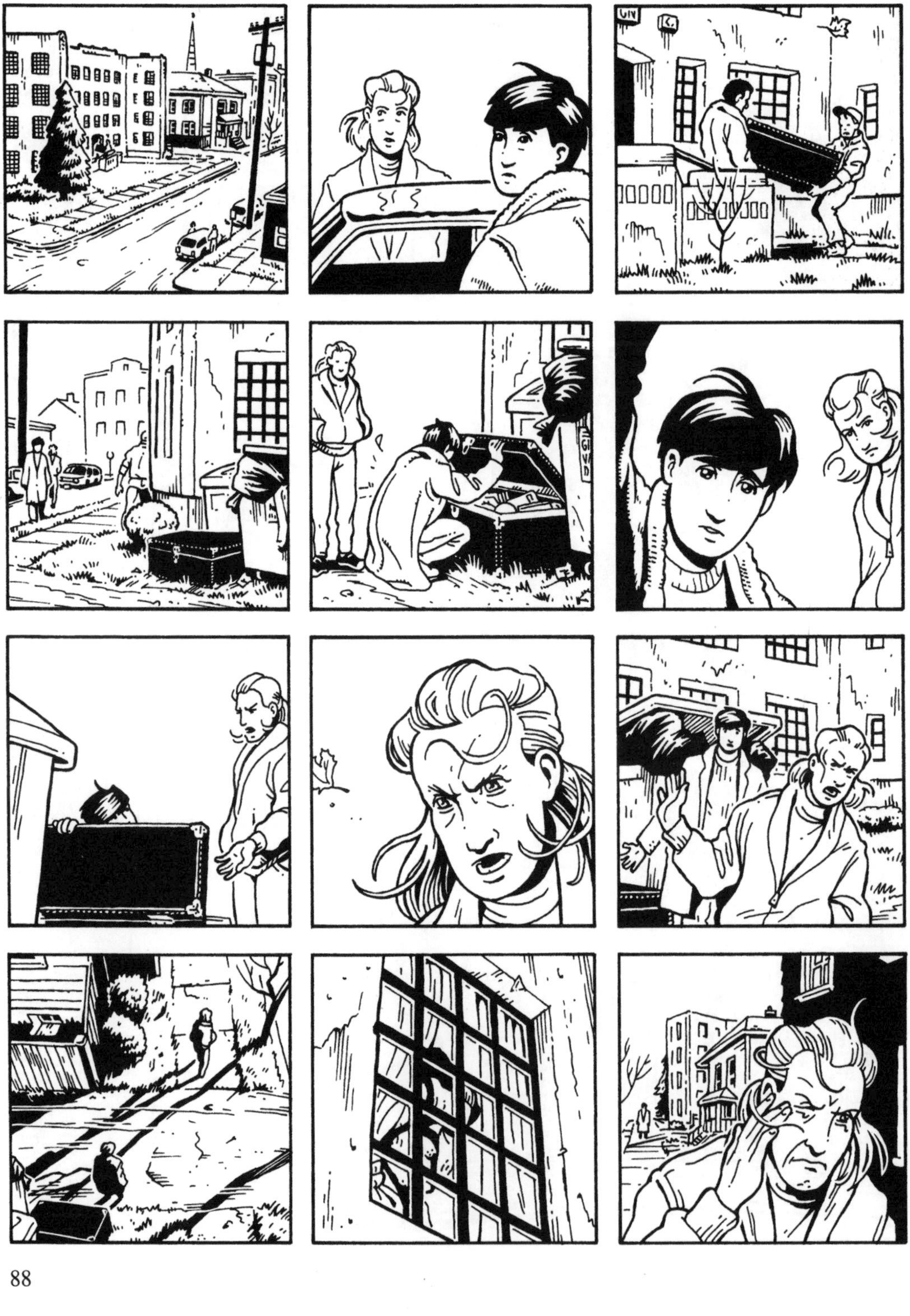

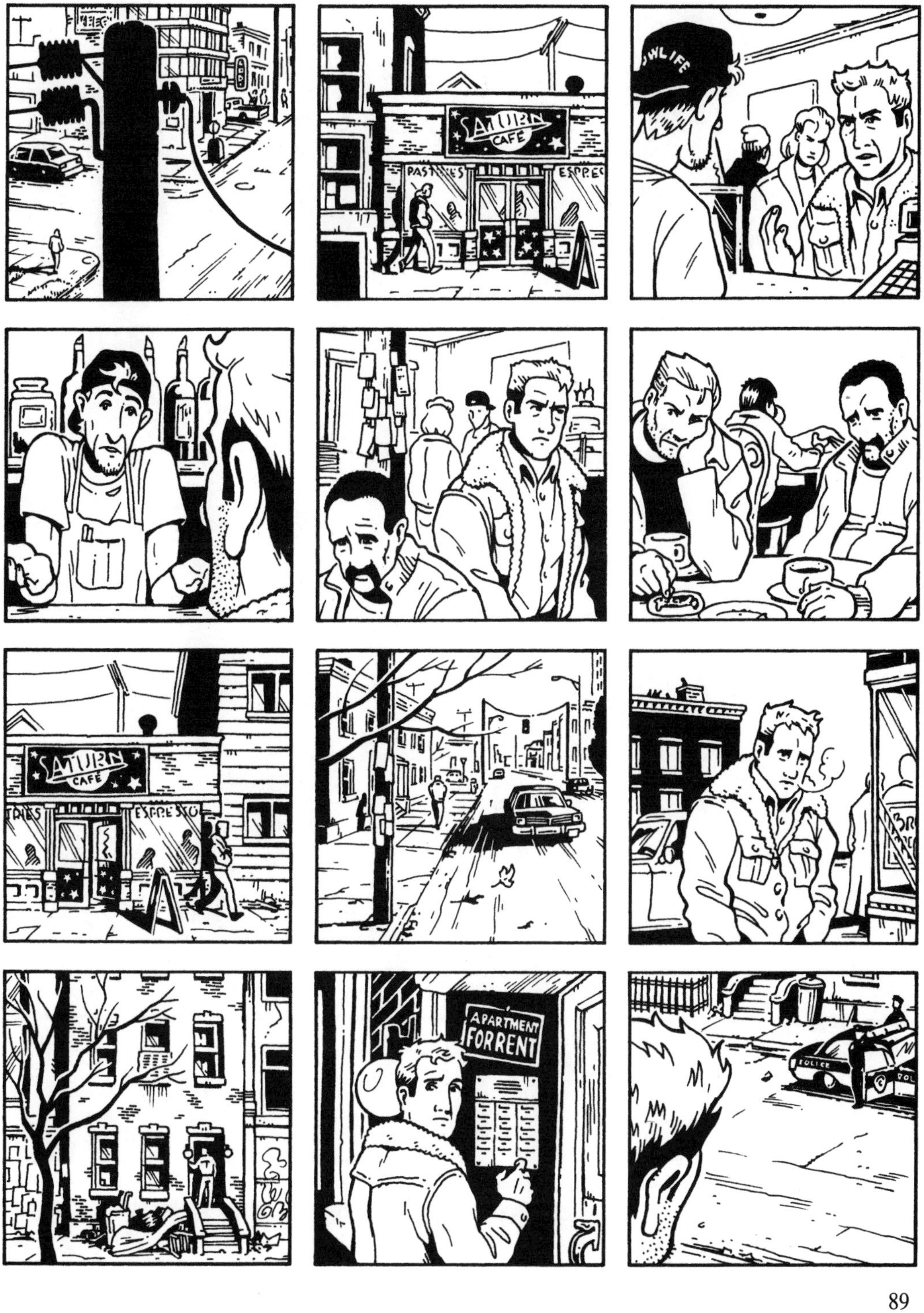
SATURN CAFÉ
SATURN CAFÉ
ESPRESSO
APARTMENT FOR RENT
POLICE

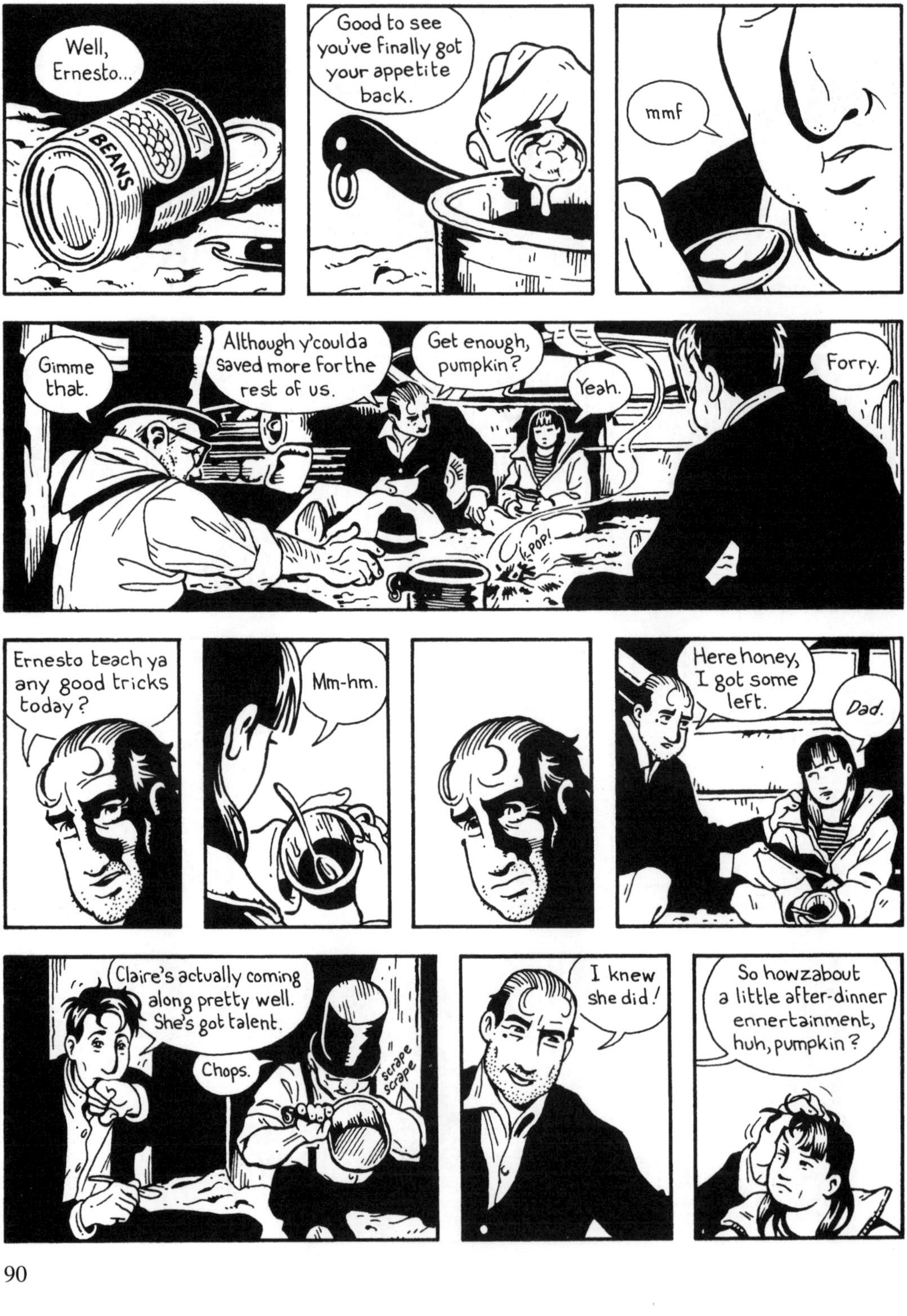
Well, Ernesto...
HEINZ
BEANS
Good to see you've finally got your appetite back.
mmf
Gimme that.
Although y'coulda saved more for the rest of us.
Get enough, pumpkin?
Yeah.
Forry.
K-POP!
Ernesto teach ya any good tricks today?
Mm-hm.
Here honey, I got some left.
Dad.
Claire's actually coming along pretty well. She's got talent.
Chops.
scrape scrape
I knew she did!
So howzabout a little after-dinner ennertainment, huh, pumpkin?

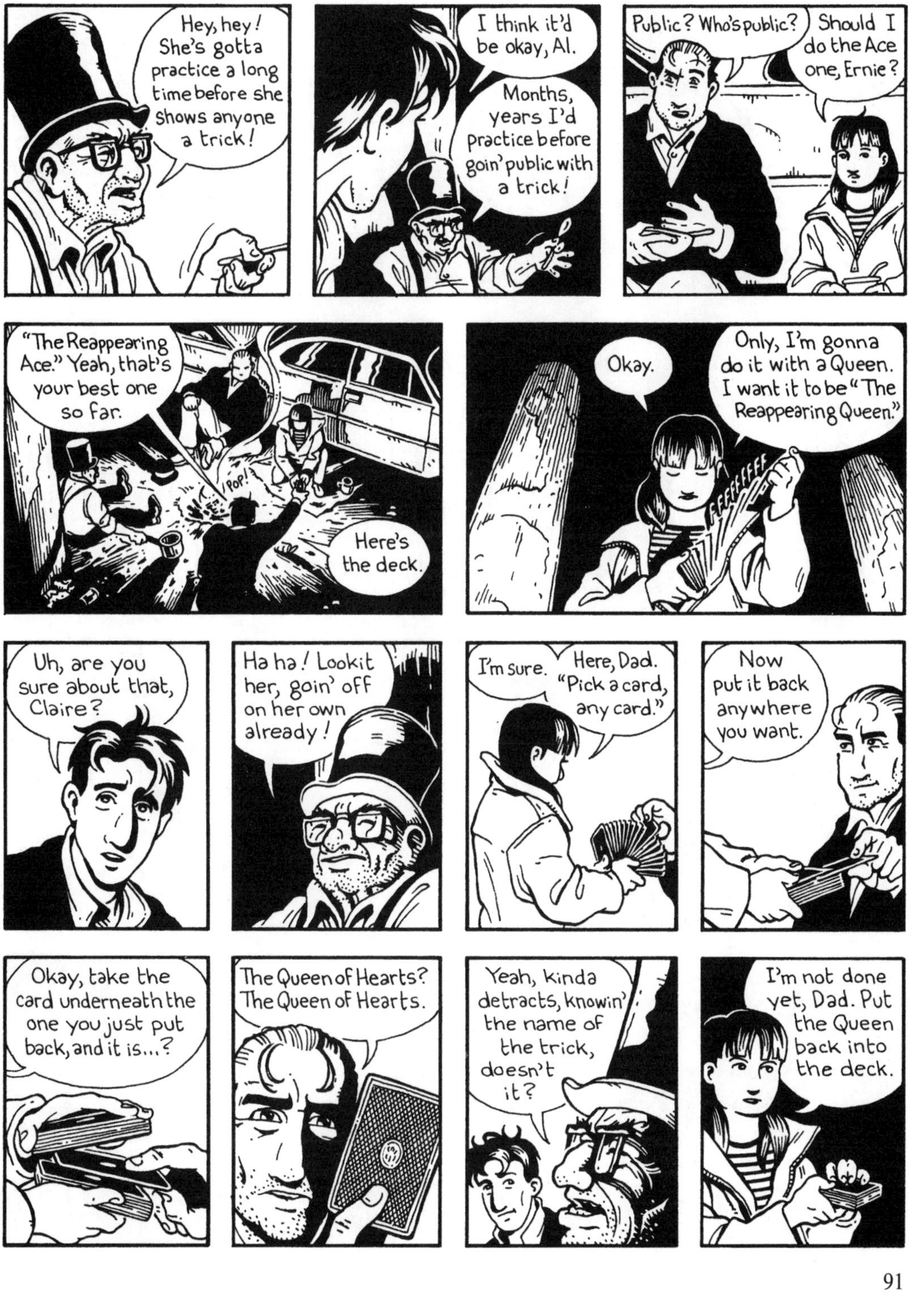
Hey, hey! She's gotta practice a long time before she shows anyone a trick!
I think it'd be okay, Al.
Months, years I'd practice before goin' public with a trick!
Public? Who's public?
Should I do the Ace one, Ernie?
"The Reappearing Ace." Yeah, that's your best one so far.
POP!
Here's the deck.
Okay.
Only, I'm gonna do it with a Queen. I want it to be "The Reappearing Queen."
Uh, are you sure about that, Claire?
Ha ha! Lookit her, goin' off on her own already!
I'm sure.
Here, Dad. "Pick a card, any card."
Now put it back anywhere you want.
Okay, take the card underneath the one you just put back, and it is...?
The Queen of Hearts? The Queen of Hearts.
Yeah, kinda detracts, knowin' the name of the trick, doesn't it?
I'm not done yet, Dad. Put the Queen back into the deck.

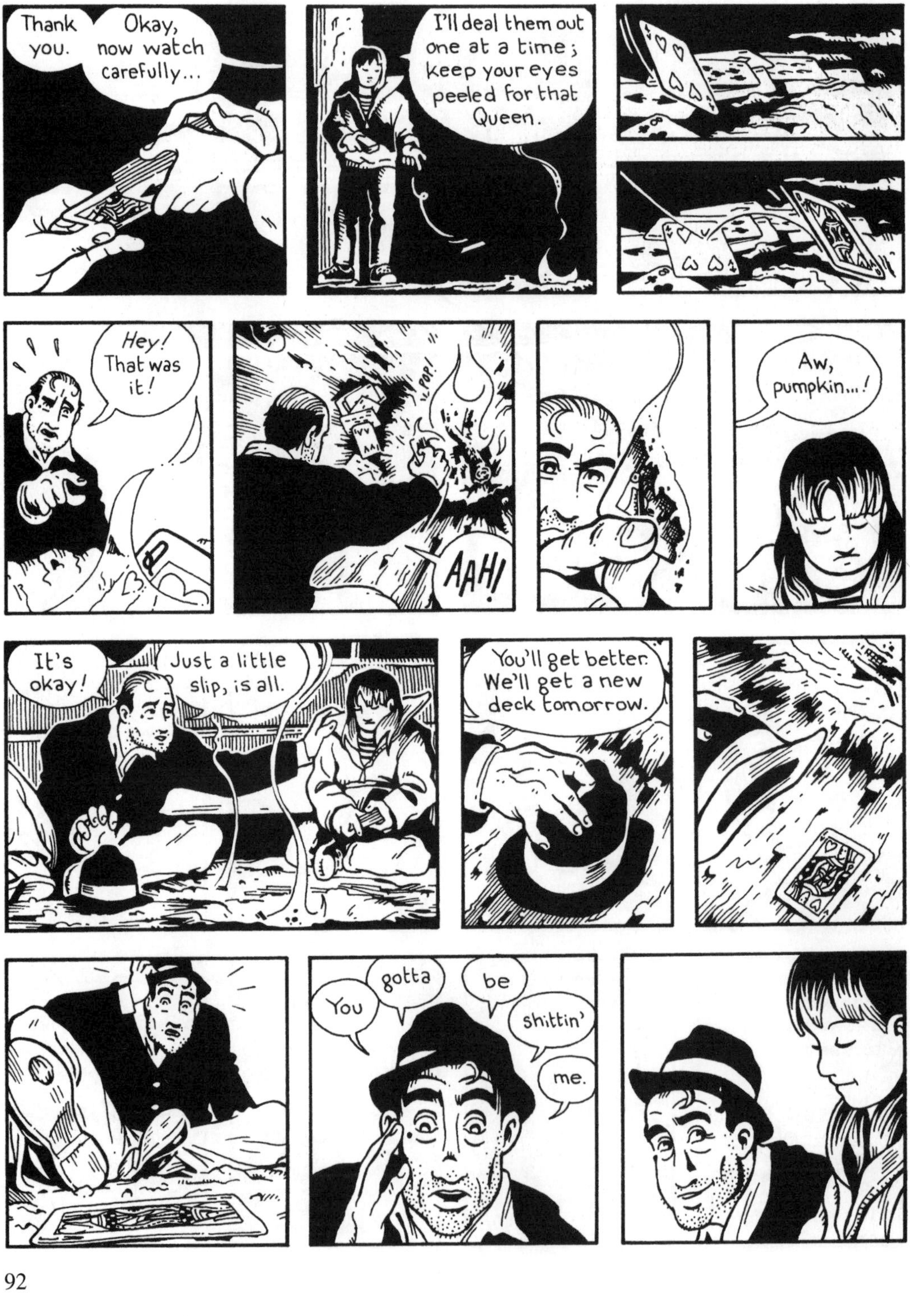

Thank you.
Okay, now watch carefully...
I'll deal them out one at a time; keep your eyes peeled for that Queen.
Hey! That was it!
POP!
AAH!
Aw, pumpkin...!
It's okay!
Just a little slip, is all.
You'll get better. We'll get a new deck tomorrow.
You
gotta
be
shittin'
me.

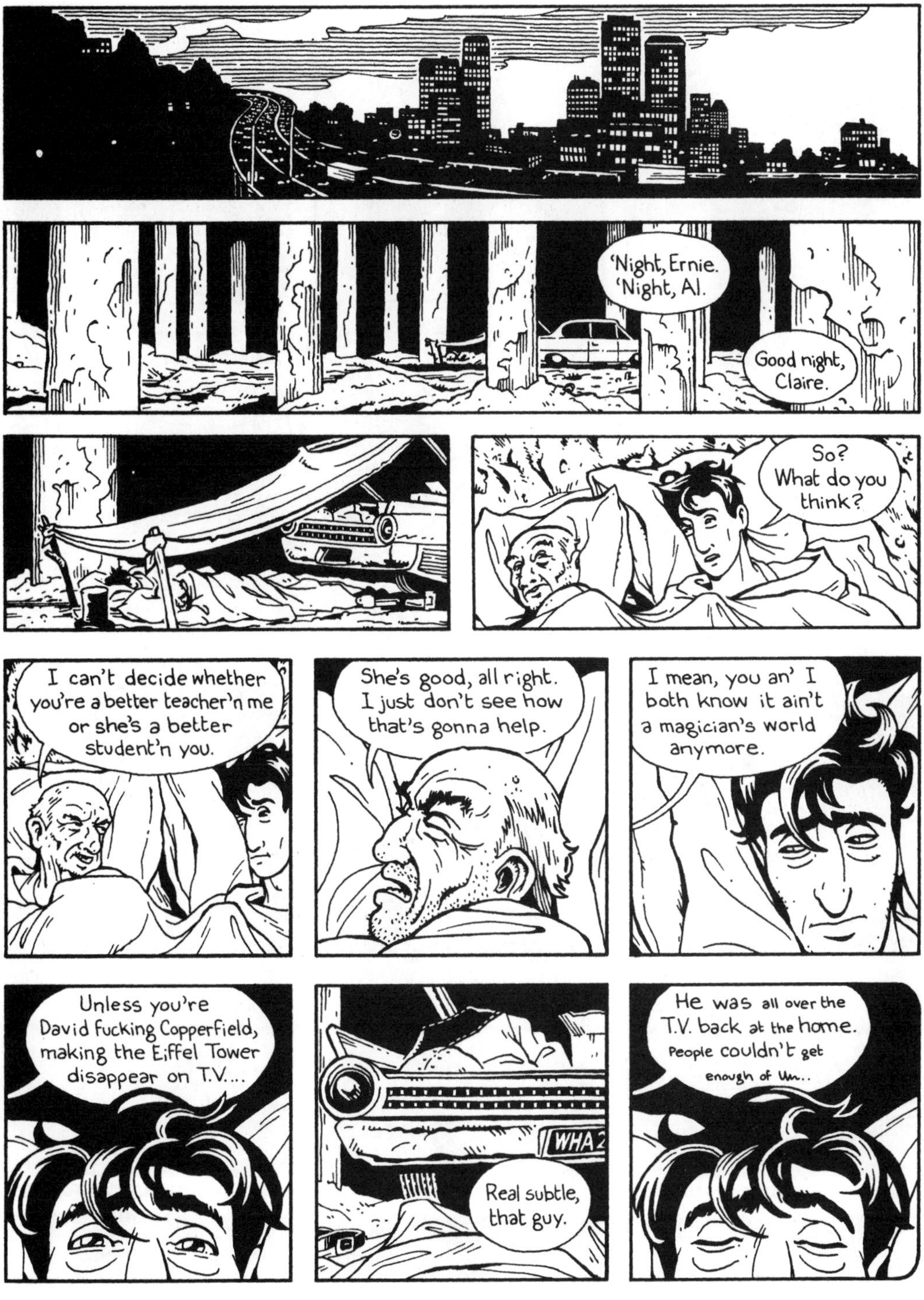
'Night, Ernie.
'Night, Al.
Good night, Claire.
So? What do you think?
I can't decide whether you're a better teacher'n me or she's a better student'n you.
She's good, all right. I just don't see how that's gonna help.
I mean, you an' I both know it ain't a magician's world anymore.
Unless you're David fucking Copperfield, making the Eiffel Tower disappear on T.V....
WHA2
Real subtle, that guy.
He was all over the T.V. back at the home. People couldn't get enough of 'im..

Ssshh...

WHA

I have just one question . . .

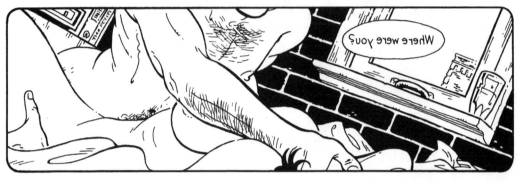

Where were you?

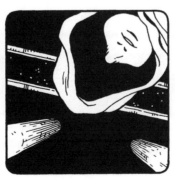

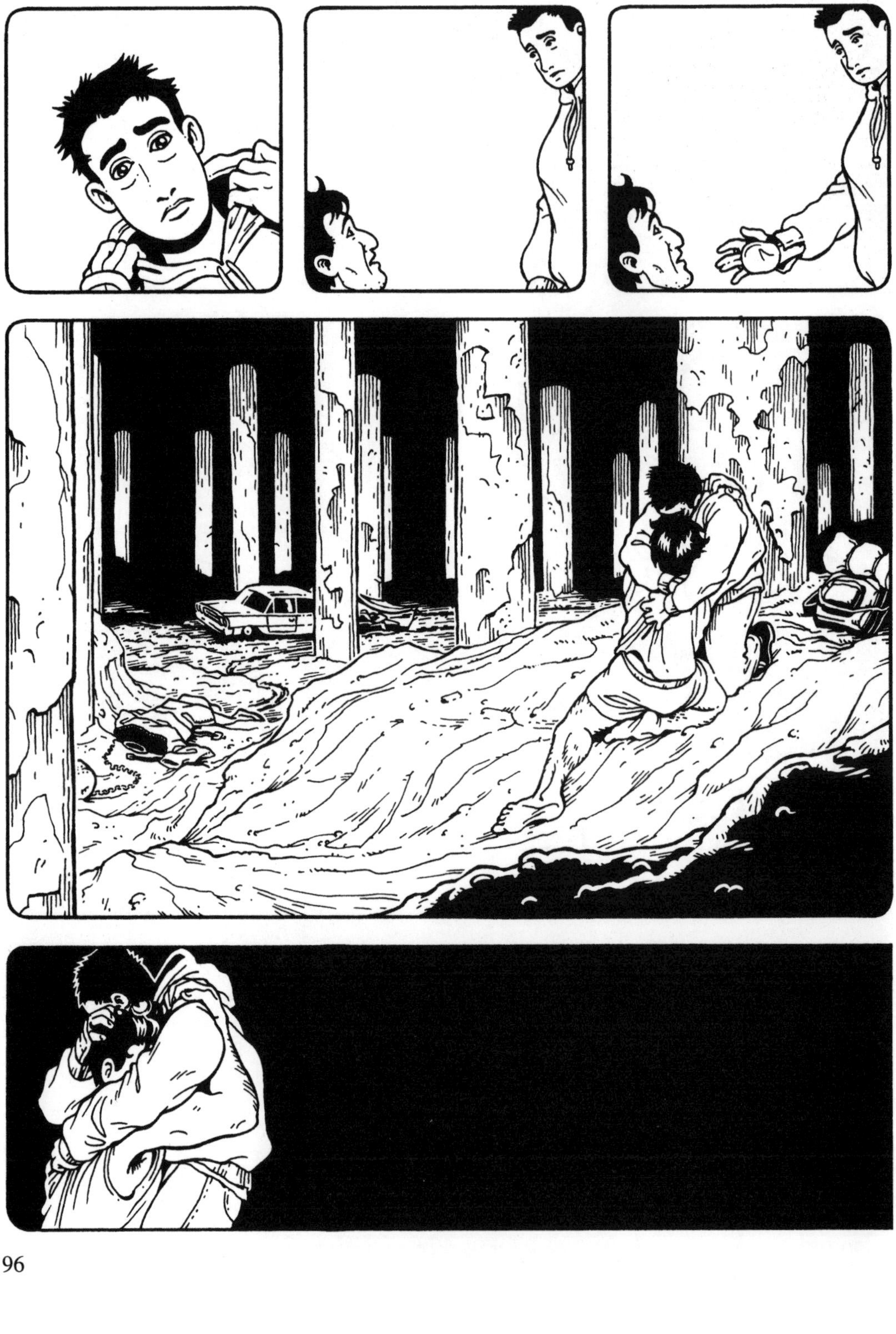

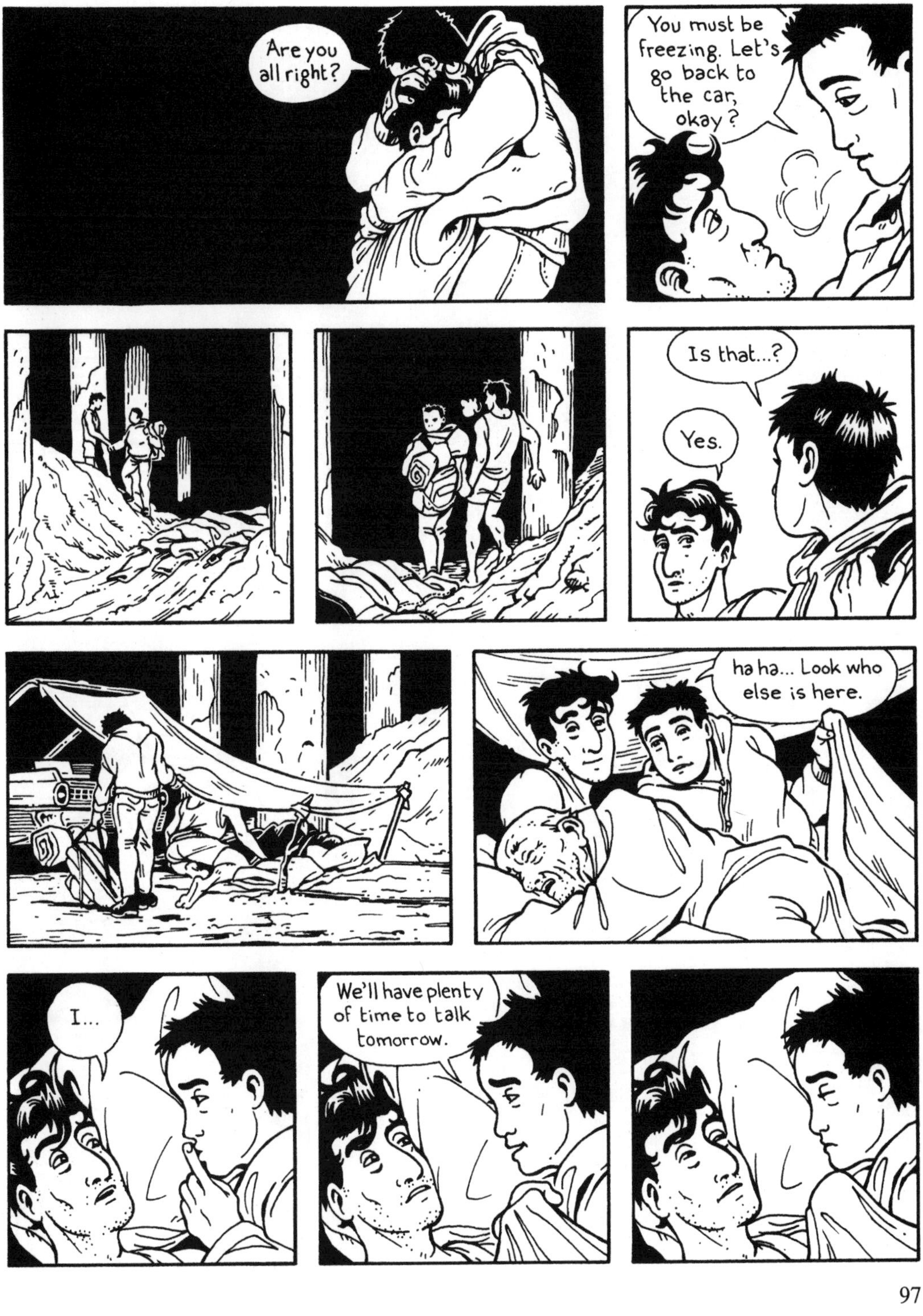
Are you all right?
You must be freezing. Let's go back to the car, okay?
Is that...?
Yes.
ha ha... Look who else is here.
I...
We'll have plenty of time to talk tomorrow.

okay Mom, okay that I will, me y...

CLICK

COOO COOO

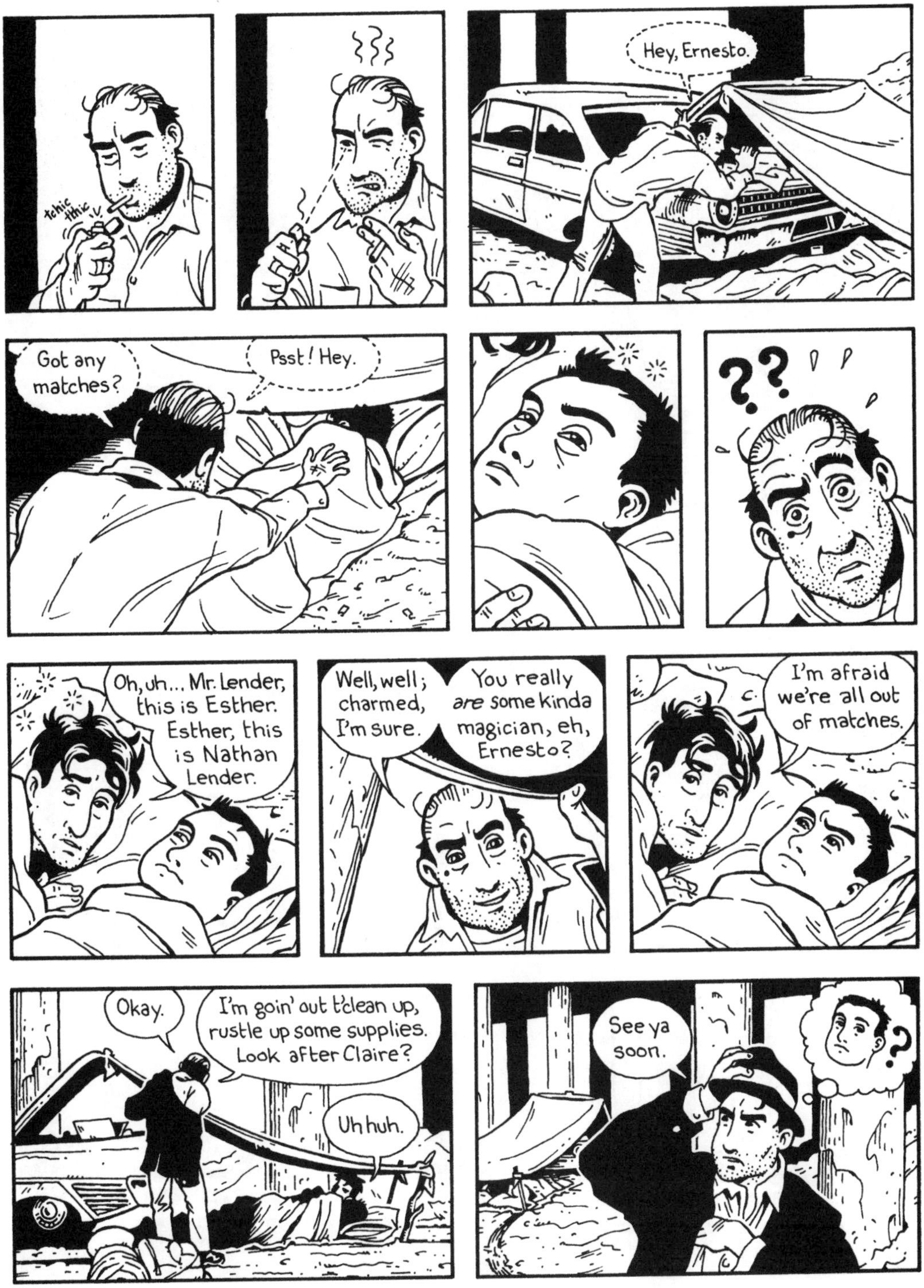

tchic
tthic
Hey, Ernesto.
Got any matches?
Psst! Hey.
??
Oh, uh... Mr. Lender, this is Esther. Esther, this is Nathan Lender.
Well, well; charmed, I'm sure.
You really *are* some kinda magician, eh, Ernesto?
I'm afraid we're all out of matches.
Okay.
I'm goin' out t'clean up, rustle up some supplies. Look after Claire?
Uh huh.
See ya soon.
?

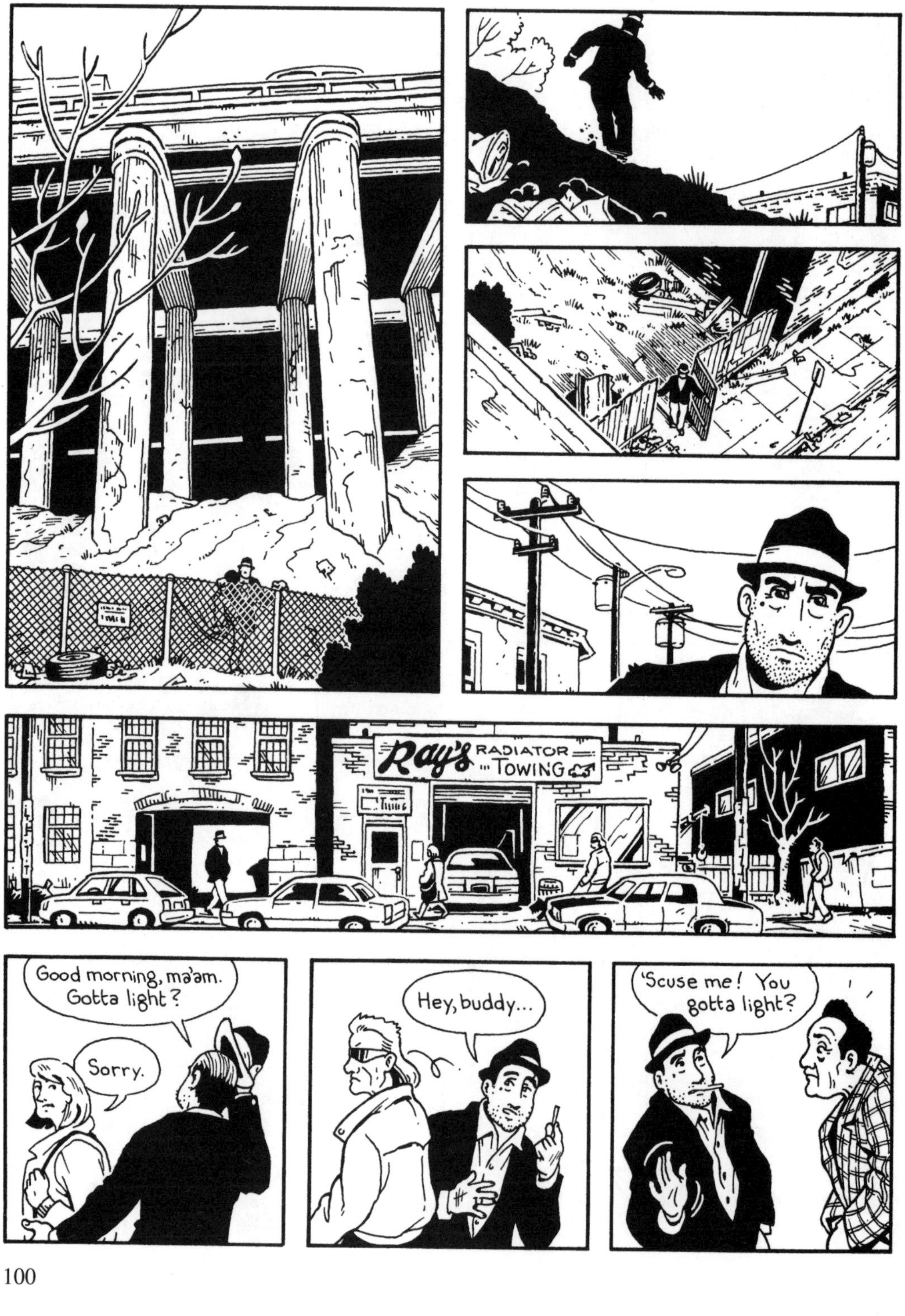
RAY'S RADIATOR TOWING
Good morning, ma'am. Gotta light?
Sorry.
Hey, buddy...
'Scuse me! You gotta light?

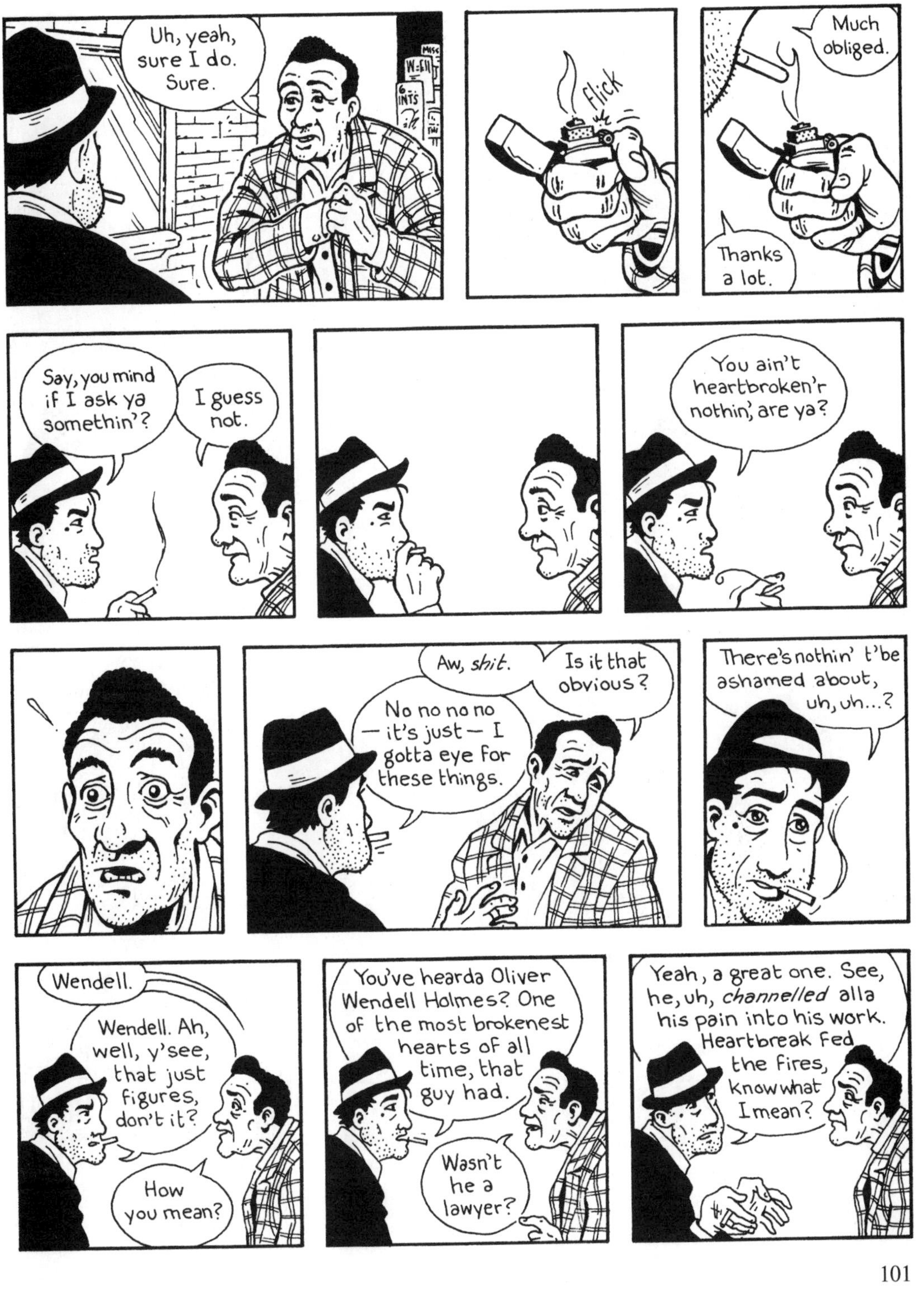
Uh, yeah, sure I do. Sure.
Flick
Much obliged.
Thanks a lot.
Say, you mind if I ask ya somethin'?
I guess not.
You ain't heartbroken'r nothin', are ya?
Aw, *shit*.
Is it that obvious?
No no no no — it's just — I gotta eye for these things.
There's nothin' t'be ashamed about, uh, uh...?
Wendell.
Wendell. Ah, well, y'see, that just figures, don't it?
How you mean?
You've hearda Oliver Wendell Holmes? One of the most brokenest hearts of all time, that guy had.
Wasn't he a lawyer?
Yeah, a great one. See, he, uh, *channelled* alla his pain into his work. Heartbreak fed the fires, know what I mean?

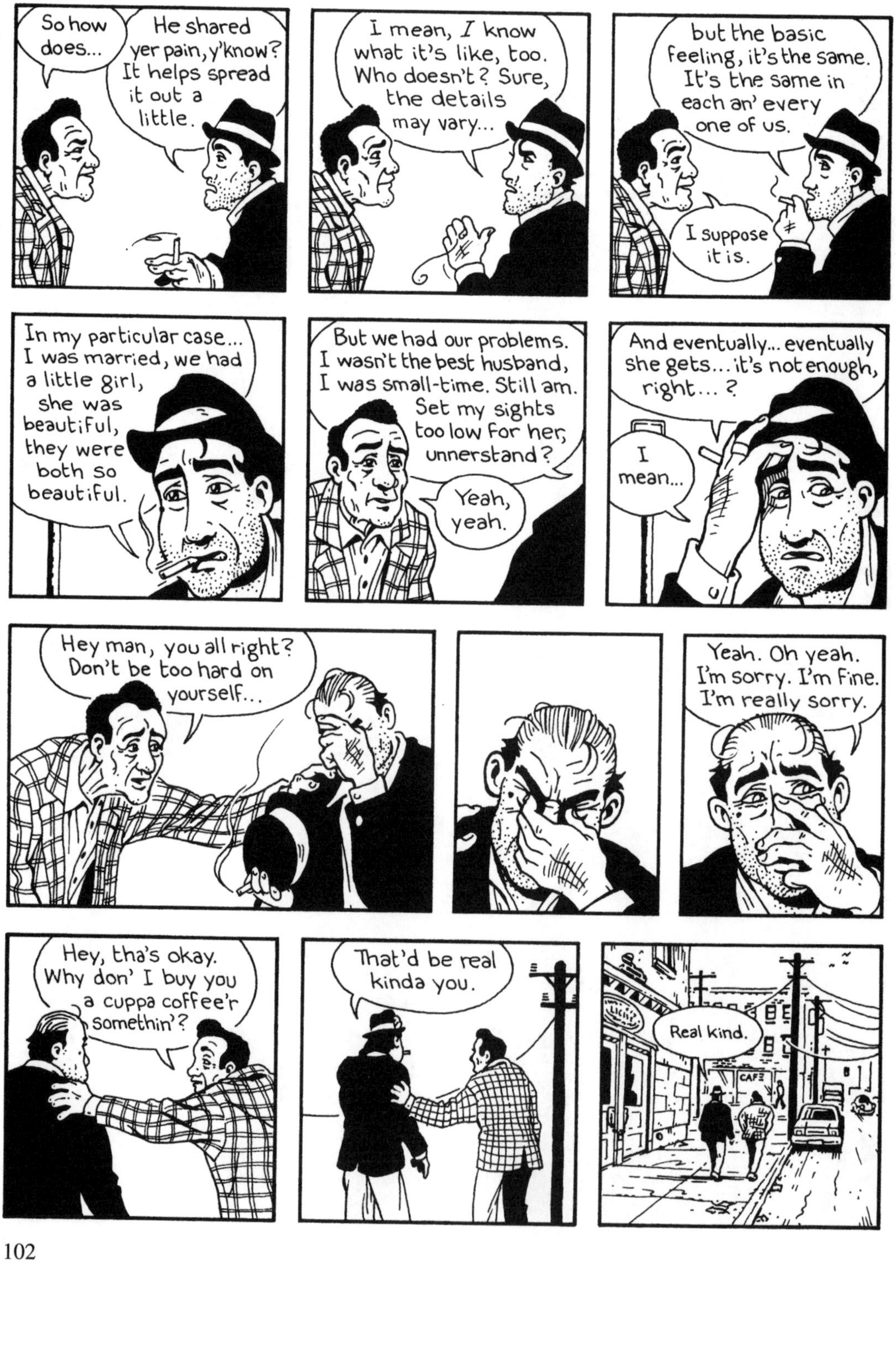
So how does...
He shared yer pain, y'know? It helps spread it out a little.
I mean, *I* know what it's like, too. Who doesn't? Sure, the details may vary...
but the basic feeling, it's the same. It's the same in each an' every one of us.
I suppose it is.
In my particular case... I was married, we had a little girl, she was beautiful, they were both so beautiful.
But we had our problems. I wasn't the best husband, I was small-time. Still am. Set my sights too low for her, unnerstand?
Yeah, yeah.
And eventually... eventually she gets... it's not enough, right...?
I mean...
Hey man, you all right? Don't be too hard on yourself...
Yeah. Oh yeah. I'm sorry. I'm fine. I'm really sorry.
Hey, tha's okay. Why don' I buy you a cuppa coffee'r somethin'?
That'd be real kinda you.
Real kind.
CAFE

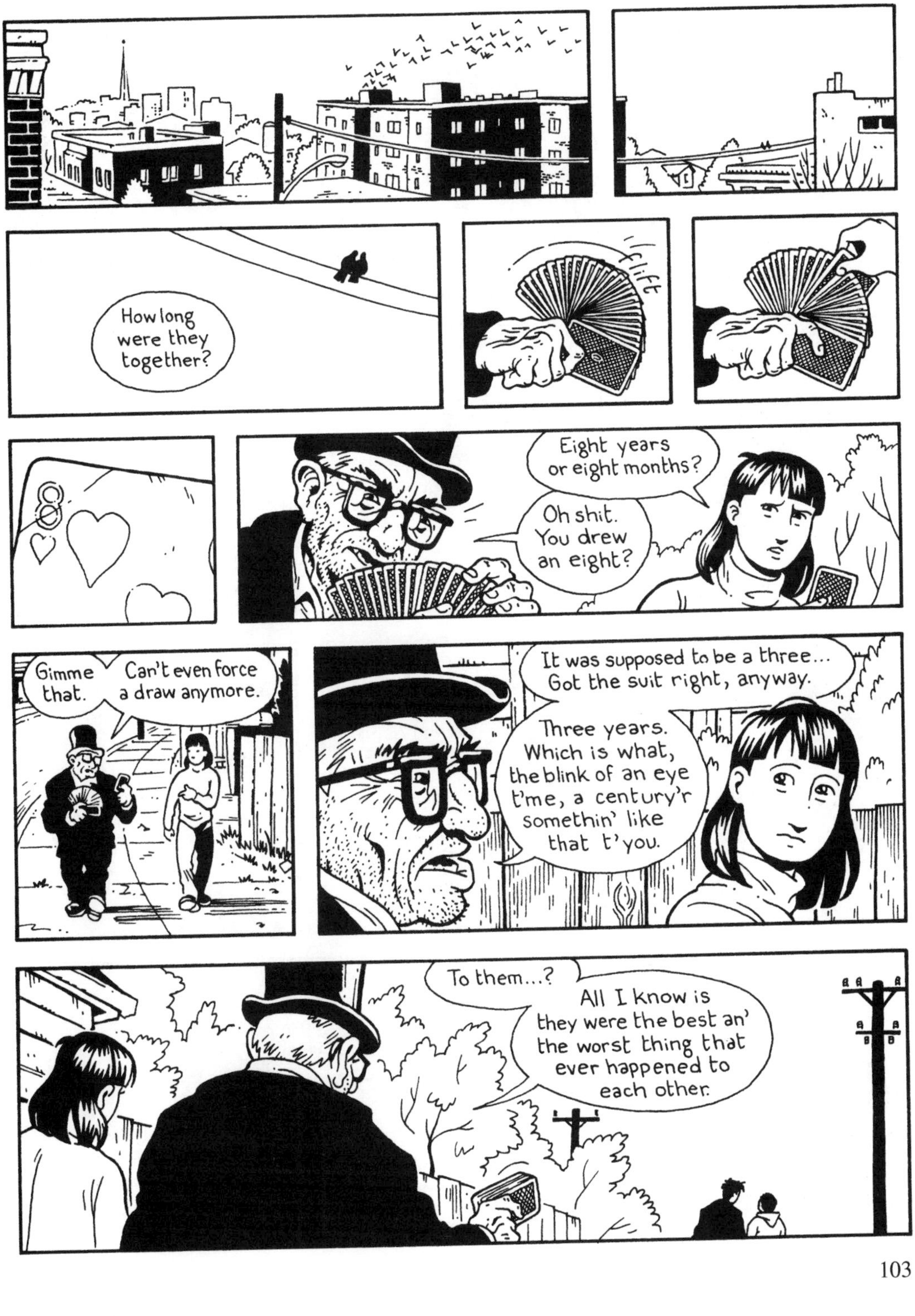
How long were they together?
flift
Eight years or eight months?
Oh shit. You drew an eight?
Gimme that.
Can't even force a draw anymore.
It was supposed to be a three... Got the suit right, anyway.
Three years. Which is what, the blink of an eye t'me, a century'r somethin' like that t'you.
To them...?
All I know is they were the best an' the worst thing that ever happened to each other.

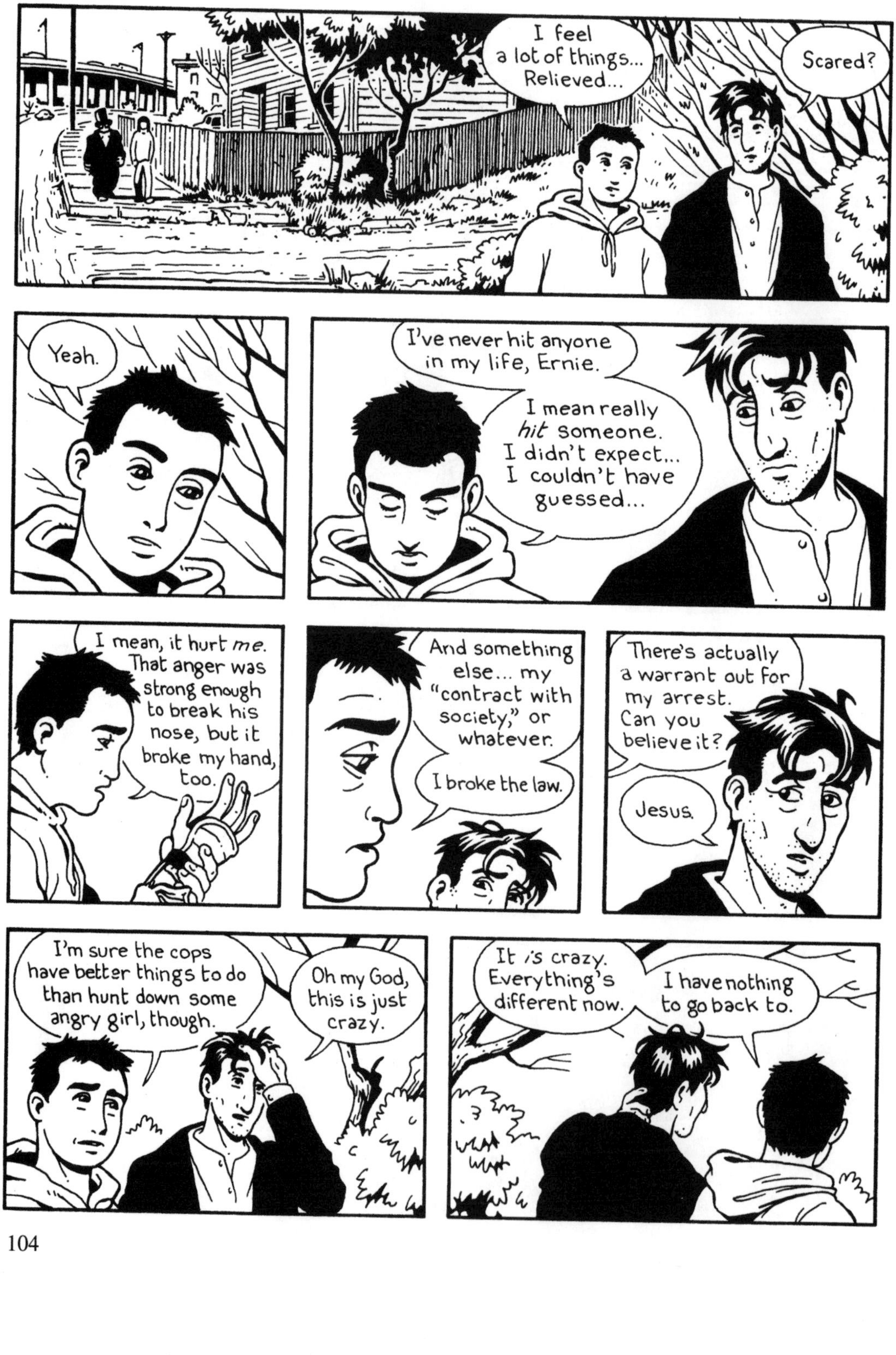
I feel a lot of things... Relieved...
Scared?
Yeah.
I've never hit anyone in my life, Ernie.
I mean really *hit* someone. I didn't expect... I couldn't have guessed...
I mean, it hurt *me*. That anger was strong enough to break his nose, but it broke my hand, too.
And something else... my "contract with society," or whatever.
I broke the law.
There's actually a warrant out for my arrest. Can you believe it?
Jesus.
I'm sure the cops have better things to do than hunt down some angry girl, though.
Oh my God, this is just crazy.
It *is* crazy. Everything's different now.
I have nothing to go back to.

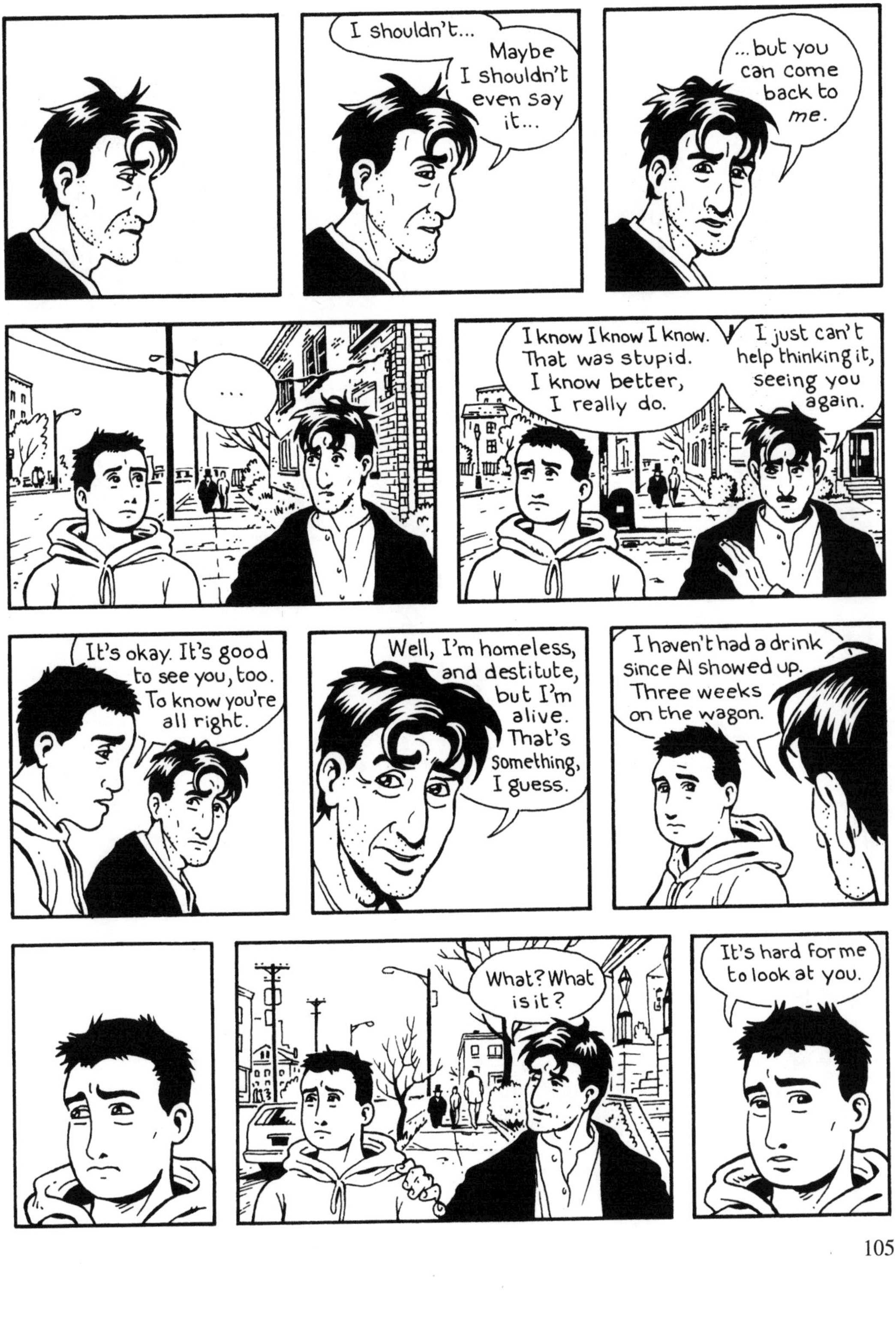

I shouldn't...
Maybe I shouldn't even say it...
...but you can come back to *me*.
...
I know I know I know. That was stupid. I know better, I really do.
I just can't help thinking it, seeing you again.
It's okay. It's good to see you, too. To know you're all right.
Well, I'm homeless, and destitute, but I'm alive. That's something, I guess.
I haven't had a drink since Al showed up. Three weeks on the wagon.
What? What is it?
It's hard for me to look at you.

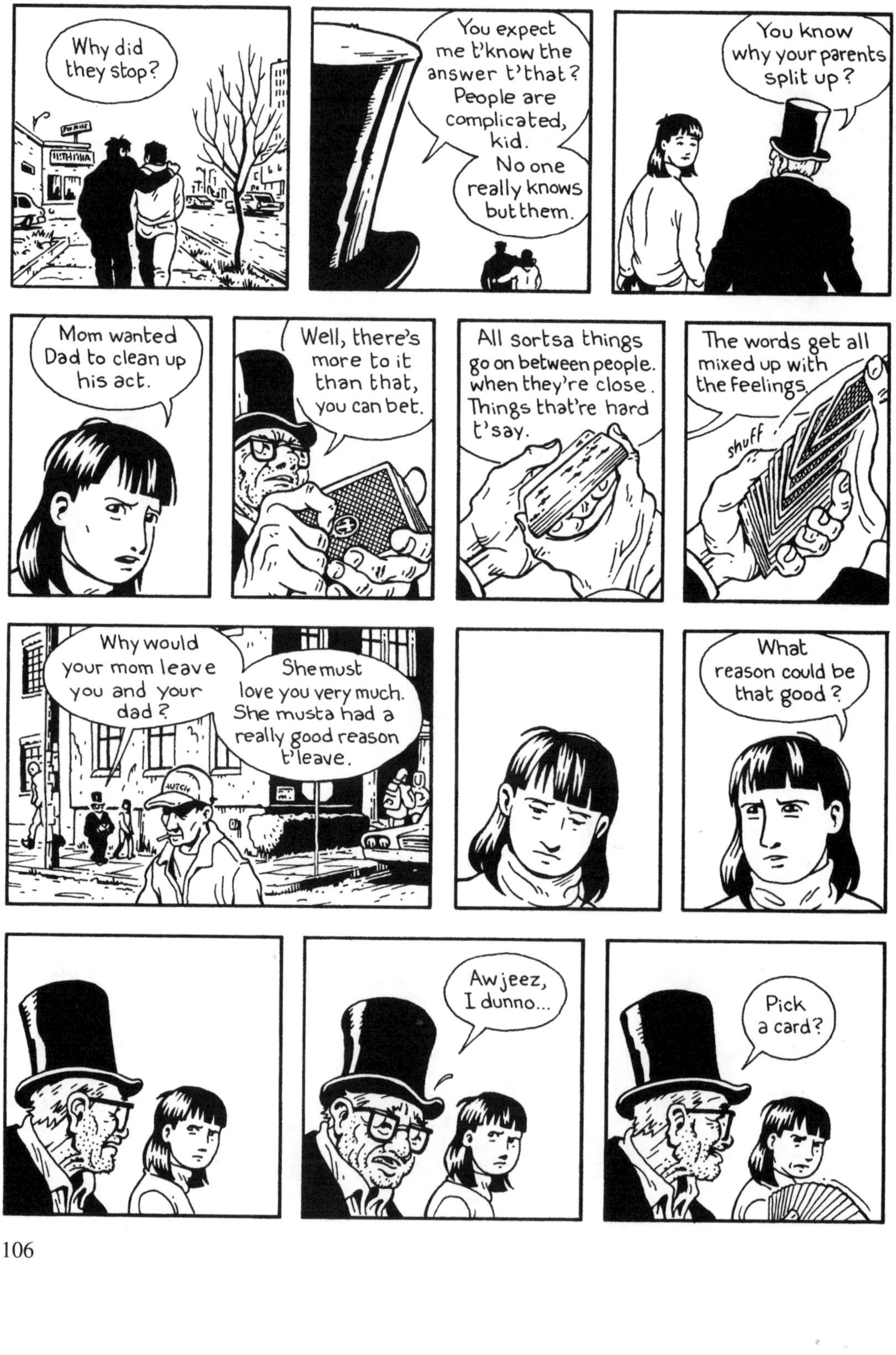
Why did they stop?
You expect me t'know the answer t'that? People are complicated, kid.
No one really knows but them.
You know why your parents split up?
Mom wanted Dad to clean up his act.
Well, there's more to it than that, you can bet.
All sortsa things go on between people. when they're close. Things that're hard t'say.
The words get all mixed up with the feelings.
shuff
Why would your mom leave you and your dad?
She must love you very much. She musta had a really good reason t'leave.
What reason could be that good?
Aw jeez, I dunno...
Pick a card?

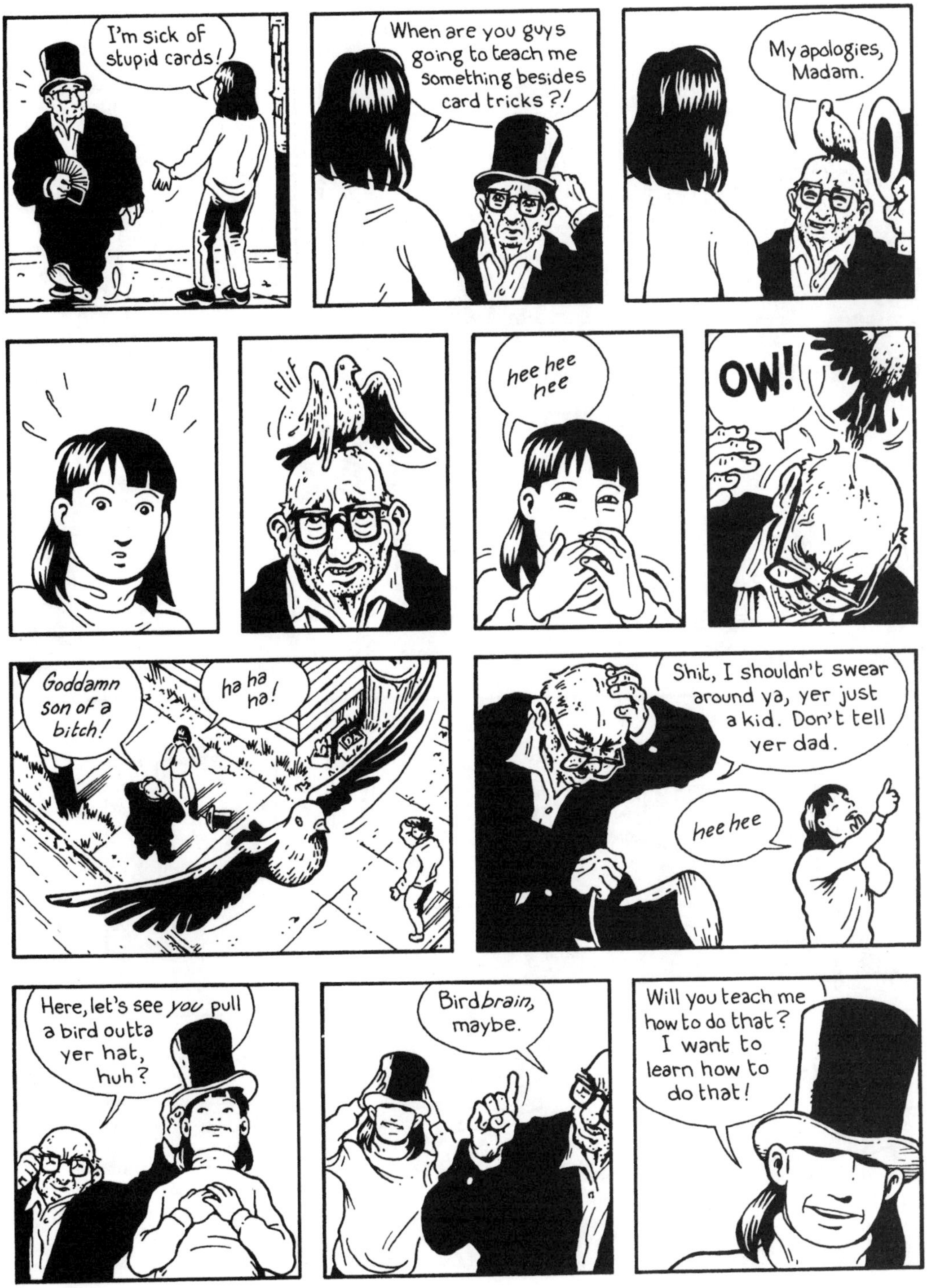
I'm sick of stupid cards!
When are you guys going to teach me something besides card tricks ?!
My apologies, Madam.
flif
hee hee hee
OW!
Goddamn son of a bitch!
ha ha ha!
Shit, I shouldn't swear around ya, yer just a kid. Don't tell yer dad.
hee hee
Here, let's see you pull a bird outta yer hat, huh?
Birdbrain, maybe.
Will you teach me how to do that? I want to learn how to do that!

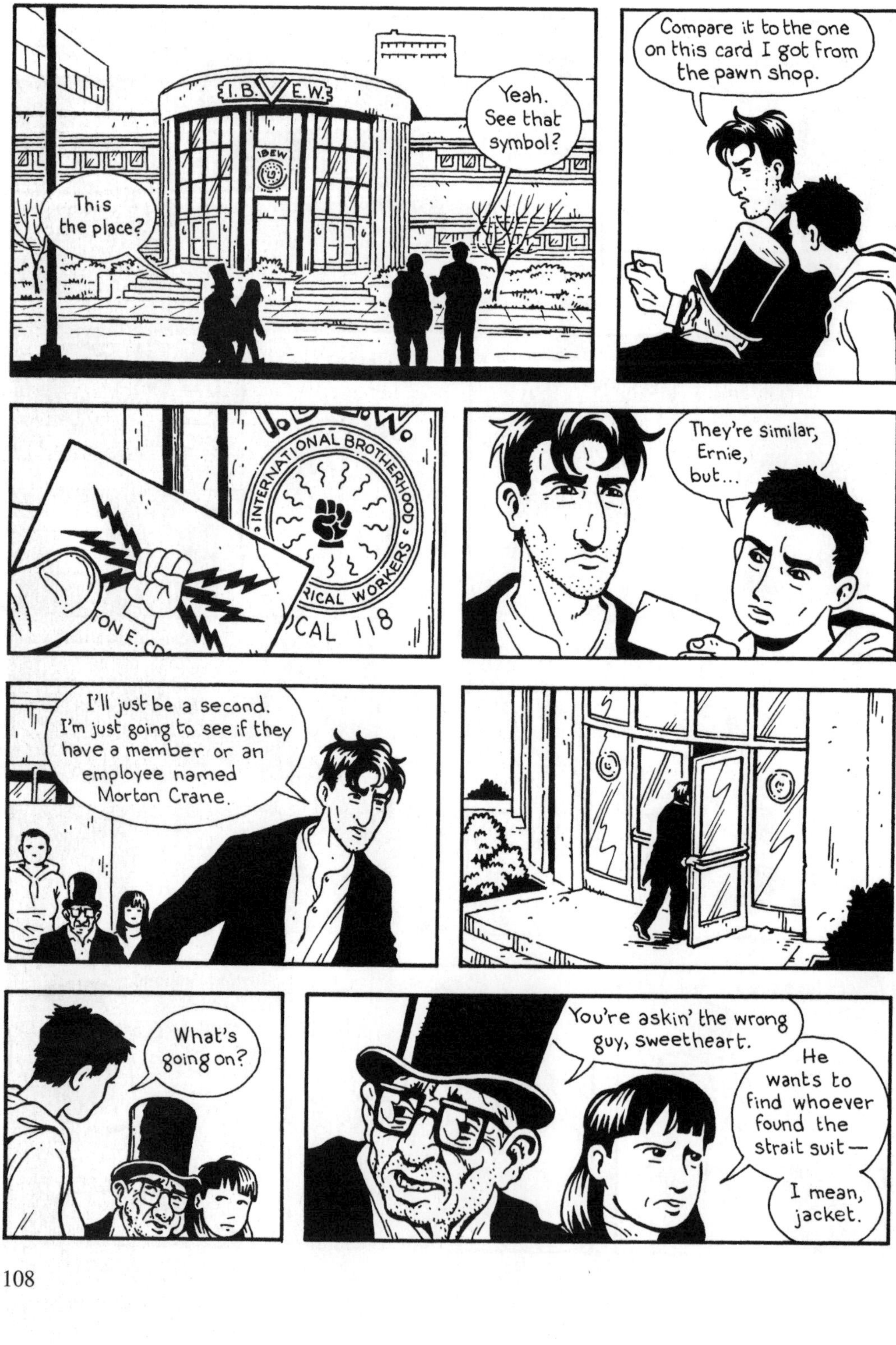
I.B. E.W.
IBEW
This the place?
Yeah. See that symbol?
Compare it to the one on this card I got from the pawn shop.
INTERNATIONAL BROTHERHOOD
RICAL WORKERS
OCAL 118
TON E. CO
They're similar, Ernie, but...
I'll just be a second. I'm just going to see if they have a member or an employee named Morton Crane.
What's going on?
You're askin' the wrong guy, sweetheart.
He wants to find whoever found the strait suit —
I mean, jacket.

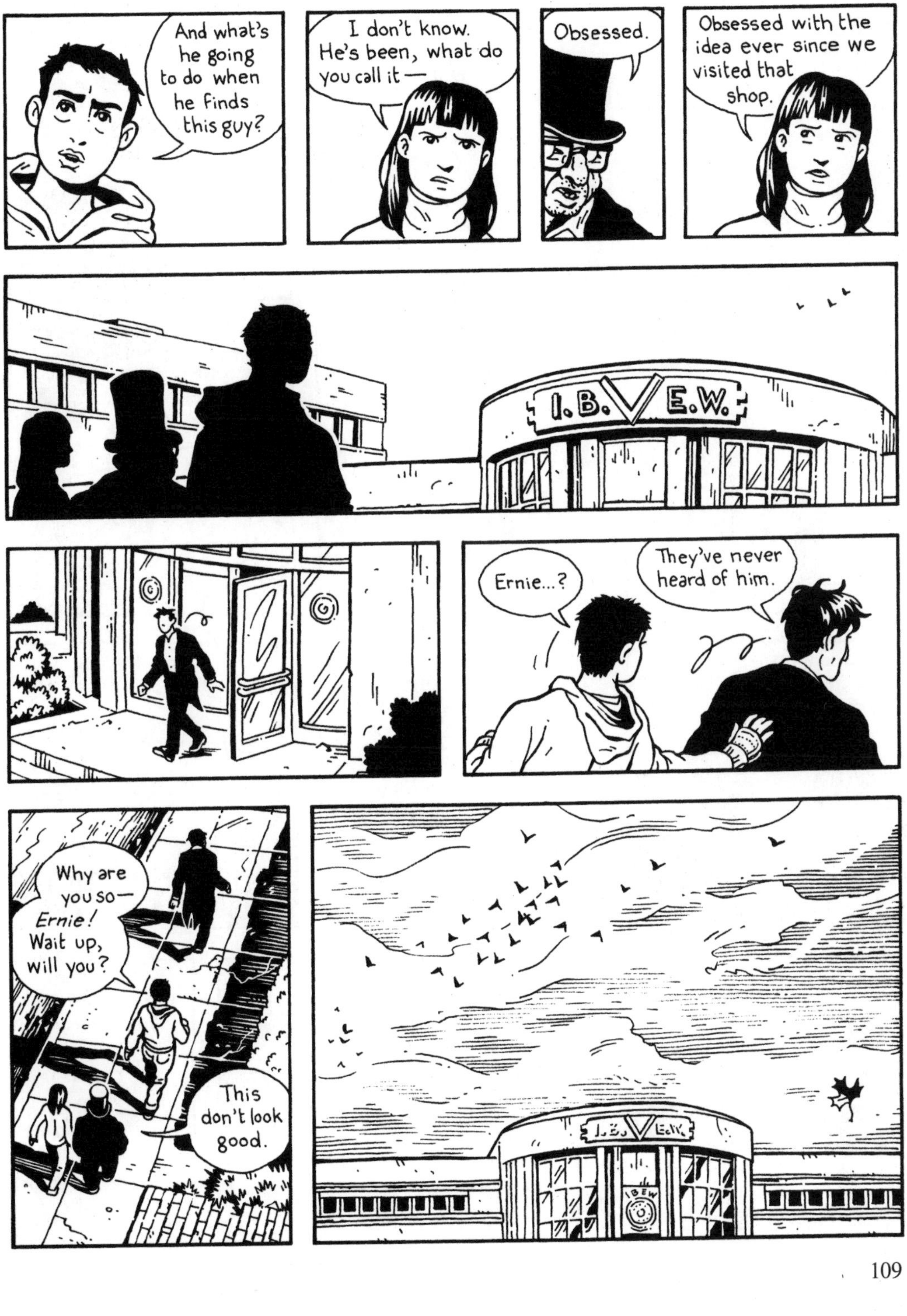
And what's he going to do when he finds this guy?
I don't know. He's been, what do you call it —
Obsessed.
Obsessed with the idea ever since we visited that shop.
I.B.V.E.W.
Ernie...?
They've never heard of him.
Why are you so—
Ernie! Wait up, will you?
This don't look good.
I.B.V.E.W.
IBEW

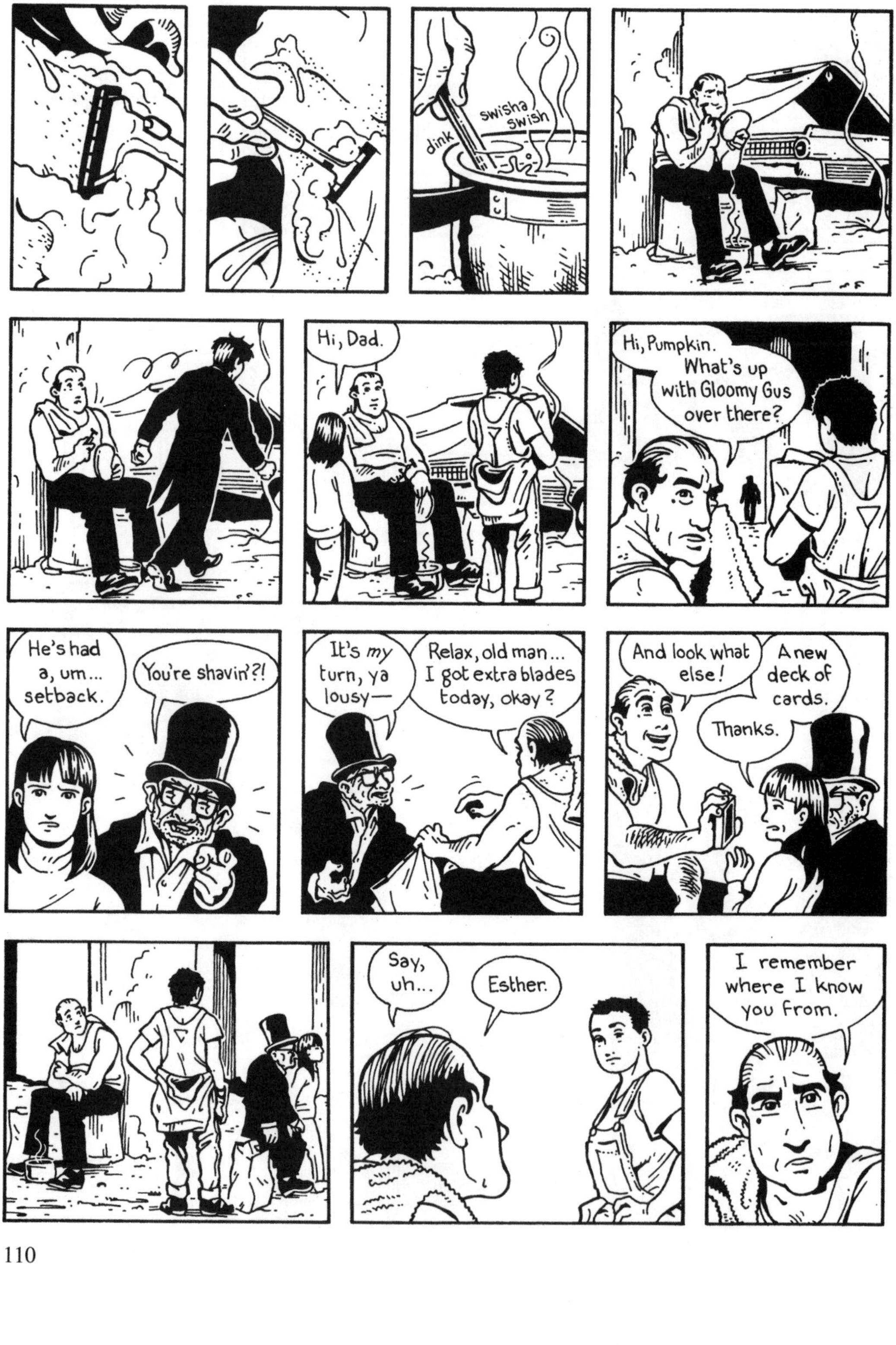
dink
swisha swish
Hi, Dad.
Hi, Pumpkin.
What's up with Gloomy Gus over there?
He's had a, um... setback.
You're shavin'?!
It's *my* turn, ya lousy—
Relax, old man... I got extra blades today, okay?
And look what else!
A new deck of cards.
Thanks.
Say, uh...
Esther.
I remember where I know you from.

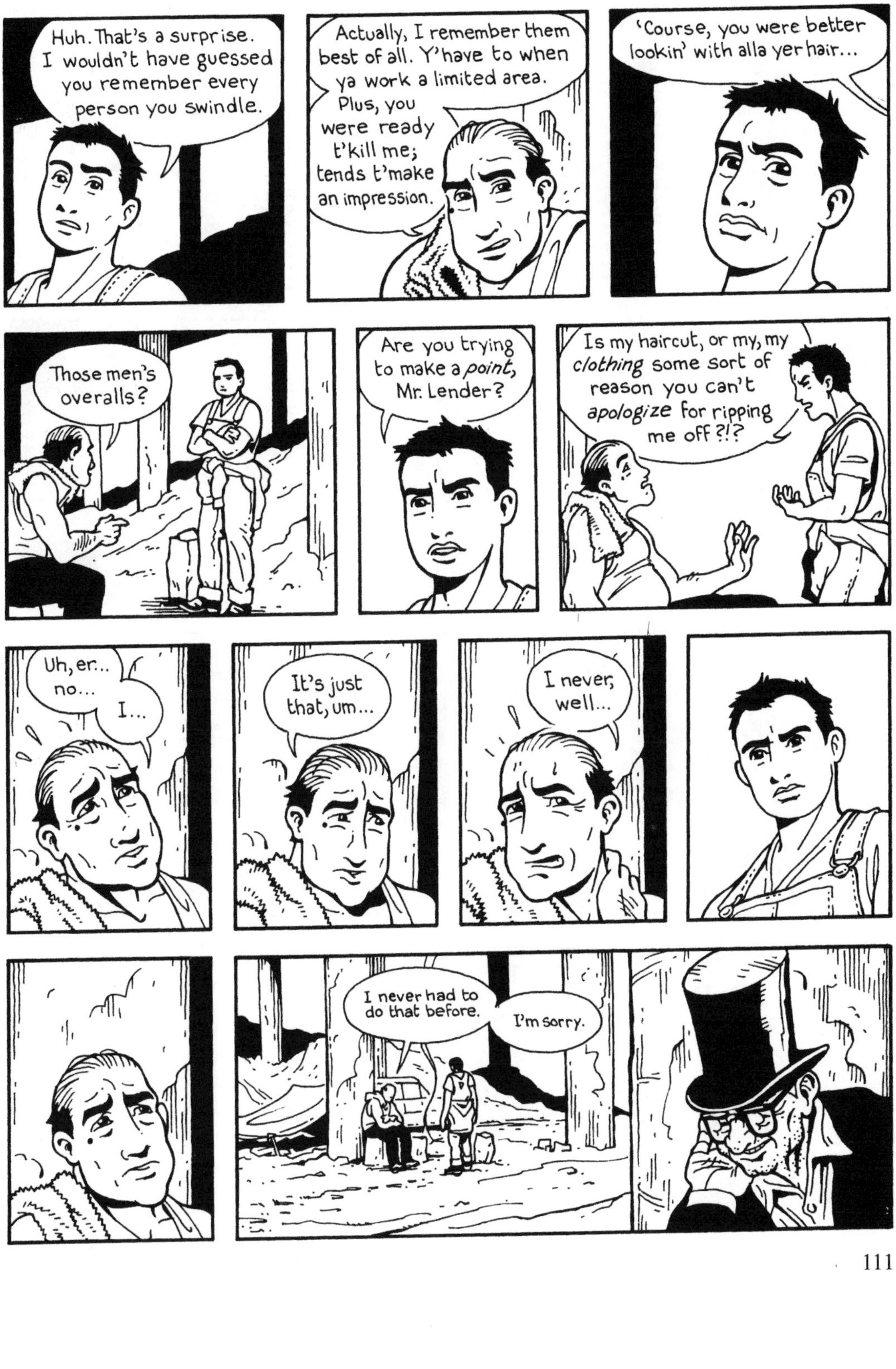
Huh. That's a surprise. I wouldn't have guessed you remember every person you swindle.
Actually, I remember them best of all. Y'have to when ya work a limited area.
Plus, you were ready t'kill me; tends t'make an impression.
'Course, you were better lookin' with alla yer hair...
Those men's overalls?
Are you trying to make a *point*, Mr. Lender?
Is my haircut, or my, my *clothing* some sort of reason you can't *apologize* for ripping me off?!?
Uh, er... no...
I...
It's just that, um...
I never, well...
I never had to do that before.
I'm sorry.

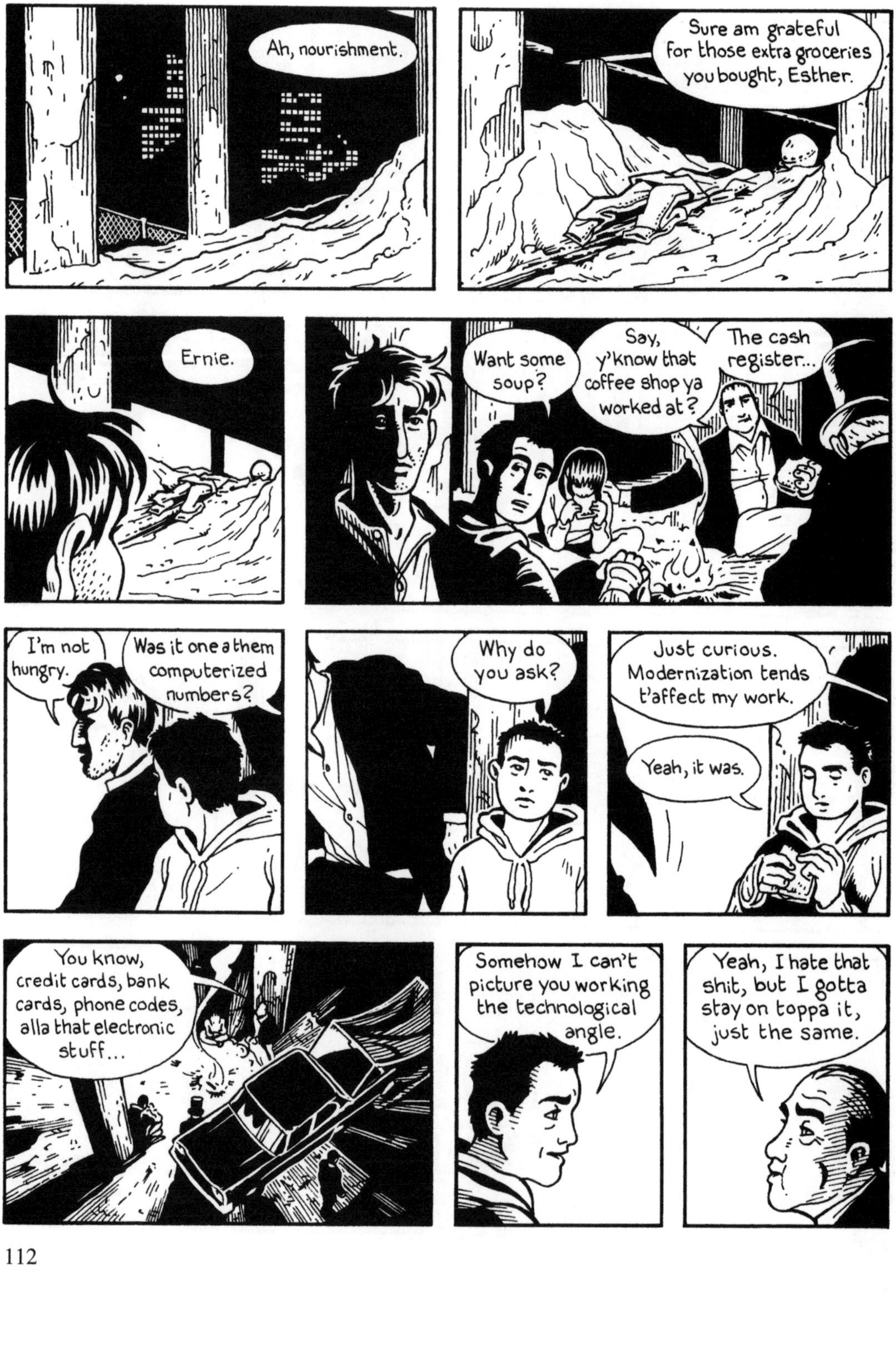
Ah, nourishment.
Sure am grateful for those extra groceries you bought, Esther.
Ernie.
Want some soup?
Say, y'know that coffee shop ya worked at?
The cash register...
I'm not hungry.
Was it one a them computerized numbers?
Why do you ask?
Just curious. Modernization tends t'affect my work.
Yeah, it was.
You know, credit cards, bank cards, phone codes, alla that electronic stuff...
Somehow I can't picture you working the technological angle.
Yeah, I hate that shit, but I gotta stay on toppa it, just the same.

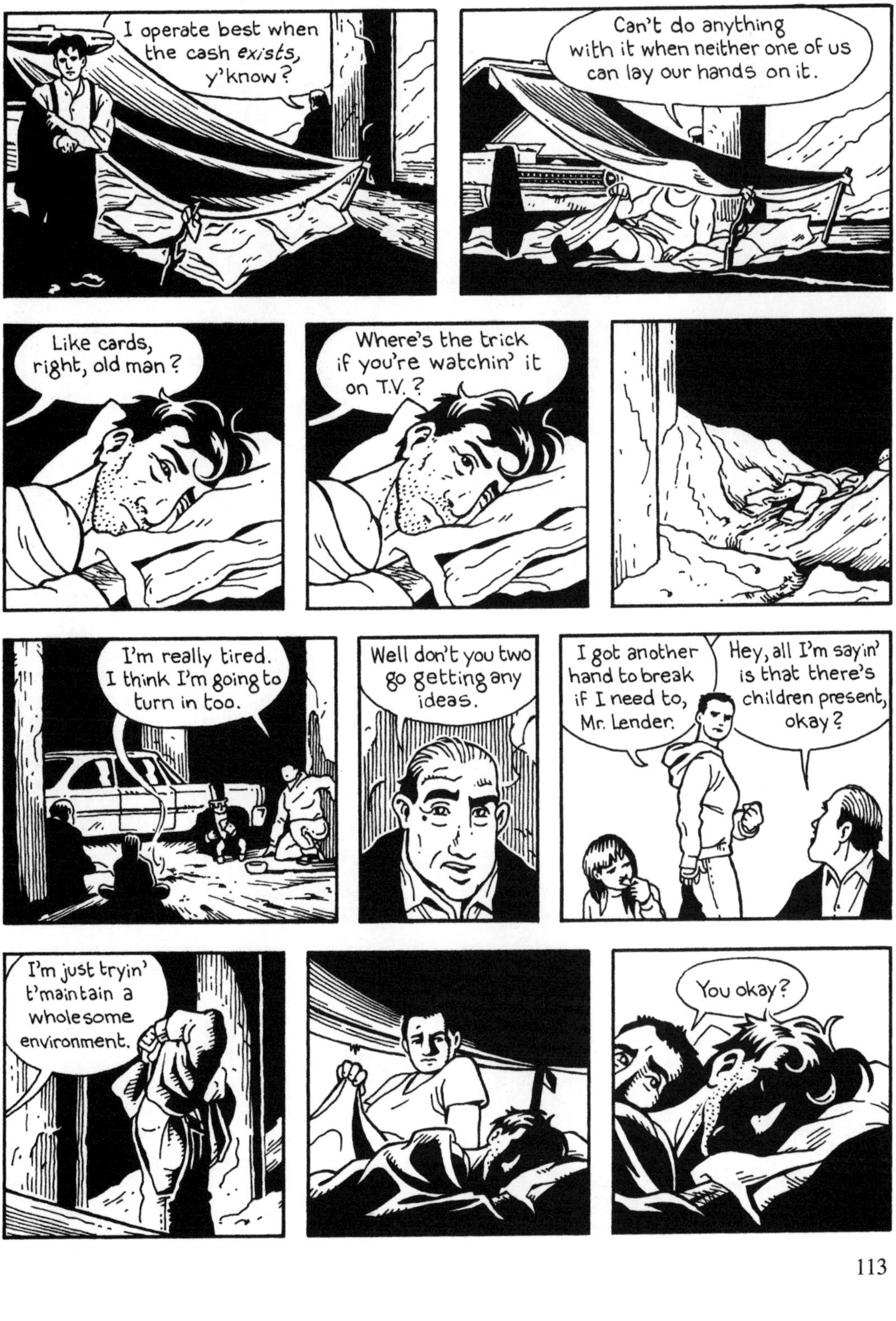

I operate best when the cash *exists*, y'know?
Can't do anything with it when neither one of us can lay our hands on it.
Like cards, right, old man?
Where's the trick if you're watchin' it on T.V.?
I'm really tired. I think I'm going to turn in too.
Well don't you two go getting any ideas.
I got another hand to break if I need to, Mr. Lender.
Hey, all I'm sayin' is that there's children present, okay?
I'm just tryin' t'maintain a wholesome environment.
You okay?

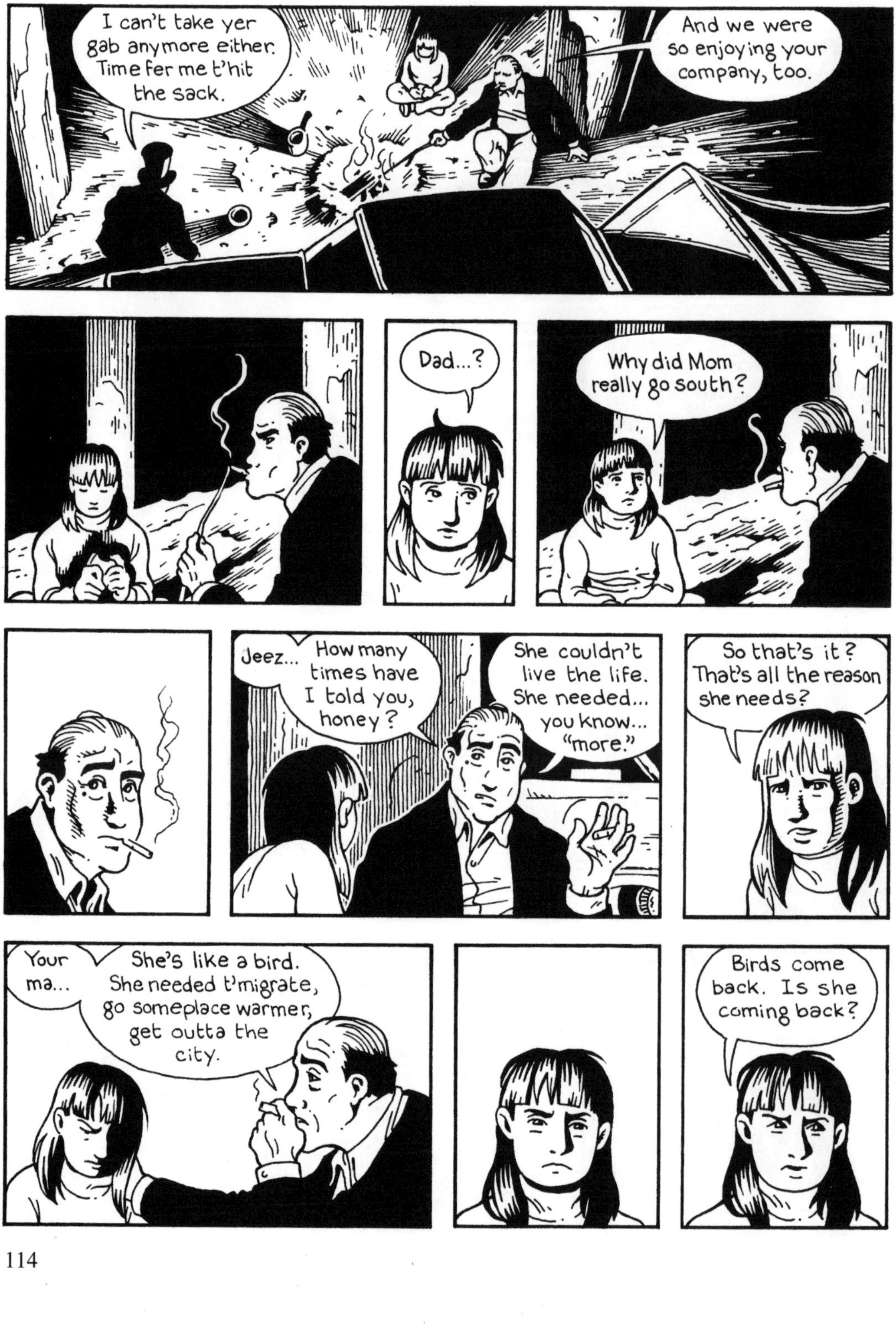

I can't take yer gab anymore either. Time fer me t'hit the sack.
And we were so enjoying your company, too.
Dad...?
Why did Mom really go south?
Jeez...
How many times have I told you, honey?
She couldn't live the life. She needed... you know... "more."
So that's it? That's all the reason she needs?
Your ma...
She's like a bird. She needed t'migrate, go someplace warmer, get outta the city.
Birds come back. Is she coming back?

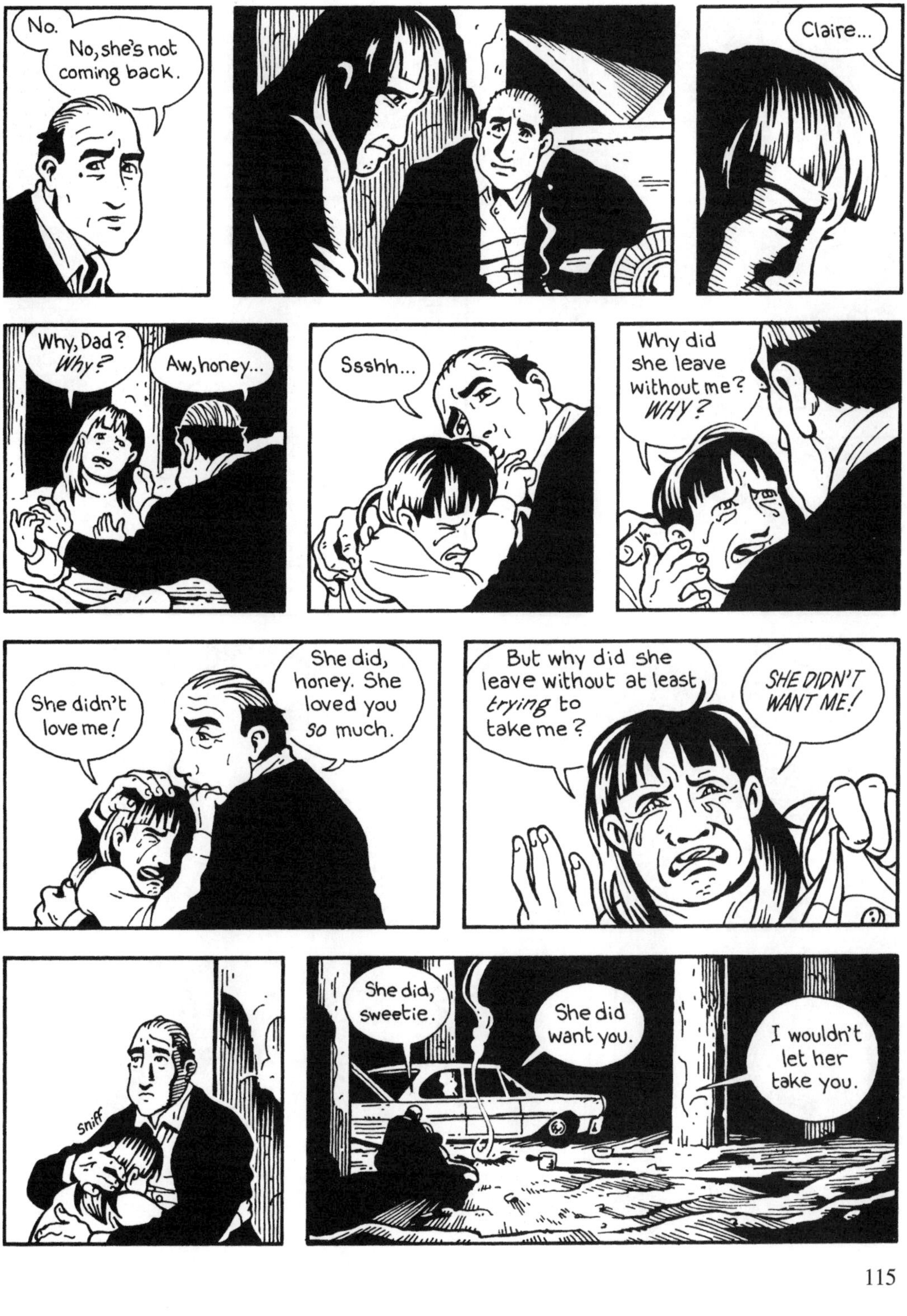
No.
No, she's not coming back.
Claire...
Why, Dad? *Why?*
Aw, honey...
Ssshh...
Why did she leave without me? *WHY?*
She didn't love me!
She did, honey. She loved you *so* much.
But why did she leave without at least *trying* to take me?
SHE DIDN'T WANT ME!
sniff
She did, sweetie.
She did want you.
I wouldn't let her take you.

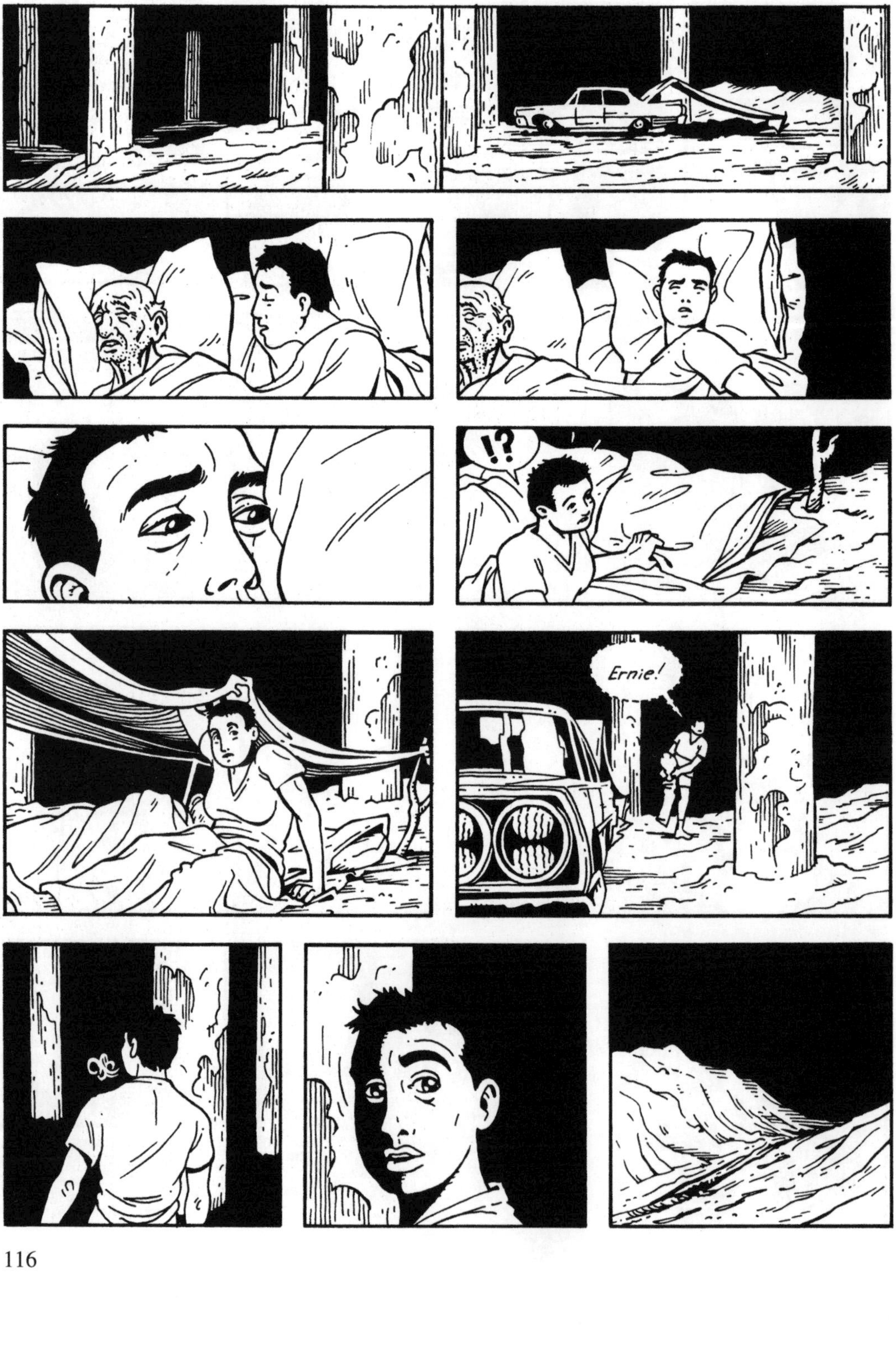
!?
Ernie!

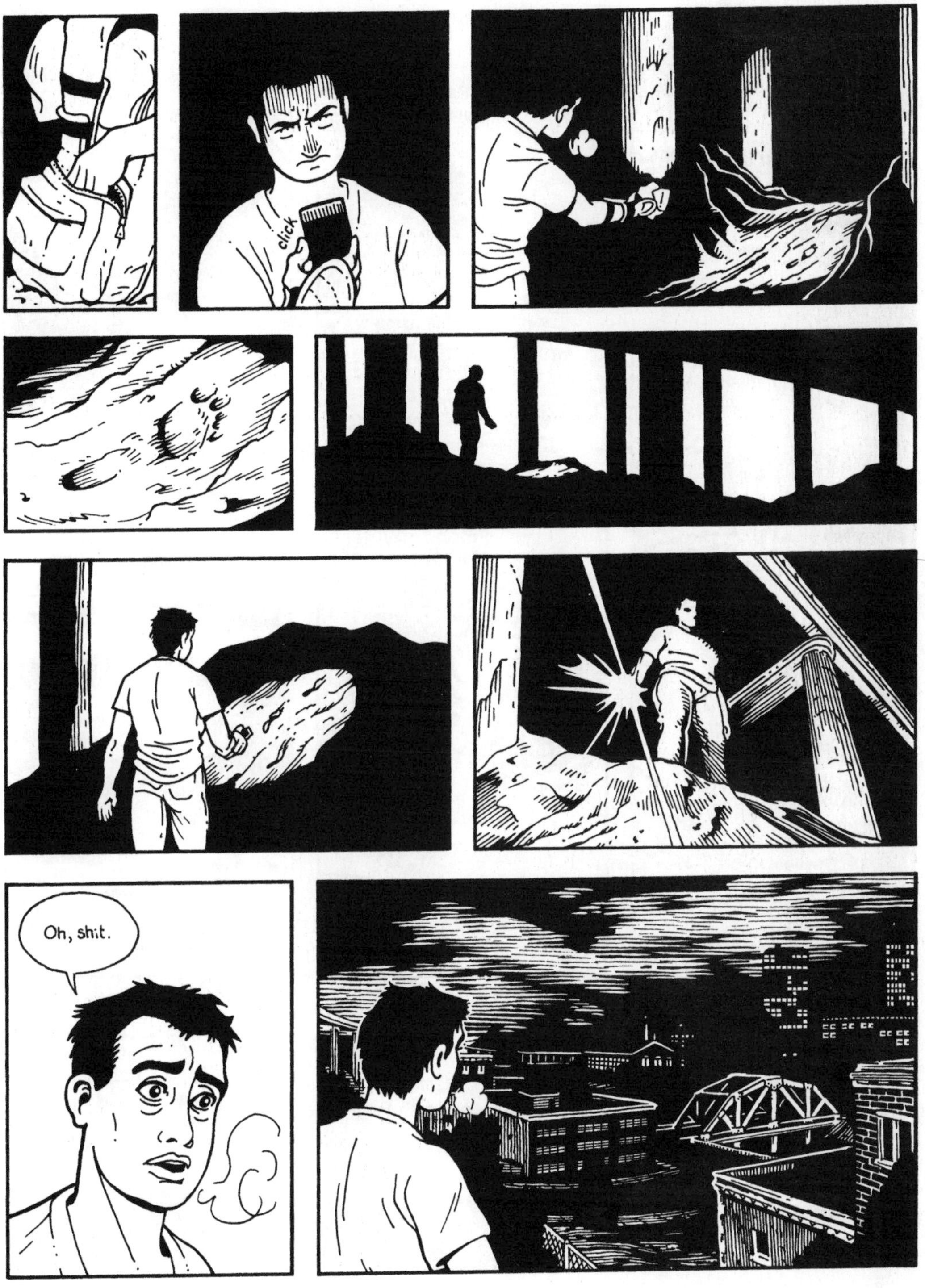
click
Oh, shit.

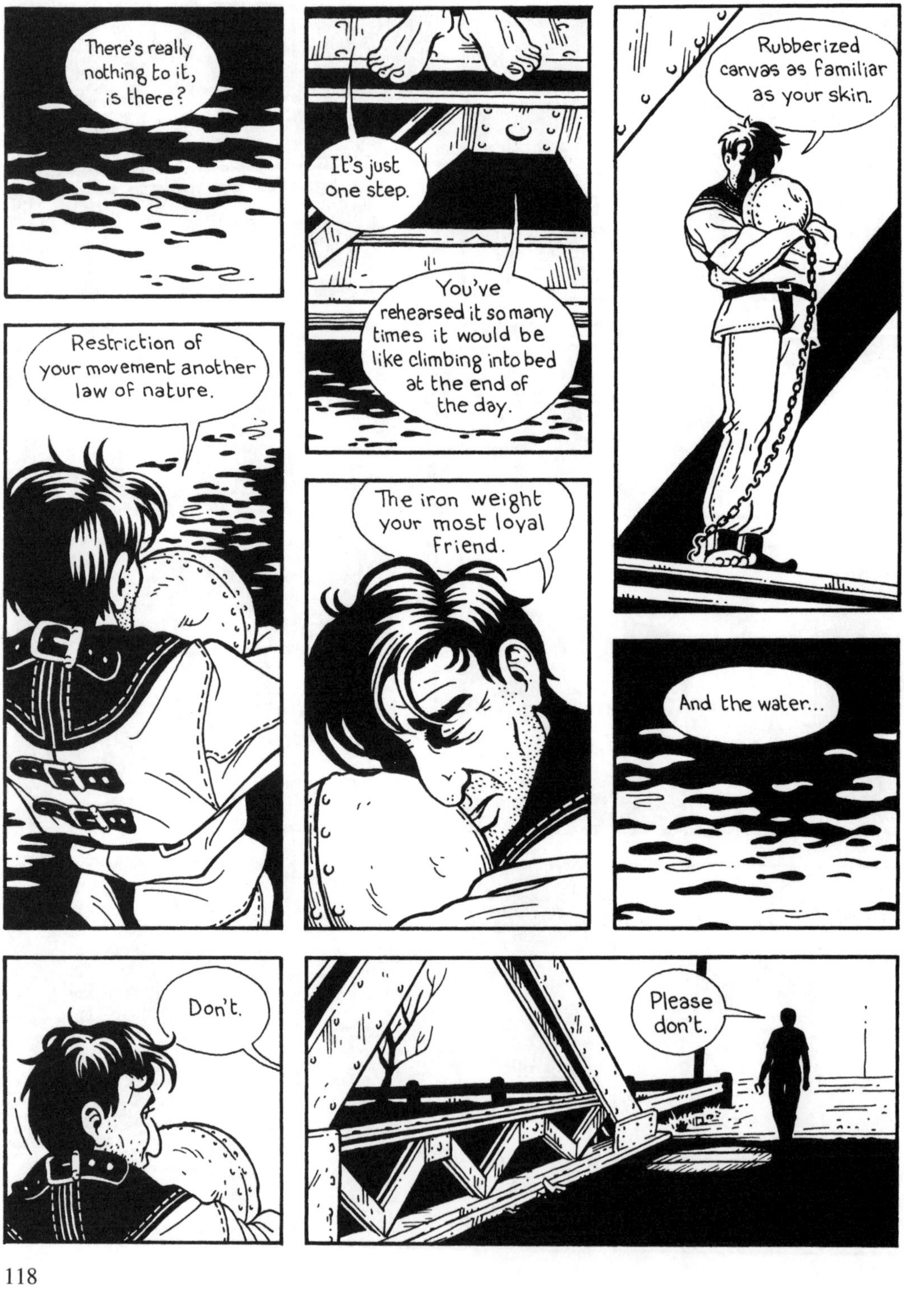
There's really nothing to it, is there?
It's just one step.
You've rehearsed it so many times it would be like climbing into bed at the end of the day.
Rubberized canvas as familiar as your skin.
Restriction of your movement another law of nature.
The iron weight your most loyal friend.
And the water...
Don't.
Please don't.

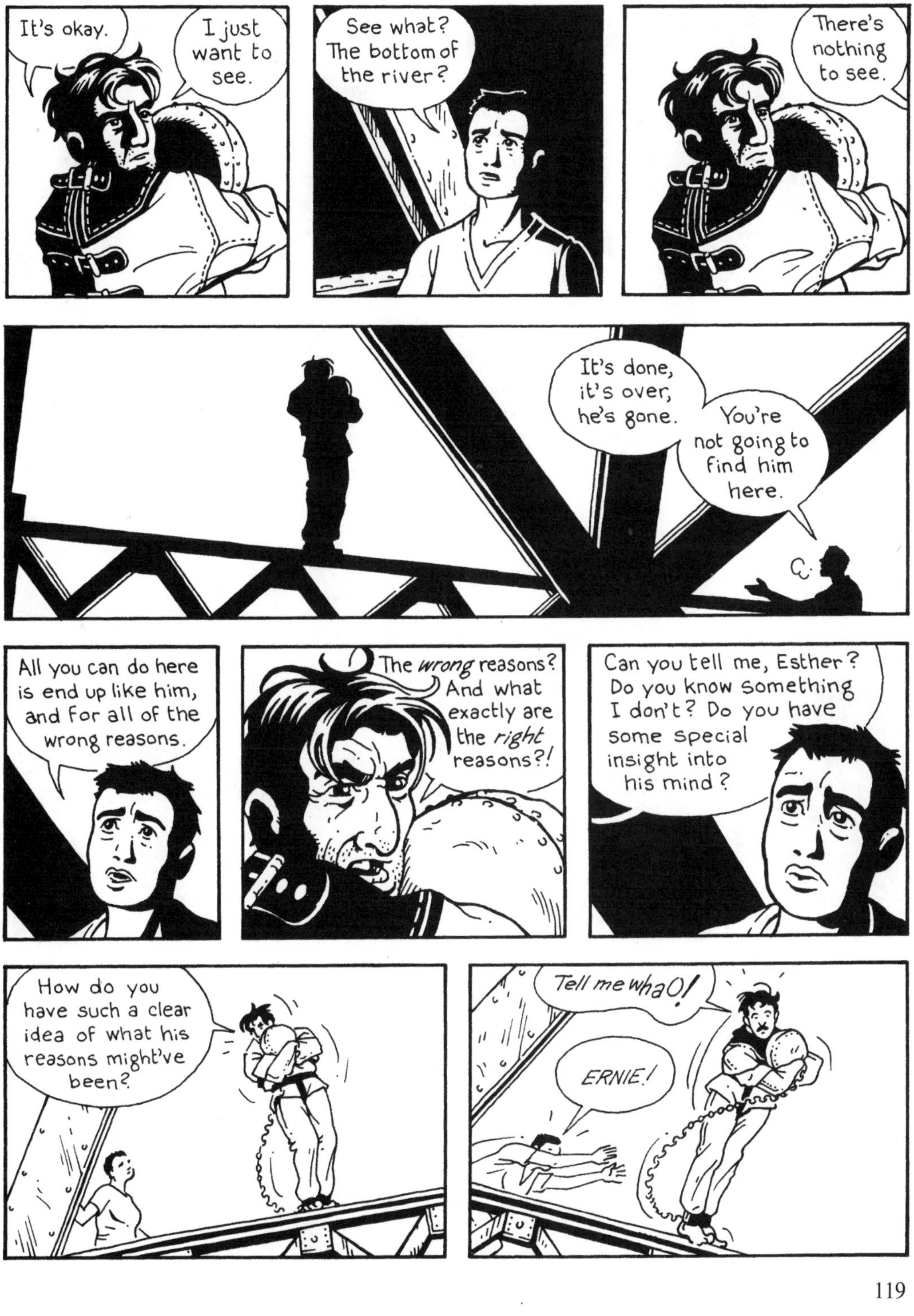

It's okay.
I just want to see.
See what? The bottom of the river?
There's nothing to see.
It's done, it's over, he's gone.
You're not going to find him here.
All you can do here is end up like him, and for all of the wrong reasons.
The *wrong* reasons? And what exactly are the *right* reasons?!
Can you tell me, Esther? Do you know something I don't? Do you have some special insight into his mind?
How do you have such a clear idea of what his reasons might've been?
Tell me whaO!
ERNIE!

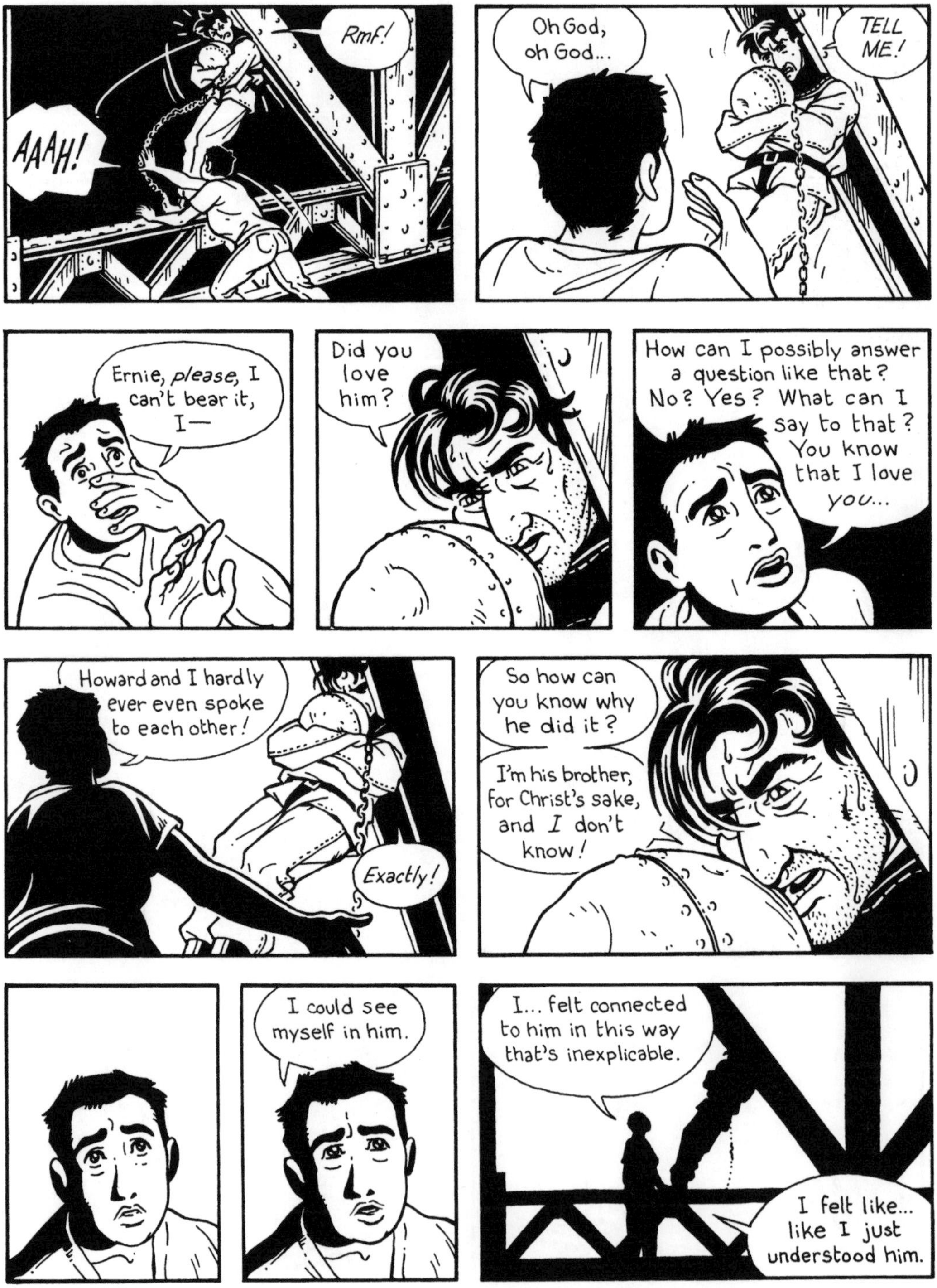
Rmf!
AAAH!
Oh God, oh God...
TELL ME!
Ernie, *please*, I can't bear it, I—
Did you love him?
How can I possibly answer a question like that? No? Yes? What can I say to that? You know that I love *you*...
Howard and I hardly ever even spoke to each other!
Exactly!
So how can you know why he did it?
I'm his brother, for Christ's sake, and *I* don't know!
I could see myself in him.
I... felt connected to him in this way that's inexplicable.
I felt like... like I just understood him.

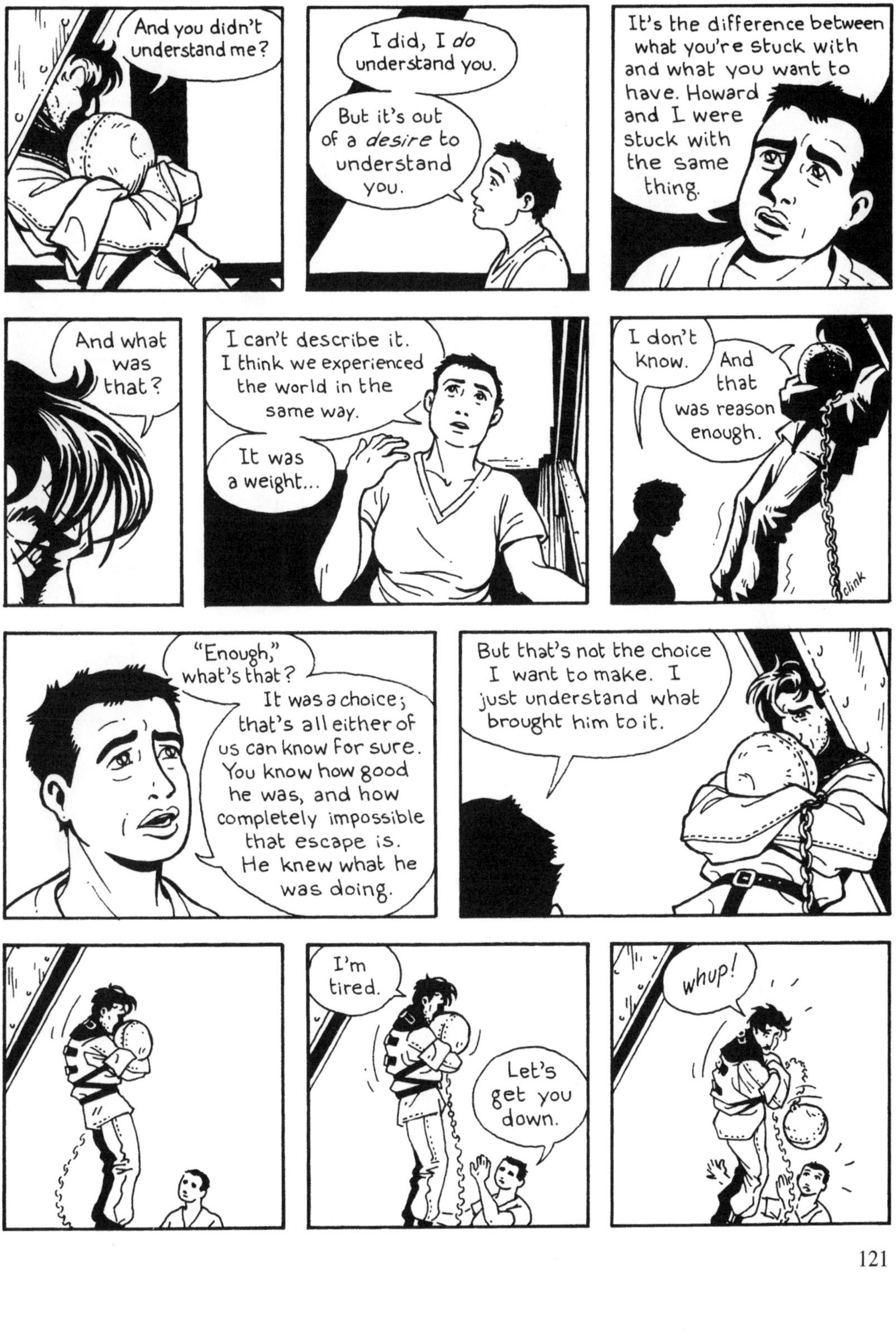

And you didn't understand me?
I did, I *do* understand you.
But it's out of a *desire* to understand you.
It's the difference between what you're stuck with and what you want to have. Howard and I were stuck with the same thing.
And what was that?
I can't describe it. I think we experienced the world in the same way.
It was a weight...
I don't know.
And that was reason enough.
clink
"Enough," what's that?
It was a choice; that's all either of us can know for sure. You know how good he was, and how completely impossible that escape is. He knew what he was doing.
But that's not the choice I want to make. I just understand what brought him to it.
I'm tired.
Let's get you down.
whup!

Ouch.
HA HA HA
HA HA HA
HA HA HA
Ha ha
ha ha
Where's
the key?
Ah!
CLICK

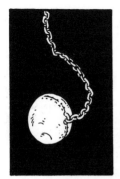

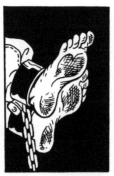

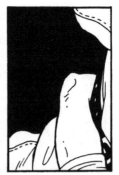

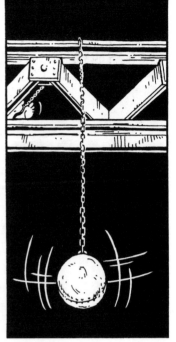

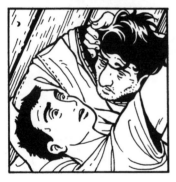

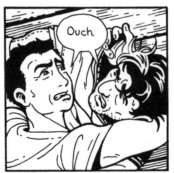

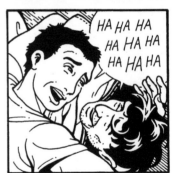

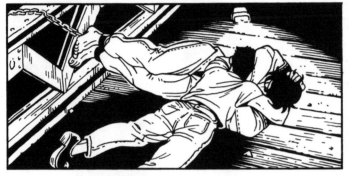

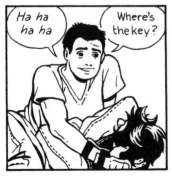

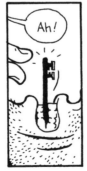

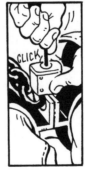

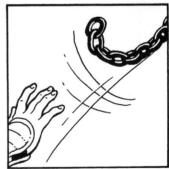

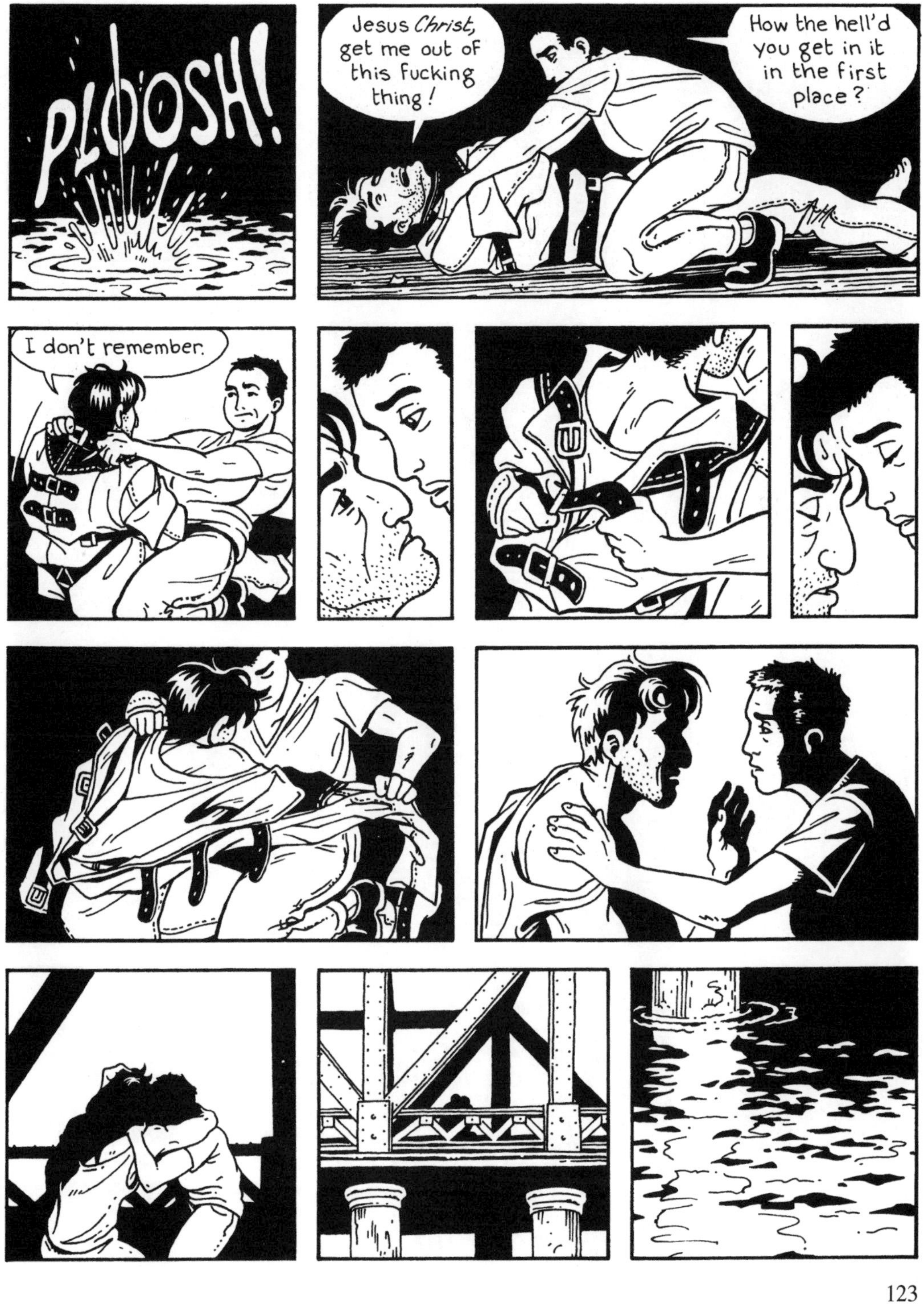
PLOOSH!
Jesus Christ, get me out of this fucking thing!
How the hell'd you get in it in the first place?
I don't remember.

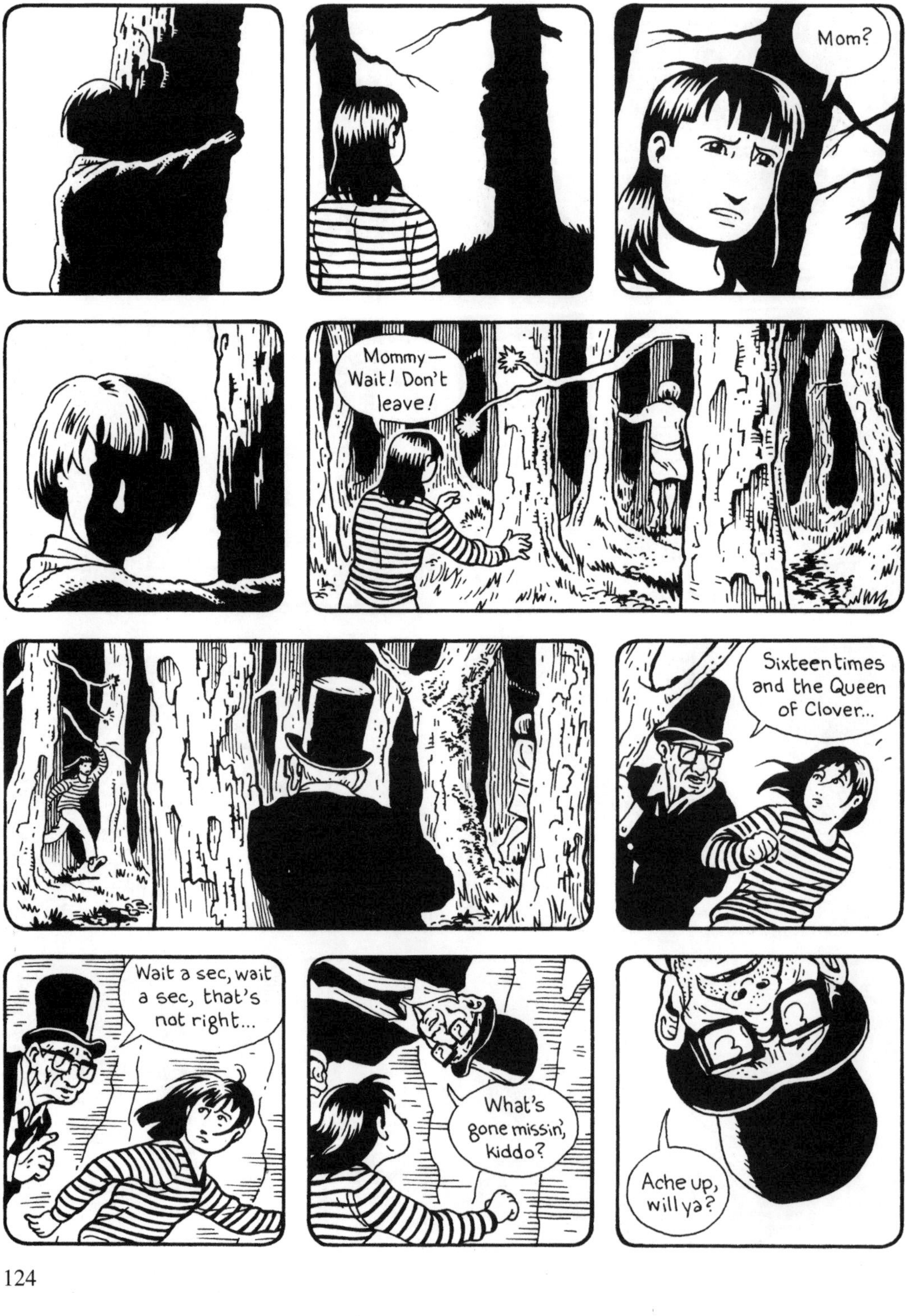
Mom?
Mommy— Wait! Don't leave!
Sixteen times and the Queen of Clover...
Wait a sec, wait a sec, that's not right...
What's gone missin', kiddo?
Ache up, will ya?

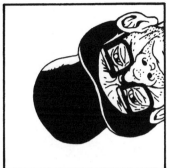

Let's go, wake up!

C'mon, c'mon. Yer dad, too.

HEY! LENDER! UP AN' AT'EM!

Huh? Whuzzat?

What's goin' on?

They're gone.

Ernie and Esther?

Whattaya wanna do about it?

I just wanted t'let ya know I was goin' t'look for 'em, okay? There's tracks off this way.

...

Uh—wait! Old man!

Hanh?

Y'got any lockpicks on ya?

Maybe I do, maybe I don't. Why?

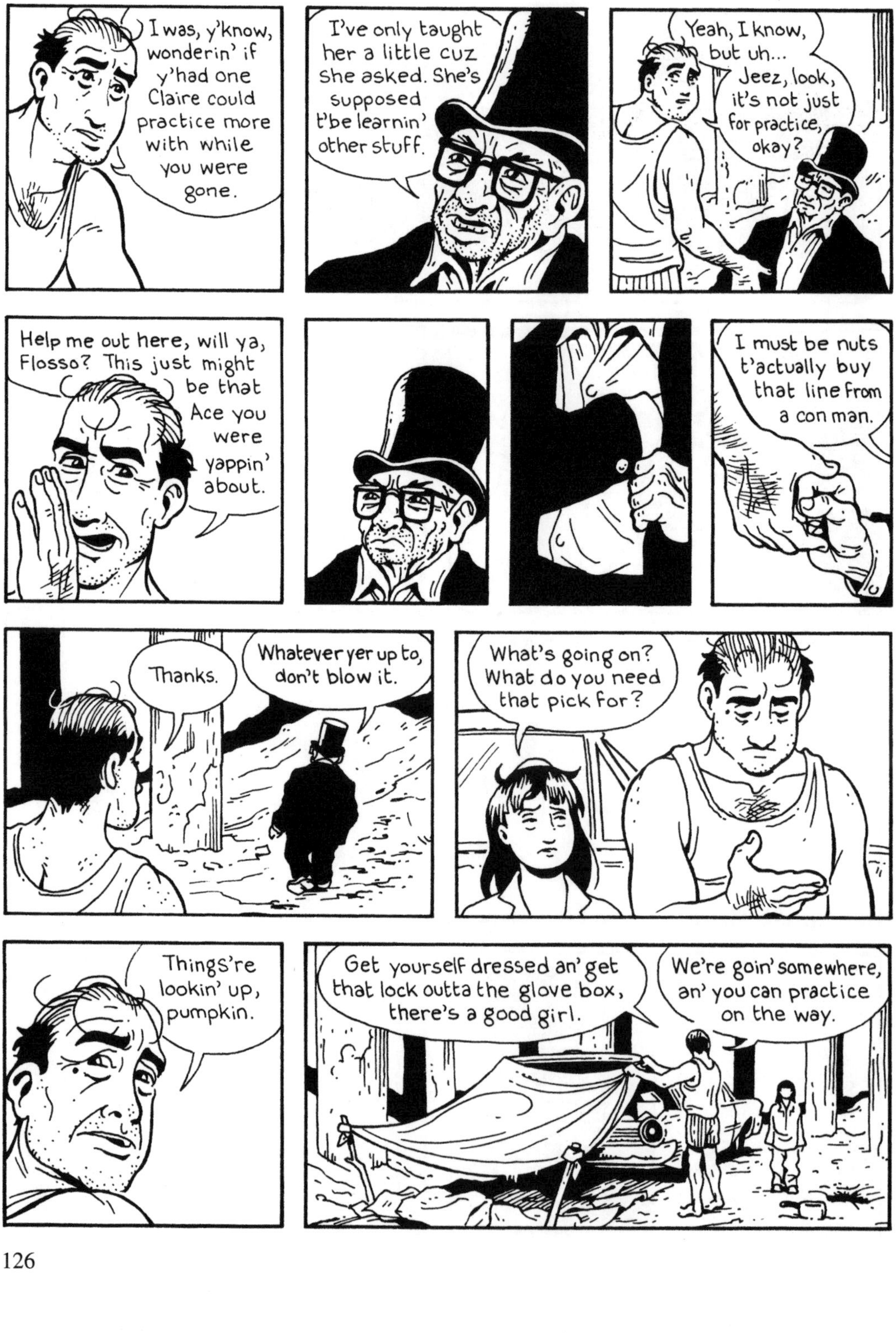
I was, y'know, wonderin' if y'had one Claire could practice more with while you were gone.
I've only taught her a little cuz she asked. She's supposed t'be learnin' other stuff.
Yeah, I know, but uh...
Jeez, look, it's not just for practice, okay?
Help me out here, will ya, Flosso? This just might be that Ace you were yappin' about.
I must be nuts t'actually buy that line from a con man.
Thanks.
Whatever yer up to, don't blow it.
What's going on? What do you need that pick for?
Things're lookin' up, pumpkin.
Get yourself dressed an' get that lock outta the glove box, there's a good girl.
We're goin' somewhere, an' you can practice on the way.

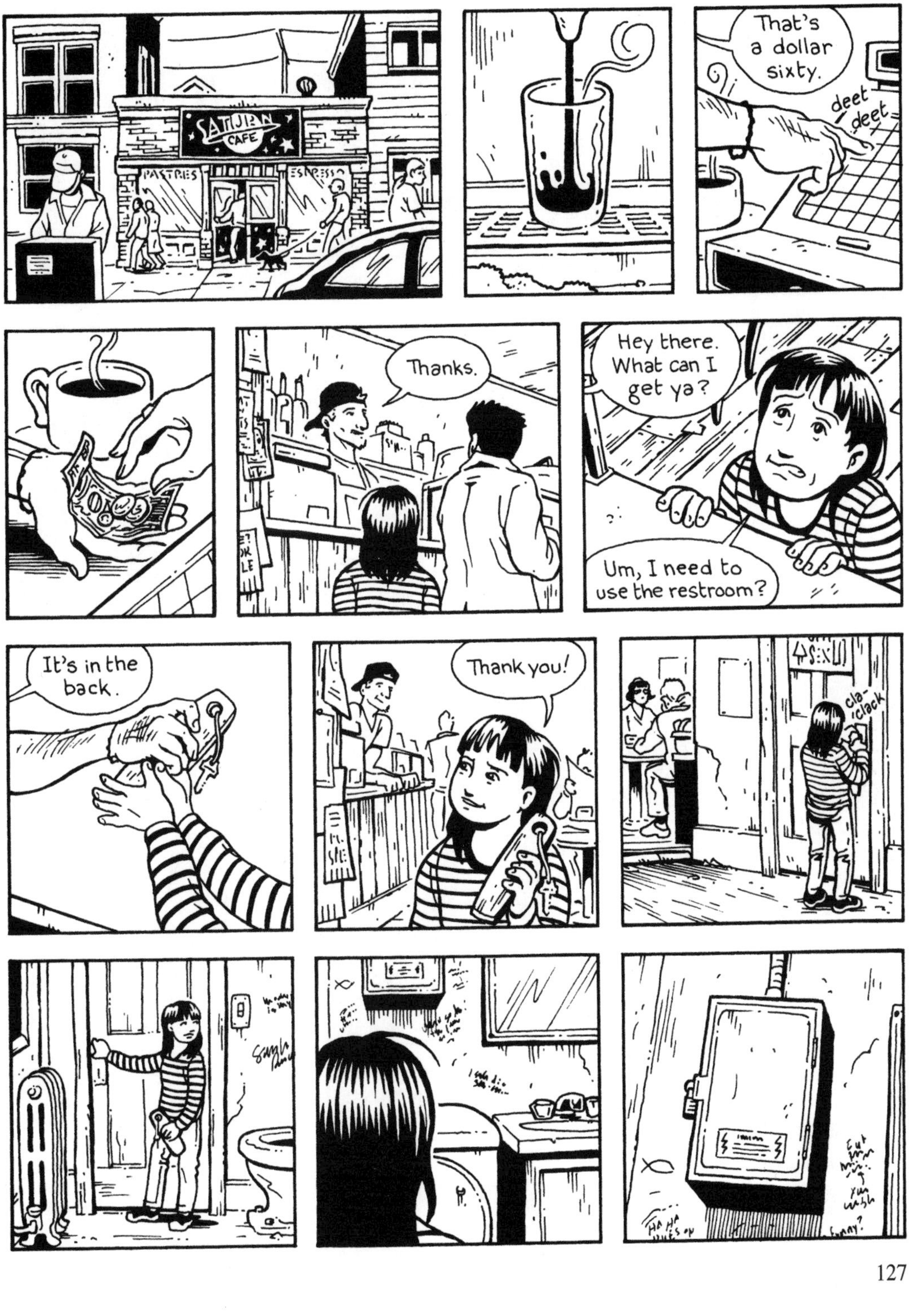
SATURN CAFE
PASTRIES
ESPRESSO
That's a dollar sixty.
deet deet
Thanks.
Hey there. What can I get ya?
Um, I need to use the restroom?
It's in the back.
Thank you!
cla-clack

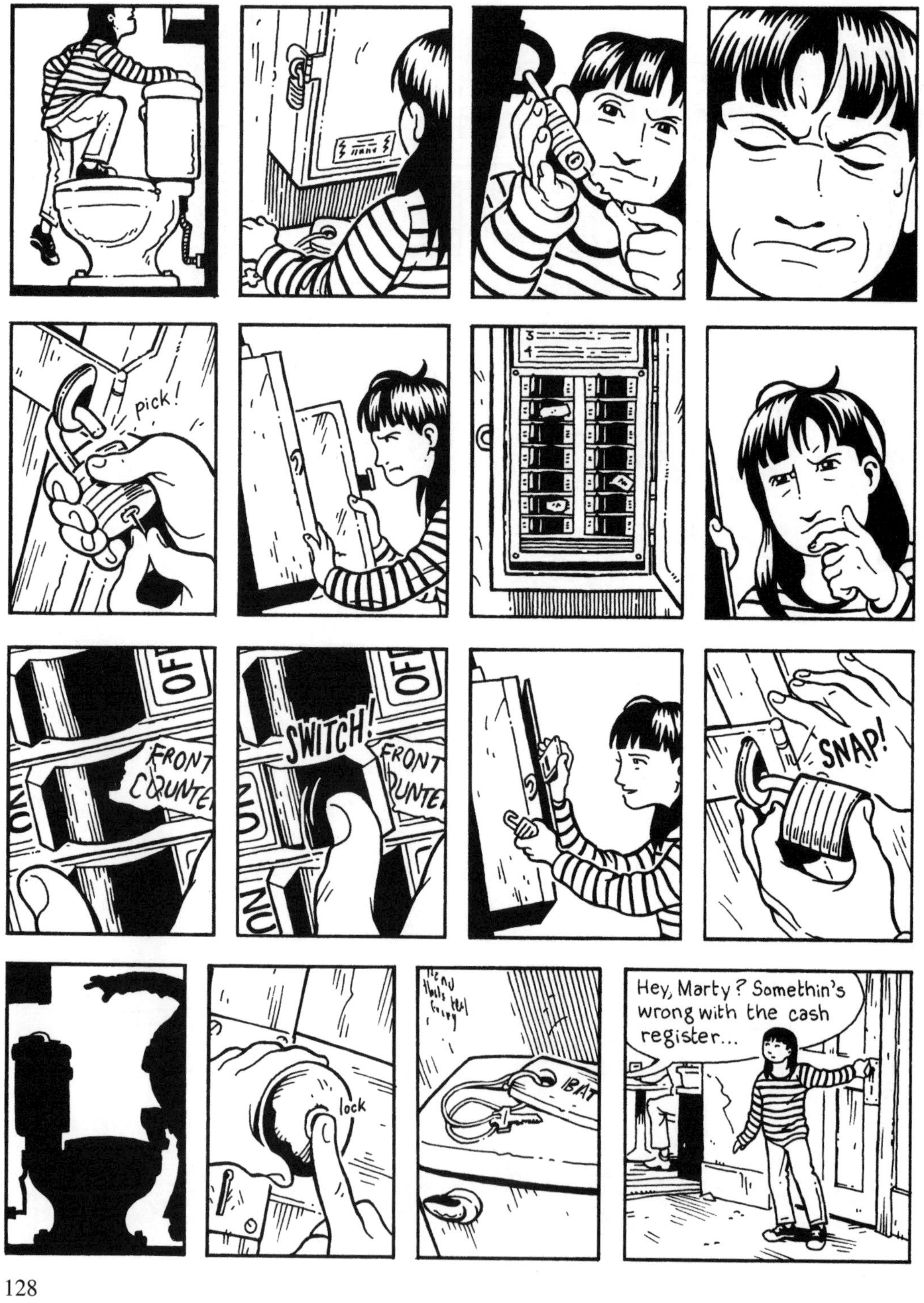
pick!
FRONT
SWITCH!
SNAP!
lock
Hey, Marty? Somethin's wrong with the cash register...

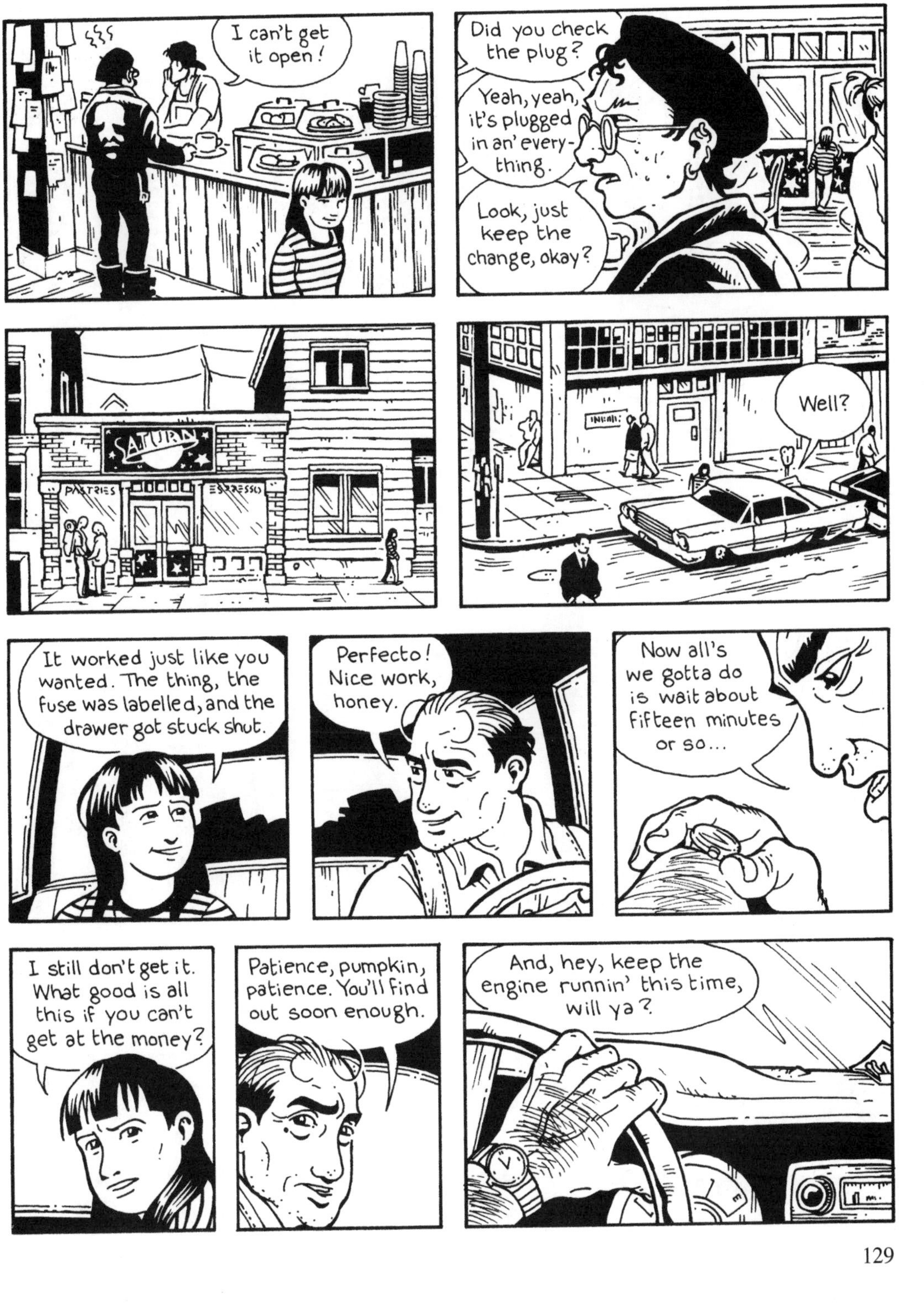

I can't get it open!
Did you check the plug?
Yeah, yeah, it's plugged in an' everything.
Look, just keep the change, okay?
SATURN
PASTRIES
ESPRESSO
Well?
It worked just like you wanted. The thing, the fuse was labelled, and the drawer got stuck shut.
Perfecto! Nice work, honey.
Now all's we gotta do is wait about fifteen minutes or so...
I still don't get it. What good is all this if you can't get at the money?
Patience, pumpkin, patience. You'll find out soon enough.
And, hey, keep the engine runnin' this time, will ya?

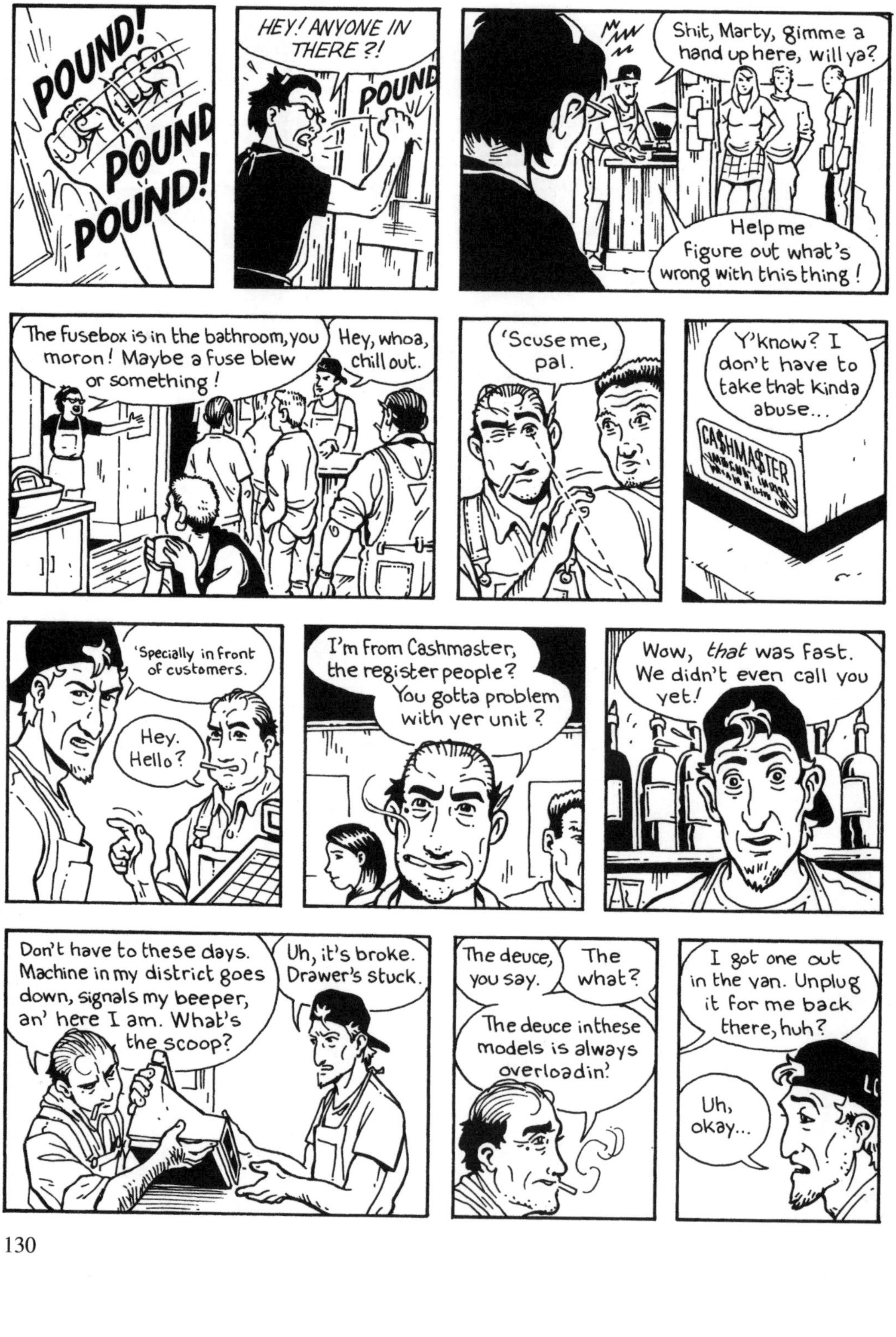
POUND! POUND POUND!
HEY! ANYONE IN THERE?!
POUND
Shit, Marty, gimme a hand up here, will ya?
Help me figure out what's wrong with this thing!
The fusebox is in the bathroom, you moron! Maybe a fuse blew or something!
Hey, whoa, chill out.
'Scuse me, pal.
Y'know? I don't have to take that kinda abuse...
CAHMATER
'Specially in front of customers.
Hey. Hello?
I'm from Cashmaster, the register people? You gotta problem with yer unit?
Wow, *that* was fast. We didn't even call you yet!
Don't have to these days. Machine in my district goes down, signals my beeper, an' here I am. What's the scoop?
Uh, it's broke. Drawer's stuck.
The deuce, you say.
The what?
The deuce in these models is always overloadin'.
I got one out in the van. Unplug it for me back there, huh?
Uh, okay...

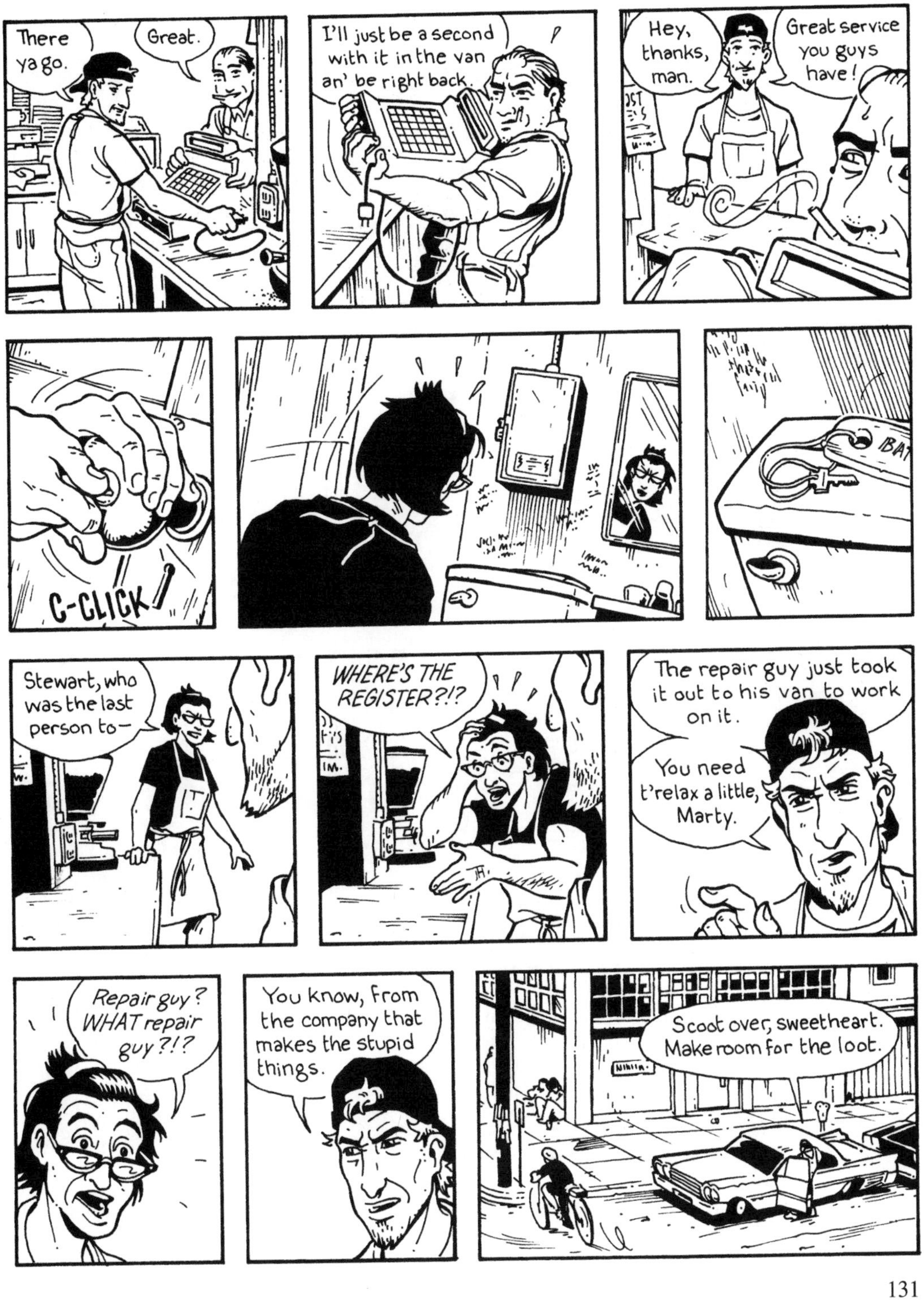
There ya go.
Great.
I'll just be a second with it in the van an' be right back.
Hey, thanks, man.
Great service you guys have!
C-CLICK
Stewart, who was the last person to–
WHERE'S THE REGISTER?!?
The repair guy just took it out to his van to work on it.
You need t'relax a little, Marty.
Repair guy? WHAT repair guy?!?
You know, from the company that makes the stupid things.
Scoot over, sweetheart. Make room for the loot.

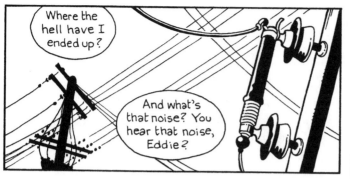

Where the hell have I ended up?

And what's that noise? You hear that noise, Eddie?

More of a feelin' than a noise. I can feel it in me.

Jesus *Christ*, it's givin' me th' creeps.

It's gettin' louder. In my bones an' gettin' louder by th' minute...

I gotta siddown, okay? I'm exhausted, I need a rest.

Where am I? I don't like this place.

It's like a fuckin' *nest*.

BANKB

That's exactly what it is, some kind of spider's nest.

An' I don' wanna be here when the owner comes home.

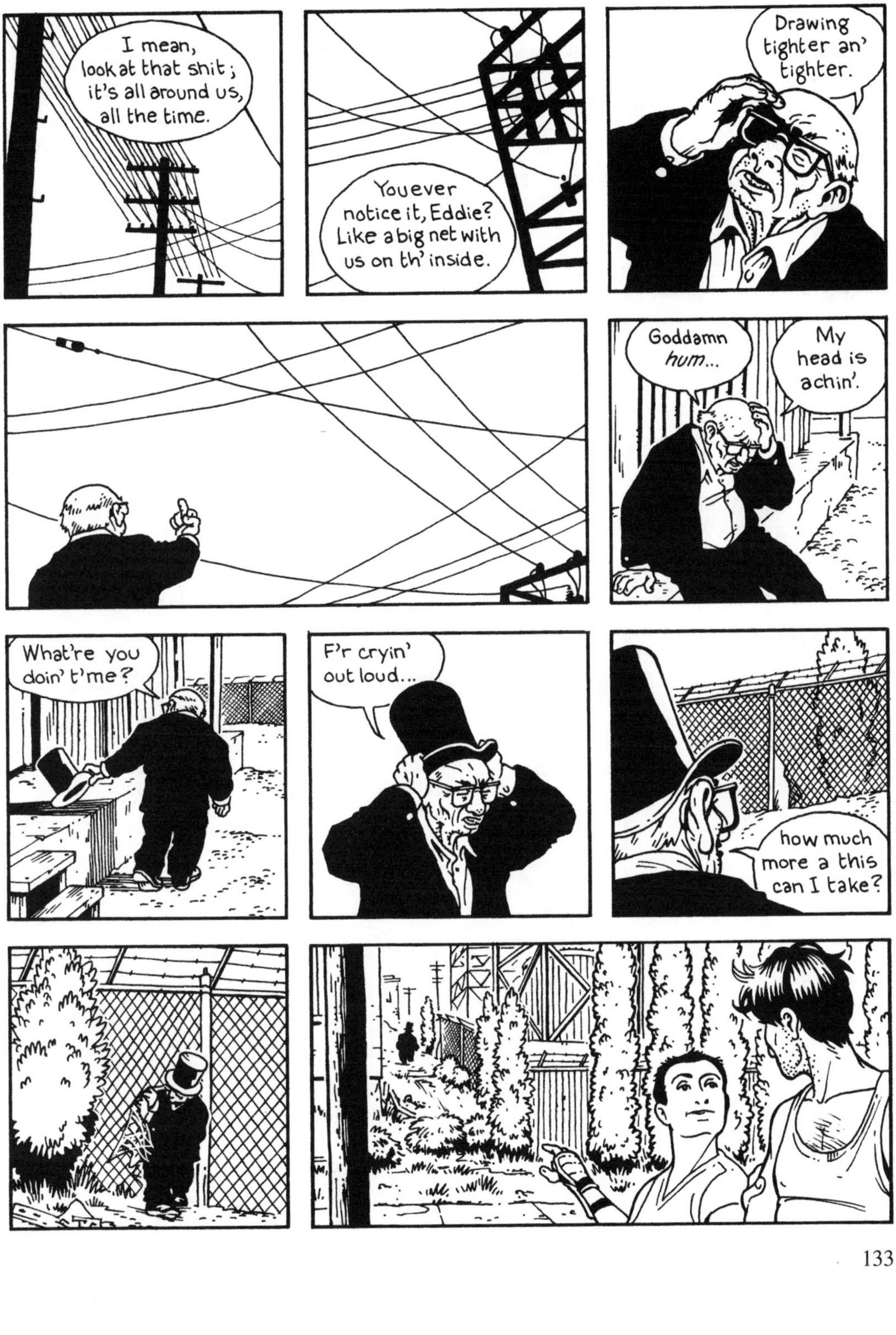
I mean, look at that shit; it's all around us, all the time.
You ever notice it, Eddie? Like a big net with us on th' inside.
Drawing tighter an' tighter.
Goddamn *hum*...
My head is achin'.
What're you doin' t'me?
F'r cryin' out loud...
how much more a this can I take?

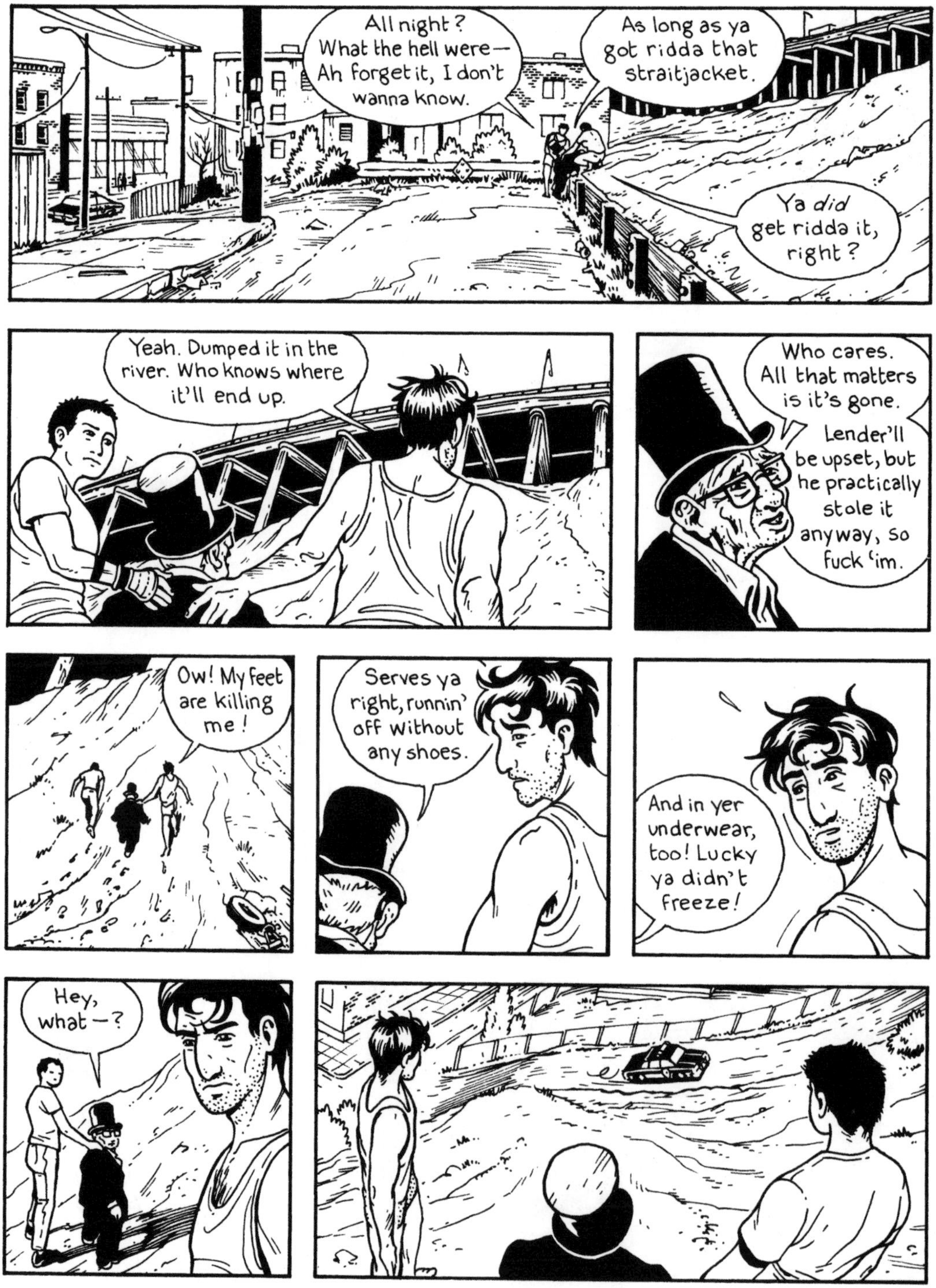
All night? What the hell were— Ah forget it, I don't wanna know.
As long as ya got ridda that straitjacket.
Ya *did* get ridda it, right?
Yeah. Dumped it in the river. Who knows where it'll end up.
Who cares. All that matters is it's gone.
Lender'll be upset, but he practically stole it anyway, so fuck 'im.
Ow! My feet are killing me!
Serves ya right, runnin' off without any shoes.
And in yer underwear, too! Lucky ya didn't freeze!
Hey, what—?

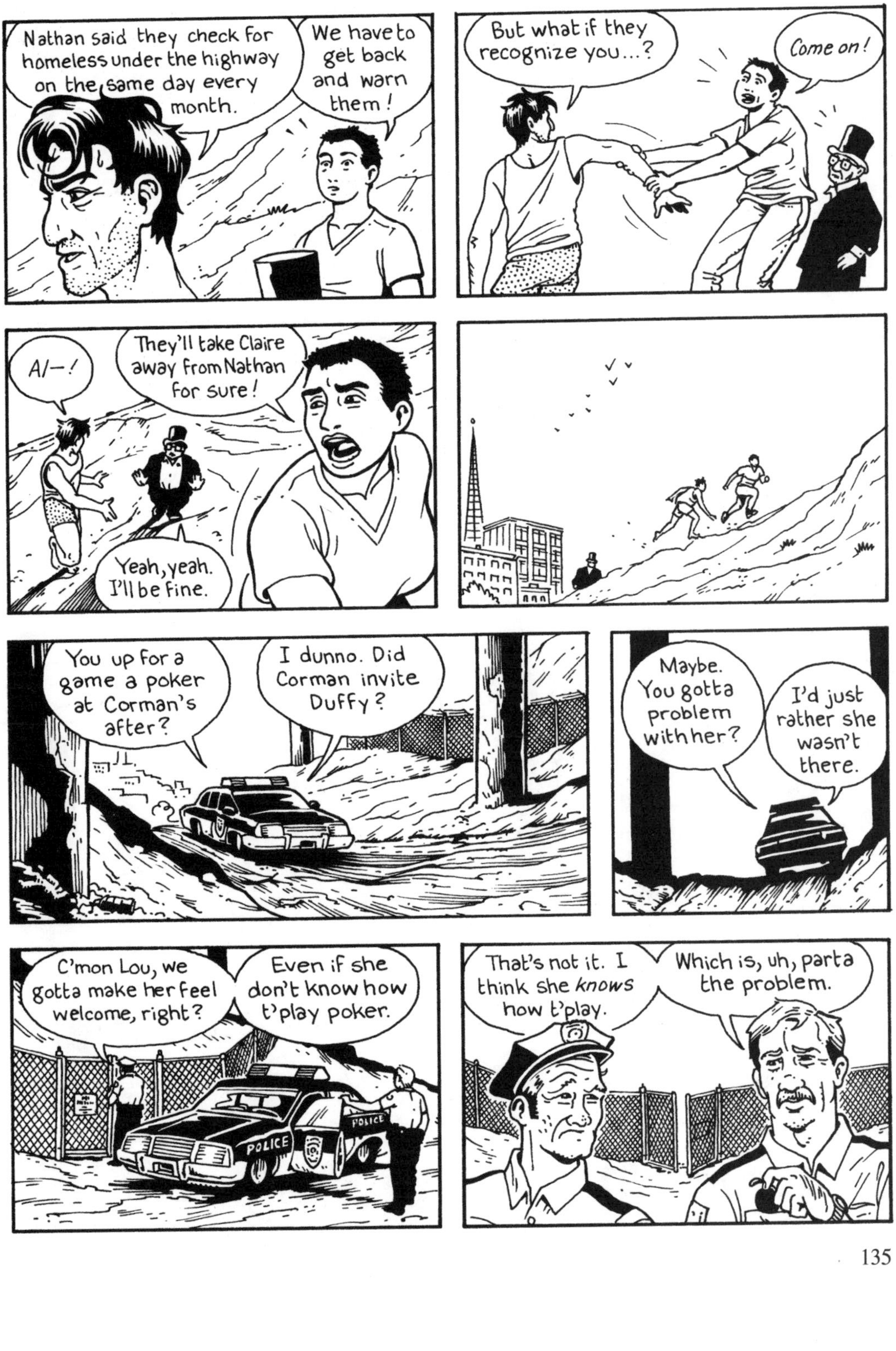
Nathan said they check for homeless under the highway on the same day every month.
We have to get back and warn them!
But what if they recognize you...?
Come on!
Al—!
They'll take Claire away from Nathan for sure!
Yeah, yeah. I'll be fine.
You up for a game a poker at Corman's after?
I dunno. Did Corman invite Duffy?
Maybe. You gotta problem with her?
I'd just rather she wasn't there.
C'mon Lou, we gotta make her feel welcome, right?
Even if she don't know how t'play poker.
POLICE
POLICE
That's not it. I think she *knows* how t'play.
Which is, uh, parta the problem.

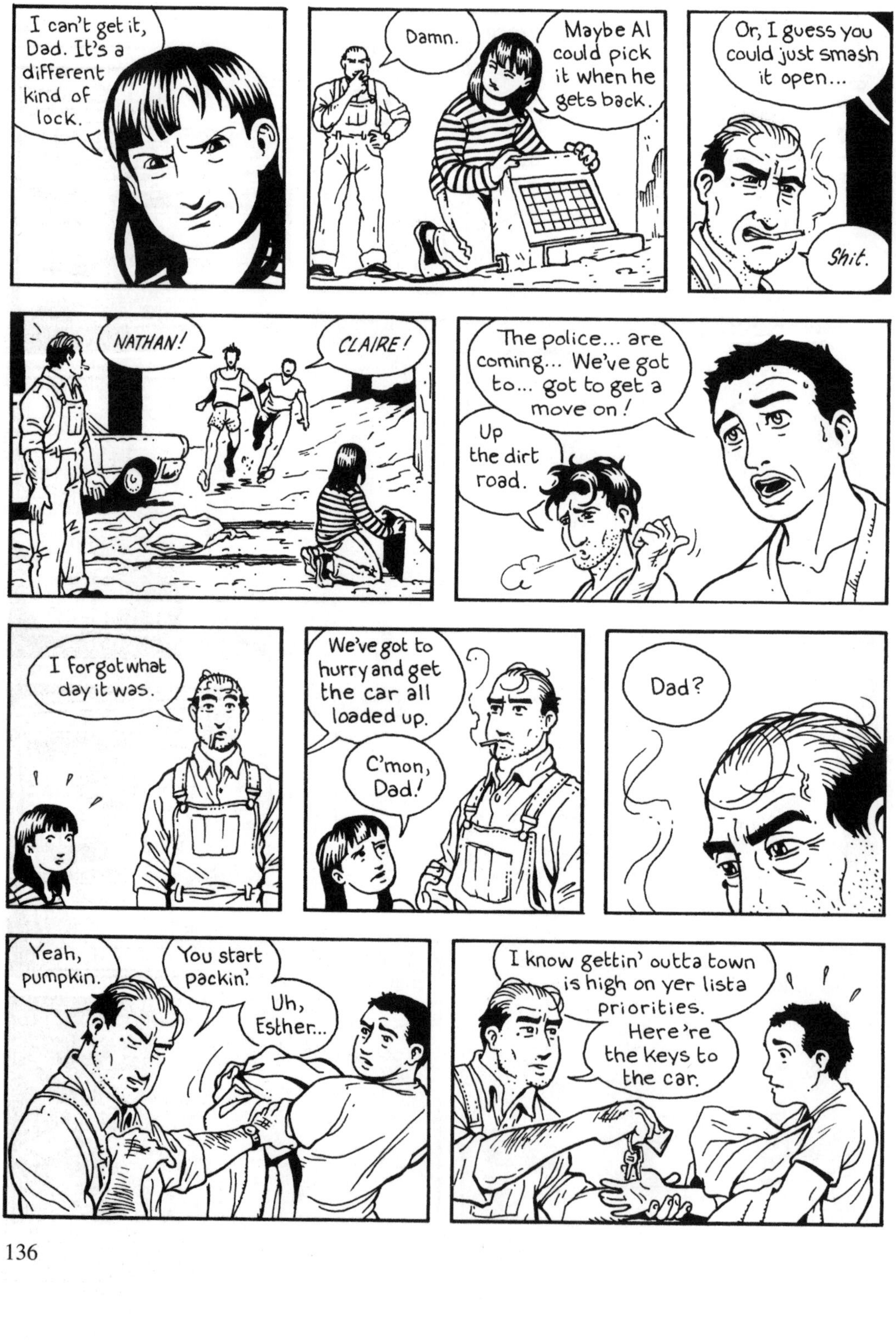

I can't get it, Dad. It's a different kind of lock.
Damn.
Maybe Al could pick it when he gets back.
Or, I guess you could just smash it open...
Shit.
NATHAN!
CLAIRE!
The police... are coming... We've got to... got to get a move on!
Up the dirt road.
I forgot what day it was.
We've got to hurry and get the car all loaded up.
C'mon, Dad!
Dad?
Yeah, pumpkin.
You start packin'.
Uh, Esther...
I know gettin' outta town is high on yer lista priorities.
Here're the keys to the car.

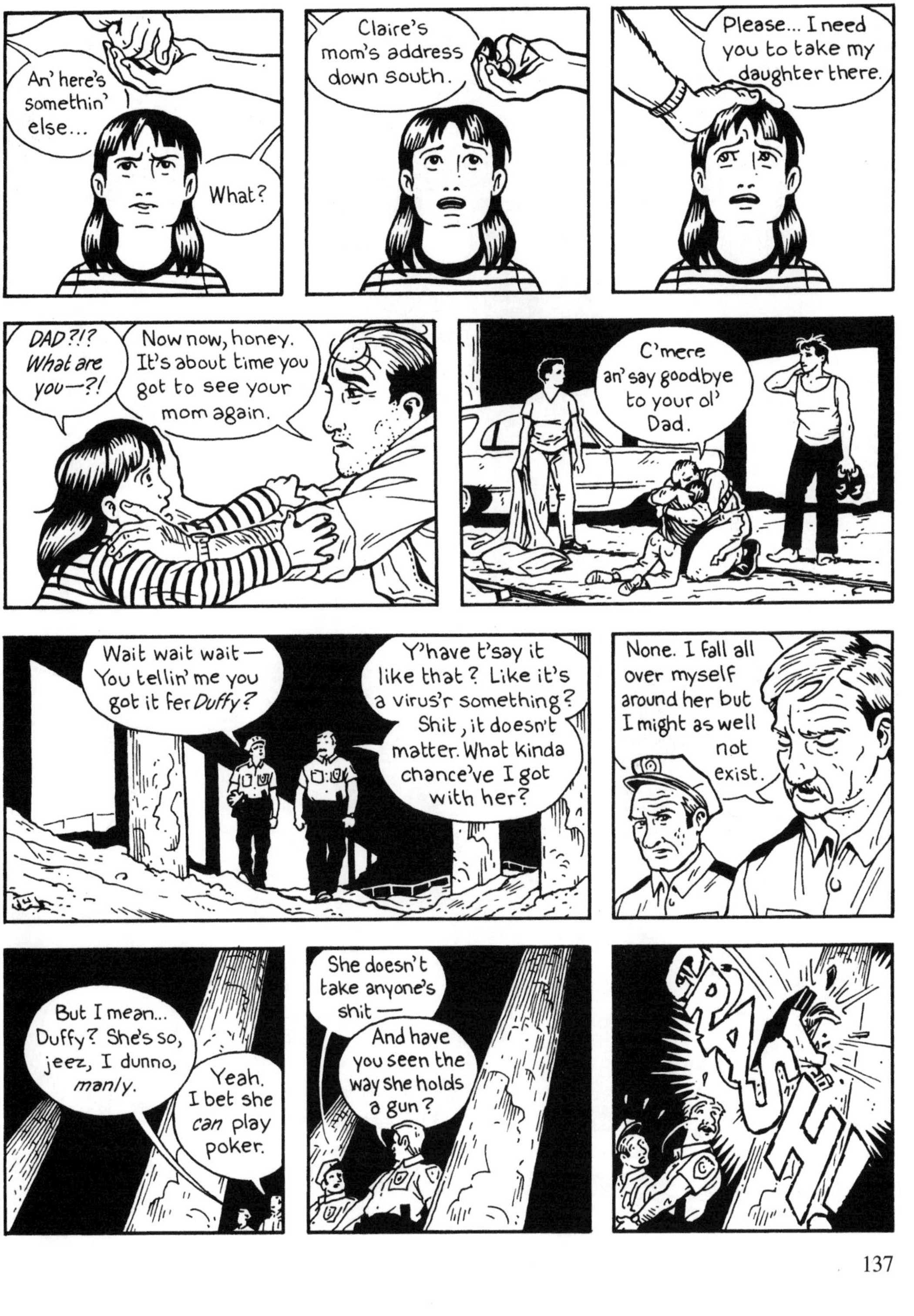

An' here's somethin' else...
What?
Claire's mom's address down south.
Please... I need you to take my daughter there.
DAD?!? What are you—?!
Now now, honey. It's about time you got to see your mom again.
C'mere an' say goodbye to your ol' Dad.
Wait wait wait— You tellin' me you got it fer Duffy?
Y'have t'say it like that? Like it's a virus'r something? Shit, it doesn't matter. What kinda chance've I got with her?
None. I fall all over myself around her but I might as well not exist.
But I mean... Duffy? She's so, jeez, I dunno, manly.
Yeah. I bet she can play poker.
She doesn't take anyone's shit—
And have you seen the way she holds a gun?
CRASH!

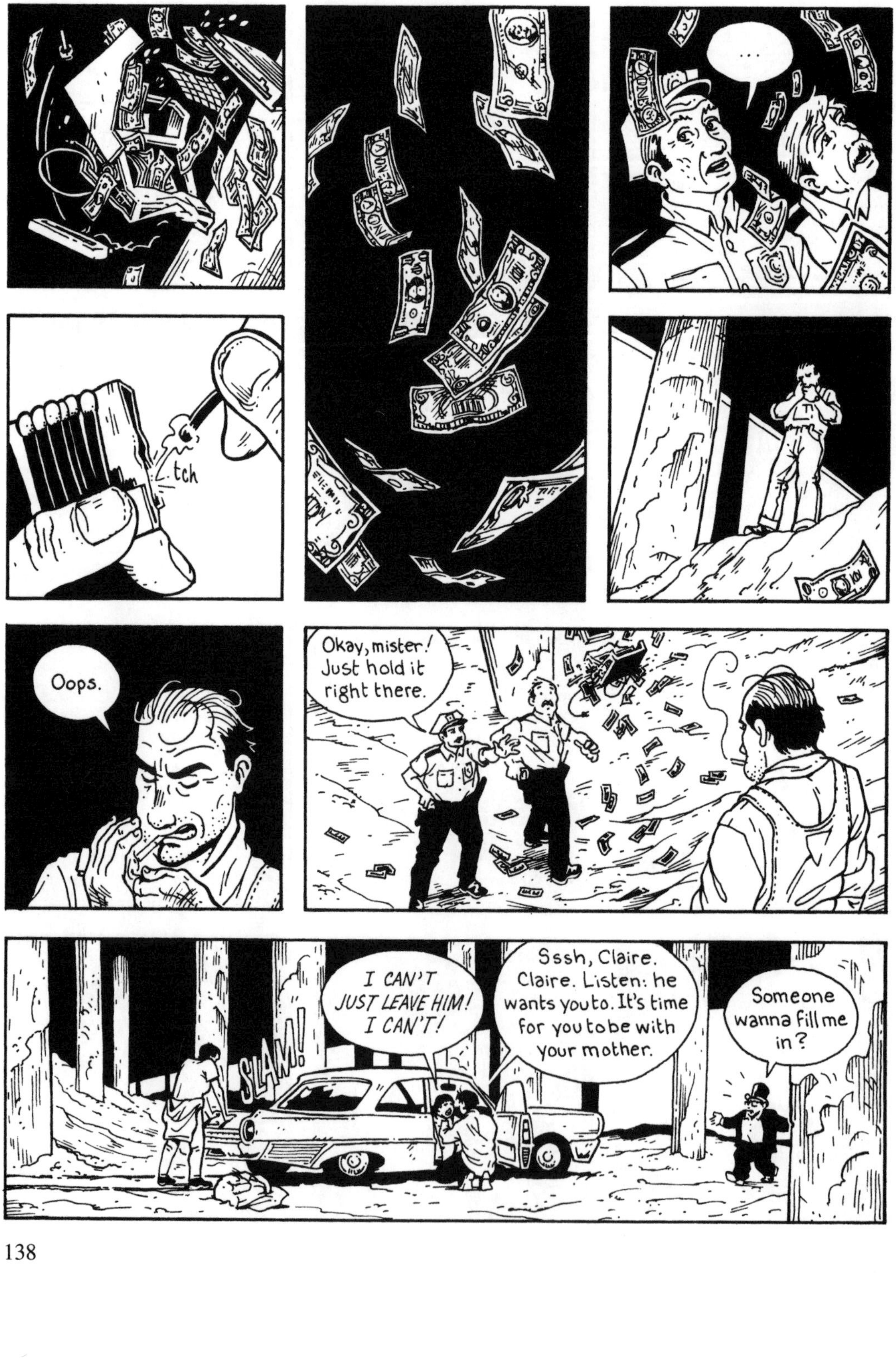
...
tch
Oops.
Okay, mister! Just hold it right there.
SLAM!
I CAN'T JUST LEAVE HIM! I CAN'T!
Sssh, Claire. Claire. Listen: he wants you to. It's time for you to be with your mother.
Someone wanna fill me in?

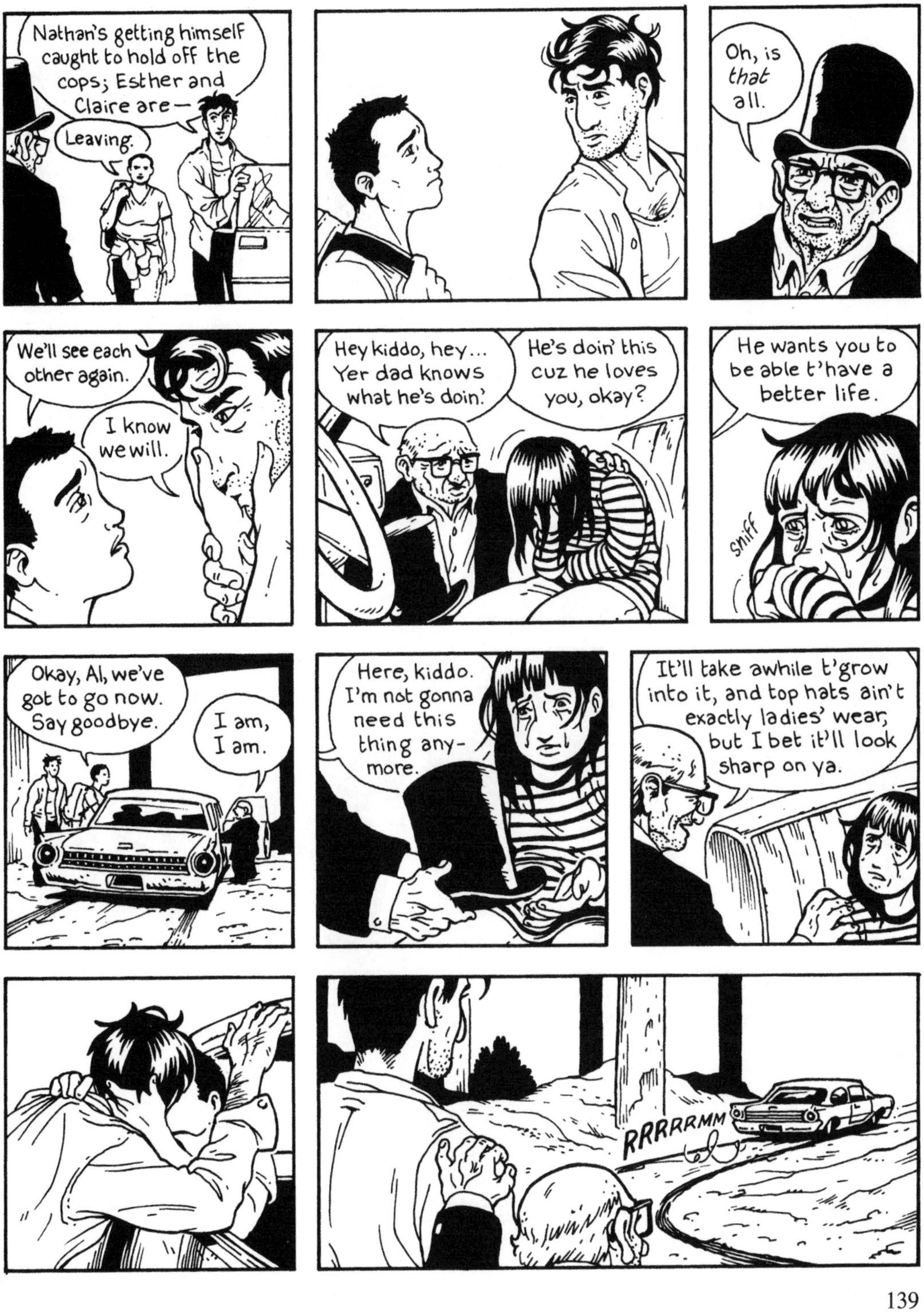
Nathan's getting himself caught to hold off the cops; Esther and Claire are—
Leaving.
Oh, is *that* all.
We'll see each other again.
I know we will.
Hey kiddo, hey... Yer dad knows what he's doin'.
He's doin' this cuz he loves you, okay?
He wants you to be able t'have a better life.
sniff
Okay, Al, we've got to go now. Say goodbye.
I am, I am.
Here, kiddo. I'm not gonna need this thing any-more.
It'll take awhile t'grow into it, and top hats ain't exactly ladies' wear, but I bet it'll look sharp on ya.
RRRRRMM

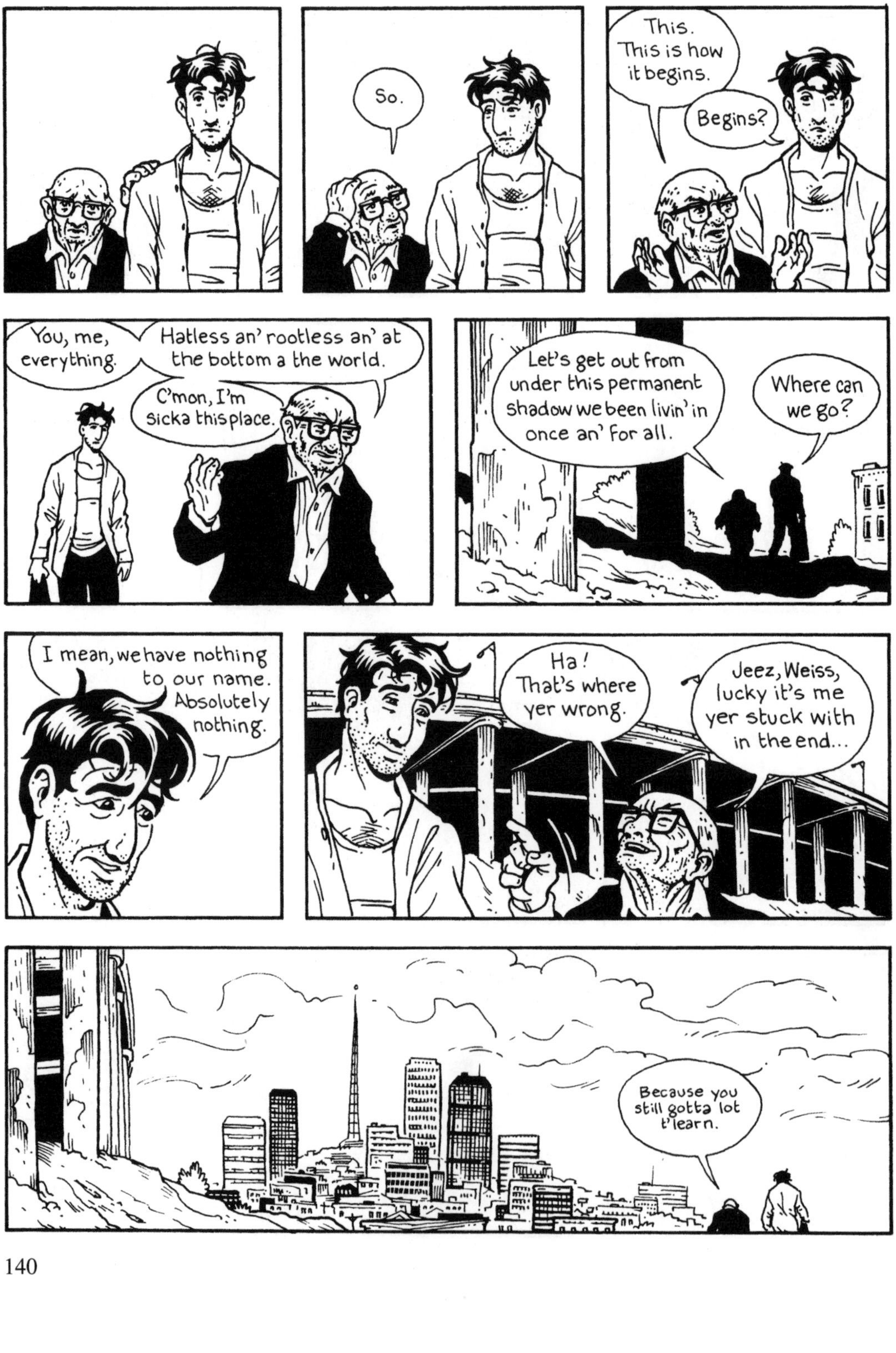
So.
This. This is how it begins.
Begins?
You, me, everything.
Hatless an' rootless an' at the bottom a the world.
C'mon, I'm sicka this place.
Let's get out from under this permanent shadow we been livin' in once an' for all.
Where can we go?
I mean, we have nothing to our name. Absolutely nothing.
Ha! That's where yer wrong.
Jeez, Weiss, lucky it's me yer stuck with in the end...
Because you still gotta lot t'learn.

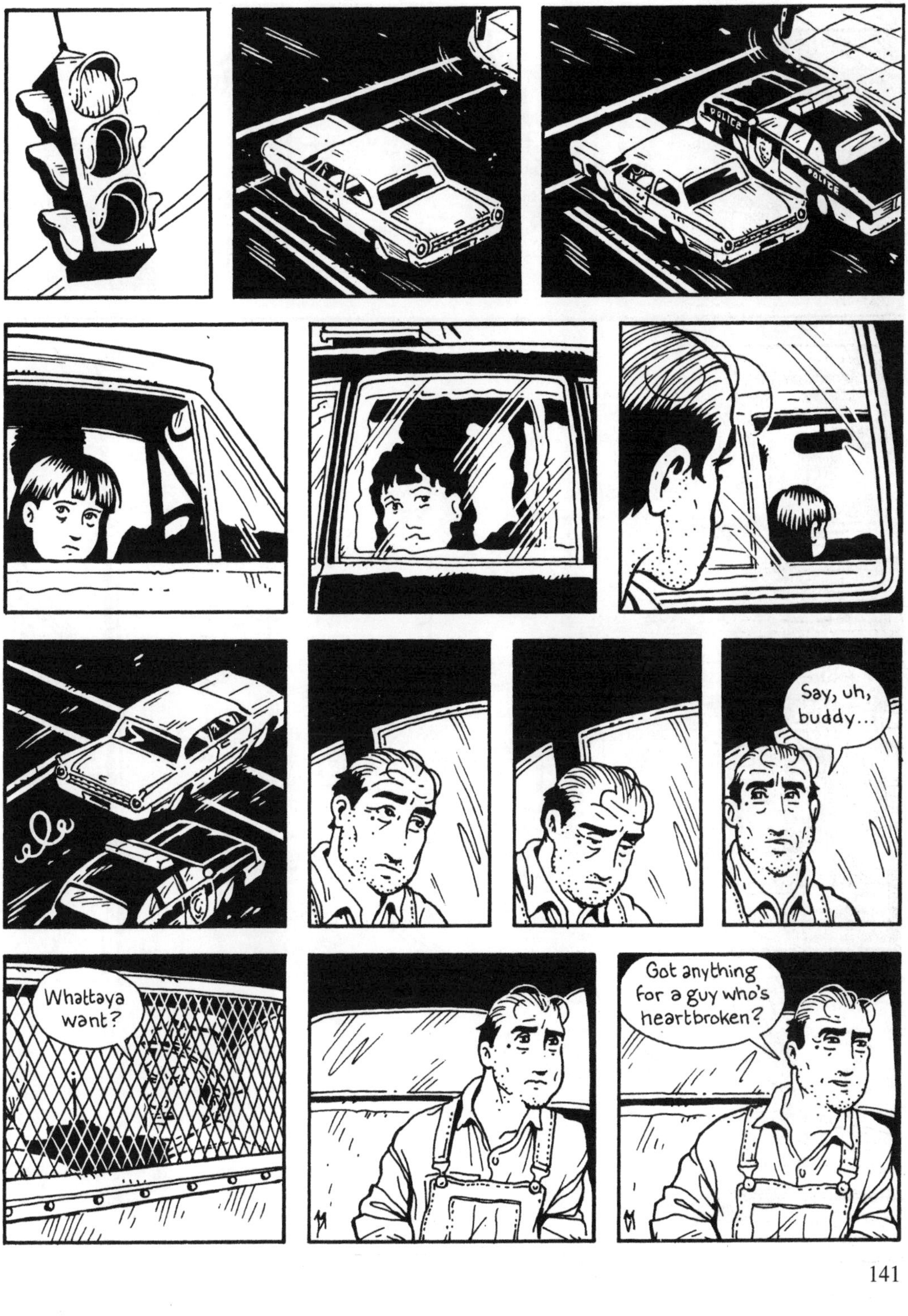
POLICE
POLICE
Say, uh, buddy...
Whattaya want?
Got anything for a guy who's heartbroken?

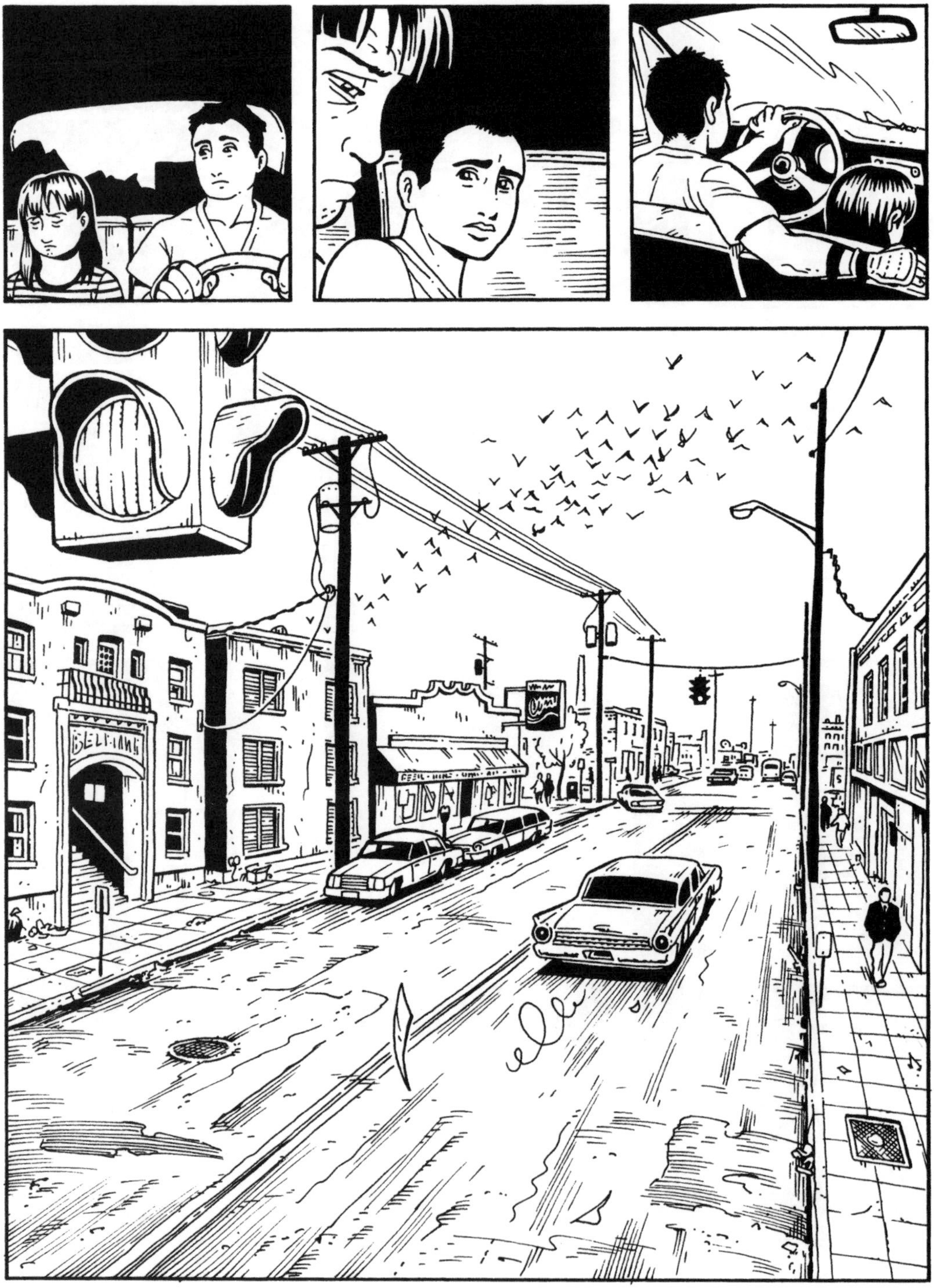

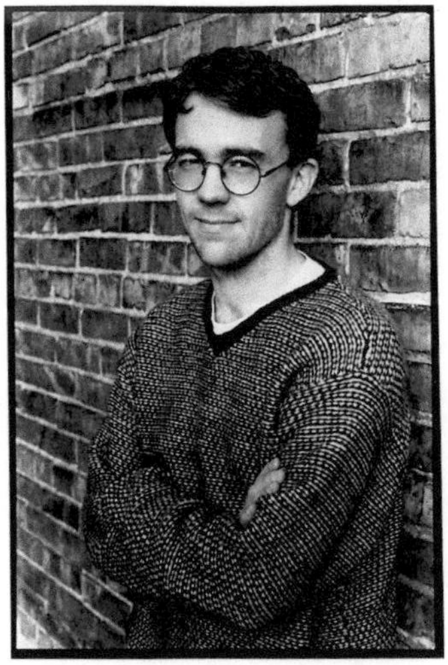

ARTIST PHOTO BY ERIKA LANGLEY

Jason Lutes was born in New Jersey in 1967. He grew up in Montana and California reading American comics, but his work has been influenced most by the European comics he discovered during trips to France as a child. He received a degree in illustration from the Rhode Island School of Design, and worked at Fantagraphics Books in Seattle for a year before becoming the art director of a weekly newspaper. His first book, *Jar of Fools,* originally appeared as a weekly comic in that paper before being collected by Black Eye Books. His current project, *Berlin,* is a lengthy story about the German city and its people between the wars.